Mic   The Stars, And You

Dottie Manderson mysteries: book 8

Caron Allan

Midnight, the Stars, and You: Dottie Manderson mysteries book 8
Copyright 2022 © Caron Allan

Edited by Lila Dawes.
Cover by Carolyn Bean.

ISBN: 9798263577254

To Alan, Alana, Aaron and Kat – it's been a tough time and I'm so grateful to you all for getting me through it.

Contents

Cast of Characters

I don't usually insert a list of characters, but this book has quite a few!

Dottie Manderson – protagonist.
Lavinia Manderson – Dottie's mother.
William Hardy – protagonist.
DS Frank Maple – friend and colleague of William's.

DI Marcus Rhodes – William's new boss.
DC Kerridge
DS Spence
Chief Super William Smithers
Chief Inspector Barrie
DI 'Foul-up' Fullerton – Frank Maple's new boss.
Miss Ellis – Chief Sup Smithers secretary.

In London:

Hon Peter St Clair St John – Dottie's former beau – loved Dottie considerably less than he loved himself.
Sir Nigel Ponsonby – another friend of the Milners'.
Lady Matilda Cosgrove – one of Christiana Milner's friends, and also well-acquainted with Sir Nigel.
Salt – Lady Cosgrove's personal maid.
John Brownlee – Sir Nigel's footman.
Sir Stanley Sissons – Dottie's biological father with whom she is building a relationship

At the Milners' residence in West Hallford, Berkshire:

Christiana St John Milner – Peter's sister.
Sebastian Milner – Christiana's second husband.
Harold Bassington MP – Christiana's first husband, deceased.
Mamie Cotton – florist and entrepreneuse, and close friend of Christiana Milner.
Anabella Penterman nee Wiseman – another close friend of Christiana, was briefly married to Dottie's other former beau Cyril Penterman.
Lord Henry Dalbury and Milo Parkes - two friends of the Milners'.
Penelope Sweeney and Florentina Coyle – two friends of the Milners'.
Major Thomas Forsythe – another friend of the Milners'.
Paul Boxhall – The Milners' butler.
Mrs Warboys – The Milners' cook.
Lucy and Janet – teenaged kitchen maids, plus others.

At Dottie's warehouse in London:

Mrs Avers – chief seamstress and Dottie's right-hand woman.
Gracie, Charlie, Patty and Millie – seamstresses at the warehouse, also work as mannequins.
Terence Whiteley – the new caretaker.

Midnight, the Stars, and You

Prologue

January 7ᵗʰ 1934 - The French Alps

Harold Bassington, Conservative MP for Halliford and Walton, was furious with his wife.

He stood in the lobby of the ski lodge, hauling on warmly padded outer-wear and muttering foul words under his breath. As he looked over the saloon-style door that led into the main lounge, he could see his wife laughing at something Forsythe had just said, whilst that snake Sebastian Milner sat at her right hand, topping up her wine and blatantly staring down the front of her dress as he did so. Next to him, his fiancée Florentina Coyle was looking down at her hands clasped in her lap, for all the world as if her heart was breaking. Nearby the new fellow, Parkes, was knocking back the contents of a small tumbler. As always, they were all deep into their cups.

Boxhall came over, his manner that of the perfect

butler even though he was unable to completely disguise his concern.

'Surely you're not going down the mountain now? Sir,' he added almost as an after-thought. He frowned as he glanced through to the lounge. Mrs Bassington was now alone with her husband's pal Dalbury and his lady-friend Miss Sweeney. Boxhall wondered where the others had gone. He hoped they weren't raiding the drinks cupboard in the kitchenette. They'd already had far too much to drink, in his opinion.

'I bloody well am. What choice do I have?'

As expected, Bassington was playing the martyr. Boxhall continued to preserve his concerned yet impartial demeanour. It wouldn't have surprised him if Bassington had instructed him to go down and fetch the bag in his stead.

'I'm sorry, sir, I still can't get through to the hotel,' Boxhall said. 'I imagine the telephone line has been brought down by this new fall of snow. It's rather a surprise that there's a line at all, right up here. In view of that, perhaps it would be better to...'

As usual, Bassington talked right over him. 'That's no use to me now, man. There's nothing more to be said. Right, I've got to go. I should be back here in about four hours. If I'm not back by then, don't waste time waiting up for me, I'll be staying the night at the hotel and returning in the morning. In fact, that seems more likely by the second. It'd be a mad risk to try to make it back tonight. The snow's really coming down out there. Hmm.' He looked like a man who'd just come to a decision. 'Yes, in fact that's what I'll do. I'll come back up on the ski lift in the morning as far as the third stage. It'll be far quicker than getting the lift right back up to the summit tonight to ski down from there like we did *this afternoon. Less tiring, too.'*

'Quite so. Very good, sir.' Boxhall bowed, saw his master out, and feeling he'd done all he could, he shut the door and returned with some relief to the kitchenette to see to the evening meal.

It ought to be an easy enough run down the mountain, Bassington thought, even with the snow falling. Might even be quite pleasant. All the same, he was pleased he had talked himself out of the return trip. Now he was already beginning to see the advantage of spending the night in the hotel. Or in the bar, at any rate. Perhaps his wife's good-looking American friend Anabella would be there. A nice informal way about her, laughed at all his jokes, and legs up to here... With Christiana out of the way, Anabella might be a little more encouraging this time, especially after a couple of drinks. Perhaps this wasn't such a bad idea, after all. And if it meant that Christiana worried a little about him, or felt ashamed over giving him so much trouble, that was all to the good. Bloody woman. He felt like wringing her bloody neck.

He'd only gone a matter of twenty yards or so, yet already visibility was down to a matter of inches rather than feet. He'd never seen snow like it. So much worse than he'd expected. This was ridiculous. And a damfool idea, into the bargain. He was likely to get killed at this rate. To continue would be tantamount to suicide.

He edged forward a little more, trying to get his bearings, and surrounded by unbroken darkness. He couldn't make out any sounds above the howling of the wind all around him. He couldn't even see the usual oil-lamp burning above the door of the lodge, couldn't hear music or laughter. Nothing. He might *have been alone on the mountain.*

He realised—too late, dammit—that he'd stepped forward but also turned, a beginner's error, and now he couldn't work out where he was. Which way was the ski lodge? He thought it should be directly behind him, but he couldn't make it out, no matter which way he looked. The damned wind howled, the snow blinded him. He took off his goggles to wipe them clear but his gloves caused him to fumble, dropping the goggles into the snow. He bent to try to find them, but patting around, found nothing but snow and more snow. A further minute of increasing impatience then he touched the hard rim, and with relief, picked up the goggles, wiped them as best he could and replaced them firmly before he could lose them again.

When he got back to the lodge, he was going to make sure his wife knew just what kind of a bloody nuisance she was. She always did things like this, and he was sick of it. Served him right for falling for that face, that figure, that bank balance. Why had he let himself get talked into going all the way back down the mountain to the damned hotel for her bloody handbag? Confounded woman. He staggered a few feet in the snow and cursed freely. Confounded snow. He should have stayed at home with his beloved ferns.

'Apparently it's got two hundred pounds in it,' Harold had been told. Two hundred pounds! What woman other than Christiana was insane enough to carry a small fortune in her handbag and then just leave it behind in a hotel room? Just lying there on the bed! Not even put away in a drawer or cupboard but just lying on the bed where any maid or footman, or Tom, Dick or Harry, could help themselves! He was fuming, and when he got back

with the blasted bag, she would know all about it.

Too scared to tell him herself, it seemed. 'I'll just bet she was,' he muttered, looking around him again. And with good reason. Oh yes, she would soon realise just how angry he was. She would probably have to invent some kind of silly little accident to explain away the black eye she'd be getting as soon as he got back to their room with her bag. But that would be tomorrow. First he intended to get pretty damned drunk, and see about the lovely Anabella.

He snapped out of his raging thoughts when he heard a slight sound behind him. He turned but still couldn't see a thing. The driving snow blinded him. Madness to be out in this, to even consider attempting it. Perhaps it was best that he left it until morning after all. If the money got pinched, too bloody bad.

Still holding his ski poles, Harold put up a gloved hand to clear the snow off his goggles again. There seemed to be a light coming from behind his left shoulder. It wasn't the lodge door lamp, there was someone there with an electric torch, no doubt Boxhall coming out to persuade him not to go. Harold began to turn. He dropped his ski pole from his icy fingers—even with his gloves he couldn't feel a thing. He bent to pick it up again, fumbling for it in the snow, the cocktails he'd drunk earlier really making his head swim.

A heavy blow hit the side of his head.

He sank to the ground, oblivious. His assailant stepped forward, and with a couple of heavy whacks, finished the job with an icebreaker. Then dragged the lifeless body across the soft snow to the edge of the run, pushing it over the teeth of the rocks and down into the abyss. The icebreaker, with blood on the business end, followed in the politician's wake.

The snow was still coming down heavily. Time to get back inside, leave the weather to cover up all traces of the murder. With any luck, it could be weeks before they found Bassington's body. If ever.

Just four months later, a small congregation of people took their seats in a chapel in Windsor, Berkshire, England to listen to the clergyman in front of the altar say,

'Dearly beloved, we are gathered here today to witness the joining of this man, Sebastian Wilcott Milner, and this woman, Christiana Glenda Bassington, in holy matrimony.'

*

Chapter One

Saturday 1ˢᵗ June 1935

Dottie Manderson was already fed up to the back teeth with parties. Admittedly, she thought, one expected parties in June. It was just that lately, life had been nothing but. Tennis parties, tea parties, afternoon dancing parties, mid-morning coffee parties, dinner parties, cocktail parties in the evening. It was endless. And now, socialising in London was giving her a sense rather too much like continually stepping over graves—those of dead relationships. Wherever she went, dragged along by either her mother or her sister, or her mother *and* her sister, to all the various events in so many hotels, houses and gardens, she kept running into people she either knew far too much about, or had heard of through other acquaintances.

This evening was a case in point. They were at Sir Nigel Ponsonby's lavish Tyne Square townhouse for dinner and dancing. Sir Nigel was having a house party for a week and had decided to invite still more guests just for the evening. Twenty-five people had been invited, Dottie and her mother included. Nobody who knew the family bothered to invite Dottie's father—he'd rather be at home with The Times and his radio, and perhaps a small glass of port.

Her mother was deep in conversation with a couple of earnest-looking ladies, probably, Dottie surmised, talking about charitable works and fundraising for the needy.

Dottie hid behind the same half-glass of rather warm white wine she had been clutching for almost two hours, and she looked about the room.

Over there by the fireplace, hanging on the arm of a man with a moustache, was the perfectly dressed, perfectly coiffed slender frame of Anabella Penterman nee Wiseman of the New York Wisemans. She had married Dottie's almost-beau Cyril Penterman only a year and a half ago, yet now if the gossip columns were correct, the couple were very publicly living separate lives. Divorce seemed to be on the cards. The woman had glanced at Dottie four times now, and although managing a social smile the first time, every other occurrence had been accompanied by a quick glance, then she'd looked away as soon as Dottie noticed. Dottie detected that the woman had lost a lot of weight, and that no wedding or engagement ring adorned her left hand. Anabella leaned in to kiss the cheek of the man she was with, a stiffly upright Military Moustache type of chap, and clutched his arm tightly, then a second later she was laughing at something he'd said. Clearly her new romance was no secret from anyone, which presumably included the divorce lawyers.

Then, on the opposite side of the vast drawing-room was Dottie's other former beau, the Honourable Peter St Clair St John, at least thirty years old as far as she recalled, yet giggling rather childishly, in Dottie's opinion, with a couple of really quite young girls.

'Far too young for him,' Dottie said out loud.

'Oh definitely, dear,' replied a woman standing a few feet away. She drew a little closer, saying in a low tone, 'I don't know what their parents are thinking, introducing them to that wolf.'

'*Is* he a wolf?' Dottie turned to face her companion, a dainty blonde woman in her mid-thirties, immaculately turned out. Dottie felt a slight flash of recognition but couldn't quite reach at the woman's name. 'I always found him a bit dull, if I'm honest. And only ever interested in himself.'

Belatedly she wondered again who she was speaking to. It wouldn't do to say that to a close relation.

'Well, absolutely. His main interest in his life has always been himself. A thoroughly tiresome younger brother, I don't mind telling you. *But once he gets a girl to himself, he's all hands, from what I hear.*'

Too late Dottie recognised Peter's sister, Christiana Milner, the widow of the Bassington estate. Her first husband, the Conservative MP for Halliford and Walton, had passed away just, what, surely it was barely eighteen months ago? And under what had always been regarded by the gossip columns as an 'odd' circumstance during an avalanche when skiing with friends in the French Alps. Yet here Christiana was, remarried over a year ago and wearing a daring dress of figure-hugging gold lame, with not a single sign of mourning about her, and a very large diamond ring on her third finger.

Catching Dottie's glance at her dress, Christiana smiled and held out her hand. 'I don't think we've ever been formally introduced, though I've seen you at a number of events over the last two or three years. Christiana, please.'

Dottie shook her hand. 'Dottie Manderson. Just Dottie. And congratulations on your recent marriage, Christiana.'

'Thank you. Sebastian is over there somewhere, chatting politics to some other chaps, I expect, and no doubt getting quite heated about it. Very dull. That's the problem when you marry a man so much older than yourself. They dance less and talk politics more.' She glanced at Dottie again, smiled and added, 'But you're not to be Miss Manderson for much longer, I hear. Many congratulations to you too.'

'Thank you. That's perfectly true. Not long now, the wedding is in August.'

'Lovely. And am I right in thinking that he's not one of our lot?'

Dottie tried not to be offended. She'd heard this a number of times in recent weeks and should really have become used to it. But still, it grated.

'He works as a police officer, I expect you mean,' she said, carefully keeping her tone neutral.

Christiana looked mortified. Her hand came out to just touch Dottie's arm before falling away. 'Oh, I'm so sorry. Please don't think I meant...' She sighed. 'I'm sorry. I really didn't mean it quite the way it probably sounded. Oh, this is a terrible start to a friendship. I'm not a snob.' Looking into her glass, she said softly, 'Believe me I know all too well how hard it is to find a good man. And when one is lucky enough to find him, one thanks one's lucky stars and refuses to let go.'

'I'm sorry too,' Dottie said. 'I'm afraid there have been a number of critical comments of late, and I'm feeling rather on the defensive. William's family used to have an estate but unfortunately it was sold a few years ago to cover—er—'

'Death duties?' Christiana suggested helpfully.

Dottie gave slight nod of the head and a wry smile. 'That. And debts.'

'Ah! Well, there are plenty of those amongst the so-called upper-crust and even the aristocracy, as we both know. In fact, I'd say it's almost compulsory. I can look around this room and tell you who is solvent and who hasn't got the proverbial penny to bless himself with. Let's start with my idiot brother, Peter. Broke,' she smirked at Dottie. 'Definitely not got a penny to his name. I'm so glad you didn't fall for him.' She discreetly pointed out two other men and two women and said, 'Stony broke,' for each of them.

'Lord Dalbury—that's him on the left, and the red-haired woman is his fiancée Penelope Sweeney with her dear friend Florentina Coyle, and the other chap is Dalbury's old school friend, Milo Parkes. All of them close friends of my husband. And all of them always up to their necks in some kind of madcap scheme. But these schemes of theirs never seem to yield any profits, so I think that speaks for itself.'

Dottie was astonished. Christiana was right. These were four people whom Dottie would have practically gone to her grave believing to be perfectly solvent, even absolutely wealthy, standing there in their elegant, up-to-the-minute attire, their jewellery and shoes glittering. Inadvertently she took a gulp of her horrid wine. She grimaced, swallowed quickly, then said,

'But my father is thinking of going into business

with that Dalbury chap and his friend Parkes. They've been having discussions all week at Father's club. Not that I've met any of those four, but I've heard of the two men.'

Christiana looked concerned. 'Oh, my word, no! Please warn your father to get out whilst he can, they will bleed him dry! I've heard of it from others. Strictly privately, you understand.'

'Really? That's terrible!' Dottie exclaimed, her eyes rounded with horror. 'I'll tell him. Thank you for the tip. It's astonishing, isn't it? As you say, one takes everyone at face value, and we make assumptions based on what we see.'

'Which prompts me to ask, Dottie. What do you think of my dress?'

'Oh, it's lovely!' Dottie didn't even have to stop and think about that.

'It's actually an old one of my mother's. Yes, honestly, it's at least twenty years old. She had some beautiful gowns and coats. Even furs. Some of them were terribly expensive, and now that she's passed away, my brother wants me to sell them. He needs the cash.'

Dottie said nothing, rather suspecting she might know where this was leading.

'We're having a house party next weekend. I know it's a terrible cheek, and horribly short notice, but I was wondering if you'd do me a huge favour. I was hoping you might know a few people who would be interested in buying Mother's things. I don't want them to go to just anybody, so if they were people you could recommend, people who *cared* about the clothes, I might not mind so much. I don't want it to feel like a village jumble sale with everyone pawing over my mother's things, they are important to me. Well, needs must, I suppose. Sebastian won't hear of me helping Peter out, I've already done it twice, twice too often in Sebastian's opinion. If I can possibly help Peter, I feel I have to do so, he's so wretchedly clueless.

'So, on that note, could you spare me the weekend to come and visit, and bring your lovely fiancé, too, of course, so long as he's not too busy, though you'd be welcome to bring some other friend with you? I'd be so grateful if you could just go through Mother's things and tell me what might fetch some cash, and who might be interested. There aren't many 'names', Mother went rather her own way in fashion, although there are some early Carmichael and Jennings items you might be interested to see. Perhaps you'll think about it and let me know? You can telephone me, I'm on Belgravia 139.' She grabbed Dottie's arm and said in an urgent tone, 'Do say you'll think about it, please. This means so much to me.'

'I will,' Dottie promised, and had only time to repeat these words as the band returned from their break, the music suddenly began, and a young man came to ask Christiana to dance.

It was an hour later, and Dottie was bored stiff. The band was again between numbers, and the guests were milling about, chatting and replenishing their drinks.

'No 'long arm of the law' with you tonight, then?' The affectedly cut-glass tones were those of the woman Christiana had pointed out as Penelope Sweeney. Dottie's hand froze as she was about to fill her glass from the punchbowl. How quickly gossip got around a room!

'I expect he's halfway along Victoria Avenue by this time of night. If we look out of the front door, we might be lucky enough to catch him on his second circuit.' This was from Penelope's bosom pal Florentina Coyle, leaning towards her friend to smirk at Dottie.

Clearly by now the whole world knew Dottie was engaged to be married to a policeman, as those within earshot smothered their laughter at that. Penelope's laugh was a penetrating false-sounding tinkle whereas Florentina sniggered through her nose in a manner anyone else would have deemed unladylike. In any case, with the way Dottie was feeling now, it was just as likely to get her a slap across the face if she didn't shut up.

Dottie contemplated a witty retort but realised she'd left it too long, and anyway, she couldn't think of anything to say. She felt like a fool and was at a complete loss for words, gaping like a goldfish. Beside her, an American drawl said,

'Oh say, Dottie, that's a great idea. I'll have some of that too.' And a glass appeared in front of her. She turned to see Anabella Penterman beaming down at her. Dottie wasn't short for a woman, but Anabella was positively statuesque. She nodded at Dottie almost imperceptibly. Dottie lifted her hand and ladled some punch into Anabella's glass, then filled her own and replaced the ladle in its perch on the edge of the bowl. She hoped no one had noticed that her hand was shaking.

Anabella's free hand came though Dottie's arm, firmly steering her away from the table towards her companion, whilst saying loudly, 'I really do think that man of yours is so terribly handsome. He reminds me of my favourite actor, Gary Cooper. And isn't William one of the Met's finest young investigators? It's not often a man is promoted to the rank of Detective Inspector before the age of thirty. He sure must be good at his job. I'd hate to get on the wrong side of him. Is it true he gets sent here, there and everywhere at the special request of Downing Street?'

Dottie found her voice at last. 'He does seem rather in demand. He was at the Houses of Parliament a few days ago. Someone very eminent wished to consult with him on an important matter.'

'Such a shame we're not allowed to know all about it. The stories he could tell us if he didn't have to sign that darned Official Secrets Act!'

The sniggering had stopped, and Dottie was pleased to note surprised, even impressed expressions on one or two faces, whilst Penelope and Florentina were blatantly looking thwarted.

Dottie and Anabella turned to smile at the man with the military moustache. Like most men, it seemed he was not a lover of punch and had opted for a glass of brandy.

'Dottie, I'd like to introduce Major Thomas Forsythe. Tom, this is Miss Dottie Manderson, soon to be Mrs Hardy, wife of Inspector William Hardy of Scotland Yard. Remember, Chris pointed her out to us earlier.'

Now did not seem to be the best moment to announce that William had been demoted to sergeant. Hopefully he would quickly be restored to his former rank, and no one would ever need to know about it. Otherwise Penelope and Florentina would feel justified in their earlier ridicule of him as a policeman on the beat. Not that it mattered, Dottie reminded herself, they were madly in love, he was a good man, and he was good at his job. His rank shouldn't matter. But even so...

Tom Forsythe beamed at her from underneath the moustache. 'He sounds like an excellent fellow, I do hope you will introduce us some time.' The major bowed over Dottie's hand with old-fashioned charm. Somehow the moustache managed to poke through her satin evening gloves and prickle her skin, but she kept her smile.

Forsythe continued, 'I'm delighted to make your acquaintance, Miss Manderson.' He glanced at Anabella. 'Is this the purveyor of those gowns that so interest you?'

Anabella swatted him on the chest. 'Now, Tom, I was building up to that. Dottie—oh, I'm sorry—I hope you don't mind me calling you that? I know we've really only met the one time before.'

'Not at all, after all you did just rescue me.'

'True! Those two are quite the team when it comes to tormenting others. But to change the subject, Christiana Milner told me that a friend of hers has one of your gowns—an absolutely ravishing burgundy satin ballgown. Apparently wherever she goes, people ask her about it.'

Dottie knew the gown, it was one of her personal favourites, she had a copy of it herself. 'I think that must be Lady Cosgrove? In fact, she has an appointment with me this week to look at some more.'

'Yes, it was her! Well, she brought it downstairs to show some of us when we were here for dinner last night. And my! It really is the last word in glamour. So I was wondering if I could join her when she comes to see you?'

'Yes, of course you can. That would be lovely. I mean, I'm sure she wouldn't object, since you and she are acquainted.'

'Wonderful! I know Christiana is longing to come by too. And I don't know if she's spoken to you yet, but she was rather hoping to enlist your help in selling on a few of her mother's things.' She turned to wave across the room at the Honourable Peter's sister, who said something to the people she was with and immediately left them to come over.

'Yes, she has mentioned it.'

It had only been a year since Dottie had inherited the fashion warehouse—*Carmichael and Jennings: Exclusive Modes for Discerning Ladies*—from her late employer Mrs Carmichael. Dottie had gone from part-time mannequin to owner and fashion designer overnight, and it had been a huge adjustment with so many new skills required of her. She'd had a lot of help and was now beginning to be more confident in her abilities. Even so it was the stuff of dreams that someone could just come up to her and start raving about one of her creations, even begging to be allowed to come and look at them. Soon, she had half a dozen women about her, all wanting an appointment.

She was telling her mother all about it on the way home later that night.

'Perhaps you ought to have another show at the warehouse,' her mother suggested as they drove home in Dottie's car. 'It might be easier to have all the ladies there at the same time and show all the gowns.'

'Yes, it would, wouldn't it? I just never expected...'

'It's marvellous, darling. And just what you deserve after all your hard work. Changing the subject, I assume, from some comments I heard, that some woman named Miss Sweeney made a remark about dear William?'

Dottie sighed, concentrating on negotiating a sharp bend before saying, 'Yes that's exactly what happened. Then her best friend, Florentina Coyle joined in, of course.'

Mrs Manderson patted Dottie's arm. 'I'm afraid

you may get quite a lot of that. Women in society are not very open to the idea of a marriage to a professional man, as I discovered myself many years ago.'

'True. Very true.'

They were home now. She began the elaborate manoeuvres that parking the car in a small space on the street entailed. As they got out, she said, 'By the way, Mother, Christiana Milner told me something rather alarming about those chaps Father is thinking of investing with. I must tell him before he commits himself irretrievably.'

But at home, her father listened with patience as she poured all this out to him, only to have him laugh and say,

'What those young fools? As if I'd invest a shilling with them! I should think after all these years I'd know a conman when I met one.'

*

Chapter Two

Sir Nigel always ensured that Lady Matilda Cosgrove—one of his oldest and dearest friends—had the Ormulu Room whenever she came to stay. In fact, he rather counted on it, because otherwise he'd have to invite fewer guests or somehow get them to share their rooms. None of the other guests would feel comfortable surrounded by so much ornate, gilded wood coupled with a rather dark marble. Oddly, Lady Matilda liked the room. As far as Sir Nigel could tell, she was the only person in existence who did like the room, and that included himself.

It was a quarter to seven on a Sunday evening at the beginning of June, just the day after his evening soirée when he had invited Dottie and her mother, among others. Sir Nigel had planned a quiet dinner with the guests who were staying with him, anticipating plenty of good food and good conversation.

Lady Matilda had just taken a seat at the vast gold

and dark brown marble dressing-table to allow her maid to dress her hair in what they both deemed to be the most becoming fashion for a lady in her mid-sixties. They were deep in conversation about which gown Lady Matilda had worn to a certain affair in the Spring of 1891, when there came a tap on the door.

Salt, Lady Matilda's maid, set down her comb and perfume bottle and turned to the door to state, 'Come,' with as much dignity as her ladyship herself.

The door opened. A timid little red-headed maid stood on the threshold looking extremely nervous, clutching the edge of the door as she peeked in.

'Well?' demanded Salt. She was a fierce protector of her ladyship's privacy.

'Begging your pardon, my lady,' the young woman began. 'But Sir Nigel's compliments and would it suit your ladyship to place your jewellery into Sir Nigel's safe for the evening? There's been two break-ins on this square in the last week, and Sir Nigel doesn't want to run any risks with your ladyship's valuables. In fact, I'm to go to all the ladies—and the gentlemen—and take their valuables down to his lordship's safe before dinner.'

She accompanied this information with a kind of bobbing curtsey, all the while nervously wringing her hands. Lady Matilda thought she seemed a sweet little thing. Rather plain. If she were one of our class, Lady Matilda reflected, glancing with satisfaction at her own reflection in the mirror, and if she had her hair nicely dressed, with good make-up, jewellery and decent clothes, she could even be quite attractive.

'And what is your name, my dear?' demanded her ladyship.

'Eliza, ma'am. Eliza Smallwood. I'm new in this establishment.'

'Well, Eliza Smallwood, I am most obliged to you. Please take my jewellery case to Sir Nigel at once and thank him for his good sense and kind thoughts. Salt, give the child the case. But make sure to keep out what I need for this evening, obviously.'

'Yes, my lady.'

Salt extracted several glittering items of great value. Once Lady Matilda had nodded her approval, the case was locked up again, the tiny key slipped into Salt's pocket, and the case was handed to the young maid.

Eliza Smallwood gave another little bob and clutching the jewellery case to her as if her life depended on keeping it safe, she said, 'Thank you, your ladyship. I'll take these to Sir Nigel directly. Good evening.'

The door closed behind her. Salt and Lady Matilda resumed their discussion relating to the precise colour and fabric of the gown worn on the evening of the Royal Gala almost fifty years earlier.

It was not long before the bell rang for dinner, and Lady Matilda descended the grand staircase to meet the other guests for a pre-dinner aperitif.

Sir Nigel greeted her with a beaming smile, taking both her hands in his and kissing first her left cheek then her right in his usual warm manner that she found delightfully Continental.

In the dining-room, Lady Matilda was seated on Sir Nigel's right hand. She lost no time in thanking him again for his invitation to stay for the week whilst George was overseas on his usual ambassadorial duties. As always, she offered her compliments on the charming Ormulu Bedroom, which had, she said, a rich glamour that one didn't see everywhere. She asked after his health, heard with patience of his sciatica and stiff knees—she was herself a martyr to her knees—and promised to let him have Salt's remedy for the relief of the discomfort. Then at last, she remarked,

'Nigel, dearest. It was so thoughtful of you to send up that sweet little girl to fetch my jewellery. I shall feel so much happier knowing my grandmother's diamonds are safely locked away. These robberies are such a worry, are they not?'

He stared at her for a second or two too long, and she immediately divined that something was amiss. But before she could quiz him about it, the door was flung open to the astonishment of all the other diners, and Salt ran in, tears streaming down her face, causing everyone to turn and stare, drinks or forks halted halfway to their mouths.

She wailed, 'Oh my dear lady, I've just found out! There isn't any such maid as that Eliza girl in the house.' Salt fell onto her knees sobbing as Lady Matilda had never seen her sob before. 'And she's gone off with all your valuables!'

And indeed she had. She had practically run down the back stairs with the jewellery case tightly clutched under her arm, knowing she had only a minute or two to make her escape. The side door was still ajar, just as she had left it. Unseen by anyone, she slipped outside, pulling off her cap and apron, then she hopped into the car waiting at the end of the drive, throwing the jewellery case and her disguise onto the floor and laughingly urging the driver,

'Well, what are you waiting for? Drive, you idiot!'

'All right, Sis, keep your hair on! You were gone ages, didn't think you were ever coming out again!'

'Put your foot down, we've got another call to make!'

They had sped off before anyone in the house had even realised there had been a robbery.

Inside the house, Sir Nigel's footman Brownlee, was telephoning for the police, muttering under his breath, 'Oh God, oh God, what have I done?'

The next morning, Monday, Lord Dalbury paid a visit to his mother. He thought he may as well get it over with sooner rather than later.

'Henry! My dear boy!'

'Mother, I'm very glad to see you looking so well.' Lord Dalbury came across the morning-room carpet to where his mother had positioned her invalid chair by the window. He bent to kiss her cheek, noticing it was cold to the touch. He took her hands in his, and crouching down beside her, he smiled his radiant, charming smile.

'So how are you, old girl? I mean, how are you *really*?'

She huffed at him, flapping a hand. 'I thought you said I looked well. 'So well', you said a moment ago.'

'And so you do. But your nurse tells me you've been very naughty. Not eating properly. Getting out of your chair. Trying to go up and down the stairs. She said she found you in the orangery yesterday.'

'I like it in there...'

'But it's cold in there, and so far from the morning-room. What if you were to have a fall onto that stone floor? You could lie there for hours before anyone found you. You know I worry about you. And now, on top of everything, I hear you've stopped taking your medicine, Mother! You know you must take it if you want to get better.'

His coaxing tone got him nowhere. She swept his words aside with an impatient,

'Oh tosh! Those pills do nothing at all for me other than to make me feel sick.'

'But Mother...' He was trying not to overdo it. He

opted for a rather half-hearted remonstrating tone. After all, it wouldn't do for the old bat to be persuaded to take the medicine again. She was sixty-eight next month. That was quite long enough to be on this earth, and he definitely didn't want her to be here next year to celebrate her sixty-ninth. He needed the money well before that. A large family home in generously proportioned grounds in a smart area of London like this was worth an absolute fortune. He added a sad, puppy-dog look, then quickly smiled at her again.

'Very well. We won't dwell on that. Now then. It's a lovely morning, would you like me to push you about in the garden for a bit?'

The old woman clasped her hands together almost as if she were pleading with him. 'Oh, Henry, dearest, would you? I'd love that. I haven't been outside for over a week.'

Inwardly he sighed, but his smile never once faltered. He gave her a mock salute, bent to let off the brake, then took hold of the handles and began to wheel her towards the hall and the side door.

He took her first to the roses as they were her favourite. Many of them were already in bloom. She greeted each one like an old friend, gently cupping the flowers to breathe in their scent. He rolled his eyes as for the hundredth time, she said,

'Your dear father and I planted this one when we came back from our honeymoon. It's a gallica rose, so fragrant, Henry, dear. It really is the best, in my opinion.'

She wittered on. Henry yawned and looked around him. The place was looking pretty good, he had to admit. Hopefully it wouldn't be too much longer... He glanced down at her, seeing for the first time how thin her grey hair had become. He remembered when he was a small boy and she'd had lustrous dark locks, curling all over her head and down to her shoulders. His father, dead for almost twenty years now, had adored her hair.

Her skin too seemed aged even since he'd seen her, what, just two weeks ago? She looked pale, her complexion having a slightly transparent tissue-paper look about it. She looked all of her age and more. It warmed his heart to think that soon she could be gone, and all this lovely property—and the lovely money it would bring—would be his. He came out of this delicious reverie when she said,

'And by the way, Henry, dearest, it was so considerate of you to send that dear girl to collect my jewellery to put into your safe last evening. She told me that there have been so many dreadful robberies in this area reported in the newspapers. Such a good idea of yours. I feel so much happier now you have them, such a weight off my mind.'

'What?' he demanded. He had a sudden sense of doom.

She paused in her sniffing of a particularly lovely *Souvenir de la Malmaison* and gazed at his reddening face with a vague sort of bewilderment.

'Henry...'

'What did you say? You gave your jewellery to some girl? What are you talking about?'

'She said she was your new maid, and that her name was Eliza. I must say, I was very glad to hear that you'd...'

He cut her off with a terse, 'You handed over your jewels to a *complete* stranger?' He could hardly believe what he was hearing. Surely she hadn't *actually*...

She gaped up at him in that frightened kitten manner that always got his back up. He felt like shaking her hard, or strangling her, his hands itched to be about that scraggy throat. He stared at her, shoving his hands into his pockets.

'Not a stranger, dear, not really. After all she *is* part of your household,' the Dowager Duchess reproached him mildly. She'd always had a soft spot for the servants, he recalled.

'Mother, dear,' he added, smiling in spite of his rage. 'I do *not* have any new staff. I most definitely did *not* send anyone to you for your jewellery. Please tell me you didn't *actually...*'

But he could see from her expression that it was only too true.

'Oh dear, oh dear, oh my dear goodness me, oh my...' Lord Dalbury's mother began to cry.

With a stifled curse, Dalbury turned and ran back into the house, leaving his mother sitting alone with her beloved roses.

Earlier that same Monday morning, Sergeant William Hardy had arrived for work at New Scotland Yard, and thanks to the traffic—a motorised coal lorry had met unexpectedly with a motorised milk lorry, and the respective drivers had decided to stand in the middle of the road and discuss the meeting in depth, causing something of a jam—he was barely on time to meet his new senior officer. As he crossed the entrance hall, he heard those words that brought a chill to his very soul.

'Ah, Hardy. Glad to have caught you. A word if you please.'

'Why—er—yes. Yes, sir, of course.' Hardy looked about him, but fortunately didn't spot anyone watching them. He lowered his voice. 'What was it you wished to see me about?'

'Not here, laddie! Pop into the office.'

Reluctantly—but with no choice in the matter—Hardy followed Chief Superintendent Smithers along the hall and into his office, straight past the surprised secretary who was just uncovering her typewriter.

'Shut the door, shut the door!'

Obligingly, William shut the door. 'Sir?'

'Now then. First day with Inspector Rhodes and his section?' Smithers was divesting himself of raincoat and hat then turned to pull out his chair.

'Yes sir.'

'Naturally they don't know that your demotion is sham and that you are looking into some highly serious accusations on my behalf. Therefore, try to keep your head down. Initially I just want you to observe him, and his men. Report back to me at the end of the week, won't you.'

'Yes sir, of course.' William waited to see if there was anything else.

The chief super was now seated at his desk, riffling through his freshly delivered correspondence. After a moment he glanced up again at Hardy.

'Well don't just stand there, laddie. Can't be late on your first day!'

'Er—no—I—er... Thank you, sir.'

'On your way out, tell Miss Ellis I'm ready for my cup of tea, will you. Now then let me see...'

And Hardy completely forgotten, he turned his attention to the first envelope, carefully slitting it open with his paperknife.

'Of course. Thank you. Sir.'

William reflected that he was now actually late, thanks to the old boy.

Two minutes later, William stood waiting for the opportunity to introduce himself to his new boss. It felt exactly like his first day in CID: he was convinced his shirt collar was too tight or not clean enough. He polished his shoes on the back of each trouser leg. He had tested the freshness of his breath by breathing into his cupped palm, and he had rehearsed what he was going to say so many times that now he couldn't remember a word. It was ridiculous to be so nervous.

At last, Detective Inspector Marcus Rhodes turned away from the other two men in the office and sent a withering glance in William's direction.

'I suppose you're my new sergeant.' It wasn't a question, and Rhodes sounded less than enthused by the sight of the new officer.

'Er, yes, that's right, sir. Hardy. William Hardy.' William held out a hand but Rhodes ignored it. William let the hand fall back to his side.

'You're late, Hardy. I don't like my men to be late.'

'I'm very sorry, sir. Chief Superintendent Smithers spotted me coming into the building and asked to speak with me.'

'Hmmph.'

William could tell that his story was dismissed as a fabrication. He repressed a childish urge to offer proof.

'That's your desk over there. Your first task is to fetch me a cup of tea. Milk. Three sugars.'

'Er...'

'Now, sergeant. Not next week.'

'Of course, sir.'

William hurried away in the direction of the canteen, digging in his pocket for the correct money, then hurried back to the office with the cup and saucer, trying not to spill the contents on his boots. The other men looked up as he entered, both smirking. He carried the drink to Rhodes's desk and set it down.

Rhodes just barely glanced at it, grunted

something then turned back to the report he was reading. William hung his coat up on the stand in the corner of the room, popped his hat on a peg, then went to sit at his new desk. He checked there were still plenty of blank pages in his daybook, and that he still had three sharpened pencils in his top pocket.

He had a feeling it was going to be a long day.

But when the call came half an hour later, there was a frantic flurry of activity.

'Spence, and what's-your-name, you're both with me. Kerridge, you too. Spence, you can drive. We're heading to St George's Crescent first about a jewel robbery, then on what sounds like an oddly similar errand, we need to go to Tyne Square immediately afterwards.'

Kerridge, who resembled a walking mountain, leapt to his feet and waited to fall in behind Rhodes. Spence and Hardy did the same.

Spence rubbed his hands together gleefully. 'Sounds exciting, boss, just what we need on a Monday morning.

William glanced sideways at the fellow, suspecting him of sarcasm, but his expression was one of genuine pleasure.

Spence drove the new police car, the warning to treat it with the same care as a newborn baby still ringing in his ears as he sped off into the traffic, swerving to avoid a brewer's dray. Beside him, Rhodes occupied the front passenger seat, whilst William chafed in the back seat next to the sprawling lump Kerridge, a newly-minted detective constable. William found it frustrating not knowing all the details, but he had to wait. He was not in charge here.

They arrived in a creditable twenty minutes, parking the car outside an attractive Georgian villa. A maid was already opening the front door for them.

'Spence! The bloody bell, man!'

Spence cursed and leaned into the car to turn off the clanging bell. The abrupt silence was deafening. Rhodes led them up the steps.

'Detective Inspector Rhodes of Scotland Yard, girl. Tell your master I'm here.'

She was not going to stand there with twenty years' experience as a head housemaid and be called 'girl' by some grubby copper. She sniffed and said, her tone dripping with sarcasm, 'I could tell him that, sir, I suppose, if I had one of they Ouijy boards. It's her ladyship's home now, and just you treat her with some respect, she's not a well lady. And mind you wipe your feet before you come in, this was all swept and mopped just two hours ago.' She turned back into the house, leaving William to close the door.

'In there,' she said, pointing. Then she marched off before they had time to ask her anything. 'There' proved to be a cramped study, sparsely furnished with a desk and chair, a lamp, and a small bookcase in an alcove to the right of the chimney breast. There was a wheelchair positioned by the window. Its occupant was the elderly Dowager Lady Dalbury, with a cosy blanket over her knees and a worried expression on her face. Across the room, an elegantly clad young gentleman halted in his pacing to look at them with a glare.

'It's about bloody time!'

*

Chapter Three

The interview room stank of sweat and cigarette smoke. It was hot, too, and Hardy wasn't surprised to see that Brownlee, the footman from Sir Nigel Ponsonby's household, looked decidedly uncomfortable. His shirt had great wet patches under the arms, he had circles under his eyes that resembled bruises, and his face was sticky-looking beneath a strong growth of dark stubble. He was in a belligerent mood, already on his feet and protesting as soon as the door opened. The duty constable shouted at him several times to sit down.

Rhodes took his seat, leaning back, his arms folded across his chest and staring at the man. Hardy decided to stay on his feet by the door. Brownlee looked from one of them to the other and back again.

'What am I supposed to have done?' he demanded, then before anyone had a chance to reply, he kicked the leg of the table, snarling, 'You can't keep me here! I'll have you! You let me go right now, or you'll regret it.' He pointed a shaking forefinger at Rhodes.

Rhodes grabbed the finger and slammed it down hard on the table, wrenching the man's whole arm so that his head almost hit the tabletop.

'Don't you know it's rude to point, Mr Brownlee? And let's not be hearing any of your threats now, that's just not polite.'

He let go of the footman who struggled to sit upright in his seat, rubbing his wrist and hand. Hardy had seen plenty of interviews during his career both in interview rooms and outside that had got completely out of hand, but he held himself in check now until he could see what Rhodes did next.

Rhodes dusted an imaginary speck off his jacket sleeve, and regarded the footman with a steady gaze. 'That's better. Now you stay nice and calm, Mr Brownlee, and we'll all get along like a house on fire. Right, we know you're behind these jewellery thefts that have been going on lately. Just tell us how many of you are involved, and what you've done with the stuff, and I will make sure to tell the judge you were nice and helpful.'

Brownlee indicated with a gesture of his right hand that this would not be his favoured course of action.

Rhodes tutted and shook his head. 'Come, come, Mr Brownlee. We've got a witness; we've got your whole plan. We just need you to fill in a few details for us. Two years, with a further two suspended. That's not a bad deal. After all, you haven't caused anyone any physical harm. That always goes down well with a judge.'

'You've lost me my job!' Brownlee snapped back, mirroring Rhodes' posture by folding his arms across his chest.

Rhodes shrugged. 'I'm sorry about that, Mr Brownlee. I'm afraid there wasn't anything we could do about that. Sir Nigel was understandably upset. You couldn't expect him to keep a thieving little toerag like you on his staff, not at a nice place like he's got.'

Brownlee clamped his mouth shut and fixed his gaze on the table-top. But after a minute he said, 'I've got nothing to say.' Another moment went by then he added, 'So don't think you can make me.'

No one said anything for quite a while though the duty constable's stomach growled loudly several times.

'Sorry sir. Missed my breakfast,' the constable said.

Rhodes gave him a curt nod. He glanced at Hardy and catching his eye, cocked his head at footman, indicating that it was Hardy's turn to ask him a few questions.

Without moving from his spot by the door, Hardy asked, 'So how did you find Eliza? And how did you get her to agree to help you?'

For a moment it looked as though he wasn't going to reply, but then, sarcasm dripping from every word, he said, 'I don't even know anyone called Eliza.'

'Well, you let the woman in that night. So you assisted her to carry out the burglary. Aiding and abetting, we call that in legal terms.'

'I've never!' Brownlee insisted, but his eyes were wary, his tone lacked conviction.

Hardy leaned forward slightly and said, 'In that case, why were you so upset when news of the theft was broken to Lady Cosgrove and Sir Nigel Ponsonby by Miss Salt? You were heard by both Lady Cosgrove and Sir Nigel to say, 'Oh God, what have I done?' That was while you were ringing for the police. Perhaps you can tell me what you meant by that?'

Brownlee glared at Hardy. For a long moment he was silent, but as before, he just couldn't help himself. He said, 'I don't have to tell you nothing!'

'True.' Hardy nodded.

'You can't make me! I ain't done nothing!'

Hardy sighed theatrically, exchanging an eyeroll with the other two police officers.

But Brownlee hadn't finished. 'You can't put this on me, I know my rights!'

'Just tell us, Brownlee,' Rhodes said in his most bored tone.

Hardy added, 'I have to say, it's one of the best schemes I've heard of. So simple. Really very clever. I almost admire you for it. Almost. And as the inspector says, you haven't hurt anyone. No one was threatened or confronted with a weapon. There was no violence. It was audacious.'

'Brilliant, even,' Rhodes added, turning slightly to quirk an eyebrow at Hardy who immediately agreed.

'Absolutely. Highly ingenious.'

Brownlee still looked wary, but it was as if he realised that was only one way out of this situation. In a sulky voice, he said,

'I was paid to do it. I didn't know what was going to happen. I just had to let someone into the house before dinner, when everyone was upstairs dressing. I had to unlock the side door. That's all I did.'

'Paid by whom?' Hardy asked.

'I don't know. Some woman that came to the house. I took drinks into the study for the men one evening, as usual, then I had to take coffee into the drawing-room for the ladies who were visiting. There were a couple of them, but the other one wasn't there, off powdering her nose or summat—and this woman was just sitting in there on his own. She asked me my name, and how long I'd worked there. So I told her, though I thought it was a bit odd. Usually, it's all you can do to get a thank you out of 'em. Then, 'How'd you like to earn a few bob on the quiet?' she says. I said I might. She just nodded and tapped her nose and said she'd be in touch. Then the other lady came back and they started talking about going to the horse racing, and what they were going to wear. That was it.'

'And then what happened?' Hardy asked.

'Well, it was about a week later, at another one of Sir Nigel 's dinner parties. He has them regular. Usually, one every week. And sometimes a midweek one but mostly there's just one on a Saturday. I'd just taken drinks in after dinner to the gentlemen, and then the coffee in for the ladies again. As I was leaving the room, this same woman followed me out. I thought she was going to ask me where the whatsit was. But she grabbed me by the arm, and said, 'Are you still interested in earning yourself a couple of quid?' So I told her I was, and she said, 'This is what I want you to do. Next Saturday, when Sir Nigel's guests go up to dress for dinner, I want you to let a young lady in at the side door. She's called Eliza. She's a lady's maid. Direct her to Lady Cosgrove's room. And Eliza will give you ten pounds. Just don't mention it to anyone, it's a dead secret. If you blab, you won't get nothing.' Well, I couldn't believe it. Ten whole pounds! And for doing what? Opening a door and telling a girl where to find Lady Cosgrove?'

'Didn't you think it was odd? You must have known there was something wrong about this.' Rhodes said.

Hardy was glad that Rhodes seemed calmer now, and he wondered if Rhodes was really so aggressive, or if he just adopted the appearance of being aggressive to get his suspects to talk. Either way, Hardy would need to keep a close eye on him.

Brownlee seemed only too willing to talk now,

relieved to get it all off his chest.

'I suppose so. But it's my job to do as I'm told, and not to ask questions or make difficulties. It didn't seem much to do for ten pounds. She said she was to hand the old girl some legal papers she wouldn't want. But all the same I never expected anything like this.'

'Legal papers? Like a court order? Or a summons?' Hardy queried.

'I assumed that was what she meant.'

'What if someone saw you?' Rhodes asked.

Brownlee shrugged. 'It wasn't a problem. I just needed to say Lady Cosgrove's maid had been sent on an errand and had just got back. But because everyone was busy with dinner preparations, no one else even noticed. It only took a minute or so, then she'd got upstairs, and I carried on taking bits and bobs into the dining-room.'

'So, the maid went up to the room... Presumably she already knew the layout of the house?' Hardy said.

Brownlee shrugged his shoulders again. 'Don't know, do I? All I said was, Lady Cosgrove's in the Ormolu Room, on the second floor. And off the girl went.'

'You didn't take her up there?'

'Nope.'

'And you did this how many times?'

'Just the once.'

'What about the other robberies, then?' Rhodes said. He looked puzzled, at Hardy felt the same. But Brownlee appeared truthful.

Brownlee shrugged. 'That weren't me. They must have someone else they use. The other peoples' footmen, their maids. I've only helped with this one. I didn't even realise what they were doing until it

happened. If I'd known, obviously I wouldn't have...'
He sank further back in his seat, eyes closed, head
shaking as he tried to take it all in.

'So this Eliza girl. Had you seen her before? Was
she a former member of staff at Sir Nigel's?'

'Not that I know of. But she could have been. I
didn't exactly spend half an hour staring at her, or
anything. Like I said, when I let her in, she came
straight past me, and said, 'I'm Eliza. Where's Lady
Cosgrove?' Then she shoved a little brown envelope
in my hand. 'This is yours', she said. And then she
was gone. I didn't hang around, I got on with what I
was supposed to be doing. I didn't see her leave. But
after I'd called the police, I remembered the door,
and I panicked and ran to lock it again.'

Hardy and Rhodes exchanged a look.

'And the woman who spoke to you, to arrange it,
what was her name?' Hardy asked.

Brownlee shrugged again. 'I don't know...'

Rhodes cut across him. 'If she was a guest of Sir
Nigel's, you must have announced her or been told to
expect her?'

'It was the butler dealt with all that. He brings 'em
in and announces them to Sir Nigel. I never heard
her name, I just carried her bags up.'

Rhodes got to his feet.

'Right,' he said to Hardy, 'I'll leave you to take all
that down.'

'Yes sir.'

For the next hour they went back and forth over it
all again, and then Hardy got the statement written
up and Brownlee signed at the bottom of the page to
say it was a true account.

'I suppose I'm going down for two years now,' he
said. He looked exhausted. Hardy felt for the fellow.
This wasn't the first time someone had tried to earn

themselves a little extra and had come unstuck.

'I doubt it will be as long as that,' Hardy said. 'You didn't really do very much. And you've helped the police, that will be to your advantage. You might even get off with just a caution.'

'What about a job, though? No one is going to employ me now, are they?'

'I'm sorry, but you held a position of trust, and you abused that trust.'

'And all for ten bloody pounds. It wasn't worth twice that.'

'About that...' Hardy held out his hand. He sighed. 'I'm really sorry, I'm going to need to take that.'

'What! Why?' Brownlee was outraged.

'It's evidence. And in any case, you can't profit from a crime.'

Brownlee got his wallet out and removed the ten-pound banknote, leaving his wallet empty. 'That's near enough the most money I've ever seen in one go. Will I get it back?'

Hardy shook his head. 'Only if you're found not guilty.'

'That won't happen, will it, now I've confessed. Cor lumme.'

'It may not feel like it, but you've done the right thing. Constable, take this man to the custody sergeant, please. Mr Brownlee, this officer will take you to be charged. Good day to you, Mr Brownlee.'

*

Chapter Four

This was how she liked it, Dottie thought, surveying the scene at the warehouse: the place was packed. Forty-six women were chatting and laughing, clinking their champagne glasses together and waiting for the show to start.

From her place in the centre of the stage, trying to ignore her usual flutter of nerves, Dottie asked the ladies to take their seats.

She had scolded and cajoled the girls into their places, and now, coming forward to stand at the edge of the stage, she nodded to Mrs Avers, head seamstress and Dottie's right-hand woman, for the curtains to be opened.

As the first mannequin came forward, Dottie glanced down at her notes, then taking a deep breath, she began:

'Welcome ladies, to this rather impromptu,' and here her audience all laughed, 'showing of our new Autumn into Winter season models here at

Carmichael and Jennings: Exclusive Modes for Discerning Ladies.'

Before she could continue, the audience erupted into a ripple of applause, and Dottie flushed with pride and pleasure. She continued:

'Our first model tonight is a charming yet practical two-piece suit in grey wool with a soft cream stripe. The jacket has padded shoulders, a double-breasted button fastening, and comes with either a matching grey or a contrasting dark grey or cream wool belt if desired. The shawl-style collar and patch pockets complete a youthful, modern look. The matching skirt has box pleats from hip-level for ease of movement and style, and this outfit can easily be paired with a snappy little matching coat for visits to Town, or for those days when the wind is that little bit chillier.' She allowed her voice to warm to a soft laugh as the mannequin stepped forward, turned to the left then to the right, then twirled slowly right around, and as she did so, aided by Mrs Avers, she slipped her arms into the sleeves to present the matching coat over the two-piece suit. 'This outfit is also available in navy blue or fawn,' Dottie added. 'Why not treat yourself to one of each?'

There was a ripple of appreciative applause. On both sides of the jutting stage, ladies began putting their heads together for hurried discussions.

'Thank you, Grace,' Dottie said as Gracie left the stage and returned to the changing area, her place on the stage taken by Charlie—Charlotte Wilmslow, a South London girl through and through, with temperamental skin but wonderful deep red hair that curled madly to halfway down her back, making her the envy of every woman at the warehouse. This evening, she wore it piled up, all the better to show the collar of the coat and skirt suit, this time in a delicate fern-green wool, that was the next model to be displayed.

Really, Dottie thought, as she said her little bit and Charlie moved across the stage, what the audience want to see is—of course—the evening wear, and the lingerie. But there had to be practical garments too. Charlie did a final twirl then returned to the changing room, smiling as Dottie thanked 'Charlotte' for her time. Next came the first of the more glamorous items: a basic evening gown in ivory silk shown by Patricia—Patty Knowles to her friends—finished with a black silk and satin wrap edged with rows of tiny gold beads that glittered in the light.

'This dress is also available in peach, lilac or pale turquoise. We can't have you all turning up in the same frock, now can we?' Dottie joked. The audience laughed too, clearly enjoying themselves. Dottie began to relax a little. She continued the narration. 'The wrap can be in grey or cream satin, or you might be drawn to a sequinned wrap like this one.' She indicated the new wrap Patricia had now exchanged for the first one she'd shown, the model slipping the wrap about her shoulders in one smoothly elegant movement, whilst the first was neatly caught and removed by Mrs Avers.

There were more comments and laughter, the audience again turning to one another excitedly. Someone made a remark that Dottie didn't quite catch, and a number of nearby ladies nodded gravely, making hurried notes on their cards, and then all three mannequins were back on the stage in new outfits, a whirlwind of colour and flowing hemlines.

Immediately the spectators clapped, thrilled to see Dottie's now-trademark ruby-coloured low-backed evening gown, plus a deep-violet gown with practically no back or indeed front, and a glittering lamé silver dance gown, fitting closely from bust to hips, but floating out at the knee to create the perfect dress for any style of dancing.

Dottie herself stepped onto the stage to show the emerald-green satin gown with tiny capped sleeves that just covered the top of the shoulders, the plunging neckline at the front that formed a deep V that came down almost to her navel, and the skirt with the waterfall style front hemline flouncing from knee to ankle in soft waves.

The audience clapped wildly.

An hour later, the show was over, and Dottie had only to mingle and—hopefully—to receive some orders. She came out to the front of the stage and with great embarrassment received far more congratulations and praise than she was really comfortable with. Coming down the steps she explained several times how indebted she was to her wonderful staff. Mrs Avers was circulating with Gracie and Charlie, offering drinks to customers and trying to get them talking about which of the models they had liked the most, whilst Patty and Millie offered canapes.

Out of forty-plus guests, Dottie was hoping for at least fifteen—twenty really, if she was honest with herself—orders.

'Good grief, it's warm,' Dottie grumbled another half an hour later. She was standing at the open front door. It was almost eleven o'clock, but the night showed no sign of cooling; there was not a breath of wind. She fanned herself with her programme notes for the show.

Coming over, Christiana said, 'I was wondering if I'd managed to persuade you to join us on Friday for a long weekend? Everyone's staying until Tuesday morning, so you'd be most welcome to do the same.

Have you had a chance to think it over? I know it's rather short notice, and you've been so busy. There's always a lovely breeze there coming in off the river, not like stuffy old London. That's not much fun in the winter of course. But in hot weather like this it's divine. Really, I'd love you to come. Anabella will be there with her new man, Major Forsythe. You met him at Sir Nigel's last weekend, didn't you? Tom is an absolute sweetheart, I've known him for years, and he is so funny once he gets to know you and starts up with all his famous anecdotes. You could bring your handsome fiancé and have a little holiday. And I know I mentioned my mother's things, but of course, there'd be no obligation, I just thought you would be the right person to ask what to do about them. But please feel free to say no, I shan't mind a bit. It would just be lovely to see you.'

'Oh Christiana, I'd love to come, I should have made that clear. But I doubt William will be able to manage it,' Dottie said. 'He's just started on a new department, and they've got a big case on, so he can't very well leave in the middle of things.'

'Oh of course! Well, look, come anyway if you can. You'd be very welcome to bring someone else if you wanted to, we have plenty of room. The more the merrier, don't they say?'

'Might I bring my mother? I'm sure she'd love to get out of 'stuffy old London' as you called it. She finds the hot weather such a trial.' Then Dottie hesitated, remembering something. 'Oh, but I can't! I have a dress fitting next week, on Monday morning.'

'*The* dress, is it?'

Dottie nodded, smiling.

Christiana grinned back. 'Well, you can't possibly miss that, obviously. But look, our place is only just over an hour's drive out of London. You could pop up to Town, have the fitting, then pop back again. How about that?'

'All right, yes, that's a grand idea!'

They beamed at each other, then Christiana gave her a quick hug before taking her leave, and Dottie remembered her other guests.

Next, Anabella came across with Lady Matilda Cosgrove to say goodbye to her. In her distinctive accent Anabella said,

'Oh Dottie, the show was just divine. I can't believe you pulled everything together so quickly. I mean, the whole thing. It was just so... Thank you so much for inviting me. I can't wait to send in my order.'

Lady Cosgrove was nodding and agreeing with Anabella, and added, 'I've already given in my order—that emerald gown was so very daring—and I know my George will love it! It's a real must-have!'

'With your figure, Lady Cosgrove, it will be perfect,' Dottie said perfectly sincerely. She knew of no woman over the age of sixty with a better complexion or a better figure than her ladyship.

'Such a consolation after what happened at Sir Nigel's last weekend,' Lady Cosgrove said, and Dottie was sure she heard a tremor in the older woman's voice. Lady Cosgrove took out a handkerchief and dabbed it quickly at her eyes.

'Why?' Dottie asked. 'What happened?'

Lady Cosgrove clutched Dottie's arm. 'Oh, my dear, haven't you heard? There was a robbery! Someone took all my jewels, apart from the ones I had on, of course. A most audacious crime—and it's left me so upset. And poor Salt, my maid, is inconsolable.'

Dottie gaped at her in dismay. 'My goodness, that's awful!'

'The police had to be called, of course. They are

looking into it. But I'm sure I shall never see my jewellery again. One feels fortunate not to have suffered any physical harm, of course.'

Dottie nodded. 'True, and thank goodness for that. But even so, it sounds awful...'

'I must admit, I felt a little worried about coming out tonight, but Salt told me to buck up and not let the so-and-so win.'

'Very true, very true, Lady Matilda,' Anabella agreed. 'A distraction is just what you needed, and a little fun. I'm sure your British police will soon find these thieves and make them pay. Don't trouble yourself over them, you'll get your jewels back, just you wait and see.'

'My dear Anabella, you're so sweet. Both of you, so kind. I hope you won't mention this to anyone? I expect everyone already knows, but... No doubt people would be sympathetic, but I'd worry they would be laughing at me behind their hands. Fancy being fool enough to actually hand your valuables over to the thief! And to thank them for taking them! My husband is devastated, of course, and understandably, it's a lot of money to lose, and some of the things are quite old, they've been in his family for generations, and he's most attached to them. Or was. And poor Nigel too, he's terribly upset. I'm so stupid..."

Lady Cosgrove patted both their arms and wandered out with Anabella, still rather distressed, only to be replaced by a pair of ladies who had questions about the evening wraps, leaving Dottie no time to ponder Lady Cosgrave's horrid experience. She must remember to ask William if he'd heard anything about it. That might even be the big case he was working on. If he was, and he didn't get Lady Cosgrove's jewels back, Dottie would feel dreadful.

After the two ladies' concerns were satisfied, another attendee grabbed Dottie's arm to congratulate her on the new season's collection, and to ask about the daywear. So it went on for almost another hour, Dottie thanking everyone, and them all thanking her too, and promising to send in their orders. By the time she finally shut the door on the last guest to leave, she felt highly gratified with the way things had gone. Gratified but exhausted.

The staff were the next to go, all calling out goodnight to her as she made her final rounds of the building. At last, at just three minutes to midnight, she locked the double front doors, and went through the warehouse to the back door, accompanied by Mr Whiteley as always.

Terence Whiteley was looking quite well, she noted, now that he had a regular income and was able to afford clean lodgings and proper food. He had been a godsend in many ways, a homeless man desperate for work when he'd knocked on the back door of the warehouse almost six months earlier. He'd seen to so many of the maintenance tasks that Dottie was clueless to tackle, and she was grateful for that. Everything at the warehouse now ran smoothly, was comfortable, and clean and tidy.

In spite of that, somehow the poor man still set her on edge. Dottie felt ashamed of her reaction to him, reminding herself for the umpteenth time that he couldn't help his limp, or the slight rasp to his voice from the gas attack he'd been caught in as a young infantryman at the end of the war almost twenty years earlier. She smiled at him now as she said goodnight and thanked him for his help. She quickly—perhaps a little too quickly, she realised later—refused his offer to walk her to her car that was garaged around the corner, and once again said goodnight to him.

She was still on edge by the time she reached the garage. The walk along the dark street and into the even darker mews, with its countless shadowy nooks and recesses, coupled with all the odd noises of the night, sent her hurrying along, breathless.

William was waiting for her by her car, chatting with the nightwatchman, his lean body and blond head immediately recognisable. The garage nightwatchman saluted them both and went back to the door of his hut.

Relieved to see William, Dottie hugged him. He kissed her cheek, her neck, her mouth. As he moved to open the car door for her, she said,

'You could have come inside, you know, you didn't have to skulk about out here in the darkness.' She slid into the driver's seat and started the car.

'I know,' William said.

Then she was waving goodnight to the nightwatchman and handing the man a shilling tip. 'Thanks a lot, Stanley.' He touched his cap and thanked her.

She allowed the car to inch forward slowly until she could see if her way was clear onto the main road.

'Do you give him a shilling every day?' William asked her curiously.

She realised he thought she was too extravagant. 'Well, I, er...'

William laughed. 'Good Lord, he earns more than I do!'

'Oh no he doesn't, you silly man, you're exaggerating. But if he did, he'd need it. He's got six children and an Alsatian to feed!'

The road was empty, though there was a figure on the pavement further along, one that moved with a halting uneven step. Terence Whiteley. Dottie turned the car in the opposite direction out of the mews and made for home. 'So,' she prompted him. 'Why didn't you? Come in?'

'I didn't feel like talking. I was tired and just wanted to mull over the day quietly.'

She spared a second to glance at him. 'Was it awful?'

His tone was one of vague surprise as he said, 'No, actually. I'm getting to rather like Inspector Rhodes. Not that he seems all that taken with me. But he's no doubt been told some story that I've made a mess of things, you know, to explain my demotion. I'm pretty sure he's all right really. Somehow, I'd imagined someone quite different to the man I met today. I'd expected more—I don't know—bluster and arrogance.'

'Oh dear. You like him?'

They turned a corner, and she pulled the car in behind a bus creeping along annoyingly slowly. 'I bet someone's rung the bell and it's going to stop,' she grumbled, half to herself.

The bus did stop. Several people began to clamber down the steps onto the pavement.

'You like him?' she said again, prompting him. Another sideways glance showed that he was half-asleep. 'Am I taking you back to my parents' house or am I taking you back to your house?'

Without opening his eyes, he said, with a slight grin, 'Our house, you mean.'

It always made her heart flutter when he said it, but she couldn't help reminding him. 'Not yet, it isn't.'

'We could go to yours,' he suggested. 'I can walk back.'

But she decided to take him straight to his home.

She wasn't dead on her feet—not quite anyway— whereas he very clearly was. By the time she halted the car in the street outside the house, he was actually asleep, his head resting against the window of the passenger door. She slid out of her seat, closed the door quietly, then went around to the passenger door, opened it carefully and leaned in to give him a gentle shake.

'Come on, sleeping beauty, this is your stop.'

He groaned and hauled himself out, reaching into his pocket for his door key. She took it from him and ran up the steps to open the door and put the hall light on.

'Go on, get yourself indoors and up to bed,' she said, kissing his cheek. 'Hopefully I'll see you properly tomorrow.'

'Aren't you coming in?' There was the usual hopeful glint in his eye.

She laughed and started back down the steps, calling over her shoulder, 'You're incorrigible! Goodnight, darling. Sweet dreams!'

He waved until her car was turning at the end of the road, then grumbled to himself about the bachelor life. He went inside and shut the door with something of a bang. So much for a romantic nightcap together, he thought. And now he was wide awake.

'Are you involved in investigating this latest spate of jewellery thefts from dinner parties across town?' Dottie asked him the following evening.

William sighed. He had hoped to keep her attention all on him this evening, and to forget about work. She snuggled into the crook of his shoulder, drawing her feet up under her on the sofa. She stroked Watson and felt the contented rattle vibrating its tiny fluffy body as it lay on her lap. It was a relief that both kittens were thriving after their difficult early days on a building site after their mother had died. Dottie had found them and rescued them, bringing them on the journey south from Derbyshire.

'Hmm. This is nice,' she added.

'It is,' he said with a pretend grumble. 'Or was. Until you spoiled things by bringing up work.'

'Sorry.' She kissed his cheek. 'It's rather brought up some nasty memories for me. As you know, I'm going to Christiana Milner's for a house party tomorrow, and Mother and I are staying until Tuesday morning. You were invited, but I assumed you wouldn't be able to get away?'

He shook his head. 'No, sorry, it looks as though I'll be working...'

She nodded. 'That's what I thought. That's why I've already asked Mother if she'd like to go in your stead. She's acquainted with some of the people and she loves to get away when she can. It's just outside Windsor in Berkshire. Do you suppose the thieves will venture that far out of London?'

His chuckle wasn't entirely humorous. 'I daresay Berkshire have their own thieves without borrowing any of our London ones.' He leaned his temple against her hair. 'I'm sure it will be all right, darling. Though I'm not surprised it's upsetting you, after what happened at your birthday party. And to answer your first question, yes, since you ask, these jewellery robberies are exactly what I'm working on with Rhodes.'

'I thought you were investigating *him*?'

'I am. But it's a case of observing him and trying to find something that isn't right. Or catching him in the act. Old Smithers was a bit cagey about what's actually going on. And in the meantime, I have to carry on being a normal copper.'

'It must be something pretty awful if Smithers was prepared to publicly demote one of his finest officers to carry out a secret investigation.'

He kissed the top of the head again. 'Thanks for calling me one of his finest—though I'm not sure he'd agree. I think he hopes I'll confirm his suspicions independently of anything he might know already. My guess is that it'll take a while for Rhodes to get used to me being around, then perhaps he'll feel safe enough to drop his guard and carry on with whatever it is Smithers thinks he's up to. I've got to keep an open mind, as well as keeping my eyes peeled. These robberies could well be something he's involved with. The perpetrators must be getting their information from somewhere. That could be it.'

'So what do the thieves do? Break into a house at night when everyone is asleep and help themselves to whatever they can find? Or do they break in when everyone is at church, or work, or something, and help themselves to the goods in broad daylight? They don't hold everyone up at gunpoint, do they? Because... Oh!'

A sudden memory of her twentieth birthday party the previous year and that chilling moment when she stared down the barrel of a gun whilst the man holding the gun laughed at her terror, made her suddenly feel nauseous. And the poor young constable, she recalled, just out on a normal night shift, and then... She shuddered, and William pulled her close, putting one soft kiss on her cheek.

'Shush darling, it's all right.' He held for a moment, stroking her arm softly. After a few minutes he continued, 'No, it's nothing like that. It's actually quite clever, though I shouldn't say so. And no one has been hurt, apart from financially, of course. At least, not so far.'

Comforting herself that she'd had another birthday party since then, on her mother's insistence, one which had been perfectly pleasant and trouble-free, she smiled, and said, 'Thank goodness for that! But what do they do?'

He reached out a hand to scratch Hastings, sprawled on the arm of the sofa, behind the ear, causing the little creature to purr loudly, its eyes tight shut in pleasure. Hastings' fur was slightly lighter than his brother's plush velvety black, being more of a charcoal grey. William wondered if the fur would grow longer, it just didn't seem quite the same as Watson's. their eyes were not quite the same either, Watson's being rounder and more golden, where Hastings' were almond-shaped and greener. Not that he'd ever imagined they were purebreds, but he wondered briefly, irrelevantly, about their parentage.

'When the guests go upstairs to dress for dinner, a maid knocks on a door to a lady's room, and asks if the lady needs any help. Then as she is leaving, she says that the host is concerned about robberies in the area and that he has offered to put all the ladies' jewellery in his safe. The maid is then given the jewellery, and off she pops, saying something along the lines of, she'll be back later to turn madam's bed down, or to light a fire, or run a bath, or something of that kind, then she leaves. She goes downstairs, letting herself out of a side door, and taking the jewellery with her. So far there have been four successful robberies along these lines, as far as we know, all in central London. Simple but effective.'

Dottie stared at him. 'My goodness! That's just what Lady Cosgrove was telling me about at the fashion show. She's been staying with Sir Nigel

Ponsonby. He's got a lovely place at Tyne Square. Poor Lady Cosgrove was in a terrible state, so distressed—and understandably. And she said her maid was also very upset about the whole thing. It was horrible. The worst of it is, Lady Cosgrove feels so humiliated. To have actually handed her own jewels to the thief. She feels like a prize idiot and worries that everyone is laughing at her.'

'It's a simple but clever, highly original scheme, that's for certain. We went to Sir Nigel's about that robbery. And to the house of a dowager duchess. It's been all hobnobbing with the wealthy and influential this week. The cases are all exactly the same, clearly the work of the same gang. I'm convinced one young woman can't be carrying out the robberies alone.'

Dottie nodded, thinking this over. After a moment she said, 'I'm actually quite impressed. I mean, if you go to a house, especially if it's your first visit, but even if it isn't, you often don't know all the staff. So if a woman wearing the right sort of maid's uniform comes to your door, and does a few helpful things, and is polite and just—you know—acts like a maid, you rather would assume that she was, indeed, a maid. I bet the women handed over their jewels without a second thought. I believe I would do the same. I'd be grateful for the extra security measures.'

'Exactly. It's quite a clever scheme, isn't it? Simple.'

'But effective. Oh yes, it is! Until word gets out, of course.'

'Hmm. No doubt they'll have to come up with a new idea now.'

'At least they haven't shot anyone,' Dottie said.

'Yet.'

'Poor Lady Cosgrove, though. I really felt for her.'

They continued to sit there, each busy with their

thoughts, but deeply contented just to be together for a short while. When the clock on the mantle struck eleven, Dottie said it was time for her to leave.

'I'll walk you home, love,' William said.

She said goodnight to the kittens, then William helped her on with her summer coat and hat, she bent to put on her shoes, and they set off along the street, arm in arm.

At the Mandersons' door, they spent quite a long time 'saying goodnight', reluctant to part, knowing it would very likely be almost a week before they saw one another again.

*

Chapter Five

The next day, the Friday, at a little after half-past three in the afternoon, Dottie and her mother arrived at the residence of Mr and Mrs Sebastian Milner in the attractive village of West Halliford, nestling on the banks of the River Thames just a mile or two from Windsor. Christiana herself welcomed them at the front door with hugs and smiles as if they'd been intimate friends for years.

'This is my butler, Paul Boxhall,' she said with a wave of the hand at a tall, well-built young man with short curling brown hair and a twinkle in his deep brown eyes. 'I'm sure he'll have your luggage brought in from the car and taken up to your rooms in no time.' She reached out a hand to just very briefly touch him on the arm. He nodded politely to Dottie and her mother then moved past them to do just that, directing a nearby maid to help him. 'If it's all right with you, Dottie, Boxhall will move your car to where the garages are at the back of the house.'

'Of course,' Dottie said immediately. 'Thank you.'
She smiled at the butler, who nodded gravely as if
receiving a great commission.

From behind them, down by the riverside, came
the honking and flapping of geese—hordes of them—
either roosting or patrolling along the banks on both
sides of the river.

Christiana shivered. 'I hope the geese weren't a
bother. Vile creatures, they terrify me. Up close, you
know, they're simply huge. Hopefully they'll be gone
soon. They are usually only here for a few weeks at
the start of the year, though this time they've stayed a
lot longer.'

Firmly repressing memories of the geese in the
grounds of the house belonging to her 'real' mother
just six months earlier, Dottie smiled politely. She
too hoped the geese would be gone soon.

Mrs Manderson said, 'Oh very true, they are quite
intimidating, aren't they? They make excellent
watchdogs, I understand.'

'No doubt. They are certainly intimidating. Boxhall
hates them as much as I do, don't you?'

Christiana beamed at the butler who gave her a
nod and a little smile back as he went past them with
the first of two suitcases, followed by the maid with a
hat box under each arm and Mrs Manderson's carpet
bag. Another maid was holding the front door open
for them all to enter. Dottie was impressed the
Milners had so many staff. Few people these days
had both a butler and several maids, usually making
do with one maid-of-all-work, and perhaps a cook. A
quick glance around her showed the house was far
bigger than it at first appeared. Presumably it needed
a large staff to run it.

'Anyway, do come in,' Christiana said, waving
them inside. 'Let's go into the drawing-room, it's

almost time for tea. I'm sure some refreshment will be welcome after your journey. Our other guests have also just arrived, people you already know, I expect, and of course, Sebastian my husband is somewhere around. Hopefully he hasn't taken himself off to his study. He's been looking forward to meeting you. Though I should just warn you, he woke up this morning with the most filthy cold in the head. I do hope he doesn't pass it on to everyone else.'

It was clearly a polite lie that he was keen to meet them, Dottie realised when, just as they were entering the room, Sebastian Milner was heard to say, rather offensively, 'Not more bloody guests!' then added something inaudible and left the room, snuffling noisily into a large white handkerchief, and practically elbowing them aside as he went. He didn't return.

Dottie was delighted to be seated beside Mamie Cotton, the celebrated florist, who, if the legends were to be believed, had made her empire as 'florist to the stars of stage and society' with her own two hands, building it up from a single hand-cart outside the Garrick Theatre on London's Charing Cross Road.

'I bet you didn't know that I was the real live inspiration for the character Judith in *Hay Fever*, that play by Mr Coward,' Mamie commented to Mrs Manderson.

She then went on to claim to have been the 'real live inspiration' for George Bernard Shaw's play, *Pygmalion*, stating without an ounce of embarrassment that she had been his mistress, and that she had also been the secret mistress of Pope Pius X, all of which claims Dottie felt seemed highly unlikely, though her mother was deeply interested and asked several questions.

Mamie's manner—and her somewhat 'individual' appearance of a rather plump, brightly-dressed figure with her hair coloured a deep violet—put Dottie greatly in mind of her old mentor, Mrs Carmichael, the founder of *Carmichael and Jennings, Exclusive Modes for Discerning Ladies*, which had been left to Dottie a year ago upon that lady's untimely death. Dottie and Mamie warmed to one another immediately and on an impulse, Dottie hesitantly raised the possibility of Mamie providing the floral arrangements: the bouquets and buttonholes, for her wedding taking place in just two short months' time.

'It would be a pleasure, my dear. I'll fit it in somehow, don't you worry about that. Will you be wearing one of your own creations for your wedding gown?' Mamie asked, her voice rasping. Dottie suspected she was a heavy smoker. The woman's fingertips on her right hand were very yellow. 'One of your own designs, I mean, of course.'

'Yes, I shall,' Dottie said. She leaned forward. 'It was quite a challenge deciding which of two or three designs to choose. I love them all, so I was rather torn.'

'It must be tempting to put a notice in the marriage Order of Service stating that the dress is available at a particular cost, and can be found in a range of sizes,' Mrs Cotton wheezed. Dottie realised this was the woman's laugh.

Dottie laughed too. 'Oh exactly! I'm already tempted to do that whenever I wear an evening gown. Luckily, ladies who know me seem to have worked out that anything I wear is usually from Carmichael's, so if they see something they like, they often ask me about it later. It can be a trial to remember, though. For example, when someone says, 'Oh that lovely red creation you wore to the Alconburys' that time...' Then I have to cast my mind back and try to work out which one it was.'

'I has the same trouble with flowers, duck. A lady might say, 'Oh Mamie, my lovely, them pink flowers you did for Lord Such and Such, what were they called?' And I have to wrack me brain. You'll have to do what I do now and keep a list in a little notebook, of everything you wear along with the date and place,' Mamie suggested, wheezing again with her earthy humour.

'That's an excellent idea!' Dottie laughed.

Christiana's butler came in at that moment with the tea tray, and everyone began to take their seats, conversation momentarily halted for the more important ceremony of choosing a petit fours or a tiny sandwich.

Mamie excused herself to 'go and powder her nose'.

Looking around, Dottie realised that here were all the same faces she had seen at Sir Nigel's home just a week earlier: not only Lord Dalbury, but also his fiancée, the loathsome Penelope Sweeney. Having noted Miss Sweeney, Dottie was not in the least surprised to catch sight of the figure of Penelope's best friend Florentina Coyle on the other side of the large drawing-room. She was simpering behind her hand at some witticism—no doubt at someone else's expense—from her companion, Milo Parkes.

The four of them began to drift over, commandeering a couple of the smaller sofas nearby, still laughing uproariously at some witty quip or another by one of their number.

'Ugh, I see that awful Parkes fellow is here as well,' Mrs Manderson murmured to Dottie as they settled themselves. Dottie nodded.

'Yes. It's all the same people we met at Sir Nigel's, isn't it? I'm afraid this weekend might not have been such a good idea after all.'

'It is very nice to see dear Christiana. I don't doubt we can put up with Mr Milner's friends for a couple of days.'

'True. Though it's not as if we have any choice,' Dottie pointed out, still keeping her voice low. She turned to smile at the moustache-wearing gentleman seated on the other side her. 'I'm so sorry, I've only just remembered your name.'

She felt embarrassed. After all she and her mother had taken their seats and completely ignored the poor man who was sitting there, cradling a cup of tea he quite clearly didn't want, foisted on him by their hostess.

He smiled. 'Miss Manderson, isn't it? I remember you from last week's shindig.'

'Yes, it is. Do call me Dottie, please. Mother, this is Major Forsythe, he was at Sir Nigel's too, though you may not have met him. Major, this is my mother, Mrs Lavinia Manderson.'

He leaned forward to shake her mother's hand. 'Do call me Tom, Dottie, Mrs Manderson. I'm glad there are a few good sports here.' He dropped his voice as he said it. 'I almost felt like leaving when I saw Dalbury and Parkes were here. But...' He halted abruptly, and only now did it seem to occur to him that perhaps Dottie and her mother were Dalbury and Parkes's dearest friends.

He blushed adorably, suddenly seeming far younger than the thirty-five or so years old he must surely be. He didn't seem to know how to recover from the *faux pas*. Dottie, sorry for the fellow, quickly said,

'Oh, I thought exactly the same, I must admit. But

as my mother says, it's only for a short while. Hopefully they won't be too tiresome.'

He looked relieved. He stared down at his teacup.

'Shall I take that from you?' Dottie offered, and he handed it to her. 'I'm surprised they didn't offer something a little stronger for the gentlemen.'

'I was offered sherry,' he said, his expression the same one her father usually reserved for cauliflower or cabbage.

'Oh dear,' Dottie laughed.

'I rather like a sherry,' her mother admitted. 'But it's not a drink popular with you young fellows, I know. Tell me, are you on leave from the Forces at the moment?'

'Yes, that's right. Two weeks' leave, long anticipated, I must admit.'

'Very good,' said Mrs Manderson. 'You soldiers, sailors and air-force chaps are greatly appreciated for all that you do.'

'Well thank you, it's very kind of you to say so.' He beamed at her.

The room was growing warm, the conversation growing louder. Mamie was now talking and laughing with Christiana, standing right by the door, whilst behind them Dottie noticed a tall, fair woman attempting to get by.

Dottie waved to her. The woman smiled, dodged around them, and immediately came over.

'Here's your Anabella,' Dottie commented to Tom Forsythe.

He gave Dottie a grin and got to his feet, ready to greet Anabella as she came over. She reached her hand out to him, he took it, but leaned forward to kiss her cheek, his lips lingering longer than conventional, and in response, her hand snaked inside his jacket to briefly stroke his back.

Caron Allan

'Oof, that was one hell of a drive, I got lost three times on these damned narrow roads,' she announced as she sat down keeping one hand on Tom's knee. Seeing Mrs Manderson wince at the bad language, she immediately apologised. 'Oh, please do excuse me, I really must mind my manners. We've met before, Mrs Manderson, though only very briefly. At my former husband's parents' home last year. I'm Anabella Wiseman Penterman.'

She stuck her hand out practically in Mrs Manderson's face, and although a little startled, Mrs Manderson shook the hand vigorously.

'Of course we did. How very pleasant to see you again, Mrs Penterman. And looking so well.'

Anabella looked about her, raised a finely tweezed brow and said, without bothering to lower her voice,

'Looks like all the old gang is here. I saw Florentina with Milo Parkes coming in just as I arrived, and now Dalbury's here with Penelope Sweeney, so I guess that pretty much completes the set.'

Tom nodded. 'Just what we've been saying.'

She looked at him, concerned. 'Did no one bring you something to drink?'

'It's either tea or sherry,' he said, pulling a face and nodding in the direction of the teacup and saucer Dottie had placed on the long low table nearby.

'Oh, nonsense.' Anabella raised her hand to wave and the butler hurried over to her, his head tilted in an attitude of enquiry. 'Boxhall, could Major Forsythe have a small Scotch please. And I'll have a pink gin, thanks.'

Golly, Dottie thought, why didn't I do that?

The butler nodded politely and instantly departed.

'See?' Anabella beamed at Tom. 'We're house guests. It's their job to keep us happy.'

She looked about her again, then leaning towards the others, in a soft voice she asked, 'Have you seen anything of Sebastian? It's odd he's not here to welcome his own guests.'

Dottie and Mrs Manderson took time to consider their reply, but Tom said,

'Chris said he's lying down. Got a bad cold or something. Under the weather, anyhow.'

'Hmm. Probably still feeling the effects of last night. How much did he drink?' To Dottie and Mrs Manderson, she said, 'Some of us were at a show last night in Town, and we went on to a club afterwards. I'm afraid we were out until pretty late.'

'Or early, depending on your point of view,' Tom added. 'Old Seb always did drink far too much, but no, this time it is a genuine cold. Chris said the doctor had been out and told him to have a hot toddy then to stay in bed and sleep it off.'

'Well,' said Mrs Manderson, bristling. 'They might at least have let us all know. The last thing I want is to catch someone's germs and be laid up for a week.'

'Oh I absolutely agree...' Anabella, leaning forward again in that urgent, confiding way of hers, her hand quite openly on the major's knee once again. She was interrupted by Christiana coming over, with Mamie Cotton clutching onto her arm.

'Might I present the famous—or perhaps I should say *infamous*,' she grinned at the woman beside her, 'Mamie Cotton, florist to the stars. Mamie, this is Anabella Penterman and her chap Major Tom Forsythe, and Dottie Manderson, and her mother, the delightful Mrs Manderson.'

'I've already met Miss Manderson and her mother,' Mamie said. 'But it's always a pleasure to meet new people.'

'I think I missed you last time, I was stuck in

London seeing some friends of my father,' Anabella responded. 'But I've heard so much about you from Chris.'

Mamie settled herself with some relief onto the sofa next to Mrs Manderson, taking up most of the two empty spaces on it. She grabbed the major's discarded teacup and gulped the tea down in two noisy slurps, then sat back with a heavy sigh.

'My Gawd, I needed that, I can tell you.'

Boxhall arrived with the drinks Anabella had ordered. Mamie eyed Anabella's pink gin. With a chuckle she added, 'Though on reflection, I could have done with one of them too! Oi, Paul, can I have one of them pink gins too? Knew his mother,' she said as an aside as the butler, a resigned look on his face, went in search of more alcohol.

As he approached a moment later, bearing the requested beverage on his tray, Mamie asked, 'How's your mum enjoying Hastings?' and to those sitting nearby, she said, 'His mum moved there last year. Nice place, though I don't care for a pebbly beach. Give me sand every time.'

'She's very happy, very comfortable, thank you.' Boxhall was spared further awkward enquiries when Christiana called to him.

Mamie immediately launched into a series of anecdotes to do with her floral services to the great and good. Dottie, listening with great pleasure, couldn't help but once again see her as a woman in the mould of her own old mentor, Mrs Carmichael.

Mamie was a larger-than-life character, just like Muriel Carmichael. Her strident East London working class accent was sharply at odds with the jewelled finery she wore in addition to the bright but careful hairstyling that Dottie could tell had cost an absolute fortune. Yes, she thought Mamie and Muriel could have been sisters.

*

Chapter Six

After they had finished tea, Dottie and her mother, and everyone else, went upstairs to unpack or rest a little before changing for pre-dinner cocktails.

They went down a little over an hour later. At the foot of the long sweep of stairs, Dottie and her mother were met by the butler, Boxhall. He gave them the slightest of bows, a very broad grin and said:

'Pre-dinner drinks are being served on the terrace, ladies. Just through those doors and outside.' He pointed towards the drawing-room.

Dottie and Mrs Manderson nodded their thanks to him and turned that way. When they had gone a few yards, checking over her shoulder that he was no longer within earshot, Dottie commented, 'He's awfully...'

'Friendly?' her mother suggested. 'It's as though he weren't a member of staff at all, but a guest. Or the host, even. He's polite, but friendly and warm. He greets us just like a host would. Or ought to do,' she added, remembering the cool welcome they had received from Sebastian Milner only a couple of hours earlier.

'Exactly! I mean, he seems very pleasant, but it's a bit odd, isn't it? Or am I just being old-fashioned?'

'Not at all, dear, especially in view of our actual host's lack of enthusiasm for his wife's friends.'

'Exactly!' Dottie said again.

They stepped through the French doors, flung wide and held in place by a chair on either side.

The terrace was broad and furnished with several lounging chairs along with a number of well-cushioned wicker armchairs. The other guests were already there, drinks in hand. The gentlemen rose and nodded politely, and all the ladies managed a smile, some warmer than others. Christiana hurried over, excusing herself from Major Forsythe with a pat on his arm and a smile. She grabbed another man by the arm as she approached, hauling him along with her.

'Dottie, I'd like to introduce you to Lord Dalbury. I know you saw each other at tea, but I didn't actually get around to introducing you properly, I'm afraid. Henry, this is Miss Manderson, she's the one with the wonderful dresses I was telling you about.' She nodded, then moved on, leaving them to talk.

He moved his drink into his other hand to shake Dottie's. 'Oh, of course! So pleased to meet you, Miss Manderson. I've heard rather a lot about your designs—my fiancée tells me has recently acquired one of your models, and I'm beginning to think that when we are married, she'll do her level best to bankrupt me for quite a few more.'

He said it with great charm, a smile lighting up his eyes. Dottie was almost taken in. Almost. If it wasn't for the things Christiana had told her about him being 'stony broke', and that he and his friend Parkes were always cooking up some scheme—which had been fully confirmed by her father—or the way Penelope and Florentina had laughed and sneered at William's job, Dottie would have been utterly fooled.

But it seemed he'd forgotten about that—or perhaps he just hoped she had. It was difficult to imagine Penelope Sweeney waxing lyrical over Dottie's designs, practically impossible to believe she had actually purchased one of them, seeing that she'd never once stepped inside the warehouse. Dottie felt sure none of this could be true. She knew her customers. She'd have known if Penelope Sweeney had purchased one of her gowns. But why make up a lie like that? It made no sense. Nevertheless, Dottie smiled back and said nothing.

He added with another broad smile, 'And please, do call me Henry—none of that stuffy Your Lordship nonsense.'

Dottie inclined her head regally rather as her mother tended to do. 'Well, in that case, you must call me Dottie, of course.'

'Thank you,' he said, covering her hand with his as she held it out to him. If she hadn't known what she did about him, she'd have said this perfectly charming gentleman couldn't possibly be a rogue. Again, she reminded herself what Christiana had said about both him and his best pal, Milo Parkes. Yet, if Christiana disliked and mistrusted them so much, why were they at her weekend house-party? Had they been invited by the gentleman of the house, rather than the lady?

'And who is this lovely lady?' he asked, turning to her mother.

Dottie waited just a second to see if he'd come out

with that trite old excuse for a compliment, 'Surely she must be your sister'. But fortunately for him, he didn't insult their intelligence with that. He bowed over her mother's hand, and Dottie could see her mother adored him on sight, in spite of the cautions Dottie had already given her.

'This is my mother, Mrs Manderson.'

'How very nice to meet you, Lord Dalbury,' her mother said amiably. 'I believe I am acquainted with your aunt, Mrs Jeremy Steinman.'

That surprised him, yet he seemed pleased. He was so pleasant, so attentive. Inwardly Dottie sighed, dismayed. It really was quite difficult to marry up what she had heard about him with the man in person. Was he just an excellent actor? Or was it simply the difference between Dalbury sober as he appeared to be right now, and Dalbury drunk as he had certainly been at Sir Nigel's London home the previous weekend. He was smiling again and saying,

'Well yes, she certainly is my aunt—my favourite aunt, as a matter of fact. When I was a small boy, she always gave me humbugs and toffees—a little bribery of that sort goes a long way with small boys! Did you know that she had a heart attack in the spring?'

Her mother was immediately concerned. 'How awful! No, I hadn't heard. I had a letter from her at Easter, but she didn't say a word about it. I hope she's recovering well?'

He nodded. 'Quite well, as a matter of fact. She was lucky to have some houseguests staying at the time, one of whom was a doctor. Otherwise, one dreads to think what might have happened. It was just after Easter that this happened. I'm sure she'll tell you all about it in her next epistle. She's in Bournemouth at the moment, on Doctor's orders, and having a high old time of it too, if her letters to my mother are anything to go by.'

Christiana returned to them now, and Dalbury drifted off, immediately grabbing a fresh cocktail from Boxhall's tray.

'I meant to ask when you came downstairs, how is everything? I do hope you have all you need?'

They assured her several times that their rooms were delightful, and very comfortable. She clutched her hands in front of her, and earnestly concentrated on their faces, as if trying to divine some hidden truth behind their compliments. She seemed anxious for their approval, like a little girl who had tried to remember her party-piece and wasn't quite sure if she'd managed it. Dottie thought it was odd that she was so lacking in confidence.

'Now then, would you like an aperitif, a sherry, a white wine, a red, a rosé? Or something else entirely?'

'A sherry would be lovely,' Mrs Manderson said. Dottie, not sharing her mother's partiality for sherry, opted for a glass of rosé wine.

Though no sooner had these been brought to them by the butler than Christiana said,

'Do let me show you a little of the gardens. They are really lovely just now. If we go out this way, we'll reach the rose walk from the best angle—it's my pride and joy.'

'What a magnificent conservatory,' Mrs Manderson commented as they rounded the end of the shrubbery and were met by the sight of a large red brick building with masses of huge dusty windows. There was a glass door at the nearest end, and like the windows that was also very dusty. 'I should love somewhere as substantial as that,' she added, thinking sorrowfully of her own small structure that smelled strongly of dry rot and lacked three panes of glass on the side nearest to the neighbour's small tennis court.

'Ah yes. Actually, that's my first husband's little fernery. He was an amateur botanist, ferns mainly, with an enthusiasm for photography and he loved to develop his own pictures. He used to send them to journals and so forth. He kept everything in there. Although the plants themselves are long gone, of course. But I must admit, even though Harold has been gone for some time now, I just couldn't face clearing it all out. Sebastian keeps saying he will do the place up and use it as—well, I don't know— something...'

Christiana was biting her lip, and with a slightly unsteady laugh, she continued, 'Well, I wasn't allowed in there while Harold was alive, and I find it hard to believe that will change!'

They laughed politely. The three ladies went to the nearest window, each using one hand to block out the light so they could peer inside. All Dottie could make out were a couple of shelves stacked with cobweb-covered bottles and jars, a long string like washing line with clothes pegs strung from one corner to the opposite end, and a table piled with equipment of all shapes and sizes. Beyond the study area, more rows of empty shelves adorned the filthy glass structure, and here and there, a shrivelled brown leaf bore witness to the history of the place.

Mrs Manderson glanced towards the door.

'I'm afraid it's kept locked,' Christiana told them, pre-empting Lavinia's request to take a closer look. 'Sebastian says it's not safe to go in there. Apparently, the roof is weak in several places and could come down at any moment. In fact, Sebastian says we're one good storm away from the whole place falling down.'

Dottie and her mother exchanged disbelieving looks as Christiana turned away to peer again through the window, but they wisely stayed silent.

'What a shame. You don't enjoy photography yourself?' Mrs Manderson was asking. 'Or plants?'

Christiana immediately shook her head. 'Oh no, I mean, I do love roses and other plants, not that I do much of the work myself, of course, we share a gardener with another family locally, he just comes here three days a week. But I don't have the patience for photography. Or indeed the artistic eye. All that measuring the light levels and the distance... Seb's not interested either. I suppose I really ought to get the fernery cleared out properly. If you really want to get a closer look...' She tried the door handle. Nothing happened. 'No, sorry, it's definitely locked. The key must be somewhere in the house, probably in Seb's study or perhaps on a hook in P—er—Boxhall's room. I must try to remember to ask him about it.' She said this last bit softly to herself, and as they moved away, still murmuring to one another in interest, Christiana pointed out the kitchen garden, proudly reeling off the names of various herbs. Clearly, Dottie thought, this was more to Christiana's taste than ferns and light levels.

'If she needs to raise funds for her brother,' Mrs Manderson murmured to Dottie, 'I believe photography equipment, even second-hand, commands quite a good price.'

Dottie nodded. 'I might suggest that to her a little later.'

Finally, Christiana led them onto the start of the rose walk, paved, weed free and smooth with no nasty traps for their heels. The rose walk was exactly that—a path edged on either side by climbing and shrub roses that meandered over a large framework that went up above their heads and down the other side to create the effect of being in a tunnel with shafts of sunlight coming through here and there. Hybrid tea roses were dotted amongst the climbers, all seemingly in flower or about to flower, spilling their silken petals and sweet scent into the air. It was like being in another world.

'Christiana, it's exquisite!' Dottie, fervent in her praise, wanted to run from plant to plant, sniffing every bloom and stroking every velvety petal. She'd never seen such a profusion of roses all together in one place.

Then Dottie became aware that she was several paces ahead of her hostess and at almost the same time she heard her mother say in a concerned voice, 'My dear Mrs Milner.' Turning, she saw that Christiana had halted and was fumbling for a handkerchief to stem a sudden flow of tears.

'I'm so sorry, Dottie, Mrs Manderson. I'm so silly. You'll think me such a rabbit. Honestly. It's so silly... I'm a fool. But it's just that I wanted the weekend to be perfect, and then the way Sebastian was so extremely rude to you both earlier... I can't think what he is about. I realise he's not feeling at his best, but really such abominable rudeness... I can't apologise enough.'

With one of them on either side of her, brows furrowed with concern, they hastened to reassure her that it didn't matter at all, that they perfectly understood.

And then a slight movement a few feet away had the three of them glancing around.

Dottie saw there was a bench, and upon it was Mamie Cotton. She had been seated—and now she had thrown aside her shawl, notebook and pencil and was lumbering over to them in her slow, heavy manner. She dragged Christiana into a tight matronly hug, and said, in a fierce voice,

'What's that so-and-so done now? Really, he is the flaming limit, Chris. I don't know why you married him, I really don't. He's as like flaming Harold as it's possible to get. And he's practically twice your age! Really, my girl!'

'Hardly twice my age, he's only fifteen years older than me,' Christiana protested, but feebly, dabbing at her eyes.

Unconcerned by this detail, Mamie continued patting Christiana rather forcefully on the back and telling her off about her husband.

Somehow this approach seemed to calm her, and Christiana got her weeping under control. With a final wipe of her eyes and a blow of her nose, she stepped resolutely out of Mamie's arms. Grumbling now, but smiling too as she retorted, she put her hands up as if surrendering.

'All right, all right. I know you never liked him, but it's too late now so you might as well get used to it.'

'Humpf,' grumbled Mamie, and her doubtful look told Dottie that Mamie Cotton and Sebastian Milner were never going to be friends.

Mrs Manderson again assured Christiana that she and Dottie quite understood that a gentleman with a heavy cold was not likely to feel particularly sociable, and that Christiana should not make herself unhappy about it.

Mamie added, not very helpfully, 'Too flaming right! Not that Seb Milner is ever in the mood for making himself pleasant to his wife's friends.'

'Mamie, please!' Christiana murmured in a tone of mild reproach.

Mamie took little notice. 'Now look here, my duck,'

she said to Christiana, 'just you go up to your room and fix your face, before anyone wonders what's going on, and I'll show these two ladies the rose walk then bring 'em back to the dining-room.'

'But...' Christiana began then glanced at her watch. 'Goodness,' she yelped. 'The gong will be sounding in less than ten minutes!'

'Go then...' Mamie flapped her hands at Christiana, who sent a final apologetic glance towards Dottie and her mother before scurrying away.

'Flaming Milner!' Mamie said to Dottie and Mrs Manderson, shaking her head and sighing heavily as she did so. 'He's a selfish fellow. Never cares about her feelings. Not now he's got her safely married to him. Or perhaps I should say, he's got himself safely married to her money.'

Dottie and Mrs Manderson stared at Mamie in shocked silence, unsure how to respond to her rather too-candid comments. Then Mamie, turning to sniff the pale pink rose on her left, said, 'This place is my favourite spot. Even my own roses at home aren't as good as these. I love sitting here. If ever you can't find me inside, I'll be out here on that bench,' and with a nod of the head she indicated the spot a few yards further on where the curved arm of a wooden bench protruded from behind a robust climbing rose that towered above them, spreading to left and right. 'Just drinking it all in, I'll be. I've been on at Chris for some cuttings and I think she has some ready for me, bless the girl. Though I'll leave that for this evening, she's got enough on her mind as it is.'

She bent to sniff another flower, cupping it reverently between her two hands. She shook her head, both eyes almost fluttering closed as she enjoyed the scent. 'So beautiful,' she murmured to herself. Dottie copied her, and had to agree these blooms were exceptionally fragrant. Mrs Manderson turned to admire a bush rose behind her, smothered by tiny white roses that gleamed like stars.

Mamie said, 'I've offered to move into the house to keep an eye on things if they go away.'

'Do they have such plans?' Mrs Manderson asked.

'Well, I hope so anyway. They did say they might pop off for a few weeks later in the summer and again in the autumn. It's my home away from home here,' she added. 'Or would be without flaming Mr Grumpy Milner. I wouldn't need to go anywhere else on holiday. Two weeks sitting here with these roses would set me up for the rest of the year.'

Before either Dottie or Mrs Manderson could reply, from the doorway of the drawing-room, there was a soft *bong* and Boxhall was heard to announce, 'Ladies and gentlemen, dinner is served.'

Dottie's soup spoon was almost to her mouth when Penelope Sweeney leaned forward, pushing a stray red lock of hair behind her ear, and said to her,

'I do like your jewellery, Miss Manderson. So elegant. I only bought my costume jewellery with me for this weekend. As you can see.' She tapped her bracelet with a crimson-painted fingernail. 'But now I wish I'd brought something rather more special with me.'

Dottie managed to swallow her soup and smile politely at Miss Sweeney, baffled by this sudden attempt at polite friendliness after all the snubs and snipes.

Miss Sweeney continued, 'But I was so worried about these jewel robberies that have been in the news. You must have heard about them?'

'Yes...' Dottie debated whether to attempt another spoonful of soup.

'But of course you have!' her new friend exclaimed. 'Is your fiancé involved in the investigation? Does he tell you all the little clues and hints that the police are following? Like the fact that the thief is a five-foot-tall bald man with limp, or...'

'Don't be so bloody crass, Pen,' Milo Parkes, seated between Dottie and Sebastian Milner, chimed in with a frown. Miss Sweeney subsided sulkily, whilst opposite them, and further along the table, Mamie commented mildly,

'Language, Milo. You're not at your club now.'

At least he had the grace to apologise with a charming smile. Dottie ventured to take another spoonful of soup, noting some of the others had already finished. She didn't want to be the one who held everybody up. The soup was a light, refreshing chicken and vegetable one, and deserved to be savoured.

Sebastian Milner, adjacent to Penelope Sweeney at the end of the long rectangular table, sniffed deeply and disgustingly, then said to the room at large, 'I can't think what people are about, hiring staff who rob their guests blind.'

He took a noisy slurp of his wine, and Dottie, attempting not to frown at him over his poor manners, as it was after all his home, debated whether or not to correct him as to the jewellery robberies' details. In the end she got on with her soup, deciding she couldn't be bothered with him.

But Milo Parkes—clearly a somewhat pedantic young man—took great pains to explain the details of the robberies to Milner who was quite obviously not listening. To Parkes' annoyance and Dottie's private amusement, Milner said at the end of Parkes' long explanation,

'All I can say is, if one of my servants did

something like that, I'd have the fellow horsewhipped then turn him over to the cops.'

It was at that moment that Boxhall leaned over to remove Milner's soup plate. There was no mistaking the look of sheer hatred on the butler's face. As he withdrew with the plate, he bumped Milner's shoulder—quite deliberately, Dottie was certain—and just as Milner immediately snapped, 'Be careful, dammit!' the butler was already saying,

'I do beg your pardon, sir.' His face was once again a bland mask.

Milner began a coughing fit, and left the table for a few minutes, returning with a small glass of some dark liquid in his hand just as the meat was being served.

'Rum and blackcurrant,' Milner commented to no one in particular. 'Excellent remedy for head colds and the like, or so I've been told. Must admit I've had two of these already. And I feel like a new man, compared to lunchtime.'

Along the table, next to Christiana, Anabella glanced in Dottie's direction, and the two women, eyebrows raising briefly, exchanged a look that said, 'What a dreadful man!'

'...and then it turned out, it wasn't my maid at all, but some imposter!' Henry Dalbury's indignant tone caught Dottie's attention. She had a good idea what he was talking about.

'Yes, dear, we know, we understand. It must have been awful!' Penelope Sweeney's hand went to her mouth, but behind her fingers she was smiling, Dottie could see, clearly enjoying his misfortune.

'Surely the police will get it all back for you?' Major Forsythe suggested mildly, and at the same time, Sebastian said:

'That's what insurance is for, old boy. Costs an arm

and a leg, but after all, we get it for the peace of mind.'

Dalbury glared at him, not appreciating the comment. 'Insurance won't pay for the sentimental value, let alone how devastated my poor mother feels at being duped in such a way right there in her own home,' he commented coldly.

There was an uncomfortable silence, but fortunately Boxhall and two maids came in and began to clear away the dinner plates. By the time they'd begun to bring in the desserts and cheese board, the matter was more or less forgotten amidst a new conversation about the situation on the Continent.

Dottie helped herself to diced summer fruits from a dish one of the maids held for her, and as she did so, she glanced up at the girl, and thought, if I encountered her in another part of the house, with no one else around, or perhaps just with my mother, and she told me that Christiana or her husband were concerned for the safety of the guests' valuables, I'd have no hesitation in handing over my jewellery.

She set down the serving spoon, smiled and thanked the maid, who bobbed politely then passed on to the next guest.

How much we take on trust, Dottie thought, and how much we take from the context of the situation.

Christiana stood to lead the ladies back to the drawing-room. The doors to the garden were still standing wide open to admit a gentle breeze as the evening remained warm. The sun, mellowed to a soft gold, was dreamily leaning towards the horizon.

'I'm going to go out and have a last look at the roses,' Christiana announced. 'They are always delightful at this time of day. You're all welcome to join me, of course.'

And so, despite Florentina's rather audible groan and the rolling of her eyes, all seven ladies strolled down the three steps into the garden, turning towards the rose walk.

Mamie immediately sank onto her usual bench, exactly where they'd found her before dinner. Florentina and Penelope kept back, deep in a conversation that no one else was privileged to hear, whilst Dottie, her mother, Anabella and Christiana wandered from rose to rose, comparing the scents and the flower colours. It was a very pleasant twenty minutes.

As they strolled back to the drawing-room for their coffee, Mamie said in a teasing voice, patting Christiana's arm, 'Don't you forget my cuttings that you promised me, young lady!'

Christiana laughed. 'Don't worry, I haven't forgotten. In fact they have been rooted and potted up for you already. The gardener is going to bring them over for you on Monday, so you'll be able to take them home then sit and dote on them to your heart's content in your own domain.'

'Oh Chris, you darling girl!' Mamie gave Christiana a kiss on the cheek, grasping for her hand and patting it with great affection.

'Come on, you daft old bat,' Christiana said, and she put her arm through Mamie's. 'Let's go and get our coffee.'

Dottie wondered how they had all come to know one another. She must remember to ask one of them soon.

Behind her, Florentina was mimicking Christiana, saying to Penelope,

'Come on, you daft old bat,' and when Penelope responded with 'All right, darling girl,' they dissolved into malicious giggles. Like two silly schoolgirls, Dottie thought, still not liking them one little bit.

It was about an hour later that the major finally joined the ladies for coffee.

'Milner sends his apologies, Chris, and says that he intends to get blind drunk in the hopes it'll shift this damned cold of his, and says not to save him any coffee, and don't wait up. Apparently, he also has some business to discuss with those other two. I don't think we'll see any more of those three tonight.'

Christiana was clearly embarrassed. 'Really, it's too bad of Sebastian. This is no way to...' She forced herself to stop, take a deep breath and smile at her remaining guests. 'Well, it's probably for the best that he keeps his germs and his temper to himself. Hopefully he'll feel much better in the morning. Now then, I'll just ring for some more coffee. Or a liqueur, if anyone would care for one? Then perhaps we'll have a couple of games of Bridge? A few rubbers could be just what we need.'

Some vague murmurs seemed to indicate that no one else was terribly keen on the idea, Dottie thought, and they'd need to have two games of Bridge running at the same time, and there'd no doubt be quite a bit of jockeying to avoid being partnered with Florentina and Penelope. Predictably though, Mamie, Penelope and Florentina were greatly in favour of liqueurs and Mrs Manderson once again asked for a dry sherry. The others were happy to just have another coffee.

Boxhall answered the summons, and Christiana went to intercept him just inside the drawing-room door. They had a whispered conversation, her expression urgent, anxious, her hand on his arm, and to Dottie, his manner appeared to be one of reassurance. As the butler departed on his errand for more coffee, Dottie was certain—almost certain—fairly sure—she heard him say softly,

'Stop fretting, love,' as he went out.

Dottie hurriedly turned away to smile at the major and asked him if he was an avid Bridge player.

He grinned and said he thought he played a passable game, though Happy Families was more his level of expertise.

Anabella, leaning forward as she slipped her arm through his, said to Dottie, 'My word, though, speaking of Happy Families, this weekend is more than usually uncomfortable, isn't it? Seb seems to have taken complete leave of his senses. I've never seen Chris so on edge.'

'He's a brute of a man,' Forsythe stated. 'I don't know how she puts up with him.'

'Or why,' Anabella agreed with a nod.

'It is all rather awkward,' Dottie admitted.

The door was flung wide open just then, making everyone start, and Sebastian, red-faced and unsteady on his feet, blundered into the room with his cronies right behind him. Christiana leapt up.

'I thought you weren't...'

He cut across her. 'Seem to have finished our business a little sooner than expected. How are we all? Everyone got a drink? Excellent.'

He fairly stumbled as he crossed the room, bumping into Mamie's chair as he went, and bent to kiss his wife's cheek, though she tried to cringe away. 'Excellent dinner, dearest. And the liqueurs too of course. Excellent.' He pronounced the last word as if it had at least one H in it, stood there swaying as he looked about him then flung himself into a chair next to Florentina, nudging her shoulder with his own and smirking at her.

Parkes, following him into the room, had quite clearly been heading for that seat, and was not pleased at having to take the empty one beside Mamie. Dalbury claimed the other vacant chair between Penelope and Christiana.

The door opened again, and this time it was Boxhall returning with a tray of liqueurs and cocktails, though he served Sebastian first with another of his tumblers of rum and blackcurrant, showing almost black through the crystal. It was too much to hope that it was a strong coffee to sober him up, Dottie thought. Behind Boxhall came a maid with a fresh pot of coffee, and behind her, another maid carrying cups, a jug of cream and dainty pot of sugar.

If Parkes had been annoyed that Milner had annexed his girlfriend, his conversation remained quiet and amiable, and Dottie noted that Dalbury too seemed sober and on his best behaviour.

Dottie was relieved. Until now she hadn't realised how tense she was, but as everyone settled down with their drinks and room filled with the hum of pleasant conversation, it seemed as though they might get through the evening peacefully after all.

*

Chapter Seven

The soft knock at her door came as a surprise to Dottie. Everyone had said goodnight and come upstairs half an hour ago, and she had been on the point of undressing for bed. Only a sudden idea for a new shape of dress sleeve had kept her up. She glanced at her alarm clock. Just a few minutes before one o'clock. With a sigh, she set aside her notebook and pencil.

She crossed the room to open the door, hoping this would not turn into an unpleasant encounter with a drunk Lord Dalbury—or his best pal Milo Parkes.

It was Anabella Penterman. She stood there in a nightgown and negligee—not one of Dottie's designs, Dottie couldn't help noticing. Anabella seemed uneasy, clutching her hands in front of her and biting her lip in a marked contrast to her usual confident manner.

'Anabella!' Dottie had been about to invite her in, but Anabella said in a panicked rush,

'Oh Dottie, I know it's awfully late, but would it be at all possible to have a little chat with you. I have something I really need to get off my chest. Although, well... I know it's awfully late.'

'Come in, it's quite all right. As you can see, I haven't gone to bed yet.' Dottie stepped back, curiosity consuming her. She was worried though. What was this thing so pressing on Anabella that she had to come here in this state of agitation?

Anabella came into the room then didn't seem to know quite what to do or where to begin. Her customary poise had deserted her. Dottie put a hand on her arm and drew her towards the two chairs at the table in the bay of the window. 'Let's have a seat.'

But Anabella halted, and unable to hold back any longer, she burst out with, 'Oh, it's been just eating away at me. Especially now we've become friends. I know you know that I stole Cyril out from under your nose. What's worse is, I even planned it. Me and my mother together. It was a despicable thing to do, and I can't begin to tell you how sorry I am. It was very wrong of me, and I feel just horrible about it, and it's just so...'

She seemed to run out of words, and she stared at Dottie, both hands over her mouth as if, too late, she tried to keep silent.

Dottie stared back. Thoughts, memories flashed through her mind as she absorbed Anabella's confession. Dottie remembered the deep misery that had overtaken her when Cyril had not come back to her that Christmas, remaining instead in New York. And then there had been the shock of the newspaper announcement, the photo with the words beneath it that had come back to her time and again: *The Honourable Cyril Penterman today with his new bride.* Dottie had been at her sister's when she'd seen it in the newspaper which her brother-in-law George had brought back to show her, feeling that she ought to know.

But Cyril and his new wife were now very publicly separated. And Dottie—well she had William, her gorgeous fiancé: constant, true, not at all the type of chap to employ concealments or betrayals. Not to mention so very attractive.

Anabella was wringing her hands.

'Let's sit,' Dottie urged again, but gently. They moved across the room away from the glare of the electric light to the nook by the window. Outside the night was still. Trees were silhouetted against a darker sky, their limbs waving gently, as if they too were sleepy. The soft swishing sound they made reminded Dottie of gentle waves lapping a shore. After a moment or two, she began to see the stars glinting here and there in the heavens.

'Oh Dottie!' Anabella said again. Her lips trembled slightly.

'Don't torture yourself,' Dottie said firmly. 'Really, there's no need.'

'How you must hate and despise me!'

Dottie shook her head. 'Not at all, I like you very much. Look, I will admit I was truly devastated when I discovered he had married you. I was only nineteen, and he was my first real love. At least, I had believed myself in love, and I was convinced that he loved me too. At any moment, I—and my family, and even Cyril's aunt—expected him to propose to me. But he didn't. He chose you.'

'But I went after him. I knew he was seeing you, and I didn't want to let him go. I sought him out, I pretty well haunted him. I *trapped* him.'

'You can't catch a man who doesn't want to be caught,' Dottie said.

Anabella sat back in her seat. She almost smiled. 'My goodness, yes, I suppose that's true. In a way. But I've just been feeling so...'

'Don't,' Dottie repeated. 'You know how happy I am with William. If anything, I was foolishly infatuated with Cyril. It wasn't real love at all. Looking back, I can see that now. So I'm glad things have turned out the way they have. I don't have feelings for Cyril anymore. William is everything to me now, you must know that. And you have the gallant major in your life now, don't you? Am I right in thinking he's more than just a friend?'

'Well, yes, I suppose we've not exactly hidden it. He's asked me to marry him as soon as my divorce is through. And he's a sweetheart, so gentlemanly and kind, and he makes me laugh. Cyril—well, he had the right look and all the right connections, and everything else really. But... I don't know. We just didn't get along. He soon got bored with me and turned elsewhere. He isn't a man to stick around when things were less than fun, I discovered.'

'I'm sorry to hear that,' Dottie said, and meant it. It had never occurred to her that he could be that type of man, though looking back now it made perfect sense, given how quickly he had attached himself to Dottie, then dropped her just as quickly. 'It sounds as though you're better off without him. You deserve someone better.'

'Oh Dottie! That's so kind of you. Thank you.'

'Don't be silly,' Dottie said, patting her arm. 'Now, tell me, how long have you known Christiana?'

'Well, we were at finishing school together in Switzerland. So we've known each other for quite a few years, ever since we were seventeen, in fact. She's my closest friend.'

'Did you know her first husband? Harold, wasn't

it?'

Anabella pulled a face. 'Oh yes, I knew him. He was a horrible man. Years older, of course. Always putting Christiana down, always sneaking around trying to start some intrigue with any woman he met, including me. Not loyal, not loving. He only wanted her fortune, and her title. It matched his aspirations, I think. He really thought he would be prime minister someday. Then take up his seat in the House of Lords afterwards.'

Dottie shook her head, not understanding. 'But why? Why would she throw herself away on someone like that?'

'Two someones like that, technically. Sebastian is so like Harold, you wouldn't believe it. Though of course, Seb has neither the money nor the breeding that Harold had. Which is not saying a lot, trust me. But Chris is not the kind of woman who gets on alone in life—she's timid, she lacks confidence. She needs someone to guide her, help her all the time, someone to lean on. And being so small and fragile-looking, she makes men feel protective of her, makes them feel powerful. She's not a woman who's made to be alone.'

Dottie nodded. She could see what Anabella meant, but Dottie wondered if she'd have been the same if she were older and hadn't met William at the young age she did. It must be hard to be alone. She knew Christiana and Peter's father had died when they were young. Perhaps that was why Christiana had a tendency to lean on an older man?

Anabella got to her feet. 'Well, thanks for being so good about it all. For what it's worth, I am sorry about Cyril, yet now I can't help thinking I did you a favour, too.'

Dottie grinned back. 'You certainly did.'

They hugged and said goodnight, and Anabella left. Dottie wondered if Anabella was going back to her own room, or to Tom Forsythe's. She scolded herself for being too nosy.

The following morning, Mamie was keen to watch the tennis match but had no interest in actually playing. She sat on the sidelines, along with Lavinia, and watched the mixed doubles match between Dottie and Forsythe against Anabella and Parkes, whilst on the second court, Dalbury played a singles game against Florentina. Penelope Sweeney was sprawled in a lawn chair, alternately watching the games and turning the pages of her magazine. Christiana had murmured something vague about needing to go indoors to fetch something and had taken herself off, wearing her seemingly habitual expression of anxiety.

The spectators, languid in the morning sunshine, called out the occasional praise or commiseration. Lavinia noticed that Sebastian Milner lay back in his lawn chair a little further apart from the others, blatantly napping beneath his Financial Times. His rather loud snores were disrupted from time to time by the excited shouts of either players or onlookers, as no one took much trouble to keep their voices down. Earlier Lavinia had noted his pale feverish look and wondered if he really ought to be in bed with a doctor at his side. Again, she was irritated by the inconsideration of inviting a houseful of guests when the host was unwell.

Dottie, poised to counter Anabella's serve—which was as immaculate as everything else the woman did—noticed that if anything the men made rather more noise than usual, as if they were determined to disturb Milner as much as possible. Dottie took two steps back and a quick leap to her left, sending the ball sailing back over the net to land just behind Parkes, where it rolled over the line to disappear under the hedge.

He cursed rather more freely than was really acceptable, and Mamie Cotton raised an eyebrow at Lavinia and said softly,

'Just goes to show, Lavvie, being rich ain't the same as being a gentleman.'

Lavinia nodded, slightly put out at being addressed by a near stranger as Lavvie, which even her own husband was not permitted to do, but at the same time, she was unable to deny the truth of the observation. Before she could say anything else, Mamie said,

'And I'd like to know where he got his money. The family was that hard up a year ago, they couldn't pay me for the flowers for his mother's funeral. And now he's all over the society papers talking about his latest adventures.'

'Perhaps he inherited the money from his mother,' Lavinia remarked, though keeping her voice low—she didn't want to offend anyone.

Mamie shook her head. She clapped suddenly, and making Lavinia jump, she bellowed, 'Oh, lovely shot, Bella, my dear! Just lovely!' Then she turned back to Lavinia and in a marginally quieter voice, said, 'No, I don't think that was it. And have you noticed that he's always with young Dalbury? Thick as thieves, those two.'

Lavinia shook her head. She told a white lie. 'I'm afraid I've only met the gentlemen this weekend.'

Mamie nodded. 'Of course. I was forgetting.'

'Although,' Lavinia added, 'Someone mentioned that they had been together at school, so they have no doubt been friends for many years.'

Both tennis matches were briefly paused whilst lemonade or iced tea was consumed, then the players changed ends, and the matches resumed. Next, Boxhall served tea to the audience.

As he did so, he grinned at Mamie and said, 'I hope you're behaving yourself, Mamie Cotton. I've got my eye on you.'

Lavinia was quite astonished to hear him speak to her like that, though she put it down to the previously mentioned acquaintance with his mother. In any case, from Mamie's girlish giggles it was clear she enjoyed such bold comments. She flapped her hand at him and told him he was a caution. Boxhall went away grinning, and Mamie leaned sideways and tapped her nose at Lavinia as if about to disclose a dead secret.

'He's a sweetheart, that fellow. So good for Christiana. The only sensible thing Harold ever did, taking that boy on. Not a word, of course. If Seb found out...'

Lavinia, shocked, nevertheless managed to indicate with a slight nod that this information would go with her, undisclosed, to her grave, excepting of course her daughter, to whom she would share this snippet at the earliest opportunity. She couldn't help glancing over to where Sebastian was asleep in his chair, fervently hoping he *was* asleep and had not overheard Mamie's dreadfully unwise comment. It was all terribly awkward, she felt, and not for the first time, she began to wish she had manufactured some excuse and avoided the visit from the outset.

Two hours later, when it was almost time for lunch, Dottie and her mother returned to the drawing-room.

On a small sofa in the middle of the room,

Sebastian sat, a soft blanket over his knees in spite of the heat. He sniffed loudly from time to time, groaning and dabbing his nose with a handkerchief. But Dottie couldn't be sure whether his red nose was due to his ill health, or the large but empty crystal tumbler placed on the side-table close by. He had two or three newspapers and two books lying on the sofa cushion next to him now but clearly hadn't felt like reading any of them.

At a table, Dalbury, Parkes and their lady companions were playing a card game. Christiana and Anabella were deep in discussion, sitting close together on a second small sofa beside a large picture window whilst the major reclined in an armchair, reading a biography of Dr Crippen that he seemed to find deeply fascinating. Nevertheless, he glanced up as Dottie and her mother entered and greeted them with a smile.

'When will lunch be ready?' came Sebastian's plaintive voice. He sounded like a sulky child, Dottie thought and tried not to roll her eyes. Then she caught sight of Anabella's face with an expression that surely mirrored her own, and she almost laughed out loud.

'Soon, dearest, soon,' Christiana soothed him. 'It's only just turned twelve o'clock. Just another half an hour, that's all.'

'But I'm so hungry,' he whined.

With a sigh she went over to straighten the blanket over his knees. 'How about another of those? What was it?'

'Rum and blackcurrant,' he grumbled. 'And get me some aspirin, would you?'

She wrinkled her nose at the smell as she took the glass, but nodded and left the room, returning a few minutes later with a freshly filled glass and two small white tablets in her hand.

'There, dear. Hopefully, those will make you feel better. Only about twenty minutes until lunch is ready.'

He reached out to grab the glass from her just as she leaned forward to set it on the table beside him. The glass flew out of her hand, its contents soaking the tabletop, the arm of the chair, and lightly splashing Sebastian's jacket and shirt front.

'You bloody stupid woman!' he bellowed immediately. 'Can't you get anything right? Where's that idiot Boxhall?'

'I'm so sorry!' Christiana was standing there, her hands to her face, her shock far greater than the mere spilling of a drink warranted, but her wide-eyed gaze was fixed on her husband who was now red-faced with fury.

'Well, don't just stand there gawping, you idiot, get me another! And where is that bloody butler?'

'I say, take it easy, won't you?' Forsythe said, attempting to sound humorous. 'Ladies present, and all that.'

'As if I care...' Sebastian began then seemed to think better of it.

Christiana was already scurrying past Anabella, who put out a hand and said, in a tone just above a whisper, 'Are you all right?'

Christiana nodded briefly and hurried on. The room was silent, no one quite knowing what to say. A few seconds later, a maid came in to mop up the mess and take away the empty glass which was fortunately still in one piece having bounced onto the rug. Christiana then returned with a replacement glass, freshly filled, and two fresh dry pills.

Her husband snatched it from her, almost upsetting it again, and grunted something that could have been thanks.

Christiana returned to Anabella who had been joined by Forsythe, Dottie and Mrs Manderson.

'Poor Sebastian,' she said to them in a low voice. 'His cold really does seem to be taking its toll. He's become terribly run-down.' But she was gripping her hands in her lap in an effort to stop them shaking.

Dottie made a sympathetic sound, whilst her mother commented that so often, summer colds were actually more severe than winter ones. She noticed that Sebastian immediately began to drink his rum and blackcurrant whilst flicking back and forth through one of his newspapers in a fussy petulant manner. He really was such a child, Dottie thought.

A few minutes later, Mamie joined them from her sojourn in the garden, and then the gong sounded for lunch.

'What's in here?' Dottie tapped on the shining surface of a vast leather box like a handleless suitcase that had been placed in the centre of a large bed in one of the empty guest rooms.

As soon as lunch was over, mercifully without incident, Christiana had approached Dottie and asked if she would mind looking through the dresses and other items that had been her mother's. Dottie was delighted, having hoped they would find time to do that as soon as possible. She loved nothing more than to look at dresses, and if she could possibly help Christiana at the same time, then it was all to the good.

'Oh that's just full of hats, I'm afraid.' Christiana's mouth turned downwards in a regretful manner. 'Mother did so love her hats. And fascinators. And all manner of other headgear, including a rather peculiar peach satin deerstalker.'

'I can't wait to see that!' Dottie laughed. 'Sadly, hats seem to be dying out, if you ask me. I often see people out in the street bare-headed these days, not just men but women too. I shall be very sorry to see them go completely, I have to admit I love hats. But I already have at least a dozen. Even so, would it be all right if I had a quick look?'

'Oh please, be my guest. It's not locked.'

There was a knock on the door. Christiana turned to see who it was. Dottie's heart sank. She hoped it wouldn't be Florentina or Penelope—or even worse, both of them together, coming to ruin what promised to be a pleasant interlude. But she heard her mother's voice, and someone else's too, which proved to be that of Mamie Cotton. They came in, and after a heaving a sigh of relief and giving them both a brief smiling welcome, Dottie turned her attention back to the contents of the leather case.

'Oh, Christiana, these are beautiful. Look at this gorgeous straw hat! The flowers and the band are silk, I should think. Mother?'

Mrs Manderson confirmed the silk theory, and Christiana took the hat and put it on, looking in the mirror at her reflection. 'Hmm. It's all right, I suppose. I remember my mother wearing it when I was quite small, but it was never her favourite—or mine.'

She took it off and almost threw it onto the bed beside the box. Dottie took it up and began to examine it closely. Mamie was already diving forwards, surprisingly agile for a somewhat plump older lady, and made a grab for a small scarlet felt cap adorned by a feather well over a foot long.

'I like this!' Mamie announced and immediately set the cap on her head at rather a rakish angle, the curling, fluffy feather sticking out in a way that reminded Dottie of an old-fashioned quill pen poking out of an inkpot. Mamie turned this way and that in front of the glass, viewing the hat with evident satisfaction.

'It's very 'me'! How much do you want for it?' she asked Christiana, her bluntness causing Christiana to blush and bluster, saying,

'Oh, er, I really don't...'

'A hundred pounds,' Dottie said firmly with a secret nod and wink at a horrified Christiana.

'Hmm,' huffed Mamie. 'I can see you're not on my side anymore, Miss Dottie. Well, I suppose I can't deny that it is worth it. All right, I'll take it. I'll contact my bank when I get home on Tuesday afternoon, if that's all right?'

Her tone was the usual forthright one, but she was smiling with delight at the hat, pulling it off to look at it, turning it around in her hands. 'I've always wanted to wear ostrich feathers.' She really was very taken with it, and it suited her flamboyant style perfectly, and Dottie immediately told her so.

'Oh shush, missy,' Mamie cackled. 'You've made your sale so you can stop flattering me now!' And she put the hat back on and had another twirl in front of the mirror.

'Very true.' Dottie laughed too. 'Now, what else do we have?' She turned to the case once more and brought out a handsome fur toque in a Russian style, with a smaller, less extravagant feather standing up from the hatband at the side. The hatband and the feather were adorned with pearls which Dottie suspected were the genuine thing.

But Mamie waved it away without any interest. She reached past Dottie to grab another item. 'Oh no this is the one for me. You can't tempt me with anything else, I'm smitten!' And she held up the peach-coloured deerstalker Christiana had mentioned earlier.

The peach deerstalker was exactly that—a deerstalker hat of traditional design, but made of a deep, vibrant peach satin. Clearly it was intended for social occasions only. Dotty giggled slightly at the thought of some chap in tweeds on the trail of a deer in such a hat.

'Oh, it's wonderful!' she said to Christiana.

Christiana laughed. 'Rather eye-catching, isn't it? In a bizarre kind of way.'

'Well, it's too late, missy, you had your chance. This one's mine now. I'm smitten.' Mamie beamed at Christiana and Dottie then ripped the ostrich-feathered cap off and plonked the deerstalker on her head. 'I'll take 'em both!'

With a laugh, Dottie nodded then turned away to put the toque down and said, 'Mother, do you see anything you like?'

Mrs Manderson was very taken with the Russian fur toque.

'I do like this one, Dorothy dear. It reminds me of one I had when I was a girl. Do you think your father would object too much?'

'Probably,' Dottie said dryly. 'But then he is the man who has had the same straw boater for at least twenty years.'

'True,' Mrs Manderson agreed, smiling at Dottie, enjoying the memory of the first time He'd worn a that boater. Herbert had taken her out, also for the first time. It had been for an afternoon tea followed by a punt along the Thames. And he snatched his first kiss from her as he'd helped her out of the punt later. Ah, so long ago, she thought with a little shake of the head and a soft smile.

Dottie and her mother each chose a hat, agreeing a

price with Christiana who was still uncomfortable with asking her friends for money. Then Lavinia and Mamie took themselves off to go for a walk amongst the roses. Unlikely friends, Dottie thought, the women were so different, but they seemed to have become quite close already, despite having only met for the first time the afternoon before.

There wasn't much left unspoken for of the entire collection. Christiana was delighted and thanked Dottie profusely for her help.

'How you had the utter cheek to ask Mamie for £100 for the little red cap, I'll never know. And then when you said the same amount for that satin deerstalker, I almost fainted.'

Dottie laughed. 'Oh, she can afford it. And she loved them both. They are probably worth more too, real collector's pieces, so she got a fine bargain. And they won't just lay in a box, they will be worn and loved by her until they fall to pieces. I hope I see her in them again.'

'Well thank you, Dottie. I'll have one of our maids help Boxhall to pack everything up and arrange for a carrier to deliver the whole lot to your warehouse next week.' She looked about her wistfully. 'Oh it's a shame to let it all go, but there it is. Needs must. Now then, about these dresses...' And she threw open both doors of the wardrobes.

It took about an hour to thoroughly examine all the dresses, skirts, blouses and jackets. There were several exciting finds, but somehow Dottie wasn't as enthused by all the garments as she had been with the hats. The hats, well, she told herself, perhaps they had just seemed more fun. The dresses and so forth were far more utilitarian, and many were not in good repair.

There were four or five walking skirts, all of the

same heavy navy or grey gaberdine or wool-tweed. In addition, there were two hobble-skirts of the same early Edwardian style, so limiting in the freedom of movement they offered to the wearer but conforming to society's expectation of womanliness especially in terms of shape. Dottie, holding first one then the other up in front of her for a better look, crinkled her nose. She doubted anyone would be interested in these as garments but perhaps to reuse the fabric for something else?

'Not very attractive, are they?' Christiana admitted. 'But perhaps they could be used to make dungarees for little boys?'

'Hmm. Possibly. I was wondering the same thing.' Dottie could just about see that they might be reworked in that way. Two pairs of dungarees or rompers per skirt, perhaps. She lay them on the 'keep' pile.

She turned her attention to the blouses: again, these were mostly the same style, typically Edwardian white cotton blouses with a thin blue stripe. They were undoubtedly made for the famous S-shaped figure that was so in vogue in the Edwardian age, though Dottie always felt they made the women look pigeon-breasted, as if they one large bosom instead of two normal ones. She fervently hoped that style never came back in vogue. The blouses had high collars, with a frilled edge, and there was room for a brooch at the throat over the button closure. She placed them on the keep pile too, reminding herself that less well-to-do mothers might be glad to have some fabric they could reuse. Some of her own seamstresses—mainly single women—had children, and she knew how hard those women worked to pay the household bills and put food on the table, so any extra help was always most welcome.

Finally, they turned to the dresses themselves. Some were marked or damaged, but of the remainder, Dottie found four delightful ones: two were as Christiana had hinted, old Carmichael and Jennings designs, whereas the final two were both designed by other warehouses, Jean Patou of Paris, and another Dottie had heard of but not seen before, Howard and Reed of Boston in the United States.

'I kept the best to last, of course!' Christiana said with a laugh.

Gleefully, Dottie grinned back at her. 'You certainly did!'

She spread the first two out across the bed, noted the familiar white label of her own warehouse, bearing the royal blue embroidered C and J, which she still used. One dress was a deep pink silk velvet, very full and long in the skirt, and embroidered all over with tiny black glass beads in swirling circles and curving lines.

Dottie blew out a long breath she'd been holding. 'Oh I love it!' she said, almost to herself.

'Isn't it wonderful?' Christiana agreed.

With reluctance, Dottie set the dress aside and took up the other Carmichael and Jennings design. It was a chestnut brown, a kind of silk, Dottie thought, but quite thick and stiff. Remarkably the hem and the end of the sleeves were trimmed with deep black animal fur, some sort of mink, perhaps. The style was rather like a gentleman's smoking jacket or Oriental-styled dressing-gown, with very little shaping, and just a fur tie about the waist. The bodice was held closed with two sets of hooks and eyes carefully hidden, and undetectable from the front.

'Not quite so keen on this one,' Dottie said. 'But it is certainly eye-catching.'

'A little larger in width and a little shorter in length and I'd have said it was perfect for Mamie!'

Dottie laughed. 'My goodness, yes, she'd love it!' She lay them on the rapidly growing pile. 'I'll definitely take these back with me. Mrs Avers might even have been with Mrs Carmichael long enough to remember making these. I'm sure she'd love to see them again.'

She turned to the other two dresses, the Howard and Reed dress was another walking dress, but designed for spring and summer wear, with a sweet shoulder cape to match, and a neat contrast fringe at the rather high waist and around the skirt at knee level. Dottie could imagine the fringe fluttering in a delightful way as the wearer moved. The gown by Jean Patou was another evening gown, in a lovely dark blue silk, with a full skirt that reached almost to the floor, and some nice stitching detail on the shoulders and the cuffs of the sleeves.

Dottie looked at these four gowns for some time, and in the end, aware now of the passing of time, she lay them on the 'keep' pile then turned to Christiana with a sense of a job well done.

*

Chapter Eight

Christiana gratefully accepted Dottie's offer to help pack everything into two large trunks to convey to the warehouse as soon as it could be arranged. It took both of them quite some time, but in the end, everything was neatly packed away, the lids were forced down tight, with Dottie leaning across each one in turn, whilst Christiana quickly buckled up the straps before the lids could pop back up again.

They sank down on the now empty bed with relief, smiling at one another to have finished the task.

'It's such a weight off my mind to have dealt with that, Dottie. I can't begin to thank you enough. I'll get these dispatched to you at the warehouse, most likely it won't be until next week. As for the other bits and bobs still in the wardrobes, well, I imagine I can send it all to one of our local welfare organisations. They'll probably cut the garments down and use the fabric for children's clothes, or something.'

They fell silent. There was an air of constraint now.

Dottie wondered if there was something else on Christiana's mind. Sure enough within another minute, Christiana said,

'Oh Dottie, this weekend party is something of a disaster, I'm afraid. I'm so sorry you and your lovely mother have been treated so rudely by Sebastian—and his friends. Why Sebastian felt he had to invite his cronies at the same time that I invited mine...' She shook her head, exasperated. 'He knows none of them get on with my friends. They are completely different in every way, their outlook, their behaviour. Not my kind of people at all, though I can tolerate them in small doses. But now... I'm absolutely certain that with the first bit of drink inside them, someone or other will cause a scene. They all drink like the proverbial fish and are not at all concerned about what they say to people. They have no qualms about causing a scene and seem determined to be as outrageous as possible. I just can't stand them. And I'm on tenterhooks the whole time they're here, waiting for the next insult to come out of their mouths.'

Dottie pulled a face. 'It does sound rather awkward. But at least you've got a few sensible ones to hopefully keep the others in check.'

'I suppose so. I mean, Sebastian's not going to be much help now he's come down with this influenza or whatever it is. I do wish I'd realised sooner, I could have cancelled.'

'At least the visitors are only here for a few days. It'll soon pass, and we'll all be off home again,' Dottie tried to reassure her. 'I take it Parkes and Dalbury are Mr Milner's friends rather than yours, then?'

'Lord, yes! Tom Forsythe is technically my friend, I suppose, or rather, I should say, a friend of my first husband, Harold. I think they met at university. Tom has always been completely charming to me, and he has made a sterling effort to try to develop a—well not exactly friendship—more like an acquaintanceship with Sebastian. For my sake, of course,' Christiana said with a smile. Then straight away giving Dottie a rueful look, she added, 'And Dalbury and Parkes were Harold's friends initially, never really mine, though they are civil enough away from Florentina and Penelope. Those two women lead them astray. Sebastian was already on the scene as Harold's friend when Harold and I first met. He was such a support when Harold—passed away. I would never have got through those dreadful days without Seb's support and his care and concern. He really was...' She gave a little smile. 'So I suppose it's not surprising that one day, after only a couple of months, I suddenly found myself viewing this supportive friend in a new, a different way. Oh, I knew that it seemed indecently hasty, much too soon after Harold's... loss. People were rather shocked. But as Sebastian said, one never knows what's around the corner, so why wait?'

'Why indeed?' Dottie murmured, thinking how hard it was to picture self-absorbed Sebastian being concerned, or helpful, or caring more about another person than himself. But of course, it had been suggested in more than one quarter that it was the money he had really set his sights on. A man with an eye for an opportunity. Rather like his friends, it would seem.

'Not that Florentina's forgiven me, of course. Another reason I wish Sebastian wouldn't invite that set here. I know she still resents me, and I can't say I blame her. And I do understand, although she's got a new beau now so you'd think she would be as happy as I am to forget the past and look to the future.'

'Florentina?'

Christiana just briefly touched Dottie's arm. 'Oh, I'm sorry, I assumed you knew. Florentina and Sebastian were engaged to be married at the time of Harold's passing. She and Seb were at the ski lodge the night of poor Harold's dreadful accident. Well, they were all there, except Anabella, as she'd sprained her ankle the previous day. But we'd gone there as a group. Of course, with Sebastian so taken up with looking after me, and helping me to get through the following weeks and months, their engagement rather fell by the wayside. She only took up with Parkes about three months ago. Though they seem very happy,' Christiana added. She got to her feet. 'Come on, I think we've earned some refreshments.'

'Goodness, yes! I'm parched,' Dottie said, following her from the room, her mind busily going over this new information.

That evening, as her mother sat at the dressing-table whilst Dottie fussed over her mother's hair, making her turn her head this way and that until she was satisfied, Dottie recounted the conversation. Lavinia had her own news to share and told Dottie what Mamie had said as they'd watched the tennis matches that morning. Dottie was immediately interested.

'Do you think she could possibly mean...?' Lavinia asked. 'Because I really think that was exactly Mamie's meaning.'

Dottie nodded immediately. 'Oh yes, I do too. What else could it be? And I'm sure I overheard Boxhall speaking to her in a rather intimate manner. Plus, she sometimes almost calls him Paul instead of by his surname. Then there's the way he looks at her at every opportunity; he makes it so obvious. And she looks at him in just that way too. They really don't take much care to avoid being seen. If there's a single person in the household who doesn't know, I'd be very surprised.'

'Well,' Lavinia said. 'That's quite the scandal. And most awkward. It puts us all in a difficult position. Besides, what will dear Christiana do if Sebastian finds out and dismisses Boxhall? Do you think she'd be heartbroken? Or furious?'

'I'm not sure. Probably both.' Dottie sat down on the edge of the bed. 'It's not as if the Milners have been married for years. Her first husband only died eighteen months ago, and she and Sebastian married, what, just four months later? They only celebrated their first anniversary three or four weeks ago, so they're still practically newlyweds. Perhaps it's all on Boxhall's side, and he's misreading her comments or behaviour towards him? Perhaps she doesn't really have feelings for him, but is just grateful for his service and support? If he's been here for years, he's very likely been a staunch support to her after her bereavement. I find it hard to believe she'd act this way in front of her husband for any—ulterior—motive.'

Her mother shook her head. 'No, I'm very much afraid that she really cares for him. I'm certain of it. And he cares for her, too. Most inappropriate. Anyway, Mamie Cotton seems to think something is going on, and she isn't the type to be discreet, unfortunately. Her mouth rather runs away with her. From other things she's said, she seems to know everything about everyone.'

'She must see a lot. She meets people when they're either celebrating or in mourning. Either way, they're at their most vulnerable and likely to say just that bit too much. And probably drink that bit too much too. She certainly does seem to be an acute observer.'

Lavinia stood up and patted her hair, nodding with pleasure at the way it sat so becomingly about her face. 'Very true, dear, and not a gift to be welcomed by everyone. Well, we had better go down, it must be almost time. I can't help wondering if it will be a quiet, pleasant dinner, or full of temperament. I do hope there's no actual shouting before the dessert comes in. Either way, my hair looks lovely, thank you.'

Just then the gong for dinner sounded, and they made their final adjustments to their appearances.

As they wandered along the corridor towards the stairs, Lavinia added, taking Dottie's arm, 'This is rather fun, Dorothy. I'm enjoying being away with you!'

Dottie laughed. 'I'm glad you're here too, I don't think I could cope with this lot on my own!'

In spite of the events of the afternoon, dinnertime arrived and brought with it a kind of contented bonhomie—everyone seemed much more relaxed. Or perhaps, Dottie thought, that was only the effect of the alcohol.

To Dottie's amusement, Mamie wore the deerstalker to dinner that evening.

Mamie was a short woman, barely coming up to Dottie's shoulder, and she was stout. She was comfortably clad from neck to feet in a flowing garment of pale pink shot-silk, with a spiralling pattern picked out in row upon row of black sequins. The hat sat on top of her piled-up hair, the domed crown making room for all those grey curls. No one else, Dottie knew, could have worn a peach satin deerstalker and silk sequinned gown with such aplomb.

'She looks like a huge overblown rose,' Florentina whispered—far too loudly—to Milo, laughing behind her hand. He leaned forward and said something Dottie didn't quite catch, but it sent Florentina into a cascade of giggles. The only word Dottie caught sounded suspiciously like 'blancmange'. Dottie turned away, disgusted and furious with them both. From Mamie's expression it was clear she hadn't heard them, though possibly she did realise they were ridiculing her. Either way she didn't seem to care.

'You look wonderful,' Dottie said with perfect honesty and taking Mamie's arm, walked with her into dinner.

Dottie sipped her wine, and as one of the maids began to go from guest to guest filling the dainty bowls with soup, the room hummed with the gentle murmur of conversation, laughter, and the soft clink of cutlery against china.

She exchanged a look with her mother, seated beside her, both of them raising their brows. Lavinia leaned towards her to murmur,

'This is very pleasant. I'm so relieved everyone has calmed down after that awful scene at lunch.'

Dottie nodded. 'Me too.'

She glanced across to where Sebastian sat at the opposite end of the table to his wife. He was laughing at Forsythe's story about eggs in a jug of vinegar, and Anabella leaned forward to listen, a smile on her face, absorbed in the conversation.

Boxhall moved along the table, pouring more wine here and there, then Dottie noticed—it was far too obvious to have missed it—how he glanced back at Christiana, and the smile that lit his eyes was directed only at her, just for her, and all too easy for her husband to observe if he should happen to glance up at that moment. The tension in the room seemed heightened.

And yet, as far as Dottie could tell, Sebastian was still deeply engrossed in his conversation. When Boxhall reached his elbow, he merely nodded and held up his glass to facilitate the refilling of it, but his eyes never left the face of Forsythe who was deep in the middle of recounting some yarn or another.

As the glass was replaced in its spot on the table, Boxhall moved on, and Sebastian's laugh was a deafening bray that grated Dottie's nerves. And not just Dottie's. The slightest of frowns crossed Anabella's face, and at the other end of the table, Christiana's look was one of undisguised revulsion.

There was, after all, a deeper level of anger here in the dining-room than Dottie had previously been aware of. She realised now that the relaxed contentment was nothing but a sham. Beneath the contentment there brewed a range of vicious emotions. As if to confirm her sudden instinct, as the butler left the room, Sebastian, still mid-conversation, turned a dark look in that direction, a look of dislike so strong that Dottie was shocked.

She now knew one thing: Sebastian Milner was completely aware of his wife's tender looks for Boxhall and his answering looks, and he was not at all happy about it.

No doubt, she thought, in the privacy of their own rooms tonight, harsh words would be exchanged. And if Boxhall was still in his position in the morning, Dottie would be very much surprised.

Alcohol must always flow freely at a dinner table, Dottie supposed, but here it definitely flowed more freely than usual. By the time their main course arrived, a number of diners were rather too drunk, considering it was still early in the evening. Florentina Coyle was one.

Florentina had barely touched her food, prodding and poking at her meat and vegetables with an expression of distaste, and the effect of the wine she had consumed was to be seen in the way she was practically hanging off Milo Parkes, giggling, pushing her hair back from her face in increasingly dramatic sweeps, and noticeably slurring her words.

Milo had to transfer his fork to his right hand, unable to use his left due to it being clutched more or less to Florentina's bosom. He appeared to be trying to prise her off from time to time, but she had the clutch of a limpet. In the end he just concentrated on eating his food before he prevented the whole table from moving on to their desserts and cheese. He addressed an occasional low-voiced comment to her, but she still clung on, giggling and finishing her glass of wine with a flourish.

Dottie just managed to catch the slight frown and shake of the head from Christiana to Boxhall, meaning of course, don't give that woman anymore to drink. But Florentina had other ideas, holding up her glass with her left hand and loudly demanding more wine from the young maid. The maid glanced at the butler, who sent a resigned look at Christiana. Christiana gave a slight shrug of the shoulders and an almost imperceptible nod.

It was a good thing there was a healthy level of conversation around the table as this had all gone unnoticed for the most part. But Milner had clearly drunk quite a bit too, as had Dalbury. Florentina's friend Penelope was hardly less drunk; she was laughing loudly and fanning herself with her handkerchief. Across the table from her, Mamie was singing softly to herself, leaning back in her chair, one hand playing with her hair. She looked completely abandoned, and to Dottie's mind, quite sweet and girlish, a sort of larger sized, older Ophelia, her deerstalker slightly crooked on her head now, and ringlets of grey hair coming down at the back. But where the ladies were loud, Sebastian was simply staring into space, speaking to no one, as if lost in a daydream. Dottie wondered if he was drunk, after all, or if he was simply suffering the effects of his 'flu or whatever it was, and the combination of his medication with his wine.

So long as he stays away from me, Dottie thought again. I don't want to spend a week in bed, ill. And like her mother, she reflected irritably on what she saw as the very bad manners of the host to be taken ill but not to cancel his weekend house-party.

Beside Dottie, her mother was looking attentively across at Dalbury, who was entertaining them with colourful and amusing stories from his recent tour of the Low Countries. Positioned between him and Christiana at the foot of the table, Mamie was leaning very close to listen to the conversation and guffawing loudly from time to time. Her glass was also empty for the third time.

The maid, clearing away the plates now that Milo Parkes had given up trying to eat his meal, retreated to just behind Dottie's left shoulder, and Dottie distinctly heard her comment to the butler,

'I don't think we'll need to bring in the afters, most of 'em is half-cut and don't know what's going on anyhow!'

Paul Boxhall snapped at her to keep quiet and get back to the kitchen, and off she scuttled, knowing she'd be in trouble later. Dottie caught his eye and grinned at him. He rolled his eyes in response, but she wasn't sure if that was a comment on the behaviour of the guests or the impertinence of the maid. He was certainly unlike any butler she'd met before.

It was a relief when at last the meal was over. Christiana stood to lead the ladies to the drawing-room, leaving the men to their cigars and, of course, their port, 'As if they needed any more alcohol,' Lavinia murmured to her daughter as they went.

They were clearly thinking along the same lines, as Christiana leaned towards Dottie and whispered, 'The sooner we get some coffee into Florentina and Penny, the better, I think.'

Dottie had to agree.

*

Chapter Nine

Back in the drawing-room once again, the ladies settled themselves on the various sofas.

The maid who'd served the vegetables and cleared away the dinner plates now reappeared with the coffee pot, followed by Boxhall bearing the rest of the coffee necessities on a huge tray that Dottie was certain measured three feet square. He tilted the cumbersome load through the doorway without disaster, with the ease borne of long practise. The traditional Butler's Tray was of ancient mahogany, with elegantly carved handles and pie-crust edging, probably itself something of an antique. The porcelain was delicate and very finely hand-painted. Too expensive and beautiful to risk coming to harm. It was a good thing that Christiana had such a strapping chap as her butler.

Dottie observed him for a few seconds. He really was *very* attractive. And very young as butlers went, certainly no more than early or mid-thirties, she thought, Christiana's own age, in fact. He set the tray down, and suddenly, aware of her scrutiny, he glanced over to meet her stare. Dottie blushed to the roots of her hair and had to look away, hoping to high heaven that he didn't think she was romantically interested in him.

Lavinia, next to her daughter, whispered, 'My goodness, I shall be so glad when this evening is over. I'd assumed we'd have Bridge or charades or something after dinner, but everyone will be too drunk.'

'Yes, indeed.'

'What a shame your fiancé wasn't able to join you this weekend.' Penelope suddenly spoke to Dottie, jerking her from her thoughts. Penelope had wandered over and now stood in front of Dottie looking down on her in more ways than one.

'Yes,' Dottie said vaguely. She waited to see what else Penelope had up her sleeve.

'I expect he talks to you about his work.' Penelope smirked. 'No doubt you hear all the sordid details about his cases.' Her glance about the room invited the other ladies to join in.

This again! Dottie, pushing down her anger, simply smiled a polite social smile, and replied, 'Not at all. The last thing William wants to do when he comes home is to talk about work. In any case, as I said before, he wouldn't be allowed to discuss police work with anyone other than colleagues. That would be a terrible breach of ethics.' Dottie felt rather than saw her mother's glance and knew just what she was thinking: that William all-too-often shared information about his work with her, and that she had interfered more than once in police work. Fortunately though, Mrs Manderson preserved a tactful silence.

'What *do* you talk about? Making plans for the future?' That sarcastic quirk of the lips again.

'Sometimes.'

'Talking about looking at houses? Or can he only run to a flat, or a little bed-sitting-room above a shop? A little love nest just for two? Before the babies start popping out, of course.'

'William already has a house.' Dottie wondered why she was even bothering to be civil.

'Ah, let me guess. Perhaps a cosy little two up and two down terraced place somewhere in—let me see— in the East End, perhaps?' Penelope's best friend chipped in.

Of course, Dottie thought with an inward sigh, Florentina couldn't keep her long nose out of the conversation for long.

Dottie just smiled politely once more and said, 'No, actually. It's a large Victorian villa not far from Covent Garden. Very convenient for theatres and restaurants.'

There was a pause during which Penelope and Florentina exchanged a look. Dottie felt they seemed surprised, perhaps even reluctantly impressed.

'Still, shame it's not actually an estate, don't you think?'

'Don't be silly, Pen,' Florentina nudged her friend and sent a jeering look towards Dottie. Dottie knew something even more spiteful was coming. Turning away, as if having no further interest in the conversation, Florentina added, 'It was his father who had the estate—right up until he bankrupted himself and the whole family.' She burst into giggles, one hand on her friend's shoulder as if she couldn't hold herself upright due to the hilarity of her own wit.

Dottie was hardly surprised to hear that. They had

clearly been doing some digging. She wondered where they had found out that information. Dottie had never mentioned anything about William beyond his job. She said coldly, pointedly, 'Yes, indeed. Like so many of the apparently well-to-do people one meets these days. Stony broke, I believe the phrase is.'

Penelope appeared stung, her cheeks blushing deeply. Florentina turned back with a flounce, furious now the tables had turned on them. She took a step towards Dottie, but Penelope grabbed her arm.

'Just let it go, Tina. It's not worth it...' And Penelope drew her away towards the tray of drinks. They each took another glass of sherry and went to talk in angry whispers in the corner of the room, casting frequent glances at Dottie as they did so.

Dottie was convinced the matter wouldn't rest there.

'And then, on top of that, my mother's jewels, just like that to-do at Ponsonby's...' Dalbury was saying, half an hour later.

'Oh, don't keep dwelling on it, Henry.' Penelope came over to him with another glass of whisky. 'Time to relax and shake off your horrid week. That's the whole point about getting away.'

'Is your mother all right, Henry? Not too shaken up?'

It was the first time Dottie had witnessed Florentina apparently concerned for someone other than herself. She saw Parkes frown as he glanced at her. Clearly, he was surprised too.

Dalbury simply shrugged. 'Oh yes, she's getting over it. Her younger brother and his wife are staying with her at present. Gives her some company, of course. Not that I'd welcome it myself. Wild horses wouldn't drag me over there while they're in residence.'

Penelope and Florentina laughed heartily as if he'd said something witty and clever.

'Well, you've got us for company now. We'll take your mind off it with some music and dancing.' Florentina went across the room to where the gramophone sat on top of a cabinet. Soon she was joined by the other three, and without asking Christiana how she felt about it, the four of them began to sort through the records from the cabinet then music—loud dance music—suddenly filled the room.

'Come on, Henry, dance with me!' Penelope grabbed Dalbury's arm, kicked back the rug and pulled him into the middle of the floor. Florentina cackled loudly, pulling Parkes up to dance.

'I didn't know we were starting with the Ladies' Excuse Me,' he grumbled, but he laughed and took her hand, twirling her into his arms.

A moment later the door of the room was flung open, and Sebastian Milner was there, white-faced and white-lipped with rage.

'What is this infernal din!' he bellowed.

Parkes ripped the needle off the record, making a horrible—and no doubt damaging—screeching sound which was followed by an abrupt silence.

Christiana, on her feet now and coming towards him, said in a reproachful tone,

'Really dear, it's just a little...'

And at the same time, Florentina protested, 'We're just having a dance!'

But it was Christiana whose comment was stopped mid-sentence as he rounded on her, lashing out and catching her across the face with the palm of his hand, his signet ring cutting her cheek.

Dottie gave a yelp of horror, as did a couple of the other ladies. Christiana fell back a step under the force of his blow, her hand automatically going to her cheek. Dottie found she was on her feet, but Forsythe got there quicker, grabbing Milner's arm before he could lash out again, and practically frog-marching him out into the hall, saying sharply,

'Hey! None of that. Pull yourself together, man!'

Anabella and Mrs Manderson rushed to Christiana's side whilst even Penelope and Florentina were too stunned to giggle or sneer over someone else's misfortune. Mamie was shaking her head in disgust and turned to watch Christiana with close concern. Dalbury and Parkes exchanged looks, their eyebrows raised but Dottie hadn't the leisure to analyse the meaning behind those looks.

'If you will excuse me...' Christiana managed to say, her voice shaking. She allowed Anabella to lead her from the room, Anabella stroking Christiana's back and murmuring soothing words as they went.

As soon as the door closed behind them, Parkes was on his feet, saying to his friend as if nothing had happened, 'Fancy a cigarette? I'm going to the billiard-room for a smoke. I might spot a few balls while I'm there.'

'Good idea...' Dalbury followed him out.

Dottie sat back down on the sofa, wondering what to do. Perhaps it would be best to just go up to bed. She glanced at her mother. Mrs Manderson was looking furious, her rouge standing out on her cheeks as bright pink dots, and she was gnawing on her lip.

'She'll need some iodine on that cut,' Mamie remarked, more or less to herself. 'I know where the medicine chest is kept. Anabella might not... I'd better take it up to them.'

She was at the door before she recalled the others,

and turned back to say, 'Excuse me for a moment, won't you.'

Half an hour later, just as the rest of them were about to give up the evening for a loss and go to bed, Christiana returned, with Anabella and Mamie on each side of her. They sat down and awaited yet another fresh batch of coffee Boxhall would be bringing in at any time now. Mamie and Anabella engaged Mrs Manderson in conversation about gardening.

Christiana just sat quietly, staring into space, hardly aware of the others around her, though she still clasped Mamie's hand. Dottie noticed that Chris now had an angry red stripe across her cheek from the ring on Sebastian's finger, a mark very similar to one that Dottie herself had received at the hand of her former beau, Gervase Parfitt, just four or so months earlier. Thank goodness she had William in her life now, she thought. But she'd never forget how the event had shaken her, not just because of her concern for poor Christiana but because it added to the all-pervading sense of meeting her own past at every turn.

Boxhall came in with the tray, followed by a maid with a jug of milk and a plate a small, sweet wafers with one end dipped in chocolate. Dottie watched to see if he noticed Christiana.

He did, of course. All pretence at professionalism fled and he practically threw down his tray on the table to go to her. He dropped down onto one knee beside Christiana, all the ladies staring at him in astonishment. He took her hand in his, and softly said, 'My God, what has that b—er—man done to you? Are you all right, dar—um—madam?'

For a moment Christiana looked as if she would

burst into tears, but she bit her lip, sat up straight and said firmly, more firmly than she could possibly have been feeling, 'Yes, Boxhall, I'm quite all right thank you.' She gave him a little nod.

He got to his feet, once more a butler. He said, 'Er—and—er... Will... will there be anything else, madam?'

She shook her head. 'No, thank you.'

'Very well.' And he turned on his heel and strode from the room. His face, as he passed Dottie, was a pale stern mask.

There were a few moments of silence, then Anabella began to serve everyone with coffee, whilst Mamie passed around the wafers.

The coffee, Dottie thought, was very welcome, and timely. It was reassuring to clutch the hot cup to her, she hadn't realised she was cold. Penelope and Florentina were laughing and whispering together again. They'd had a few more sherries during the last half-hour.

As Mamie approached them with coffee cups, Florentina began to giggle rather loudly, pointing directly at Mamie in an outrageous manner and laughing.

'You look just like my old nanny. She looked like a fat old frog too!'

There was shocked frisson around the room. Anabella gasped.

'Florentina!' Christiana was horrified and shocked out of her introspection. She immediately began to make apologies to her older guest.

Mamie wheezed heavily and batted the apology away. She set down the cups. 'Don't you think nothing of it, Chrissie, my dear. It's not your manners what's wanting.' Lifting her voice in reply to Florentina, Mamie said, 'Seems to me your old nanny should have smacked your bottom for you a few more times. Then perhaps you'd have learned how to behave like a lady and be less of a trollop.'

'Oh, and you know how to behave like a lady, do you, you old cow! Common as muck!'

'Takes one to know one,' Mamie immediately countered, turning to the coffee tray.

Christiana was looking from one to the other of the women as if she just couldn't believe what was happening. Before anyone could say a word, Florentina had tottered across the carpet, unsteady on her high heels, and slapped Mamie across the face, the sound of it echoing like a gunshot, then she'd promptly turned and been violently sick all over the coffee table.

There was a stunned silence. Penelope grabbed her arm and hauled Florentina from the room with neither a word nor a backward look. The remaining ladies stared at one another.

'My... Oh my... Mamie, are you all right?' Lavinia asked.

Mamie now also sported a red mark across her face. She held her fingertips to it as if feeling for any damage. She appeared very shocked, Dottie thought, which was hardly surprising. Christiana seemed frozen to the spot, her mouth gaping in horror at what had just happened. Lavinia, coming closer, put an arm about Mamie's shoulder, whilst Anabella, on her feet and taking charge again, said,

'Ladies, let's move to the morning-room. We'll be more comfortable in there. Come, Chris, let's go. Chris. Christiana!' And their hostess seemed to shake herself then followed Anabella from the room.

They moved across the hall to the morning-room, never normally used after lunch. Christiana hardly seemed to know what she was doing. It had to have been the worst evening of her life, Dottie thought. Certainly it was a house party that would be mentioned with horror for years to come.

'I'll ring for more coffee,' Anabella said.

When Boxhall came, very noticeably puzzled to find them there in the wrong room, as it were, it was Anabella who went across to meet him by the door, to ask for more coffee and to explain in low tones what had happened.

He directed a worried look at Christiana, who was clearly on the verge of tears.

'She's all right,' Anabella assured him. 'But could we please have a cold compress for Mrs Cotton?'

He nodded and left almost at a run. No one spoke. They were all just looking at one another. With the other two gone, it was intimate enough that no one bothered to be polite or to make any kind of pretence.

'God, what an absolute bloody disaster,' Christiana said, pulling herself together. She reached out to squeeze Mamie's hand. 'I can only apologise to you all, girls. And especially to you, Mamie. Really, I cannot believe...'

Mamie assured her again that it wasn't her fault. The coffee came in—for the fourth time that evening—and the maid brought a cold compress for Mamie to apply to her cheek, halting for a moment to take it all in. Dottie knew the staff—as well as the guests—would be talking about this evening for years to come.

Half an hour later, neither the men nor the other two women had reappeared. Clearly there was no point in continuing to salvage a wrecked evening. Anabella and Mamie chivvied Christiana upstairs to bed.

Dottie sighed and exchanged a look with her

mother.

'We may as well...'

Lavinia got to her feet, seemingly relieved. 'Yes indeed, dear.'

As they went out of the room and began to climb the stairs, Dottie glanced back to see the door of the study was standing open, and Boxhall, frowning deeply, was carrying in a tray of glasses filled with either brandy or whisky, and another of the dark stuff that had become the master of the house's favourite tipple. In the room beyond him, Dottie could see Forsythe and Dalbury standing beside a slumped figure in a chair pulled up to the desk.

'Let's hope they belt some sense into him,' Mrs Manderson said crossly, not troubling to lower her voice.

There was no lamp beside the bed, so Dottie padded barefoot across the room in her nightgown to turn out the overhead light that evening.

On her way back to bed, she turned towards the window, slightly ajar, and stood there for a few minutes looking out, enjoying the sensation of the soft breeze cooling her face. She admired the dark majesty of the sky above, dotted with tiny pinpricks of stars, here and there overlaid by the softer, lighter colour of assembling clouds.

That dark curve beginning beneath her window was the rose walk, of course, and both to the right and left beyond it were the lighter flat expanses of lawn, with the path that led through the arching hedge into the kitchen garden.

Somewhere further away, the harsh voice of a fox sounded, coming to her on the breeze, along with the promise of rain, making her suddenly chilled. She shivered. The sound seemed so alien, so strange. The night made all things seem other than they were, and tonight no moon beamed cheerily down on the grounds of the Milners' home. The property could have been anywhere, there was no sign of another home within summoning distance, no hint of neighbours cosily at hand. Everything seemed isolated, dark and cold.

Then she saw a glow, orange-red, tiny. Someone was in the rose walk and smoking a cigarette. A gentleman, almost certainly. Dottie felt oddly comforted by the sight. The man must be walking up and down the path as he smoked. She wondered if he was aware of the lovely fragrance of the roses, or if the smoke from his cigarette overpowered all else.

Dottie remained at the window, watching the smoker. Although she could see next to nothing, her imagination filled in the details from the way the glowing cigarette tip moved. He had taken the cigarette from his mouth, his arm falling to his side as he took a step forward. Then the cigarette was up to his lips again, the tip glowing brighter in the night as he drew on it. She lost it for a few moments— clearly he was walking away from her—and then, there it was again, moving towards her from the other end of the walk, now and then blotted out by the trellis-work and stems of the roses.

She wondered who it was. Sebastian Milner didn't smoke, and besides, with his illness and all the alcohol he had drunk that evening—and all the morning and afternoon too—it seemed unlikely he would be well enough to be strolling up and down the walk at well past midnight.

It was most likely one of Milner's guests. But there was no way to know who it was—Dalbury, Parkes or the major, or possibly even Boxhall, angry or upset about the events of the evening. It could have been one of the ladies, of course, as Dottie knew some of them also smoked. Not that it mattered who it was, Dottie admitted. Nor was it any of her business. She was just curious.

The orangey glow fell to the ground, and a soft scraping sound told her that the dog-end had been extinguished underfoot. Almost immediately she heard the scratching of a safety-match and saw a quick bright flame flare into life. Another cigarette was lit, and that done, the walk continued.

Tired now, and ready for her bed, Dottie was about to step back from the window when she heard voices. A man's voice. And an answering, softer murmur, male or female she couldn't tell.

The man murmured, 'I thought I might find you out here.' But still she couldn't tell who it was that spoke. The voice was soft, quietened, no doubt to avoid disturbing anyone in the house.

Peering through the darkness, Dottie stared in the direction of the rose walk, but although she could clearly see the glowing tip of the cigarette, she could make out nothing else. A darker than dark shadow seemed to move. She thought—she wasn't *certain*— but she thought perhaps it was another man who had joined the smoker. The soft rumble of their voices went on for a few minutes, then she realised the second cigarette had been thrown down and trodden out just like the first, and the shadowy form of the smoker melted away.

But to Dottie's surprise, it was Mamie's voice that called out goodnight after him.

In the hall downstairs, a door banged. Soon, footfalls mounted the stairs and went softly along the corridor. Mamie's slow, heavy tread, Dottie guessed, and the quieter, quicker movements of someone else. She resisted the urge to crack her door ajar a little and spy on whoever was coming along the hall.

First one door and then another closed quietly, and all became still.

She had missed her chance and regretted it immediately. Feeling irritated that she didn't know who had been in the rose walk with Mamie, she let the curtain fall back in place, and she got into bed, shivering a little and snuggling down under the covers even though it had been a hot summer's day.

But what a day!

*

Chapter Ten

A scream roused the entire household from their sleep early that Sunday morning.

Dottie, practically falling out of bed with the shock, sat for a moment wondering if she'd really heard a scream, or if it had been a part of some dream she could no longer remember.

There were voices in the corridor, and the sound of running feet. Putting on her bedroom slippers, and reaching for her wrap, she prepared to go and see what was happening. Even without leaving her room she could hear the low tones of Boxhall's voice, soft but urgent in the hall below, and the higher pitch of a woman's voice answering him. At the same time, also from downstairs she could hear the sound of another woman sobbing.

'What on earth...?' Dottie was saying to herself as she threw open her door, only to see her mother at the open door of her room opposite. They looked at one another but neither of them had any answers.

She hurried to the top of the stairs, where Dalbury and Parkes, pyjama-clad, were already gathered and staring down into the hall. Almost immediately they were joined by Mamie Cotton in a scarlet flannel dressing-gown, men's socks instead of slippers, with a scarlet headscarf tied about her violet hair.

'What was that racket? It scared me half to death!'

No one answered her. Dottie peered past Dalbury to look over the banister, hoping to see what was going on. A maid was crying in the arms of the cook, who had clearly come running from her domain, the strings of her apron still hanging down untied.

Boxhall, in just his shirtsleeves, was running up the stairs towards them. Christiana was coming out of her bedroom, moving in a jerking, hesitant fashion, as if sleepwalking. She wore only a revealing night-gown, with no negligee.

Boxhall took her by the arm and tried to lead her back into her room. She clung to him, confused, and he bent to speak to her, his voice low, directed only to her. Dottie saw Christiana's hand come up to her mouth and she began shaking her head violently.

'No, no, no... No, it can't... No! No, I tell you!' But she subsided that same instant, almost falling to her knees if he had not caught her.

They all just stood there watching, apart from Mrs Manderson who returned to her own room, retrieved her black lacy evening shawl and hurried back to hold it out to Christiana, who just stared at it blankly.

'She's in shock,' Boxhall said. 'I've just had to tell her...' He took the shawl from Mrs Manderson and began to tenderly place it around Christiana's shoulders, standing in front of her to shield her from everyone's view. He pulled the garment across her front and pulled the ends together into a loose knot to keep the garment in place, all the while saying softly,

'Come along, my love, let's get you into this before you catch cold, and get you back to bed. There's nothing you can do for him now. The doctor is on his way.'

Once the shawl was secured, he stepped back, though Dottie could see clearly that his arm was still around Christiana's waist.

Christiana didn't seem to quite know what to do. She looked from one to another of them, as if she had no idea who they were or where she was. Then, finally, as Dottie was on the point of asking Boxhall what on earth had happened, Christiana took a few deep, steadying breaths then found her voice.

'I want to see him.'

Dottie and Mrs Manderson exchanged a look. Beyond them, Anabella—with Forsythe behind her in burgundy and white striped pyjamas that he was still buttoning the jacket of—were coming out of a bedroom at the far end of the corridor, having quite clearly been together.

'What the hell...?' Forsythe was saying.

At the same time, Boxhall said to Christiana, 'Do you think that's a good idea? It's not a pleasant sight. In any case, the doctor will be here shortly. Let him take a look first.'

'No, Paul, I want to see him. I must.' She clutched his arm. 'But stay with me, won't you? Promise me you won't leave me.'

He patted her hand and nodded. 'Of course I won't. He's in his study. Been there all night, I'd say.'

Shocked and silent, everyone followed Christiana and Boxhall down the stairs, the guests halting in the hall as Christiana, still clutching at Boxhall's arm as he opened the study door, went inside.

'Mrs Warboys, please take Susie and go back to the

kitchen, if you would,' Boxhall said, his tone gentle. 'I think everyone could do with a good strong cup of tea.'

'Yes Mr Boxhall.' The cook took the maid through the baize door to the kitchen. Perhaps having something practical to do would help the girl to pull herself together. Seeing guests were coming downstairs, Boxhall suggested they all go into the morning-room and make themselves comfortable.

The doorbell rang, and a maid hurried to let in the doctor, taking him directly to the study at the back of the hall.

The guests, coming into the morning-room, found Florentina there, sobbing on Penelope's shoulder. Both women were also still in their nightwear.

Everyone found a seat and sat about in an awkward silence, staring at the floor or exchanging looks with one another, brows upraised in astonishment. Florentina continued to weep loudly, and no one wanted to be the first to ask what was going on.

Not for the first time since it had happened, Dottie relived the dreadful moment when Florentina had slapped Mamie. The sharp sound of it seemed to echo in her brain. But of course, she reminded herself, that had been in the drawing-room, not here in the morning-room. She wondered if the drawing-room was now once again fit for use after the mess Florentina had made. She glanced at Mamie, sitting in all her colourful glory on a small sofa which she filled. There was no mark visible across her cheek. Mercifully, Dottie thought.

'He was such a wonderful man,' Florentina sniffled into her handkerchief.

It took Dottie—and probably everyone else too—a moment to realise she was talking about Sebastian

Milner. She had to be talking about him, Dottie thought. Everyone else was accounted for. Dottie reflected with surprise at the idea of anyone referring to Milner as a wonderful man then she guiltily remembered she had hardly known the fellow, whereas Florentina had once been engaged to marry the man.

Florentina added, 'I don't know what I shall do without him!' Then, her voice rising nearly to a wail, she turned back to a bored-looking Penelope and flung herself onto her shoulder once again, sobbing uncontrollably.

The door opened and the cook herself came in with pots of tea on a tray.

Anabella said to the cook, 'Is Mrs Milner all right, or does she need me?'

The cook shook her head. 'I really don't know, madam. She's still in the study with the doctor and Mr Boxhall.'

Anabella seemed to be on the point of asking something else, but just at that moment, two maids came in, one with the cups and some plates and cutlery, the other bearing toast, bacon and sausages.

It was another half an hour before Boxhall came into the room alone and said, 'Ladies and Gentlemen, as I'm sure you've realised, something dreadful has taken place. I regret to inform you that Mr Milner has been found dead in his study this morning. The doctor has been here and has stated that in his opinion, Mr Milner suffered a heart attack sometime late last night. Arrangements are being made to have Mr Milner's—er—remains taken away. So I'd be grateful if you could all remain here whilst that happens.'

'What about Christiana, how is she? Does she need me?' Anabella was on her feet, ready to go to her friend immediately.

'The doctor has just given Mrs Milner a strong sedative, and we've helped her back to her room and her bed. She will be asleep very soon, if she isn't already. I'm sure she would be glad to see you later, but for now, I'd be grateful if everyone could afford her some peace and quiet.'

'Of course,' everyone murmured, concerned, subdued. Florentina wept silently now, her handkerchief placed over her eyes.

Boxhall departed and they were left to stare at each other once more, no one sure what to do next.

It was late on Sunday evening. For the houseguests, the initial shock seemed to be fading, leaving behind concerns in their minds as to whether they should stay to offer support, or go home and so leave Christiana to her privacy in order to come to terms with what had happened. Lunch, and then dinner had been understandably subdued affairs. Of the guests, only Florentina seemed to be really grief-stricken. Anabella, along with Tom Forsythe, Mamie, Dottie and her mother lingered in the morning-room after the others had gone up to their rooms somewhat earlier and considerably more sober than usual that night. Almost the second they had gone, Christiana had reappeared, wearing a good thick gentleman's dressing-gown over her nightgown. She was pale but seemed composed.

'I'm so sorry to have abandoned you all for the whole day,' she began as she came over to where they were seated on the two main sofas.

Immediately everyone began to tell her not to be silly, that they perfectly understood, and she sat down with an air of relief, reaching for the cup of coffee that Anabella had already poured her.

'To be honest I couldn't face the others. I'm afraid that I deliberately waited until I heard them all come upstairs. I'm a horrid person, I know,' she added with a slight curve of her mouth.

'Don't be silly, ducks, I'd have done the same thing meself!' Mamie assured her, patting her hand. 'Can't stand 'em at the best of times.'

Christiana gave her a full smile, grateful. 'Hmm, well, yes. I'm afraid I never really fitted in with my husband's friends. I heard them calling me a black widow, earlier, when they thought I wasn't listening. They were on the lawn outside, practically right under my window, so how could I not have heard them? But I suppose that's what everyone thinks, and they may be right.' Her voice wavered a little. 'First Harold, and now... and now... Perhaps I really am bad luck.' Christiana bit her lip, looking down at her hands. 'To think that Sebastian had been there all night. The whole night. And I didn't even know. It was a maid who found him this morning—she went into the study to tidy up as usual after his evening in there with the other chaps—and—and there he was. I know we weren't on the best of terms, but he was so good to me when Harold died. And this is how I repay him! I *am* a black widow!' She began to weep softly.

Mamie patted Christiana's knee rather vigorously, whilst Anabella hugged her and soothed her. After a few minutes, Christiana began to pull herself together a little, wiping her eyes and attempting a smile at them.

'Sorry about that. I think it just suddenly hit me all over again. That keeps happening. I just can't seem to shake that idea out of my head. That it's my fault, that I should have done better. All those hours alone in his study. How could I not have known?'

'Rubbish!' said Tom Forsythe bracingly.

'Nonsense!' Mrs Manderson said at the same time, a comment often heard by her daughters.

'If you don't mind me asking,' Dottie began tentatively, wondering if this really was the time, but feeling she may not get another chance. 'Just what did happen to your first husband? Surely no blame can be attached to you?'

Christiana hesitated. 'I don't know. I suppose—I suppose no one blames me directly. Certainly, Sebastian never said a reproachful word to me about it. But I think a few of Harold's friends and business acquaintances held me morally responsible at the very least.'

'But why...?'

'Well, he told everyone that it was due to my stupidity that he had to go back out again that evening.'

Tom Forsythe leaned across to place his hand over Christiana's. 'He had no right to say that about you, dear. No right at all. It was his own fault things went the way they did. Wasn't it, Anabella? No amount of common sense could have overcome his pride that night and let him say, do you know what, perhaps you're right and it would be better to wait until the morning after all.'

'Absolutely,' Anabella nodded vigorously in agreement.

'That's very kind of you both, but really, it was true. You see,' Christiana said again, turning to Dottie and her mother. 'We were on a skiing trip to the French alps with Harold's friends—the usual people,' and here she nodded upwards as if to say, those people upstairs. 'Dalbury, Parkes, Penny and Tina. And Tom, you were there too, of course. We were all staying at the lodge.'

'All except for me. I was still at the hotel in the valley,' Anabella put in. 'I'd sprained my ankle in a fall on the skating lake the previous day, so I couldn't ski for a few days.'

'That's right. Well, I had forgotten my handbag. Or rather, I'd decided that I wouldn't need it up at the lodge, and so I left it in the hotel room. A stupid thing to do, I know that now. We had got the ski-lift up right to top of the run, and then we skied down to this lodge for an overnight stay.'

'Renowned for the difficulty of the runs,' Forsythe butted in. 'But the run down to the bottom of the valley in the dawn light was really something special. So we stayed overnight in the lodge to do the main run down in the morning.'

'Yes,' Christiana agreed. 'It was the sole reason for the trip, really, it was reputed to be such a beautiful sight.'

'But that first section from the lift to the lodge was rather demanding. I'd say it really was for experienced skiers only,' Forsythe added, with an encouraging smile at Christiana.

She nodded ruefully. 'Exactly. It took most of the afternoon to get to the lodge. I was quite a new skier, so I held them up rather. We arrived just as evening was drawing in, we were all quite tired. Then, we went to get changed out of our gear and into ordinary indoor clothes. As I was looking through my haversack for my things, Harold said something like, is that all you've brought with you. He'd wanted me to wear a proper gown, an expensive one he'd bought me. But I hadn't bothered to bring it with me. The lodge was not exactly a grand hotel, so I thought ordinary, warm and comfortable clothing would be the most suitable.'

Dottie agreed. 'I'd have done the same, I think. Not

that I ski. But those lodges can often be so draughty and somewhat basic, from what I've heard.'

'Just what I thought,' Christiana said with a nod. 'But of course, Harold was angry with me, said I would be showing him up. I pointed out no one else would be dressing for dinner as such, even though Paul—I mean, Paul Boxhall had come up with a maid by the back road to prepare us a rather good evening meal and make sure the beds were aired, that sort of thing. Anyway, Harold was furious.'

'He was a swine to you, Chris,' the gallant major chipped in. Dottie could see he was still angry, even after almost eighteen months had passed.

'Even so,' Christiana said. She sighed. 'We had a bit of a scene, I'm afraid. I'm fairly sure everyone in the place heard. He said something like, you haven't even got evening shoes or a wrap with you. Then he noticed I didn't have my usual daytime handbag with me either, so of course, he turned on me about that. I told him I hadn't brought it up with me as I didn't think I'd need it. He said words to the effect of, well I hope it hasn't got any money in it. Then of course I remembered. And as soon as I remembered, he guessed what I'd done, it must have been written all over my face.

"It has, hasn't it, you stupid...' Well, I won't tell you what he called me. I'm sure you can imagine it for yourself. He never did have much control over his temper. And of course, I had to admit to him that there was a little over two hundred pounds in my purse. Which when he completely lost his temper. Understandably, I know. I know I was a fool. I just hadn't thought about it... I hadn't known what to expect, it was my first skiing trip.' She hung her head.

As before, Forsythe was furious on her behalf.

'It was absolutely beyond the pale, the way he spoke to you that night. I've never heard such vile language from a so-called decent man in all my life. And to his own wife! I wanted to come in there and punch him in the mouth. Really, it was disgraceful. True, he paid a heavy price for it that night, but even so, the way he spoke to you was unforgiveable.'

'Oh Tom, it wasn't quite that bad. His bark always was far worse than his bite, or at least, usually it was, though I must admit it upset me at the time.'

There was a long silence. Outside, a blackbird sang a tribute to the sunset that was spreading red and gold ribbons across the summer sky.

'To cut a long story short, Harold immediately got all wrapped up, huffing and puffing, and said he had to go out again, though I tried to persuade him to leave it as we were going straight back to the hotel the next day, but he wouldn't listen. He was certain some chambermaid or chance thief would help themselves to the money.'

'He skied back in the dark?' Mrs Manderson asked, unable to keep the astonishment from her voice.

'Well, yes. Of course he was a very experienced skier, far better than me. And he'd done that run a few times. As I said, I'd held them up quite a bit on the way there, they'd had to help me to find easier stretches and wait for me and so forth. But he should have been all right, though it does seem like rather a mad idea, especially with the benefit of hindsight. It had started snowing again and there was a stiff breeze, but in any case, Harold was never a man to listen to reason, so...' She sighed. 'Well, it seems that he somehow came off the ski run and—no one really knows how—ended up going over the edge, over a cliff on the mountainside. His body wasn't found until several days later, in a deep gully.'

There was a silence as Dottie and her mother absorbed this. It was broken by Forsythe saying gruffly,

'Cracked his head on a rock, broke his damned neck.'

His rather forthright manner caused Christiana's eyes to flicker closed for a second. But she nodded, her lips pressed together in distress.

'My goodness, how awful!' Dottie exclaimed.

There was another long silence. Eventually Anabella said,

'But a few months later, you married Harold's closest friend Sebastian, and he was a great comfort to you. Or at least...'

Christiana nodded again. 'Yes, he was. At the time, he was seeing Florentina. I believe they even had an understanding. But now of course, she and Milo... Sebastian was very kind to me, helping me deal with the legal side of everything, and helped me to—just to cope with everything and everyone. He was such a comfort and a support.'

The unspoken words, now he has gone too, seemed to echo around them, Dottie thought. How unfortunate—incredible even—for a woman to lose two husbands in a mere matter of a year and a half. As if she was thinking exactly this, Christiana said in a soft voice,

'So you can see it was all my fault that Harold died. And now—Sebastian too. I didn't take his cold seriously enough. I should have insisted on fetching the doctor. Or—or he should have been taken to hospital. Or something. I just didn't think... Again! Oh it's too terrible!' She leapt to her feet and ran from the room.

They listened to the sound of her hurrying feet as she ran up the stairs.

Anabella said, 'But Sebastian was just like Harold. A bully, and a man of absolutely no common decency. Oh, at first he played the part, when he could be bothered. Just until he was sure enough of her. But he treated her like an imbecile, whilst making free with her money.'

'He had no money of his own?' Mrs Manderson queried.

'None.' Forsythe's mouth was a grim straight line. 'Anabella's hit the nail on the head right there. Milner and Bassington were two peas from the same pod—selfish, bullying, greedy men with terrible tempers and not an ounce of love for that wonderful woman. She deserved so much more, didn't she, dearest?'

He kissed the back of Anabella's hand as she said, emphatically,

'Oh, my goodness yes. I do hope that one day Chris will meet a really decent, caring man. It's about time.'

'Amen to that!' said Forsythe fervently. The others all agreed.

Very early on Monday morning, Mamie was leaning back against the wooden pillar behind her favourite bench on the rose walk. She closed her eyes, enjoying the warm sensation of the early morning sun on her face. She had drunk far too much last night, and her head was pounding. She should have known better than to spirit away a decanter to her room. But with what had happened, she'd needed something.

'Oh dear. Did we overdo it last night?' Someone came and sat beside her on the bench.

'My mouth feels like the bottom of a budgie's cage,' she said without bothering to open her eyes. She put her hand to her forehead. 'And my head feels like someone is crashing cymbals on it every five seconds.'

The other person laughed. 'So that's why you're sitting out here instead of going in for breakfast? Not that I blame you, I had a few too many myself last night. But a spot of bacon and eggs will soon set me right. Or I may have a kipper.'

Mamie's hand went to her mouth. 'Oh no, duck, stop talking about food before I disgrace myself!'

The other person laughed even more heartily, causing Mamie to wince at the sound, her head pounding. She glared at the person and they patted her arm.

'What you need is a little 'hair of the dog', as they say. What say I go and grab you a little glass of something? That'll pick you right up.'

'That's not a bad idea, duck. And very kind of you to offer, don't feel as though I could even move right now.'

The person departed. Mamie, groaning, and wondering if she should simply just go back to bed, leaned back against the pillar once more. She closed her eyes again, and very soon was drifting into sleep.

All at once, the other person was back, holding a glass out to her and saying, 'Gin and tonic, wasn't it? And easy on the tonic? Get that inside you and you'll feel like a new woman. You'll be knocking back the bacon and eggs in no time. Fried bread and mushrooms too, I dare say.'

Mamie took the glass, holding it against her forehead, even though it wasn't particularly cool, as there was no ice, the fine crystal of the tumbler still soothed her hot weary skin. In a muted tone she said, 'Probably a bit of dry toast and a good strong cup of tea will be enough.' She gulped down the contents of the glass in one go then pressed the empty tumbler against her forehead again. 'Thanks. I think that might have done the trick.'

'Glad to be of service.'

Already feeling better, Mamie turned to look at the other person. 'While I've got you here,' she began. 'About that little matter we discussed. I know you've been very naughty. I saw you when I was out here on Saturday night enjoying the evening air. The question is, do you want other people to know just how naughty you've been? Because I do love to chat to people, as you know. I'm a very sociable person. And as we both know, sometimes things that should be kept quiet seem to just tumble out. If that happens, sadly people aren't always as understanding as we would like, are they? It could be very bad for you. The police would get involved, obviously, as it's not the kind of thing that can be just swept under the rug, now is it? And if you get arrested, well... You don't need me to tell you the likely outcome. Not nice. Not nice at all. That'll put an end to all your plans, and I'm sure neither of us would want that to happen. So anyway, I'd like to help you, and you can help me, too. Seb got what was coming to him if you ask me. About time too. I'm grateful for what you did. At least promise me you'll think about my proposal.'

The other person was frowning slightly, leaning back on the other pillar, apparently relaxing, just as Mamie was doing. She had expected anger, or perhaps strenuous denials. But then, even yesterday when she had broached the subject, a calm good humour had greeted her words. She wondered if perhaps her veiled threat was not being taken seriously. Perhaps she should make her meaning even clearer.

But the other person simply shrugged and, getting up, said, 'My dear Mamie, let's discuss this later, shall we? For now, I understand what you're saying, and I'm convinced we can come to an amicable solution. I shall of course need to visit my bank to make arrangements. Perhaps you will be kind enough to give me a little time? And now, breakfast is calling. I think I shall have the bacon and eggs after all. What about you? Are you ready to come in and eat?'

She had her hand to her forehead again. 'Not just now, dear. I feel worse than ever now I've had that drink. My head is swimming. No, I'll just sit here a little longer. You go ahead, and I shall see you later.'

'Very well. See you anon.'

Looking back, the other person could see Mamie smiling to herself, clearly satisfied, as she bent to take in the scent of a lovely double-flowered deep pink rose, before clapping a hand to her forehead as if suddenly dizzy, then sinking back onto her bench once more, eyes closed as she leaned back against the pillar.

*

Chapter Eleven

Dottie and her mother arrived very early at the warehouse on Monday morning, early enough to avoid inconveniencing either customers or staff. Apart from Mrs Avers, that was.

Dottie's stomach rumbled. They'd left at seven o'clock. If they had still been at Christiana's home near Windsor, they would have been tucking into a generous breakfast by now. Dottie thought she might suggest to her mother that they head directly to a Lyons' tearoom after the dress-fitting, there was no way she could drive all the way back to Christiana's on an empty stomach.

Mrs Avers met them at the door, wringing her hands in despair. 'Oh my dear Miss Dottie! I've been trying to call you on the machine. But they said you'd already left. I'd hoped to spare you a wasted journey. I'm so sorry, my dear.'

Dottie felt a shock of anxiety. 'Why? What's happened? Are the girls all right?'

Mrs Avers managed a flicker of a smile. 'Oh yes, the girls are all fine, don't you worry about that. No, Miss Dottie, it's your dress. We haven't managed to get the lace stitched in place. There was a problem with some of the machines.'

Dottie wasn't sure what she meant. '*Some* of the machines?'

'Yes. Four of the sewing machines have somehow lost their tension assemblies and can't be used. And the other machines were needed to keep up to date with the orders. I wasn't sure whether to prioritise your dress, but I thought you wouldn't want that.' Mrs Avers was looking worried again.

Dottie hastened to reassure her. 'No, you were quite right. The orders must come first. Obviously with the missing parts, the stitching won't interlock on the garments.' She thought for a moment or two. 'But how can four tension assemblies be lost all at once?'

Mrs Avers' lips thinned in annoyance. 'Exactly, Miss Dottie. They can't. Not by accident.'

'A deliberate act?' Dottie was astonished at that—it felt too great a leap of supposition. But then, what other explanation could there be? 'Surely not. Although... But who? And why?'

Mrs Avers could only shrug in response. 'Come and look.'

Dottie and her mother followed Mrs Avers' neat form along the corridor to the sewing-room. They greeted the ladies who did the sewing for the warehouse. Some were busily working on the six remaining machines, but four machines were unattended, silent. Dottie and Mrs Avers surveyed them.

'You see, Miss Dottie? We've checked the floor for any loose parts that could have fallen down, even gone through the dustbin and we've found nothing. But I really don't see how...'

Dottie nodded. She stared at the silent machines, chewing her lip. 'No, nor I.'

'One machine, I could imagine—just about. But for it to happen to four machines all at the same time.' Mrs Avers shook her head. The girls in the room were silent, they continued sewing but there was none of their usual merry chat. They glanced from time to time at Dottie and Mrs Avers.

'And when was this discovered?'

'First thing this morning. I came in early to open up. And Jenny was in early as she needs to leave early this afternoon. She was on this one,' Mrs Avers pointed to one of the damaged machines. 'Then she realised it wasn't sewing right, and saw that the tension assembly was missing. So she called me, and as we looked around, we discovered three other machines were the same.'

'But everything was locked up as usual when you arrived, Jenny?'

'Yes, Miss Dottie,' Jenny told her, looking up from her work. 'Mrs Avers had to let me in with her key.'

'Thank you, Jenny.' Dottie couldn't immediately see what they could do about it. She nodded. 'Well, thank you, everyone.'

Then Dottie, her mother and Mrs Avers left the seamstresses to get on with their work.

'I've checked the storeroom,' Mrs Avers told them, once out in the corridor. 'There were three spare tension assemblies on a shelf in there, but they are gone too. I'm terribly afraid, Miss Dottie, that someone has done this deliberately to cause harm to the warehouse's good name.'

Dottie nodded again. 'So it would appear. And it was someone who knew what they were looking for.

And where to find it.' She bit her lip, thinking. She had to make a decision, and quickly. 'Right, here's what we'll do. We'll order some more to replace the missing pieces. I'll leave that with you, Mrs Avers. And, if you would, please ensure that the assemblies are all removed from the machines when everyone leaves at the end of the day. You could take them home with you, perhaps. It'll be a nuisance to have to replace them each morning, but otherwise, I'm just not sure what to suggest.'

'I think that's all we can do, Miss Dottie. Now then, when will you return for the dress fitting? Perhaps Wednesday, at the same time? We should have had time by then to finish attaching the lace.'

'Thank you, Mrs Avers. Wednesday will be perfectly all right.'

They went into Dottie's office for a further conference, and a cup of tea, which would have been most welcome. But they didn't get a chance to drink the tea because a few minutes later there was a call from the Milner residence. It was Anabella.

'Oh Dottie, I'm so glad I caught you,' she immediately began, and it was obvious from her tone that this was something important.

'What on earth is it?'

'It's Mamie! About half an hour ago, Tom went to see where she'd got to, as she hadn't turned up for breakfast.'

Dottie's heart felt chilled. 'And what...?'

'Oh Dottie, she's *dead*! It looks like a heart attack! Tom found her slumped to one side, on her favourite seat in the rose walk.'

'My God! That's just...'

'There was nothing that could be done for her, it was too late for that. The doctor has just left. Christiana is beside herself, as you can no doubt imagine. And I'm not feeling any too happy myself.' Her voice choked on those last words.

'We'll head back right away. We'll be about an hour and a half.'

In fact they were slightly quicker than that: the traffic in London was light, and the weather fine. Dottie's thoughts as she drove simply went around and around in her head until she felt it was too much to take it all in. Her mother was also deep in thought, silent beside her, and although she sent Dottie the odd reassuring smile or a pat on the arm, they hardly spoke for the entire journey. It was relief to arrive and see Paul Boxhall rushing out to meet them as soon as Dottie halted the car in front of the house.

'I understand Mrs Penterman called you in London and told you of the sad event?' He was wringing his hands. 'I just don't know what to say. Mamie... She was so...' He broke off, unable to put the words together. Mrs Manderson patted his shoulder.

'Let's go in, shall we?' she suggested gently.

The rest of the day was spent constantly asking one another how it could have happened, reminding one another that Mamie had seemed in reasonable health for an older woman who smoked like a chimney and drank heavily too. They kept telling one another what a dreadful shame it was. If anything, Dottie reflected later as she was getting ready to go down for dinner, Mamie's death had eclipsed Sebastian's. It was Mamie's death that Christiana and even Anabella were weeping for, Sebastian all but forgotten in the face of this new disaster.

The evening was a quiet one, passed with Christiana recounting anecdotes about Mamie and her adventures, the others simply listening. The dreadful four, as Dottie now always thought of them, had made their excuses and left immediately after lunch. The house was a more companionable relaxed place without them.

Up rather early on Tuesday morning, Dottie was making her way downstairs when she overheard Boxhall in the front hall talking severely to two of the maids. He looked thoroughly annoyed, Dottie thought. She saw him wave them away, and the two young girls scurried off through the baize door to the rear quarters of the house, relieved expressions on their faces.

Dottie gave him a look of enquiry as she reached his side. 'Anything wrong?'

He ran a hand through his hair, and groaned, apparently frustrated. 'Sorry, Miss Dottie. I'm afraid I rather lost my temper with the girls. Yet I shouldn't have. They only said what I'd been thinking myself.'

She continued to look at him and waited.

'Coming downstairs to find Mr Milner dead on Sunday morning. And then again, yesterday, when poor Mamie was discovered. Well... I know it's stupid, and just pure superstition, I suppose, but I was half-expecting...'

'Another dead body? My goodness, I do hope not!' Dottie looked about her in alarm. She shivered a little.

'Exactly that. Then I heard the girls saying the same thing, and I just snapped at them before I could stop myself. And I've always prided myself on my control, even with the greatest of testing. I know it was idiotic of me, but as I say, I almost expected to find another body. My mother always says things run in threes.'

Dottie nodded. 'Mine too. I can understand how

you felt. It's a natural reaction, really. Quite incredible to think that only two days ago, Mamie was cackling away at someone's jokes.' Her voice broke as she said that, and she had to pause and take a breath.

He touched her shoulder in a consoling gesture, more like that of a friend than a member of staff. 'She was larger than life, or so I always thought.' His demeanour sobered abruptly, and he looked down at the ground. Shook his head gently. 'Poor old girl. I was very fond of her. She was really quite something.'

Dottie could hear the faint sounds of someone moving in the upstairs hall. Boxhall glanced up. Anabella was coming out of her room, the major right behind her. Then, once more the perfect butler, Boxhall said, 'Well, Miss Dottie, I'll bid you good morning. Breakfast is waiting for you in the dining-room, just let me know if there's anything else you need.'

And he gave her a slight bow and took himself off to his back-of-house domain.

In the privacy of his own sitting-room that evening, Boxhall poured himself a small brandy and settled into his armchair. The radio was on quietly, just to give a little background noise as he sat there and thought about things.

It was only a few minutes later that the telephone rang. He got up to answer it.

A man's voice said at the other end, 'Is that the residence of Mrs Christiana Milner?'

He told them it was.

'I'd like to speak to Mrs Milner, if I may.'

'I'm afraid Mrs Milner is in bed. She has taken a sleeping draught on her doctor's advice and gone to bed early. She isn't to be disturbed. I'm Boxhall, her butler. May I pass on a message to Mrs Milner?' It wasn't true that she was asleep, but he refused to disturb her.

'Yes, very well. I'm calling from the police station in Windsor. I just wanted to inform Mrs Milner that the police will be calling on her at ten o'clock tomorrow morning.'

'The police?'

'That's correct. With two sudden deaths at that address in as many days, we are required to ask a few questions, make sure everything is above board. Officers who are travelling down from London will be with you at ten o'clock tomorrow.'

'But...' Boxhall floundered. It had been a tricky couple of days, and he had felt in a continual state of flummoxedness. As he did now. He took a breath, and pinched the bridge of his nose, willing himself to find his composure. 'The doctor confirmed that both deaths were due to heart attacks. Natural causes. Why do the police...?'

'Like I said. Ten o'clock tomorrow, mate. Pass it on to the lady of the house.' And the line went dead.

Boxhall dithered, unsure whether to speak to Christiana now while she was relaxing and having a pleasant time with her guests. If he left it until later, she might not sleep too well, and then she'd definitely need to take a sleeping draught. If he waited until the morning, she might be annoyed with him for not letting her know sooner. He'd just lied to save her from having to speak to the man herself, but would that turn out to have been a disastrous decision?

He decided to leave it until the morning. First thing, that should do it. Unless she rang for him this evening. He glanced hopefully at the clock on the wall. He hoped she'd ring for him, though he knew she was afraid of their situation becoming known by her guests, even though he was fairly sure everyone knew, in any case, but it was her desire to maintain the appearance of things, more particularly because she had not yet held Milner's funeral. After that, who knew? He hoped that somehow they'd find a way to be together, but he wasn't sanguine. Though, he told himself for the dozenth time, if she marries yet another brute of a man, I shall leave.

He went back to his sitting-room shaking his head at his idiocy. He knew he would never leave unless she told him to go.

*

Chapter Twelve

It was just after half-past eight in the next morning, the Wednesday. This time, nothing untoward had occurred to prevent the lace being attached to Dottie's wedding gown. She emerged from the changing-room and presented herself to her eager audience of two.

The full, flowing sleeves of fine lace reached exactly to Dottie's wrists. She looked critically at the dress in the mirror. Was the shoulder seam slightly out of line on the right? Or was it just the way she was standing? She straightened herself up and looked again. Was it a little better? She was annoyed with herself for forgetting to bring her wedding shoes with her, it made it almost impossible to get the exact length for the gown. But she thought the length of the dress seemed right. She'd need to bring the shoes with her when she came back to work next week.

'What do you think?' she asked, turning to the left, standing sideways on to the mirror. Yes, she thought, she was right. That shoulder seam was just a little lower than it should have been where it joined the sleeve, by perhaps just half an inch, but she noticed it all the same and having done so, wouldn't be able to ignore it.

Mrs Avers was on the point of replying, but Mrs Manderson, thinking Dottie was addressing her, said,

'Oh Dorothy, dear, it's quite lovely.'

Mrs Avers smiled. It always did her good to hear the work praised—she would pass that on to the girls. Her girls, as she thought of them. She believed in encouraging them for the long hours of careful work they put in, misplaced shoulder seam notwithstanding.

She and Mr Avers had never been blessed, so she also enjoyed, from the outside as it were, the mother-daughter relationship and the supreme importance of the wedding gown. Wedding gowns were her favourite garments to work on. Excepting the new range of baby and toddler clothes they were now doing. But everyone loved working on those, not just Mrs Avers. They were so sweet and tiny, it wasn't like real work at all.

In the glass, Dottie met Mrs Avers' look with a smile.

'Yes, Miss Dottie, it's perfect for you. Apart from that shoulder seam, of course, but we'll see to that in no time at all.' She ran a practised eye over the line of the nape and the sweep of the sleeves, the neat curve of the hips and the final flare to the floor. 'I'm quite pleased with it, otherwise,' she added.

Dottie nodded. 'So am I. It's very good indeed. I love it! Please thank the girls for me.'

She began to inch her way out of the gown, Mrs Avers and her mother coming forward to help.

What a pity, Dottie thought, that Mamie Cotton

would not now be able to provide the floral arrangements. Dottie had been very much looking forward to discussing bouquets with Mamie, she had been such a character and so passionate about flowers

It was a little like losing Mrs Carmichael all over again. Obviously, she hadn't known Mamie anywhere near as long as she'd known Mrs Carmichael, but she had appeared indomitable, a larger-than-life character, and it was hard to believe that she really was gone. A grievous loss to all who knew her.

'I wonder if she had any family?' Dottie murmured as she stepped out of the gown and reached for her skirt.

'Who, dear?' Mrs Manderson asked but immediately realised her daughter must be speaking of Mamie Cotton.

'Mamie,' Dottie said, just as Mrs Manderson replied,

'Oh yes, poor Mamie Cotton.'

Mrs Avers' ears pricked up. 'Mamie Cotton? Why? What's happened to her?'

'She passed away during the night on Sunday, it's believed. She was found sitting on a bench in the garden first thing on Monday morning,' Dottie said. 'That was why we left in such a rush on Monday. That phone call.'

'Yes, of course.'

'We were staying with the same people in Berkshire for the weekend,' Mrs Manderson explained.

'And she's dead?' Mrs Avers asked, shocked. She crossed herself. 'The poor lady.'

'Did you know her?' Dottie asked.

'She was a friend of my mother's,' Mrs Avers said. 'She used to be at our house all the time when I was a girl. Though I haven't seen her for twenty years at least, I should think. But she'd become such a success, quite celebrated in the society pages. I used to read any little snippets I could about her. Even read them to my mother before she passed on.'

Dottie nodded. 'I'm sorry that I just blurted it out, I didn't realise you knew her. She was a new acquaintance of ours, but I liked her. Very much. She reminded me of Mrs Carmichael.'

'There's another one that went too soon,' Mrs Avers said, crossing herself again.

'Dorothy had been hoping to have Mrs Cotton to do her wedding flowers,' Mrs Manderson told Mrs Avers. 'I know our troubles are minor in comparison with the poor woman's death, but it's such a shame you'll have to find someone else, dear. It would have been tremendous fun to plan the flowers with Mamie.'

'Bridgers of Broad Street,' Mrs Avers said. 'They do lovely flowers—bouquets, buttonholes for the gents, you name it, they do it.'

Dottie nodded. 'I'll remember that, thank you.'

'A pleasure, Miss Dottie. How did she die? Mamie, I mean?'

'They seem to think it was most likely a heart attack,' Dottie said. 'Mamie was really very merry the night before, and in great spirits. Well, at least it was amongst her beloved roses that she passed away.'

'My gawd, poor lady,' Mrs Avers said, crossing herself again and adding, 'Mind you, that does sound like Mamie Cotton—always had a bit too much of anything not good for her. But then, she always said life was for living. Better than denying yourself all the time, I suppose. At least it was quick, from the sound of it. No lingering on for months on end in pain and suffering. That's something.'

'True,' Dottie said, buttoning up her blouse. 'Although just the day before, the gentleman of the house, a Mr Milner, he died too, very suddenly.'

'What? Two deaths in one weekend? And at the same house?' Mrs Avers asked. She stood as if frozen to the spot, her expression one of horror.

And Dottie, thinking about it that way for the first time, could see now how peculiar it appeared. Two deaths. In two days. Both from heart attacks. 'Very odd,' she murmured to herself, her brow crinkled in puzzlement as she turned away to collect her jacket that matched her skirt.

One of the seamstresses ran in at that moment and said, 'Begging your pardon, Miss Dottie, but there's a Mr Boxhall on the telephone. He says could you please return at once, as the police want to speak to you.'

'The police? But... Why, yes, of course we shall. I'll come right away and speak with him.'

As soon as Dottie and her mother reached Christiana's house, they were told that an Inspector Rhodes wanted to see them in the study. *Immediately*, the constable added, as if that would make them hang up their hats and put on their house shoes any more quickly.

So they took their time, hanging up their outdoor things and pulling off their outdoor shoes, then finding their indoor ones, popping to the bathroom, and adjusting face powder and tidying their hair as necessary. It was at least ten minutes later that they went into the study—without knocking—and found Rhodes seething behind the desk.

'About bloody time!' he snapped at them, not bothering to do them the courtesy of getting to his feet as they entered.

Dottie's mother, of course, frowned at the man. Then said, quite firmly, 'Kindly moderate your language, inspector. We are not some street-corner riff-raff, you know.'

From his place in the corner, William disguised a snigger as throat-clearing, and nodding politely to both ladies, took his seat once more, notebook and pencil in hand. Dottie, having forgotten his new senior officer's name, managed to hide her astonishment on seeing him. She wasn't sure whether to acknowledge him or not. She decided perhaps it was better not to. If he didn't say anything, clearly she shouldn't either.

Mrs Manderson noticed that, unlike the first time she had met him when he really had been a sergeant, this time he was equipped to make notes. She gave him an affectionate smile. He might now be a sergeant again, but to her he would always be 'William, dear'.

Fortunately, Rhodes didn't notice the maternal smile. He gave them a half-hearted apology, and in an attempt to reassert himself, said rather loudly, 'Now then, where have you been? I've been waiting almost three hours to speak to you—along with everyone else in the house—only to find you and half of the other guests have disappeared.'

'We informed Boxhall that we were going out, how long we'd be gone, and what time to expect us back, inspector. Had we known you were coming, of course we would have put off our business in town and remained here.'

'Mrs Manderson, what you told Boxhall is neither here nor there. You should have asked my permission.'

'You weren't here,' Dottie pointed out.

'I was here at ten o'clock on the dot, young lady, I

can assure you.'

'But our appointment in London was for nine o'clock,' Mrs Manderson informed him. 'Therefore, we had to leave at soon after seven. And kindly remember to refer to my daughter as either Miss Manderson or madam.'

He stared at them both, furious that she had made a logical point and knowing he was being unreasonable in attempting to pursue the matter, but a dogged determination to do exactly that rose in him.

'So I ask again, where have you been?'

Dottie noticed William smirking. But Rhodes, seeing her glance that way, snapped,

'And it's no good looking at him, miss, he can't help you.'

She almost rolled her eyes, but remembered she was an adult, and such things just weren't done. Sadly.

'I had a dress fitting,' she told him.

'A—a—*dress* fitting?'

She thought he sounded as if he just couldn't believe it. This was confirmed when he went on to repeat: 'A *dress* fitting? I did hear you correctly?'

She nodded.

He glanced from one woman to the other. Trying to intimidate us, Dottie thought, and to undermine our confidence. Then he turned briefly to Hardy and said,

'Did you hear that, sergeant? They left this house where I am conducting a murder enquiry, and no one is allowed to leave. And for what? A dress fitting, sergeant!'

Dottie's slight gasp and Mrs Manderson's, '*Murder*!' were ignored.

William's expression was one of mild enquiry.

With the utmost politeness he said, 'You left here just after seven o'clock, I believe you said, Mrs Manderson?'

Collecting herself, Dottie's mother nodded. 'That is correct, W—er—sergeant.' She glanced at her daughter. They exchanged a look over the near slip. Mrs Manderson was simply glad not to have accidentally called him 'Sergeant, dear'.

Rhodes seemed disappointed in Hardy's calm response. But he left that for now in order to return to his questioning of the women.

'And so this incredibly important dress fitting just couldn't wait, it seems?'

'No.'

'Why?' he demanded.

'Because it was for my wedding dress and therefore of great importance to me.'

He nodded, not entirely satisfied, but even the long arm of the law had to admit to the importance of a wedding dress fitting.

'So you're getting married. Congratulations,' he said, and Dottie received these wishes with a cool nod. 'When is the big day?'

'Saturday the third of August.'

'Very nice.' He nodded and gave an approximation of a smile.

Insincere and trying to get back in my good books, Dottie thought.

'And—er—who's the lucky man? Anyone we know? That could be important to my investigation, you know, miss.' He was smiling now, looking at William as if inviting him to join in the joke.

Dottie looked at William. He gave her an almost imperceptible nod.

'William Hardy.'

'Oh, that's interesting,' Rhodes said, grinning at

William again. 'He's got the same name as...' He saw William's expression and his voice faded away. The grin faded with it as realisation set in. Then, 'Ah,' said Inspector Rhodes.

There was a moment's pause then Rhodes told them,

'Very well, ladies, that will do for now.' He got to his feet this time as they rose to leave the room.

At the door, Dottie glanced back towards William, concerned that she was the cause of him getting into trouble with his new boss.

As soon as the door closed behind the two women, Rhodes turned to Hardy.

'Why didn't you tell me you were involved with suspects in this case! You could have compromised the entire investigation. Not to mention making me look like a prize-winning idiot into the bargain!'

You did that yourself, William thought, but wisely didn't say that. They glared at one another, both momentarily angry.

Then Hardy said, forcing himself to keep his tone deferential: 'I'm very sorry, sir. I had no idea my fiancée and her mother were in the house. I knew they'd gone away for the weekend, of course, but I didn't make the connection. When we got here, I was told that two ladies had left the premises but I'm afraid I didn't ask for their names, just instructed that they'd be told to come and see us as soon as they returned.'

'*If* they returned!' But Rhodes thought for a moment and presumably decided it wasn't entirely Hardy's fault, for he said in a more considered tone, 'Right, well, anyway, is there anyone else we haven't yet spoken to?'

'No one. Unless you want to check Mrs and Miss Manderson were where they said they were?'

'Oh, I think we'd better, don't you?' But almost at once his sarcasm was replaced by a marginally more reasonable tone. 'But not you. Spence can do that. At some point, you and I can go to the dead woman's home and see what we can find out, but it looks like it was most likely a heart attack that killed her. Her age, and the over-indulgence of the weekend caught up with her. We won't waste any more time on this than we need to.'

'Yes sir.'

'The doctor was right though. Damned odd coincidence. Two deaths in one weekend. Definitely a house-party to remember.'

'Indeed.'

Dottie and her mother joined everyone else in the morning-room. Seeing at once that Dalbury, Parkes, and the two women had also returned, Dottie's hopes for a pleasant afternoon were dashed.

'Ah Dottie, Mrs Manderson, do come and sit down. Did you get the third degree?' Forsythe asked. He fetched chairs from the other side of the room, bringing them over so that the Mandersons could settle themselves. Across the room, the other four were playing a card game at the table, and for once the drinking vessels beside them were just coffee cups. They glanced up briefly to nod in the direction of Dottie and her mother but said nothing. Dottie noticed Florentina was watching them, clearly interested in anything she might manage to overhear. The others urged her to put her card down, and so she turned back to the game.

Christiana said softly, right away, keeping her social smile in place, 'As you can see, the poisonous four are back amongst us. Commanded to return by the police.'

'As were we,' Dottie said.

'I'm sure it can't be true that there's anything suspicious in Sebastian or Mamie's deaths. I know it seems a little odd, but the doctor said quite plainly that they were both heart attacks. Neither Seb nor poor Mamie were in the pink of health.' Christiana looked troubled.

'I'm sure I saw your tame copper with the other inspector who came this morning. Why do they need two inspectors on this case?' Forsythe commented, resuming his seat between Anabella and Christiana, no doubt hoping to change the subject slightly, but it was the last thing Dottie wanted to hear.

Unwilling to mention William's demotion, Dottie hedged rather, simply saying, 'Oh you know, they can't take any risks when an unexpected death takes place in the home of an eminent family. Let alone two deaths.'

'Of course,' Christiana nodded.

Anabella shot Dottie knowing grin, and Dottie just prayed that Anabella would say nothing until they were alone. It was obvious, Dottie thought, that Anabella knew or thought she knew about the demotion—and had no doubt already told Tom.

'I'm sorry to come back to such an unhappy topic,' Mrs Manderson said to Christiana and Anabella, 'But did Mamie Cotton have any family who the police would need to inform? I've often thought that must be such a difficult task.'

Anabella said, with a shake of her head, 'Oh, I really don't know.'

Forsythe simply shrugged.

At the same time Christiana said, 'Not that I've ever heard. She never married, though she claimed to have had a number of mostly eminent lovers. I must admit, I always rather took those claims with a pinch of salt. I know she had no husband—or not currently, anyway—and no children. I suppose there could be siblings or even aged parents, not that it seems likely, as Mamie was in her late sixties. But we never discussed it.' Her voice faltered. 'You know how it is, you always think there's plenty of time to talk about everything. Poor dear Mamie.'

They nodded solemnly.

She leaned a little closer and said in a low voice, 'I feel terribly awkward with the men, and Penny and Tina here again. They arrived just before you returned, and behaved for all the world as though they'd just been invited back after a lovely weekend. I do hope they won't need to stay here for long. No mention, of course, of 'the incident' with Florentina.'

Dottie was not surprised to hear that and said so.

Christiana continued, 'I was in two minds whether to tell the police all about that. But in the end, I decided there was no need. I don't want to make things awkward for anyone, even if it is Penny and Tina. And surely that couldn't have triggered poor Mamie's heart attack.'

Mrs Manderson wisely made a remark about the display of cheerful pink and white cosmos on the coffee-table, and this led to a new discussion about flowers which kept them busy, and before they knew it, Boxhall was coming into the room to let them know lunch, already slightly late, was now ready.

It was only three o'clock, but Spence was already in trouble. The cook, Mrs Warboys, was banging her cast iron pans about between the table and the stove in an ominous manner.

'Coming into my kitchen,' she was saying to herself, but perfectly loud enough for anyone to hear, 'and accusing me to my face—*to my face, mind you...*'and here she banged a large cast iron pan down on the stove, practically deafening those nearby. 'Of *poisoning* one of the guests with my soup, my special mushroom soup, the receipt for what has been in my family for nigh on three hundred years, and what my great-great-great-grandmother almost got burnt at the stake as a witch for. Like I don't know how to make a good, rich, nourishing mushroom soup, and neither do I know what to put in it, if this one's to be believed!'

Hardy, standing just inside the kitchen door, hid his smile, afraid she'd turn her wrath on him next. Her voice had been rising, along with her indignation, and the deep flush of her cheeks, until she reached the end of this remarkable speech, and Hardy allowed a few seconds to elapse as he waited to see whether Spence had the good sense to placate the woman. Hardy glanced across the kitchen to where two young girls, only fourteen or fifteen years old, stood solemnly dicing vegetables, their aprons brilliantly white, their caps straight on their heads, their faces bent down to concentrate on their tasks and hoping—it was a slim possibility—they might escape the notice of the Duchess of the Lower Realm and another scolding.

Mrs Warboys huffed to herself and dumped a jugful of hot beef stock into the pan on top of some butter and began to whisk it furiously, darting a sideways glance at Spence every so often and, Hardy was certain, breathing some kind of dire incantation upon the sergeant's head as she did so.

Spence appeared to realise he had mishandled things but seemed not to understand how to mend matters. Sensing disaster, Hardy cringed as he heard Spence say in his most sarcastic tone,

'Well, it's been done before, duck, so perhaps you

did just put some bad ones in. By accident of course.'

'Not by me, it hasn't been done. And,' she said, turning, a hot and dripping whisk raised in one furious fist, a massive knife in the other, 'if you ever, *ever* have the gall to come into *my kitchen* and call me 'duck' again, young man, I shall personally turn you into a young lady! *Now get out!*'

At the roar of her voice, one of the girls jumped with shock and dropped her knife. Mrs Warboys swung around to glare at the girl who was frozen in place, crouching on the floor and not daring to get back up.

'Lucy!' bellowed Mrs Warboys, then remembering justly that her quarrel was not with the youngster, she continued in a milder tone, 'Just you fetch me two onions and a stick of celery, there's a good girl.'

Relieved, Lucy bobbed a half-curtsey and ran at full pelt for the vegetables.

Spence had gone when Hardy glanced back, which was the first sensible thing he had done all week, in Hardy's opinion.

Hardy pulled out a tall stool from under the end of the twenty-foot long, well-scrubbed table, and sat on it. Mrs Warboys glared at him as if she couldn't believe his temerity. He just got out his notebook and pencil. Then he glanced up, giving her a cheeky grin.

'You remind me of someone who was a great friend of mine when I was a child.'

'Oh yes?' she countered, but her manner was already softening. 'And where is this great friend now?'

His smile grew sad. 'She died, I'm afraid.'

'I dare say she died waiting for you to get to the point, young man.'

He had to laugh at that. Lucy, back with the onions and celery, looked horrified, as did her colleague.

He said, 'Look, I know a skilled and experienced cook such as yourself would never make a mistake of such an elementary kind. That's just for the storybooks. But we police have to ask all these stupid questions just so that we can get to the real cause of death, for the sake of the friends and the loved ones, and for the victim herself, of course. No one is trying to blame you for anything, I can promise you that. I can see that you're good at your job and are not someone who has only been working in a kitchen for just a week or two. So please, can you help me, Mrs Warboys?'

'Hmm. I can see you know exactly what you're doing too, young fellow. What was it you used to talk her round for, this friend of yours? Shortbread? Or cherry buns?'

'Oh shortbread, every time.'

'Hmm.' She nodded knowingly, eyeing him closely. Then she said, 'Janet, fetch the gentleman some shortbread and a good strong cup of tea for him and one for me too. Lucy, come over here and stir this. That's it,' she said approvingly as the girl took her place by the stove. 'Gently now, don't whip it to a frenzy, just keep it moving slowly. And when I tell you, I want you to carefully pour in that little dish of sherry, then Janet can bring you the rest of the veg.'

In a few minutes, Mrs Warboys was sitting beside him with the tea and shortbread. William took a finger of the sugary, crumbly treat, hesitated for a moment to take in the warm sweet scent of it which took him right back to eight years old and the kitchen at Great Meads. Then he bit into it, closing his eyes in appreciation. The sweetness hit his tongue and the short pastry melted away. After a second bite, which was enough to finish the finger, he said,

'Mrs Warboys, in all honesty, that is the best

shortbread I have ever tasted. It is superb.'

She blushed with pleasure at his praise, and with her cap lying on the table, her fair hair loose to her shoulders and the pink in her cheeks, she looked young and carefree, and he realised she was nowhere near as old as he'd originally thought. He doubted she was on the wrong side of fifty. She pushed the tin towards him. 'Here, you'd better have another piece then. Now, what is it you want to know?'

'Perhaps we can start with you telling me where you get your mushrooms?'

'They come fresh twice a week from the greengrocer, and he gets them direct from a farm in Ireland.'

William noted this down. 'And I imagine you inspect all the items that come into the kitchen carefully?'

'Yes, I do. I inspect everything myself, and if I'm not happy with it, it goes straight back. I've been buying from that same greengrocer for twenty-six years.'

'Excellent.' William made a note of that too. 'And were mushrooms used in any of the other dishes that evening?'

'No,' she said decisively. 'Just the soup. And Mrs Milner said not to make a lot, as some of the guests didn't care for mushrooms. One of them was the poor lady that died.'

'Mrs Cotton was known to dislike mushrooms?'

'Yes. And she never took none of that soup because of it. I made her a little bit of oxtail soup. Her and his lordship both had it, he didn't want the mushroom neither.'

'Mr Milner was that?' Then he reminded himself they weren't talking about the night after Milner had died, the Saturday night. This was Sunday night, when Mamie Cotton had passed away.

But she was already shaking her head. 'No, I'm taking about Sunday. It was one of the guests. Lord Dalbury, his name was.'

'Lord Dalbury?' He raised one eyebrow for her confirmation.

'That's right. They both had oxtail soup.'

William wrote all this down and thanked her profusely for her time. As he got up to go, he swiped one last finger of shortbread, and thanking her again, he took his leave, her vigorous laugh following him into the hall.

Definitely *not* the mushrooms, then. Not that he'd really thought that either death was due to natural causes, or accidents. A new theory seemed to be growing from strength to strength. Two deaths, two days, one household.

*

Chapter Thirteen

After a surprisingly pleasant and amiable lunch, Dottie was approached by Boxhall as she crossed the hall. He said, 'One of the policemen would like a word with you. He's in my sitting-room through the door there.' He indicated the baize door to the back quarters of the house.

Dottie, feeling excited, followed him. It had to be—surely—William who wanted to see her. There could be no reason why the 'other fellow', as she thought of Inspector Rhodes, would want to see her.

Boxhall opened a door to announce: 'Miss Manderson is here, sir.' Then, with a curious glance at Dottie, stood back to allow her to step into the room before closing the door behind her. He was walking past the sitting-room window onto the hallway when a quick glance in showed Dottie was now in the man's arms and they were kissing.

'Well, well,' Paul Boxhall said to himself, and went into the kitchen smiling.

'How is the case going? If it is a case at all?'

William grimaced. 'I'm not too sure at the moment. Rhodes has already made up his mind that it's murder, of course. But we haven't had confirmation of that as yet. I mean, I'd agree that at first glance, two sudden deaths in two days at the same house seems a most unlikely coincidence, but then...' He raised his hands then dropped them again. 'Unfortunately, coincidences do happen. There isn't any real proof at the moment that it's anything untoward. This is all based on the local doctor's suspicions.'

'But I thought he said they were both heart attacks?'

'Yes, he did, based on the appearance of the bodies. But at the same time, he admitted he felt uneasy and thought there should be a further investigation, as he was not aware of any history of unhealthy heart conditions in either case. Apparently, he had attended Mrs Cotton last year when she had bronchitis. And so the Yard got summoned. Before we even knew if there was any real reason to summon us. Autopsies have been requested, but nothing has come back yet, it's far too soon. We probably won't have anything conclusive for several days. More than a week, even, that would not be unusual. So far, we've got nothing other than our nasty police intuition.' He gave her a stern look. 'Unless there's anything you can tell me?'

'I?' She laughed. 'As if I would know anything.' She made herself comfortable in Boxhall's armchair, leaving William to sit on the hard upright seat. He grinned at her.

'I wouldn't mind betting you've been sticking your nose in.'

'Not exactly sticking my nose in. More like, condoling with the widow who is a friend, and staying here because we were told to stay put by you.'

'Ah yes. Sorry about that. Changing the subject, how did the dress fitting go?' He lounged back on the chair as much as he was able, crooking an arm over the back.

'Very well, the dress is practically perfect. It should have been ready on Monday but when Mother and I got there, Mrs Avers told us there had been some damage to several machines and so it wasn't ready.'

William looked puzzled. 'What sort of damage?'

She leaned forward, keen to tell him, though it was hardly a matter for Scotland Yard. 'The tension assemblies on four machines had been removed. And so had the replacements that were kept in a store cupboard.'

He frowned now. 'What, someone deliberately made the machines unusable?'

'It looks that way. We can't think of any other way it could have happened. Those things don't just fall off every five minutes. Nor can they magic their way through a locked door.'

'Odd. And what do these tension thingummies do?'

'They create the tension on the thread that causes the upper thread and the lower thread to interlock properly, forming a stitch. Without that, the stitches won't stay in place on the fabric, the cotton thread just pulls off in a long line.'

'It sounds like sabotage.' He was leaning forward now, the frown pinching his eyebrows together.

'Exactly.' She bit her lip, worried all over again now. What on earth could be behind it, that was what she kept coming back to.

'Do you want me to get someone to look into it?'

She shook her head. 'Not yet, darling, but thanks

all the same. I think I'd rather wait and see what happens. *If* anything happens... I'm hoping that it turns out to be some kind of isolated occurrence. Probably silly of me...'

'That's fine. So how have things been here? Anything useful you can tell me?'

'Am I your spy now?'

'I might as well make use of your nosiness.' He grinned at her again. And of course, she thought, it was perfectly true. So she told him all about Sebastian's illness and bad temper, about the truly dreadful evening they'd all had on Saturday with tempers flaring and the two separate slapping incidents. She was a little disconcerted when he got out his notebook and wrote it all down, with occasional whistles of surprise and shakes of the head as he began to see just how awful the weekend had been.

Finally leaning forward and lowering her voice in case the butler or any of his staff should be nearby, she said, 'Boxhall is terribly attractive.'

William teased her with a mock frown. 'Oh, you think so, do you?'

She slapped him playfully on the arm. 'There's no need to be like that. I just meant, butlers are usually several centuries old and completely decrepit. Not handsome able-bodied young men.'

'And?'

'And, I'm fairly sure, and it's not just me saying it...'

'And?' he prompted her again.

Dottie said, 'I think perhaps something is going on between Boxhall and Christiana Milner. In fact, I'm certain of it.'

'Really? They're having an affair? Interesting.'

'Exactly. They're not terribly discreet. Which

makes me wonder...'

'Wonder...?'

'Well, I rather wonder whether Sebastian Milner knew. Or at least, suspected. I mean, that could make things difficult, couldn't it? In fact, judging from the looks he gave Boxhall at dinner on Saturday, coupled with Sebastian's anger towards his wife, I believe he did suspect. Perhaps him lashing out at her wasn't anything to do with the spilled drink at all.' She fell silent, mulling the scene over in her head once more.

'Hmm, I suppose so.'

With a touch of impatience, Dottie said, 'Think about it, darling. Boxhall could have lost his job, and he wouldn't have got a reference from Milner, so there's goes his chance of getting another one easily. Or Sebastian could have started divorce proceedings, citing infidelity, and then Christiana's reputation could have been in tatters... Not that reputation means much these days, but even so, her name would have been dragged through the courts and splashed in the gossip columns. They both had an awful lot to lose.'

'Now that is interesting. Of course, we don't know for certain that Sebastian was aware of anything going on, if anything *is* going on. It may turn out that there isn't anything to know, although it does sound rather likely. But I'll certainly mention it to Rhodes. I can't do anything without his say-so, unfortunately.'

He got to his feet and kissed her again. 'Sorry, my love, I really have to get back. I'll try to let you know where I am and what I'm up to. In the meantime, I think it's probably safe enough for you and your mother to stay here. If that changes, I'll drive you back to London myself. Thank you for the information. Behave yourself.' And with a last kiss he opened the door and escorted her back to the hall.

Lord Dalbury stretched his long legs out in front of him and yawned widely and loudly.

'Damned awkward, isn't it?' he remarked in a general way.

No one said anything, so he continued to elaborate on his thoughts, leaning his head onto the back of the chair and gazing up at the blue sky.

'I mean, when you've lost your husband, you could normally expect to be entitled to a bit of privacy. And yet here we all are, crashing in on the new widow and eating her out of house and home, all because those wretched police are making a mountain out of a molehill.' He lifted his head momentarily to slurp from his cocktail glass, then let his head sink back again.

'Two molehills, technically,' Parkes pointed out.

Dottie caught her mother's eye. Mrs Manderson's mouth was a straight disapproving line. Penelope put out a manicured hand to pat and stroke Dalbury's chest in a far too intimate manner for polite company. She'd also had several cocktails. As had her friend. And Parkes too. If they stayed any longer, it seemed likely that fresh stocks of alcohol and mixers would be urgently required.

'Oh Henry, sweetheart, do stop fretting.'

Dottie almost laughed. It was quite clear no one was fretting, certainly not Dalbury. They were all just fed up with being hauled back here.

Tom Forsythe was coming towards them across the lawn, stepping carefully between the markers of the previous afternoon's clock golf.

'How is Christiana?' Dottie asked him.

Penelope cast a resentful look in Dottie's direction, leapt to her feet and almost shoved Forsythe down into her seat, saying loudly, 'Yes, Tom, do tell us how things are. Poor Christiana must be completely prostrated with grief. Not just about Dear Seb of course, but Poor Mamie too.'

He frowned, not really at her, but at the situation. 'She's resting. Anabella is with her.' He shook his head then, adding, 'It's a bad business. And the police—I know they've got to do their job, but, well I'm afraid they really are making things worse. Even poor old Seb's doctor told her it can happen like that, a chap is a bit low health-wise, and the heart struggles to keep up—it doesn't even need to be an abnormal amount of exertion, as it could quite likely have been caused by a relatively small defect that's gone unnoticed for years. And suddenly... the poor chap's gone.' He shook his head.

'But having the police about the place, poking into everything, disrupting our lives. It's no wonder Christiana is in such a state. They are just putting all these foolish ideas into her head. Making her worry over every little thing that's happened of late.' Florentina yawned and stretched in her chair as if she hadn't a care in the world. She drained her glass and stood it on the grass beside her chair.

'Dottie, surely you can do something?' Penelope suddenly said, startling Dottie.

'I? But...? How on earth could I...?'

'Well, your chap is one of them, isn't he? He's one of the police that are in the house. He's the driver or something, isn't he?' She made a poor job of disguising her malicious enjoyment of this little gem. With a quirk of her mouth she added, 'He's obviously not the inspector you said he was, after all, from the way the real inspector sends him here, there and everywhere.'

'Er—well, no, he's—er...' Dottie, flustered, said. 'He may possibly be here, I'm not sure. But in any case...'

'Correct me if I'm wrong, but I rather had the impression that a chap was supposed to make his way up through the ranks, not down?' This was of course Florentina's idea of humour and a good way to needle someone she clearly didn't like.

Dottie stared at her, unable to think of a response that didn't involve unladylike language or violence.

'Oh come on, Dot,' Milo remarked lazily from his lawn chair. Then, on spying Boxhall approaching with another tray of drinks, he hastily gulped down the last of his cocktail. 'Why can't you do something? Tell them to back off and leave Christiana alone. It really is too bad, them badgering her in this way at a time like this. You would think the police had better things to do, like solving a few crimes for a change, rather than pestering a young widow. You could point out to him that Seb's death was quite simply due to a heart attack, as his doctor can confirm, and if they had any decency, they'd leave Christiana alone.'

'I'm afraid I can't do that,' Dottie's tone was frosty. She still didn't like Parkes. Or Dalbury, if it came to that, and she certainly didn't like them calling her by her first name in such an informal manner. My goodness, she thought, casting another glance to her left, I'm turning into my mother. Flora said that would happen. Dottie huffed, and her fringe gently lifted with the breath then settled itself again in place.

Parkes didn't seem to notice her tone, he was probably already thinking about his next drink. Boxhall bent to bring the tray level with Milo's reclining nose.

'Drink, sir?'

'Don't mind if I do.' Parkes selected a large whisky and soda from the back of the tray.

Dottie sighed inwardly and again caught her mother's eye. At this rate, Dottie thought, all the guests would be well and truly plastered by the time they went into dinner. Again.

'Anyway,' Penelope demanded, narrowing her eyes. 'What do you mean, you're afraid you can't do that? Can't? Or don't want to?'

'Both,' Dottie said. Her tone was firm—perhaps a little too firm. Too late she realised she ought to just have laughed it off, but now everyone was staring at her.

The major, unfailingly gallant, came to her rescue. 'Oh no,' he said. 'Of course, she can't. Unfortunately, there are procedures for these sorts of occasions. They are there to protect us all, really, and have to cover every type of situation. So of course, our trusty police force have to be seen to do their bit, just in case. One never knows, from the point of view of the police. Someone could have slipped poor old Seb something. For example a Mickey, or Mickey Finn, as they say in the films.' On seeing the shocked faces of some of the ladies, he added hastily, 'Not that anyone would, of course. But the police don't know that. It's their job to make sure. Let's hope and pray that they will be gone by tomorrow and we shall all be able to get on with our lives.'

'Just as well,' Dalbury grumbled, on his feet now. He kicked one of the golf balls across the lawn. It disappeared under a sprawling plant on the edge of the herbaceous border. He took his glass and wandered off.

There was a little ill-natured muttering, and Penelope and Florentina became immersed in another of their low-voiced conversations. Dottie couldn't make out what they were saying, but it clearly centred on her or William, or both of them, to judge by the resentful looks they cast now and again in her direction. Dottie sighed again. She hoped that Forsythe was right, and that by the following day they would all be allowed to leave. It was becoming too severe a strain on her temper; the weekend house party had now lasted almost a week.

Boxhall was near Mrs Manderson, collecting up the used glasses, and Dottie heard her mother ask, 'How is Christiana?'

He nodded, and said, keeping his voice low, 'She's all right, considering, thank you Mrs Manderson. Mrs Penterman is with her at the moment. I'm grateful for that, I didn't want her to be left alone. She did ask me to tell everyone how sorry she is that you've all been detained, though...' He looked over his shoulder and nodded in the direction of the others. 'I must admit I'm reluctant to pass the message on. If that lot have been inconvenienced, then all I can say is, good, I'm glad!' He turned back to Mrs Manderson and Dottie. 'Sorry, ladies, that's not very kind of me, is it? And I'm doubly sorry you've both been lumped in with that lot. But I know Mrs Milner would feel more like leaving her room if they weren't still here.'

Mrs Manderson nodded sympathetically. There didn't seem to be much else to say. She looked at the drinks on the tray.

'These two are lemon cordial, ladies, or I can bring you some tea?' He nodded at two tall glasses on the right of the tray.

'Lemon cordial is perfect, thank you.' Dottie beamed at him and took one. Her mother did the same, and he gave them both a smile before turning to serve Penelope and Florentina with yet another cocktail each.

'My word, it seems a long time until dinner,

doesn't it, dear?' Mrs Manderson said.

'It certainly does, Mother.'

The dressing gong sounded an hour later, and with relief, they went up to dress.

Dinner was not so very different from previous dinners in the house, but without Sebastian's volatile presence, seemed rather more relaxed, even though there were two empty seats to serve as a constant reminder.

After dinner they made their way to the drawing-room, now fit for use once more. A light rain was falling, and so the party had to remain inside. Dalbury asked if Christiana would mind if they put on some music.

'Certainly you may,' she responded immediately. 'I know some would say it's disrespectful in a house of mourning, but what else are we going to do? Cards or conversation would be no better than dancing. And I think we can all guess what Mamie would say.'

"Enjoy yourselves, ducks,' I should think,' Forsythe said.

Christiana smiled. 'Exactly.'

Florentina and Parkes found some dance records, Christiana rang for drinks, and the mood turned into a celebration. Somehow Dottie found herself dancing with Dalbury, then Forsythe, then Dalbury again, and even, surprisingly, Parkes.

She was feeling a little tipsy, even though they had only eaten their meal a short while before. But almost without thinking she had consumed three cocktails in a short space of time, and now, as one of her favourite songs began to play, she danced with enthusiasm alone as the others all were dancing with their usual partners. After the introduction, they all began to sing along with the well-known chorus:

'Five foot two, eyes of blue, has anybody seen my gal?'

Even Christiana and Mrs Manderson were clapping along to the music, laughing and exchanging comments.

Then the door opened, and in came Sergeant Hardy.

In her high-heeled silver evening sandals, and with a half-empty martini glass in her hand, Dottie executed a little dance around an amused, grinning William. Not noticing that everyone else had stopped dancing to look at the policeman, she was singing her own variation of the song.

'Six foot two, almost. Eyes of blue, a *gorgeous* blue. Has anybody seen my Bill?' Dottie, slopping a little of her drink down her dress, giggled.

As she came around the back of him to his other side, she collided with Inspector Rhodes, just coming in at the door, and looking rather bemused.

'Dottie, darling,' William said, hiding a smirk. He raised his voice slightly. 'Everyone, if you could give us your attention for a moment, the inspector would just like a word with you all.'

'Oops,' Dottie said rather loudly and clapped a hand over her mouth. Dalbury stopped the music. Dottie stopped dancing abruptly, her head swimming gently but pleasantly from the alcohol, and like the rest of the guests, she waited to see what the inspector had to say.

'Yes, well, er, thank you everyone. I'm sorry to interrupt your evening. I would just like to say we have concluded our initial interviews with the staff, and the guests as well of course, and we are returning to London tonight to report to the chief inspector and to carry out further checks, but we shall be back either tomorrow evening or Friday to continue our investigation. In the meantime, please do not leave the premises, and be assured that I shall leave two constables on duty at all times for everyone's protection.'

He paused and glanced around the room solemnly, commanding everyone's interest. Dottie found her heart was suddenly pounding. She thought she knew what he was about to say. Her hand to her mouth, she held her breath. He mother, beside her now, put her arm through Dottie's.

Rhodes continued in his grave tones: 'We are now officially treating both Mr Milner's and Mrs Cotton's deaths as murder, although we have not yet confirmed the means of those murders. However, I expect to have that information very soon. That is all, and er, thank you, and good evening.'

His words were greeted by a silence. No one knew quite what to say, it seemed. Rhodes nodded to Christiana and left the room, William dithered awkwardly, and in the end, contented himself with kissing Dottie quickly on the cheek, murmuring, 'Sorry to spring it on you, didn't know myself until ten minutes ago that we were going back to London.' Then he hurried after Rhodes.

The guests remained rooted to their respective spots, no one knowing what to say, the gramophone remained silent. After a moment, Dalbury put the records away. In twos they began to say goodnight in muted voices and left the drawing-room to go upstairs.

A short time later, Dottie knocked on her mother's door, then turned the handle to go in. The door moved an inch but bumped against something solid and moved no further.

'Mother? Are you in bed?' Dottie called.

She heard a sound on the other side of the room, and smothered the brief flare of concern when she heard the reassuring sound of her mother's voice, perfectly normal-sounding if a little ruffled, calling back,

'Oh one moment, dear, let me just...'

There was a bumping sound and then the door was opened. As Dottie entered the room, her mother, looking a trifle sheepish, said,

'I expect you'll think I'm over-reacting, but I felt a little nervous.' She had her hand on the back of a chair that stood right by the door. Clearly she had been using the chair back to wedge the door shut.

'Not at all,' Dottie said. She closed the door behind her and replaced the chair-back under the handle. 'I think it's a very good idea. Don't forget to turn the key in the lock, too when I leave.'

They sat down in the bay of the window, one on each side of the little table. Dottie was glad to note that although her mother was wearing her dressing-gown and slippers she had yet to remove the discreet make-up she wore, nor had she plaited her hair.

'I'm glad you're still up. I didn't feel like going to bed,' Dottie said. 'It's just the shock of that inspector's announcement, I expect. I did think that two deaths in as many days in the same house was a little odd. I can't seem to get the word 'murder' out of my head. To hear it put into words by someone official, that's a bit different to thinking it in your own head. It's shaken me up.'

Her mother was nodding. 'Oh yes, dear, I quite agree. Murder! Two of them! It's so shocking. Too shocking to contemplate, really, because of course one immediately thinks of the other people in the house, and wonders...'

'Yes, exactly! I keep thinking of each person in

turn, and asking myself, was it him? Or was it her? The only person I'm certain of is you. Well, and myself, obviously.'

A ghost of a smile passed over her mother's face. 'I'm glad you're sure of me!' She drew her dressing-gown closer about her as if she was cold. 'I wonder what the police will do now? Obviously, they've already interviewed all the suspects, as the inspector said. But if they've done that, and don't have any other evidence, what do they do next? Is that why they're going back to London, do you think? This is all rather old hat to you, after your recent experiences ever since you found that poor fellow in the street...'

'True,' Dottie said. 'But that doesn't make it any easier. Though at least I have half an idea what to expect. They'll talk to solicitors, I expect, to find out about wills. Then the police will get an approximate time for when the deaths occurred, so they'll be back again to ask all of us where we were at those times, and whether anyone can corroborate that. So they will speak to everyone again tomorrow or Friday when they come back. And they'll be looking into the friendships, fallings-out, grudges, personal lives and business arrangements to try to find likely suspects or motives.'

'Hmm,' her mother murmured. 'Florentina's behaviour towards Mamie, for example.'

'Good Lord, yes!' Dottie was lost in thought for a moment or two, remembering that scene. Then she said, 'I'm not sure if I did the right thing, but William wanted to see me earlier, and we talked about what was going on, and well, I told him all about Sebastian slapping Christiana and then later, Florentina slapping Mamie. I rather wish I hadn't, now, but I didn't want to keep anything back from him that might be helpful to the case. Or cases, I should say.'

'Hmm,' her mother mulled. 'Yes, two cases. Two separate cases.' She shook her head, deep in thought.

Rather startled, Dottie said, 'Two cases? Or just one, do you think?'

Her mother sighed, looking down at her hands. 'No, you're probably correct. Surely it has to be one case? Two deaths in one weekend at the same house, it seems too much that there would be more than one killer. Though I suppose one can't be sure until all the facts are known. Perhaps one death was due to natural causes, and the other was an accident, or it was only that one that was murder?'

Dottie stared at her now. 'My goodness. It's as if I'm seeing you for the first time. You're detecting too, aren't you! I thought it was just me.'

Her mother laughed. 'One can't help noticing things sometimes. But yes, let's hope it's just one murderer, and not two.'

Dottie shook her head. 'However many it is, I still feel rather mean telling William about Florentina, though as far as I'm concerned, Sebastian deserved whatever he got for being so vile.'

'I do hope that young lady will mend her ways. Sooner or later one can't help but feel that she really will find herself in difficulties beyond anyone's help.'

'Do you suppose she is in the habit of taking some kind of drugs? I mean, as well as all the alcohol she drinks. I suppose that could explain her erratic behaviour. Because the others drink an awful lot too, but she seems more affected by it than they are.' Dottie's tone was doubtful though. 'But what I find surprising is how little—relatively—she was upset by Sebastian's death. She was, after all, his fiancée until just eighteen months ago, but now that the initial shock has worn off, she seems no more grief-stricken than the rest of us.'

Her mother was nodding. 'Mamie said something to me about that, she'd heard it from Florentina herself. Apparently, Sebastian broke it off with her almost the second Christiana's first husband died in France. Surely that must have hurt her? Or at least made her angry or resentful?'

'Yet she and Milner seemed to be on good terms, along with the other three in their little clique. It's most odd.'

'Perhaps she just disguises it? If one is used to hiding one's feelings, it can be easy to play a part. But a little alcohol can undo even the strongest of defences.'

'Hmm. Interesting, yes, that could well be. And speaking of drinking, I wish I hadn't had so much earlier and done that ridiculous little song and dance around William. He must have been so embarrassed. Honestly! And I criticise the others for their drinking!'

'Oh, I don't know. I think William thought it rather sweet and amusing. He certainly smiled. And you hadn't had many cocktails, certainly nothing like the number the others drink practically all the time. Really dear, I don't think you should worry about it. I thought it was quite clever myself, the way you adapted the words of the song.' And Mrs Manderson smiled at her daughter fondly, thinking, oh to be so young again.

*

Chapter Fourteen

Relieved to be back in London for the night, even if it was rather late by the time they arrived, William headed to his fiancée's parents' house, and spent a pleasant hour with his future father-in-law, Herbert Manderson, drinking port and telling him a little more about what was going on in Berkshire than Mrs Manderson had been able to report in her short telephone call.

Then at last William went home, fed the kittens a little extra, and not wanting to bother with going all the way upstairs, he collapsed onto the sofa and slept, the kittens curled up with him.

The next morning, he arrived early at Scotland Yard for a tedious day of meetings with various people. First of all, he had to report to the chief super.

'Not that there is much to tell you,' Hardy commented. 'I still haven't seen anything untoward in Inspector Rhodes' conduct. He seems to be doing exactly what I would do. He has a lot on his plate, with the jewel robberies and the murders in Berkshire.' Hardy looked at the man sitting opposite him.

'Hmm.' The grunt was the only response he received, so after another minute, Hardy said,

'It would help to know what it is I'm looking for, or what Rhodes is believed to have done.'

There was another grunt, followed by, 'Very well, keep in touch, Hardy.'

Hardy left feeling irritated and dissatisfied by the old boy's lack of response or indeed, useful information.

Later, there was a meeting of Rhodes, Spence and Hardy with Chief Inspector Barrie and Chief Superintendent Smithers. Rhodes told the two senior officers what they had so far discovered, little differing from what Hardy had already told Smithers, and that they had no case until the results of the autopsies were known.

They were dismissed with a short, 'Right, well you'd better get on with it,' from the chief inspector, and the chief super said he would do what he could to encourage a speedier result from the two pathologists.

As the three detectives stood to leave, Smithers said, 'Not you, Hardy. We'd like a word with you.'

'Of course, sir.' Hardy had no choice but to stay behind, and as he went past, Spence said in a low voice,

'Oh dear, who's been a naughty boy then? You're not the golden boy anymore, are you?' He smirked maliciously, smoothing back his rusty locks in a self-satisfied manner. He couldn't resist jolting William's shoulder as he went by.

When the door was shut, Smithers motioned

William back to his seat.

'I've been thinking about what you said earlier, and on discussing it with Barrie, we've decided to give you a little more information.'

William nodded. 'Thank you, sir.'

'Barrie, over to you...'

Barrie nodded and leaned forward, as if about to divulge a state secret. 'So, Hardy. Obviously this is for your information only and must not be shared with anyone else without my permission.'

'Of course, sir.' William was on the edge of his seat.

Barrie sighed. He looked down at his hands, clearly reluctant to pass on the 'dirt' about one of his officers. 'We've had complaints from more than one quarter indicating that Rhodes has been assisting some criminals—well-to-do ones, mainly, or those in a position of influence—to avoid being charged for various offences, in exchange for a fee. That's really all we have, but the fact that these complaints have come from more than one quarter seem to indicate there could be some truth in the matter, and therefore we are most concerned.'

Hardy nodded. 'I see.'

Barrie added, 'You can see how we're placed. The police cannot be above the law, there's already been far too much of that. We need the public to know we are a body of men who can be trusted. We need to be seen to uphold the law at all times, as a body of men, and as individuals."

'At the same time,' Smithers said, 'we don't want to dismiss the man out of hand without being sure of our facts or giving him the chance to speak up.'

'Absolutely, sir.' William was saddened by the revelation and didn't quite know what more to say. 'I'll do my best, sir.'

'Good man,' Smithers said with unusual approval.

'Well, off you go. Keep us informed.'

William returned to the detectives' common office and took his place at his desk.

'Humpf,' responded Rhodes. 'You're still with us, then. I suppose they just wanted to remind you to behave yourself?'

'Something like that, sir, yes.'

'Right, well see that you do. Now then, Spence, you're with me. We're going to see Mr Milner's solicitor. Hardy take Kerridge, go and speak to Mrs Cotton's solicitor. Find out who the beneficiaries are, and what assets she had to dispose of. They've agreed to see you at eleven o'clock. Whitstable and Charles of Queen Charlotte Avenue in Kensington.'

'Yes sir.'

Mr Milner's solicitor, looking excited to be part of a real-life drama, even if only in the manner of a bit-part actor, folded his hands on his blotter and leaned forward towards Rhodes and Spence in a confidential manner.

'And you think Mr Milner was murdered? Not a heart attack after all? My, my, how ex—I mean—how extremely distressing for his poor wife. And her so young. So very handsome.'

His thoughts strayed away to the charms of Mrs Milner, and failing to note any parallel with Mrs Milner's real life, he enjoyed a short-lived daydream in which, as he read her husband's will, Mrs Milner, delicately weeping into a lace handkerchief, allowed him to pat her hand and promise to be by her side to help her through the difficult weeks and months ahead—during which time they would, naturally—become close, and then after a year or so he might declare himself, and she would receive his vows of love with a gentle pleasure, then in the fullness of time, he would lead her to the altar, and...

'Just tell me who inherits the estate, would you? I'm in rather a hurry, as you can no doubt imagine. I have other people to speak with today.' Rhodes jolted the man out of his fantasy and bought him rather rudely back down to earth.

'Oh, er, well... that is to say, if I can be assured of your secrecy... the will cannot be read before the funeral...'

'The funeral's not likely to be in the immediate future, is it, if the results of the autopsy indicate murder. As it is, a police investigation is now underway, and that must take precedent. We need to know the way things stand.'

The policeman was a little rough and ready, the solicitor thought. Rather too brusque. The solicitor cleared his throat and consulted the document on the desk in front of him.

'Of course, of course. Very well. I've been advised that there is unfortunately a considerable overdraft attached to the bank account of Mr Milner, which I will be required to settle from his estate, so there are no funds to go to his wife, but there are a few smaller assets lodged with his bank, jewellery, I believe, and a painting by Stubbs, so that should partially ameliorate the overdraft.'

'How big is the overdraft?' Rhodes butted in.

The solicitor frowned at the interruption, but said, 'About eight hundred pounds. Now, coming back to the disposition of Mr Milners assets. There are a number of small bequests to friends and acquaintances, again, mostly to settle small debts. The monies for these are held by myself and will be dispersed after the funeral when the will has been read officially.'

'Yes, yes, but the residue. The property...?'

'The main family home in Windsor was inherited by Mrs Milner from her first husband, the late Harold Bassington, MP, and so it was already her property before her marriage to Mr Milner. But other than that, there is a townhouse in London, and a small family retreat in Devon, both of which come from the Milner estate, and which were Mr Milner's sole property.' The solicitor removed his pince-nez and peered at Rhodes myopically. 'Altogether worth a very considerable sum, I might add.'

'Excellent, thank you.'

'Though there is a considerable mortgage on the townhouse in London, and another, slightly smaller loan outstanding on the Devon property too. Mr Milner's directions were that the London townhouse and the Devon property should be sold and the mortgages repaid, and the residue divided equally between a Lord Henry Dalbury and a Mr Milo Parkes. There are no details about why Mr Milner made these stipulations. But Mr Milner had, I believe, considerable debts. Considerable. Though I am not able to shed any light on those, I'm afraid. I was not privy to Mr Milner's business affairs, apart from the little he had told me, although one may conjecture that he owed a very considerable sum to both Lord Dalbury and this fellow Mr Parkes, if the terms of the will are any indication.'

Rhodes was already halfway out of his seat. He sat back down. 'Debts? And that's all you can tell me?'

'Considerable debts, Inspector. And no, I cannot shed any further light, I'm afraid... I believe you will need to contact Mr Milner's bank, which is, I believe, Dullards of Threadneedle Street.'

Rhodes and Spence got to their feet, said goodbye, and the solicitor returned to his rosy thoughts of Christiana Milner, weeping delicately into a lacy hankie.

Outside, in the street, Spence said, 'If he'd said 'considerable' one more time, I would have punched him.'

Rhodes laughed. 'How many times?'

Spence laughed too. 'A considerable number.'

Meanwhile, Hardy and Kerridge arrived in the upper rooms of a building which contained on the ground floor, a butcher's shop, and above that, an employment agency for domestic staff. The stairs creaked, and there was no window or lamp to give light as they went.

'I thought it would be a lot posher than this, I can tell you, Sarge,' Kerridge said as they reached the door and knocked.

'So did I. It seems even Kensington has a few back streets.'

The door was opened by a young woman. They explained why they were there, and she brought them into a small waiting area. She left for a few minutes, then returned to offer them tea.

'Mr Kent won't be long. He's just making a telephone call.'

'Not Mr Whitstable or Mr Charles?'

She smiled. 'They don't exist. The company is run by Charlie Kent. On his own.' She leaned closer and said in a low voice, 'He thought two posh surnames sounded more professional. But he is a proper solicitor though, don't you worry about that.'

'I don't doubt it,' said Hardy, who did.

Just then Mr Kent appeared at his office door and invited them to step inside. His sharp suit was a little too sharp for the usual solicitor, his hair a little too neat, too well Brylcremed and slicked back. In a different setting, Hardy thought, he could be on the other side of the legal equation completely. Hardy had seen many a polished gangster or loan shark or other criminal turned out in just such a way. Mr Kent smiled a perfect smile, his teeth immaculately even and white enough to dazzle.

'Do come in,' Mr Kent said, and they followed him inside, Kerridge closing the door behind them.

Kent took his seat behind a wide, polished desk and motioned for them to sit.

'Now then, I think you're from the police, and you want to ask about Mamie Cotton's will?'

The 'th' of 'think' was more of an 'f', and the 't' at the end of 'about' was missing entirely, as were the two 't's' in Cotton. He was, as Hardy suspected, a working-class lad made good, no doubt by his own hard work. His place at law school would not have been achieved by his father having a discussion with some acquaintance at his club. Mr Kent was his own man, and his position earned on his own merit.

'That's correct,' Hardy said. 'Unfortunately, Mrs Cotton died a few days ago at a friend's weekend house party.'

'Poor old girl,' Kent said, his brow furrowed. 'I didn't realise she was ill. I haven't seen her for a while, but she always seemed so full of life. I'll miss the old bird.'

Hardy said, trying not to give too much away, 'We don't know the cause of death as yet. We're still waiting for that information.'

'From the autopsy,' Kerridge piped up helpfully. Hardy frowned at him, and Kerridge had the decency to dip his head in acknowledgement of the mistake, then he got out his notebook and pencil.

'What, you think it was foul play? Oh, my good God, surely not?' Kent looked from one to the other of them in sheer disbelief.

'I'm afraid I can't say any more at this stage, Mr Kent, but it would be useful to know the provisions of Mrs Cotton's will. I was told that she had made one.'

'Oh yes, yes, she did. I have it here. Got it ready for you.' Kent pulled the document out of his drawer, slit the seal and unfolded the paper. He cast his eyes over it then said,

'Mrs Cotton had no relatives to speak of, nor children. She owned the flower shop and the premises behind and above it outright, and she owned a small house not far from there. The only provisions she made were that her personal belongings should be given to charities to help the needy, that her staff at the flower shop—three ladies named here—er, do you need the names or addresses, Inspector?'

'Not at the moment,' Hardy told him. He smiled; he was warming to the fellow.

'In that case, er, where was I? Oh yes. The three ladies were each left a generous bequest of £1,000. The remainder of Mrs Cotton's estate—her property, and her financial assets which are with her bank in Regent's Terrace, the London and Home Counties Bank, something in the region of twenty-five thousand pounds, were left in entirety to Paul Boxhall, whose mother is a dear friend of Mamie's, and this bequest is his to do with just as he chooses. I have Mr Boxhall's address here if you need it?'

'Is it in West Halliford, in Berkshire?'

Kent seemed surprised but nodded. 'Yes, that's it. I believe he's a butler by profession.'

'He is.' Hardy was already wondering how long Boxhall would continue as a butler once he received this legacy. Not long at all, was Hardy's guess.

'And that's it.' Kent folded the will document and placed it back in his drawer.

'Excellent. Well, thank you for that. If we do need further information, we'll be in touch.'

'Very good. Well, I'll say good day to you.' Kent got up, trotted round to open the door for them and shook both their hands as they went out.

Before Hardy and Kerridge left, Kent added, 'Oh by the way, would it be possible to let me know when her funeral is held? I'd like to be there, if that's all right.'

Hardy nodded. 'Absolutely. Could I have a business card? I'll phone you with the date.'

Kent provided one, and they said goodbye.

Outside, slipping his hat back on his head Kerridge remarked, 'Well, don't that blooming beat all!'

'Don't it just,' Hardy agreed ungrammatically.

They returned to the office to find that Rhodes and Spence had also only just arrived back, and the four officers discussed everything they had learned.

'I think we should arrest Boxhall right away, sir,' Spence stated.

'What! Why?' Hardy responded, then too late, remembered his place.

Rhodes frowned at him, and at Spence. 'It's a little premature for that, sergeant, we'll need more on the man than just him inheriting Mamie Cotton's estate. We need to know what his motive would be for killing Milner.'

Spence shrugged. 'Bring him in, question him, perhaps he'll crack under interrogation.'

Rhodes frowned at him again. 'This isn't some kind of spy novel, sergeant. If we bring him in, we'll have to have a damn good case against him, or his solicitor will throw it out. As will Barrie and Smithers.'

'What if he knew what he was in line to inherit? Perhaps he thought if he got rid of Milner he could have Mrs Milner too; they're having an affair as it is.'

Hardy was wondering how Spence knew that, but all Rhodes said was, 'I'm telling you, we need more. Right anyway, let's call it a day for now. Tomorrow, I want us to leave here at ten o'clock promptly to be in Berkshire at a decent time. We'll see what Mr Boxhall has to say for himself then. Before we leave, Hardy, go to Mrs Cotton's bank and talk to the manager, find out all you can. Spence you do the same for Milner's bank. Kerridge, get it all typed up. Good night to you all.'

'Yes sir,' they chorused.

As he was leaving, William went to seek out his good friend and former sergeant, Frank Maple. On the way, he passed a noticeboard; pinned to it was a newspaper clipping. The headline ran: *Bank Robbers Foiled by Scotland Yard*. It was almost two years old, but the most important thing for William was the grainy photo of several police officers, including, in the back row, Spence, and right next to him, nice and clear, Marcus Rhodes. It was just what Hardy needed. Glancing to left and right in the corridor, William saw that no one else was around. He quickly unpinned the cutting, put it in his wallet, then continued on his way.

Frank was covering his typewriter and locking his desk drawers, about to leave the office, when he glanced up to see William standing there.

'I thought you'd swanned off to Royal Windsor.' Frank beamed at him.

'I did. But we're back again until tomorrow. Had to see a few people, not least both the chief inspector and the chief super. Then the solicitors of the deceased. Got time for a chat?' William asked. 'Perhaps at the Rose and Crown?'

'You're buying.'

William laughed. 'I thought you'd say that.'

William bought the first round, then he and Frank settled themselves at a quiet corner table where they would not be overheard.

The first ten minutes of their conversation was necessarily taken up with enquiries about one another's love interests. Then the next ten minutes centred around Frank and Janet's pride in the early achievements of their four-and-a-half-week-old son, Michael Francis, their firstborn, who was clearly destined to be a child prodigy, despite having his father's nose. The fond father recounted all the things the little fellow could already do. Such as holding his head up, smiling—which might be wind, Frank admitted—and waving excited tiny fists when catching sight of his parents—especially his mother, Frank senior was forced to concede. He was also sleeping for long periods of time during the night, enabling Janet to catch up on her own sleep and regain her strength following the lengthy labour.

These important things out of the way, the two men, now settled with their second pints of beer of the evening, turned their conversation to work.

'Did you see that bit in the evening paper?' Frank asked. 'Said, and I quote, "Police are baffled by these ingenious crimes." Makes me mad, it does.'

Hardy nodded. 'Though I have to admit, I agree that the crimes are ingenious. Clever, simple, and showing a good understanding of how humans think. I take my hat off to them.'

They glanced at the spare chair at their table where both of their hats—Maple's flat cap and Hardy's trilby had been set aside, along with nearly identical raincoats. Maple's tie was hanging out of his coat pocket, which made it easy to distinguish his.

'Perhaps now everyone knows how they are done, there won't be any more. The robber or robbers know that everyone will be highly suspicious of all maids in posh houses. Still, it's a blooming nuisance. And of course, the papers can't resist having a go at us coppers,' Maple pointed out.

Hardy had to agree with that too and took another gulp of his beer. There was an amiable silence as they were occupied with their own thoughts. The time had come, and Hardy leaned forward, and keeping his voice low, said,

'Frank, I need you to help me with something. Can you ask around—discreetly, of course—and see what you can find out about Inspector Rhodes. As dictated by the chief super, I've got to try to work out what's going on there, and I'm not getting on very quickly. All the old boy's told me is that they've had contact from someone who claimed that Rhodes has been accepting payments to let people off charges. It's all a bit vague. I get the impression they don't want to tell me too much in case it clouds my judgement.' He sighed heavily and took another drink of his beer. Then he remembered the press cutting and took it out of his wallet to pass it to Frank. 'Look, I swiped this from the noticeboard. If you find anyone who might be able to help you, show them this and see if they recognise Rhodes, will you? There might be a solicitor or a copper who knows or has heard something and is willing to talk. And see a couple of people from old cases if you can.'

Frank nodded solemnly. 'Of course. I'll see what I can find out. Could even be a colleague who worked with him on a previous case?' He glanced at the cutting then folded it carefully and put it away inside his wallet which he placed back in his jacket pocket. 'What's he like to work with?'

'At first, Rhodes was pretty standoffish, but he seems to be softening a bit. I think, given a little more time, he might confide in me. I sense he has something on his mind,' William said. 'But it's taking him a while to feel he can trust me, which is hardly surprising, seeing that he thinks I've been demoted for dodgy dealing. I really hope he hasn't done what they think he's done, I'm beginning to like the fellow. As far as police work goes, he seems very capable and does everything by the book. I can't fault him there.'

'It has only been a couple of weeks... but if anyone can get him to open up, you can.'

'Thanks. I hope so. He seems like a decent chap, though of course, that's likely the whole point. What's really going on, and how is he pulling the wool over everyone's eyes? But in any case, this Spence character...' Hardy shook his head. 'I don't like him. Not that that means anything, but there's just something about the fellow. It may be just my dislike of him colouring my judgement, I don't know.' He took a drink of his beer then shook his head. 'No, there's definitely something off about him. I'm convinced he's up to something, though again, I've no idea what.'

'I'll do some digging on him too,' Maple promised.

'Thanks, I appreciate it. And how's life with DI Fullerton?'

Maple huffed and took another long draught of his beer, draining the glass to the bottom. 'He's all right, I s'pose, but he's just so... Like you with Rhodes, I just don't know what to make of him. It's like he's never done this before, yet he must be in his mid-fifties, and he joined the police as soon as the war ended, so not far off twenty years ago. He keeps asking me what I suggest. He doesn't seem to know what to do, or how to talk to people. You know we're looking into this profiteering racket, smuggling by any other name. But Fullerton, he's terrible at procedure and just says whatever pops into his brain regardless of who he's talking to. The stuff he's let slip to our main suspect! It's no wonder the bloke's got a good alibi—Fullerton told him exactly when the crime was committed and where, and how.'

Hardy condoled, saying, 'I've heard about Foul-up Fullerton a few times. They say the chief super practically has a stroke every time his name's mentioned.'

'I'm getting that way meself. I don't know why they haven't got rid of him. So I will do everything I can to help you out, in the hopes that it'll mean you'll be back in your old job, and I can go back to being your bagman instead of Fullerton's. Now, how about another swift half before we call it a night?'

'Good idea. It's your round.'

*

Chapter Fifteen

'Right, we now have all the information about the wills of the two deceased, and about their bank accounts and transactions. And whilst we now know that both victims were poisoned, we are still waiting for confirmation about which poison in particular,' Rhodes announced.

'We'll need to find out who amongst the household or guests had any knowledge of poisons and also were able to get their hands on them.'

Rhodes stared at Hardy as if he had just grown a carrot for a nose, whilst behind him, Spence laughed and came forward to toss a folder onto the desk, standing there with his hands on his hips and that jeering smirk on his face.

Spence said, 'You are kidding, Hardy? Honestly!' He shook his head in a pitying manner then turned to the inspector. 'Sir, do you want to talk to Boxhall again, or shall I just proceed straight to charging him with the murders?'

Hardy said, without thinking, 'What? You can't possibly be serious. On what grounds?' Then remembering—yet again—that he was not ostensibly an inspector but a lowly sergeant who was just there to do as he was told, he hastily added, 'I apologise, sir. But I don't feel we have sufficient evidence.'

Jerking a head in Hardy's direction, Spence said to Rhodes, 'Who does he think he is?' Again, Spence gave his disbelieving laugh. He perched on the edge of the desk, hands in his pockets now, whether accidentally or deliberately mimicking his superior, Hardy wasn't sure. But in essence the two of them were allied against him.

Or were they?

Rhodes, a frown of concentration on his face, stood up and began to pace back and forth. He halted opposite Spence and said,

'What actual evidence do we have that Boxhall had anything to do with the deaths of Mr Milner or Old Mother Cotton?'

'But sir! Of course he did it. How much of a coincidence would it be to have two lots of miscreants in the same household, carrying out two different crimes but in exactly the same way? That's frankly ludicrous. Boxhall stood to inherit all that money from the old woman. It means he could chuck in his job and go off to live on the Riviera. Get a butler of his own.'

Hardy said nothing, but waited, chewing his lip, arms folded across his chest.

Rhodes rounded on Spence. 'But evidence, sergeant! As Hardy says, it doesn't matter what we think happened, we need solid proof. It's got to stand up in court. Evidence, sergeant!'

'I can't believe you're even listening to him, inspector. Lest we forget, he's been demoted for not doing his job properly. Don't you think it's a bit of a coincidence him being here when all this is going on? In fact, if you're looking for a coincidence, then there it is, standing right there! Why, his fiancée is conveniently already in the house, no doubt able to pass on any information about our investigation to the other guests.' His voice rising with his temper, Spence pointed his forefinger right at the centre of Hardy's chest.

Hardy stayed where he was, forcing himself to remain calm. He knew he didn't need to say anything, he could already see that Spence had lost Rhodes' trust by acting in this kind of childish manner. As if they were kids picking sides in the playground. Spence might just as well have said, 'You like him more than me, so I'm not your friend anymore'.

Rhodes frowned. 'Lest we forget, *sergeant*,' he said with careful emphasis, 'Sergeant Hardy was placed in this department by none other than the Chief Superintendent himself. So unless you're prepared to question Chief Superintendent Smithers' authority and accuse *him* of conspiracy to murder Mr Milner into the bargain, I think we will have to dismiss your idea. I'm sure that can't be what you're suggesting, sergeant, so let's just forget you said anything, shall we?'

'Sir.' A sulky Spence shuffled his feet.

'Right, gentlemen, I think we'll leave this for now. I want to think about it a little longer. Hopefully we'll have some firm evidence tomorrow from the pathologist.'

Rhodes grabbed his hat and plonked it on his head. He patted his jacket pocket and heard the reassuring jingle of his door key. 'Goodnight Spence, Hardy. I'll see you both bright and early tomorrow morning.'

'Sir,' Spence repeated, still every inch the resentful eight-year-old who had been found out in his mischief.

'Sir,' echoed Hardy, reaching for his own hat, and checking his own pocket for his door key. 'Goodnight,' he said to Spence. Spence made no reply.

Hardy decided he would go to the pub nearby, one that was often visited by policemen on their way home after a long or difficult day at work. He was not especially surprised to find Rhodes already there in the pub, as if waiting for him. The inspector was at the bar, buying two pints of bitter. He nodded towards an empty table.

As soon as they had both sat down, Rhodes said, 'Do you think the robberies are separate from the murders?'

Hardy took a drink and wiped his lip on the back of his hand. 'I needed that. Yes, definitely two separate crimes. Or rather, two separate series of crimes. I'm certain the robberies are unrelated to the murders. Also, the robberies took place in London, the murders in Berkshire.'

'But many of the same people were involved, and it's not that far away,' Rhodes reminded him. After a second's pause, he said, 'So do you reckon the footman Brownlee for the robberies?'

Hardy shook his head. 'No. I think things happened exactly as he described them.'

Rhodes was frowning. 'Hmm. He was rather convincing. But on the other hand, he was perfectly placed to organise the robberies. He knew who was in the house that night.'

'Not really,' Hardy pointed out. 'He wasn't as well-informed as the butler, for instance. No, he was just an idiot who thought he could make a sly ten pounds.'

'Convince me.'

'If he'd been more deeply involved, he'd have stayed calm, and either kept out of it altogether or brazened it out. He wouldn't have lost his head and said, 'Oh God what have I done?' in front of witnesses. And—he wasn't at the other robbery venues—so he had no way of knowing who was staying at those places, nor what room they were in. Unless he had connections with other staff, perhaps. But he'd have to get them to let in the robber--he wouldn't be there to do it himself.' William shook his head. 'No, that makes it too complicated. He was just one little cog, and if we enquire, we'll no doubt find other cogs who also were offered ten pounds to let someone in.'

Rhodes nodded now. 'Very good. You've convinced me. We'll talk to the staff at the other households again. I'll get Spence and Kerridge onto that tomorrow.' He took a drink.

Hardy had finished his pint. He stood up, glass in hand. 'Another one?'

Rhodes looked regretful. 'I shouldn't really. Bad for the digestion, so they say.'

'Just a half, then.' Without waiting for a reply, Hardy went to the bar.

When he got back, he sat down and immediately said, 'Now what about the murders?'

Rhodes sighed. 'Well, two murders by poison, if it is poison, which seems likely. More than likely, according to the pathologist. Although he now knows it wasn't the same poison in each case. Even so, got to be the same perpetrator, surely.'

Hardy nodded. 'My thoughts exactly.'

'Poisoning is such an odd way to kill someone. I

know this will sound strange, but to me it's a very sneaky, underhand crime. Give me a good old-fashioned bludgeoning any day of the week.'

'I know what you mean. Bludgeoning seems more honest somehow, lashing out, losing one's temper in the heat of the moment. You can almost understand someone doing that.'

'Just so. Whereas poison...' Rhodes sighed again. 'And not just any old poison either, it seems. I mean, everyone knows about cyanide being used for wasps, or too much of a dose of heart medicine.'

'Or weedkiller.'

'Exactly! But these appear two quite unusual choices. I mean, you'd have to *know*. And plan well ahead how you were going to get the stuff into the victims.'

'I don't think the girl who carried out the robberies would be likely to have the ruthless streak one would need to murder Milner or Mamie Cotton. To put the poison into some of their food or drink then just sit back and wait for it to take effect—that's a very different action to the brazenness of walking into a house and conning wealthy ladies out of their jewels. So that's another reason why I don't think the robberies and the murders are connected. Plus, they'd need access to the kitchen, and then there's the risk of poisoning the wrong person...'

'Yes. It's too complicated. There's the staff in the kitchen, but I can't imagine the cook being involved, because where would be her motive? And as for the young kitchen maids...' Rhodes shook his head. 'No, I can't imagine some young girl doing the kind of thing that would mean the gallows if they got caught.'

'Same with Brownlee,' Hardy pointed out. 'Surely ten quid for opening a door isn't worth putting your life at risk for. Even if it was a hundred pounds, it's too much of a risk for too little reward.'

'To be perfectly honest with you, I don't see this Brownlee fellow as doing anything so calculating. He's more the brash, salesman type. I could picture him being convincing when it comes to some kind of con, but planning not one but two murders? In another household? And knowing the attributes of the poisons? Not to mention getting hold of the stuff then putting it into something. Yes, you're right. I just can't see it.' He lit a cigarette and took a long draw on it. The smoke was a perfect blue-grey ring in the air in front of his face as he said, 'We'll definitely need to get some answers tomorrow. From all of them. I'd like you to sit in with me to interview both the women, and Parkes too. I'll get Spence to do Brownlee again, he'll be in London anyway. Kerridge can sit in on it with him.'

Hardy nodded. With a short laugh, he said, 'Spence will love that, he'll try and bully Brownlee into a confession.'

'That's why I want Kerridge there. He's not very experienced yet, but he is very hot on procedure and prisoners' rights and so forth.' Rhodes got to his feet. 'All right, I'm off. Thanks for the drink. See you tomorrow.'

'Goodnight, sir.'

Dottie and her mother were having a very similar discussion about poisons and people using them.

'Well, who might have done it?' Dottie had begun with.

Mrs Manderson shrugged. 'It could have been anyone.'

'Anyone in the house at the time. Poison is not the kind of weapon some passing criminal would just happen upon and make use of. There could be no benefit to them, unless they were completely unhinged and just wanted to kill someone for the joy of it. Which seems most unlikely. At least, I hope so. Anyway, how would they get into the house?'

'True. Do we think it likely to have been a member of staff?'

Dottie was already shaking her head. 'No, surely not. Why would they? I could almost accept Boxhall killing Mr Milner. But why would he kill Mamie?'

'Boxhall was upset over Mr Milner's treatment of Christiana. Boxhall obviously has feelings for her, so it may be that he was determined to protect her. Perhaps even wanted to free her so that she could marry him. If she would do that.'

Again Dottie shook her head. 'I don't believe it. And again, we come back to Mamie. He was clearly fond of Mamie, I doubt he would hurt her.'

'Then that leaves us with the guests. Surely that seems more likely—to me, at least. Lord Dalbury, for example.'

'They appeared to be the best of friends, spending a lot of time together closeted away in the study or the billiard-room. I've never seen them have any kind of falling out. Even when Sebastian hit Christiana. But again, why Mamie? And even if Dalbury did kill Sebastian, perhaps if he was angry over some business deal not going the way he wanted it to go, would he use poison?'

Lavinia was already shaking her head. 'It's very difficult, dear. Let's consider the women: Florentina seemed on good terms with Sebastian—possibly rather too good—but she disliked Mamie. Penelope—presumably she had a cordial relationship with Sebastian as they were all such a tight group, and she probably disliked Mamie in the same way that Florentina did, but was it enough to make her feel she had to kill her? And again, why use poison?'

'Parkes keeps harping on about poison being a woman's weapon,' Dottie said. 'As if that means only women use it, and that it's the only weapon they would choose.'

'An irritating young man,' Mrs Manderson commented.

'But he has the same motives—or lack of them—as his pal Dalbury. Then there's the major. Soldiers are trained to kill, but I don't believe he would be likely to choose poison. Besides, he'd known Sebastian for some time, and he and Mamie got on like the proverbial house afire.'

'It's most frustrating,' her mother agreed.

'I could imagine Anabella killing Sebastian if she was extremely angry or upset, especially if it was over his behaviour towards Christiana.'

'Yes, but once again, I'm sure she wouldn't mess about with poison. She'd probably shove him down the stairs and call it an unfortunate accident,' Mrs Manderson said. 'She could just say she slipped and fell against him, or something like that. No one would be any the wiser there.'

'And we're back to Mamie again,' Dottie pointed out, and groaned. 'Because no one seems to have a reason to kill both Sebastian and Mamie.'

It had been a tedious afternoon of endlessly making small-talk and trying to avoid four guests in particular. All Dottie wanted now was just to be allowed to return home. She hoped William would be back soon, and that he'd be able to find a little time to see her. Away from London, from the warehouse, and William, she felt isolated and anxious.

They enjoyed a long walk in the gardens after tea, then Dottie and Lavinia just had time to quickly change their dresses. They hurried into the house and up the stairs.

When the maid came in to turn down the bed ten minutes later, as Dottie was putting on her earrings and necklace, Dottie couldn't help herself. She subjected the poor woman to very close scrutiny. The maid noticed, of course, and in a shocked voice, said,

'Oh madam, please don't think I've got anything to do with those robberies in London. I would never... and I've been with Mrs Milner for almost five years, she and Mr Boxhall will both vouch for me.'

Dottie relaxed. 'I'm so sorry. Of course you're not involved. I don't know what I was thinking.'

'Though it is a good thing that you're being wary, I suppose, madam. I must admit, I'd likely feel the same. But anyway, I'm not a redhead, so it can't be me!' She patted her fair curls proudly.

'The thief had red hair?' Dottie asked. 'I hadn't heard that part.'

'I had it from my friend Betty who is in Sir Nigel's household. When we're at the London house, Mr Boxhall always lets me have the same evening out as Betty and we go to the bingo together at the church hall. She's my best friend, and it was her that told me, having got it from Miss Salt, Lady Cosgrove's maid.'

Dottie nodded. 'Interesting. I wonder why Lady Cosgrove didn't mention the red hair?'

'Well, madam, Miss Salt, Lady Cosgrove's lady, told Sir Nigel's staff that she didn't think her ladyship would have noticed, as she was facing the girl, and the girl had her cap on right over her forehead. But Miss Salt was behind the girl at one point and saw some of the hair poking out from under her cap at the back. And, Miss Salt said, the girl had that really milk-and-water skin with freckles that often goes with red hair. Anyways, madam, I didn't mean to give you a fright. Are you sure it's all right for me to turn down your bed?'

'Yes, of course, please do.'

As the maid bobbed a curtsey to Dottie, she said, 'And will there be anything else, madam?'

Dottie said no thank you. The bedclothes arranged to the maid's satisfaction, the maid wished Dottie a good evening and departed.

It took Dottie just two ticks to finish getting ready, and she came out onto the landing and waited there for her mother to join her. There was a tray of dirty dishes on a side table in the hall. It had been there when she had gone into her room, and it was still there now. She wondered where the maid was.

A little further along the hall, the door of Christiana's room stood half-open. Dottie wondered how Christiana was. She walked the few steps to the door then halted abruptly. She was shocked—and yet not especially surprised—to see Christiana in a man's arms. They were kissing. Passionately. Christiana opened her eyes at that moment and turning slightly to see Dottie there on the point of making a hasty retreat, she pushed Boxhall away. He immediately reached for her again.

'Paul...' she cautioned him, glancing in Dottie's direction.

He turned and saw Dottie. 'Ah.' For a second he appeared discomposed then he shrugged his shoulders.

'I'm so sorry...' Dottie began, half-turning away.

Paul just sent a laughing look at Christiana, not at all concerned, and said, 'Perhaps I'd better go.'

'Yes, perhaps you better had.' She swatted at him and made a shooing motion with her hand, smiling at him in a way Dottie had never seen her smile at her recently deceased husband.

Boxhall went past Dottie with a grin, not at all embarrassed, and said, 'Excuse me, Miss Dottie.' He disappeared along the hall, presumably taking the tray with him.

Dottie remained in the doorway, chewing her lip, and wondering whether to stay or go.

'I expect you're horribly shocked?'

Dottie shook her head. 'Not shocked. A bit surprised perhaps. But only a bit. I had been wondering...'

'You'd better come in,' Christiana said.

It was a large room but decorated with a sparing hand. Nothing was over-elaborate, fussy or ostentatious. It was a calm, quiet room for relaxing away from the eyes of the world. Or at least away from the prying eyes of smart society.

'Shall we sit down?' Christiana closed the door then led the way across to the window, to where a pair of chairs had been set either side of a small table, exactly like the setting of Dottie's room, and her mother's, the group positioned to make the most of the early morning sunshine and lovely views of the garden.

'I know I'm asking a lot,' Christiana said the second they were seated. 'But I'm sure you understand I have no wish for this to come out. Not yet, at any rate. I know it's selfish, but people just wouldn't understand. I wouldn't be able to hold my head up, and as for poor Paul...'

Dottie was already shaking her head. 'I wouldn't dream of saying anything. It's none of my business, in any case.' She thought for a moment, then asked, 'Does Anabella know? Although I really don't think it's much of a secret. Mamie hinted at it more than once.'

Christiana nodded. 'Oh yes, she's known for a while. Knew, I should say. As has Anabella. I'm afraid I haven't been at all discreet. But you see, I love him. I know it seems far too soon after Sebastian, but this is different.' Christiana suddenly seemed on the defensive.

Dottie held up a hand to stop her. 'It's all right. You don't have to explain anything to me.'

Christiana smiled. 'It... It's not a new thing, we've been having an affair for some months now. I used to think we could never truly be together. But now... Oh I don't know. I can only hope, I suppose.'

'What if you were to move away?' Dottie suggested. 'You could go somewhere where no one knows you. Or rather, where no one knows Mr Boxhall.'

'Then what? Return a year or so later with yet another new husband on my arm and hope no one notices?' She shook her head. 'That would never work.'

They were silent for a moment. Dottie leaned forward to sniff the flowers in the dainty glass bowl in the centre of the table.

'These carnations are lovely, aren't they?'

Christiana smiled again. 'Yes, they are. Paul cut them for me. He knows how much I love them. He's so sweet and thoughtful. Unlike Sebastian. Or Harold, come to that.'

Dottie nodded. It really sounded as though she and Boxhall were besotted with one another.

'I was fond of Sebastian in the beginning,' Christiana said. 'At least, I thought I was. Perhaps it was only gratitude, I don't know any more. But he wasn't the faithful family man I wanted, or that he pretended to be. He's had affairs, and expected me to turn a blind eye, like wives are supposed to. Harold was the same. He thought he could act as if he was a free man and still expect me to wait at home for him like the good little wife he demanded. It was Harold who took on Paul a few years ago when our old butler retired, and at the time I just thought he was a charming, helpful and efficient young man. Gradually though, he became an ally, then a confidante, and then... Once Seb started to go his own way, and began to lash out, well, I found myself being offered comfort by Paul, at first in quite small, caring ways, but gradually I started to see him with new eyes. It just sort of happened. I never thought I'd be an unfaithful wife, and I *am* ashamed of that, but I do so love Paul.'

'Do you think Sebastian knew?' Dottie had her own idea about that, but she waited to see what Christiana would say.

Christiana shook her head. 'I'm sure he didn't. He barely noticed me, let alone a member of staff like Paul. As far as Seb was concerned, Paul was merely part of the furniture. He'd have no more thought about Paul as an actual human being with feelings or ideas than he would this table.' She rapped on the polished surface, then sighed. 'All the same, for Seb to die like that...'

Dottie wondered if Christiana really believed what she was saying, or if she was just lying to herself to spare some sense of guilt. But all Dottie said was, 'A terrible shock for you, Sebastian dying so suddenly.'

'Oh yes, it was. My goodness, it was horrible, and I felt so helpless. Just thinking of him all alone. So like Harold's death in that respect. Seb was already dead when Paul gave me the news, and... I felt so guilty, as if I should have sensed something, or known somehow. For it to be all over by the time I found out, and too late to do anything to help him...' She shrugged, reliving that sense of hopelessness. 'It seems worse than if I'd been with him and not been able to help, but just to be there.'

'Horrid for you.'

'It was awful. But with the case still not solved, there hasn't been any time to just—come to terms with what's happened. And now, look, I know it's awfully selfish of me to worry, but I'm afraid the police will think I did it. I mean, it was bad enough when I thought it was a heart attack or some kind of seizure, perhaps brought on by his cold. But now! I mean, who could possibly want to kill him apart from Paul or myself? I'm just so scared. And don't they always say in the detective books that it's usually the wife who kills her husband, or the husband who kills his wife? It's all too terrible. I just don't know what to do. I feel like running away!'

'Well, you mustn't do that,' Dottie assured her. 'That would definitely arouse suspicion. But it's so odd that your doctor said it was his heart.'

Dottie thought to herself, the police might have had more information by now, some clue as to the actual poison that caused Seb and Mamie's deaths. She had to try to prise that information out of William. Not that he'd be happy about that, of course, but he might be willing to tell her a useful snippet or two, anything that could put Christiana's mind at rest.

'Well, they did ask if I thought he could have deliberately made away with himself. I told them he'd never do that, absolutely not. He was the centre of his own little universe, and he enjoyed his life— wealth, comfort, everyone coming running as soon as he snapped his fingers, and women falling at his feet. He loved the adulation he got from his circle of friends. No, he'd never commit suicide, and an accident seems equally impossible. If it wasn't his heart, then... A few more days, your nice man said, and they should know more.'

'Oh, William said that, did he?' It was exactly what he'd told her too. 'I suppose it could have been an accidental overdose of some medicine that Sebastian was taking for his cold?'

'Possibly.' But Christiana sounded doubtful. 'Though I honestly don't see how. He was only taking aspirin, surely that couldn't have such a terrible effect? He was taking the dose shown on the bottle, he's—he was—fussy about things like following instructions and so forth. Oh, I don't know. Surely it can't have been the aspirin? Well... No doubt we'll soon find out. Whatever it was, it must have acted pretty quickly, which is rather awful to contemplate, isn't it? But anyway, I worry that the police will find out about Paul and I. If they do, they may decide that gives us a motive for bumping Seb off—you know, so that we could be together. Oh, it's silly of me to worry, but you do sometimes hear of people being charged for a crime they didn't commit.'

'True,' Dottie said, guiltily remembering that she'd already told William her suspicions about the affair. But William was good at his job, and wouldn't just arrest someone on a whim, merely because they were in the right place at the wrong time. Although of course, there was a different man in charge of this case, and who knew how he would view things? She felt sick with the worry of it. If only she'd kept her mouth shut and not told any of this to William!

'Oh Dottie, I do appreciate you listening to all this. This weekend—or rather *last* weekend has been a total disaster, hasn't it? I can't apologise enough to you and your lovely mother.' She smiled at Dottie, then glanced down at her watch. She was immediately on her feet in a panic. 'Oh my word, we really ought to change and go down, I'm sure Paul will sound the gong at any moment.'

'Odd about poor Mamie, too,' Dottie added, murmuring it as if to herself.

Christiana shot her a direct look. 'What? What about Mamie? What have you heard?'

Slightly startled, Dottie said, 'Well, it's odd to have two poisonings just one day apart. I can't seem to get that thought out of my head. Surely, if one of them turns out to be not a heart attack at all but poison, the same must apply to the other. Who could possibly want to kill both Sebastian and Mamie?'

Christiana stared at her. 'My God! Do you really think...?'

'I don't know. It just seems... Have the police asked you about Mamie's death?'

Christiana shook her head. 'No, not at all. I've been expecting it, so perhaps that's something they are planning for tomorrow. I'm sure they must have suspicions about who did these awful things, but they are hardly going to share them with us until they are ready to arrest someone.' She took a long breath in, and sounding a little surprised, she said, 'Well I never did, as my old nanny used to say.'

Dottie smiled. 'Yes, mine too.'

Christiana went on, 'Good Lord, if they were both killed somehow, then *why*? Who on earth could do such a thing?'

Dottie shook her head. 'I've no idea.'

'But this might mean they believe me when I say I didn't kill Seb. Because why on earth would I kill Mamie too? I adored her!'

'More importantly,' Dottie said, 'That seems to point to the killer being one of your guests.'

Christiana stared at Dottie open-mouthed. 'My God. I hadn't even thought of it that way. They must still be here. Downstairs. And we're about to go down to have pre-dinner cocktails with them in the drawing-room.'

*

Chapter Sixteen

Dottie left Christiana to finish getting ready, and darted along the hallway to tap on the door of her mother's room then went straight in. The chair was no longer in front of the door—it seemed her mother's momentary panic had passed. Dottie wasn't sure if that was a good thing, but she was amused by how excited she felt about letting her mother know what she had discovered.

Dottie immediately said, 'Guess what, I just saw Christiana and Paul in a clinch in her room—kissing!'

Mrs Manderson stared at her, open-mouthed, but not exactly surprised. 'What did she say?'

'Just that she loved him, that she didn't think anyone knew about it apart from Anabella and Mamie, and that she hoped it would stay that way. She says Sebastian didn't know.'

'Hmm,' her mother said. 'I really think she's fooling herself there.'

'So do I.'

She sat on the bed and watched as her mother brushed her hair at the dressing-table.

'I do think my hair is growing terribly grey, Dottie,' Mrs Manderson commented, frowning at her reflection. 'Do you think I should try a brightening wash?'

'You'll need to ask your hairdresser to recommend one that would suit your colouring. You don't want to go too bright! I've also got a little snippet I learned from the maid just now.'

And she told Mrs Manderson what the maid had told her.

'Isn't it astonishing that two maids having an evening out at the bingo can elicit clues that have evaded the police?'

'Exactly my thoughts,' Dottie agreed. 'I'm assuming the police don't know this, or I think William would have mentioned it.'

'Are you going to tell him?'

'Absolutely. It's a small thing but could be vital.'

'Oh definitely.' Mrs Manderson set down her hairbrush, deftly twisted her hair into a decorative loose bun on the back of her head, clipped on some earrings, arranged a long rope of pearls about her neck—still taut, still smooth and not at all jowly—then clasped a bracelet about her wrist and stood to her feet just as the gong sounded from the hall below.

'Ready to go down?' Mrs Manderson asked her daughter.

At last—mercifully—the grim news programme gave way to dance music, and gentle waves of a romantic melody filled the air. Dalbury offered his hand to Florentina, and Milo Parkes came to ask Dottie to dance, with no trace of his usual sarcastic smirk. Almost too surprised to decline, Dottie found herself doing a waltz in the drawing-room with him whilst Tom kicked aside the rug then led Penelope to join the little group. Mrs Manderson moved to sit beside Christiana and Anabella to watch the dancing and chat.

'One of the coppers who have been here asking questions is your young man, I understand?' Parkes said. He kept his voice low, just for her ears alone. She hoped he was simply being discreet and not attempting to flirt with her. She thought the phrase 'your young man' sounded oddly old-fashioned coming from someone only a few years older than herself.

But she simply smiled and said, 'Yes, that's right. He's with Inspector Rhodes at the moment.'

'I see.' Parkes appeared to think for a moment. Dottie couldn't quite understand what it was he saw, exactly. They'd already all talked about this, and ended up with ridiculing at Dottie and 'her chap'. The song ended, and another, more familiar one took its place. They continued to dance, Al Bowlly's voice crooning, *'The very thought of you...'*

Dottie shivered. The last time she had danced to this song, she had been in William's arms, and it had all been so wonderfully romantic, but now she felt tense, on her guard.

'Does he ever discuss his cases with you?'

She shook her head. 'Oh no. As I told you a few days ago, not until they are solved. He doesn't like to talk about anything current.'

'A stickler for the rules, is he?' Parkes laughed a little, but she didn't think he was mocking William's integrity, it seemed rather the reverse. For once it seemed that malice was not on the agenda.

'Very much so. He is a firm believer in procedure.'

'He sounds like a fine fellow. And a very lucky one,

to be engaged to a lovely lady like yourself.'

Dottie glanced at him, surprised. But he still seemed perfectly sincere. The second song came to an end. Parkes, with a slight bow stepped back, and Dottie found herself partnered now by Dalbury, whilst Parkes turned to Florentina, who went right into his arms, one arm about his neck, her other hand clasped tightly in his, as the next romantic waltz began.

'Makes a change to liven things up a bit, what?' Dalbury commented as they moved off. She thought he sounded stuffier than usual. Why was that, she wondered. What was he up to? Were he and his friend working together to pry something out of her. How many times did she have to tell them she knew nothing?

'Yes. It's difficult to get the tone right in a house of mourning,' she replied.

'Very true, very true. I must say, I hope we can all get away soon. Tomorrow or the day after at the latest. Keeping us all cooped up here is really too ridiculous. If they don't let us go tomorrow, I shall have a word with the man at the top, I think. Don't like to pull rank too often...'

'No indeed,' Dottie murmured, only half attending.

'...but for goodness' sake, this has gone on long enough. Anyway, enough of that. Nice to be cutting the rug with a pretty girl.'

He beamed at her.

She sighed inwardly. More compliments that she doubted were sincere.

It was only now that she was dancing with him, she realised he was the same height as her—not terribly tall for a man. His manner seemed to indicate he felt he was doing her a kindness, getting her up to dance, instead of letting her wilt sadly away in the corner. He had glanced at her bosom quite noticeably twice. She began to think perhaps she had been correct in her distrust of him.

Then, to make matters worse, he said, 'Don't suppose your chap has said anything, has he? They must have some idea by now, surely, about poor old Seb. And Mamie, of course. Mark my words, it's all a damned mare's nest, and they're just being difficult, flexing their muscles just because they can. Damned interfering jumped-up nobodies, the lot of them. Got a touch of the hunger for power.'

Not again! Was it some kind of conspiracy to wear her down and get her to tell them everything? Dottie said nothing, but employed the cool stare perfected by her mother to encourage men to realise they'd said the wrong thing. It failed miserably. Dottie reminded herself such a skill obviously took decades to really hone. She must remember to practise in front of her mirror.

'I expect your fellow is quite pleased with himself, having a member of the nobility like me going to him cap in hand and begging to be allowed to leave.'

Dottie doubted Dalbury had ever gone cap in hand to anyone. She doubted he even possessed a cap. She said, as coolly as possible, 'I'm afraid my fiancé doesn't discuss police matters with me, as I've already explained. Several times.'

The music ended, and before the next tune started, Dottie took a very definite step back, inclined her head to Dalbury with a rather artificial smile—also taught by her mother—and turned away.

Anabella put her hand on Lord Dalbury's arm, saying, 'Say, Henry, I do believe this dance is mine!' To which the gentleman readily agreed, stepping back from Dottie with a slight bow, his eyes not meeting hers as he turned to find his next partner.

Major Forsythe, holding out his hand to Dottie, said simply, 'May I?'

With great relief she began to dance a foxtrot of sorts with him in the limited space available. She only hoped he too would not try to prise information from her about the police and their investigation.

'Ever since I slapped that old bag, you've hated me. You think I killed her!'

It was an hour later, and Florentina had just bumped Dottie and stepped on her foot. Dottie had assured her it was all right, but somehow things had gone from bad to worse.

Now Florentina's face was crimson with rage, and just as on the awful night she'd mentioned, she was swaying as she stood facing Dottie, the smell of alcohol so overpowering it seemed to be leeching from her every pore. What on earth had the woman been drinking?

On the other side of the room, Anabella and Tom were on their feet, and Dottie's mother said, 'What on earth are you...?'

Dottie attempted to placate Florentina, taking a seat so that they weren't nose to nose, instinctively sensing that might calm things down a little. Keeping her voice low, she said, 'I think no such thing, Florentina, I...'

'Oh, you make me sick, talking to me in your quiet polite little voice, dear sweet little Dottie, the calm one, the sober one, the perfect Little Miss Prim. How you look down at your nose at us, don't you? Don't trouble to deny it, I know what's been going on in your head. You...'

From the corner of her eye, Dottie could see some of the others exchanging horrified looks.

'Come, come, Florentina, let's keep things friendly,

shall we? It's not easy for any of us, being cooped up like this. How about a nice walk on the terrace, my dear? It's a lovely evening.' Dalbury intercepted Florentina, grabbing her arm and turning her toward the French doors. Dottie wondered if by doing so he had prevented Florentina from actually lashing out at Dottie just as she had at Mamie.

'That young woman definitely has a problem with alcohol,' Anabella said in a low voice, patting Dottie's arm in a display of comradeship that Dottie greatly appreciated.

'Oh Dottie, are you all right?' Christiana said, keeping her voice low so as not to reach the ears of Parkes or Penelope who were still moving as one to the music. 'What on earth could have caused Florentina to act like that? Really, her whole personality transforms. It's rather unsettling. I shall be so glad when she leaves. She was always more Seb's friend than mine, that whole set is, and I'm very happy to know that soon I need never see her again.'

'I have no idea,' Dottie said. 'She just—blew up like a firework.'

'It's a disgrace. Talk some sense into your girlfriend, can't you, Parkes? She looked for all the world as if she was on the point of hitting Dottie just like she did Mamie the other night. What on earth is the matter with her?' Forsythe said, his anger making his voice rise to reach to where Parkes and Penelope had stopped dancing to look at them.

Parkes simply turned, shrugged his shoulders, and in a bored voice said, 'What the hell am I supposed to do about it? You know she's got a problem, but she won't get help for it.'

'Well, then keep her away from the booze, why don't you?'

'It's not up to me. She's not a child after all. She can decide for herself if she wants to have a drink or not. In any case, if I say anything, I just get my nose bitten off. Think I'll go for a walk, get some peace and quiet.' He turned on his heel to go out through the same French doors Dalbury and Florentina had just exited. Penelope hurried after him. The remaining company looked at each other.

'My, my,' drawled Anabella in an amused tone. 'You certainly see another side to people once the house party becomes a prison.'

There were some murmurs of agreement. Christiana suggested a game of bridge, but Mrs Manderson said she was sorry, but she felt she'd like an early night, and Dottie took the opportunity to say the same, following her mother out, and leaving Christiana, Major Forsythe and Anabella behind.

'My goodness, Dorothy dear, what a nightmare this is all turning into. I do hope we'll be allowed to leave soon.'

'I hope so too, Mother. I'm sure everyone feels just the same. But I've had a worrying thought. Suppose we have to stay until after the inquests? That could be another whole week! I don't think I could bear it.'

She followed her mother into her room and sat down on the edge of the bed. 'It's horrid not seeing William. And not seeing Flora or the children, or going to the warehouse, talking to Mrs Avers... I feel so... Rootless and purposeless. Oh, It's completely ridiculous.' She threw herself back onto the bed, staring up at the ceiling, frustrated. 'What on earth can the police possibly gain by keeping us all here? Cooping us up here with a murderer. It's madness.'

Mrs Manderson was removing her shoes, then her stockings, and putting on a comfortable pair of slippers. This done, she sat in the chair beside her bed. 'I completely agree, dear. But surely they can't keep us here too much longer—everyone is feeling the tension of it too badly. They must realise that people have lives to go back to, even jobs, possibly.'

'I'm not sure anyone here has a job apart from the major. But, yes, there's likely to be another murder if they don't let us leave. All joking aside, it really does feel so—unsafe. The tension! When we were dancing earlier, Dalbury told me that he was going to speak to someone about it. He didn't say who, but the implication was someone high up in the police. The Commander of the Met, perhaps. He seems to think he can pull some strings and insist on us being 'released'.'

'Good,' Lavinia Manderson said decisively. 'I don't generally approve of that sort of boys'-club carrying-on, but for once I'm glad someone has the power to be able to do it. I just want to go home.'

Sitting up, Dottie said, 'I wonder if we will ever find out what actually happened to either Sebastian or Mamie? Perhaps they really were just natural deaths after all, and it's only because they both happened in one weekend that it seems so odd and suspicious. Perhaps it is still possible that the doctor's first opinion was correct.'

'I do hope you're right, dear, but I'm afraid...'

'Yes. Me too. I know I'm kidding myself,' said Dottie. 'The police must be right, and it's a double murder, surely? Nothing else seems believable.' Feeling increasingly astonished at the reality of the situation, and her emotions rising, she gestured impotently at the door to the hall, unable to really find the words to match her meaning. 'And one of these people—*one of these people right here with us*—they were the one who did it!'

Her mother came to her, and put an arm about

Dottie's shoulder, and it was all Dottie could do not to weep with the abandon of a five-year-old.

Lavinia Manderson said, 'There, there, Dorothy dearest, we'll get to the bottom of it, and you can tell William everything, and then we can all go home.'

'Except the murderer,' Dottie reminded her.

'Well, yes. Except the murderer.'

Hardy arrived back in Berkshire rather later than expected. Rhodes' plans to get away sooner had been scuppered by various things. Chief Inspector Barrie had wanted yet another word with them all, mainly telling them to hurry up and get to the bottom of things. It was an infuriating delay, achieving nothing useful so far as Rhodes, already irritable and on edge, could tell.

More usefully, there was some slight news from the pathologist. It was confirmed beyond doubt, he said, that both Mr Milner and Mrs Cotton had been poisoned. Most likely by something they had eaten or drunk, as there were signs in their mouths and throats. Two different somethings. This wasn't a case of inhaling a chemical or absorbing anything through the skin. Each poison had been taken orally, although whether taken knowingly or whether concealed in some way, it was too early to say. But two deaths with the same or similar cause pointed away from suicide and towards wilful murder. Further information would be available in a day or two, when more tests had been run. The pathologist was confident he could narrow it down to a specific poison or family of poisons.

A further meeting with Barrie had resulted in him instructing them to proceed on the assumption that both victims had been murdered, which they were already doing. Rhodes made the decision that they needed to speak to Boxhall again as a matter of supreme urgency.

'But not until tomorrow morning,' Rhodes had added, not seeing the irony in his words. Hardy hid a smile.

They had been authorised to arrange overnight accommodation in the area so that they wouldn't have to drive back to London the same day. He had left Spence, Kerridge and Rhodes enjoying a drink after their meal at a small hotel ten miles away and driven to West Halliford in the unmarked police car to see Dottie. He wished he could have done both: seen Dottie, obviously, but he also felt a regret at losing the chance to spend some time off-duty with his colleagues. He might have picked up something useful or at least built some bridges with them. But he knew that if it came to a choice, he wasn't going to miss any opportunity to spend some time with the woman he loved.

He parked at the rear of the Milner property where one of the two stable blocks had been converted into garages several years earlier. He didn't put his car inside any of the garages. It seemed a private enough spot, and so he parked in front of the doors. The upper storey of the house was hidden behind some spreading oak trees and there were no neighbouring houses within view, so they would be safe from prying eyes.

Not that they'd be doing anything they shouldn't, he reminded himself. Unfortunately. But he didn't want anyone from the house to see them together, or they might get the impression that Dottie was some sort of spy in their midst.

Through the trees, he saw the back door of the house open, the constable stationed inside the house was standing there, glancing this way and that as if checking all was well, then Dottie came out, nodded to him and followed the path through the garden. William lost her behind the trees for a few seconds then he caught sight of her—her wavy dark hair just bobbing into view as she came between the trees, her tall, slender figure swaying as she moved.

'My word, she's beautiful,' he murmured appreciatively. He reminded himself yet again that this was just a quick half-hour's conversation.

He leaned across to push open the door for her, then wondered if he ought to have got out to open it for her properly, like a gentleman should.

Dottie got in, beamed at him, said, 'Oh William!' and leaned into his all-too-willing arms for a kiss. A long one. She settled back against his shoulder, her hair tickling his nose, her delicate floral scent teasing him.

'How are things in there?' he asked, nodding in the direction of the house.

She crinkled her nose up. 'All right, I suppose. We've divided into two groups. Mother, myself, Christiana, Anabella and Major Forsythe are one 'faction', if you like, and the other four are the other. It's jolly strange at mealtimes, we all just sort of look at one another as if we've grown another head or something. People are talking about the weather, but that's about it. It's become so awkward. Everyone is on edge. Darling, when can we all go home?'

He shook his head. 'Sorry, not just yet. I'm afraid there's not much we can do about it at the moment. Rhodes has been told to keep everyone together while we're looking into things.'

'Even though one of us is likely to be a killer, and may strike again?' Dottie couldn't resist saying. Then felt horrid for taking it out on him. It wasn't his idea, his fault, or his case. 'Sorry, dear.' She wriggled around to kiss his cheek. 'I suppose it's out of the question that one, or both of them, died as the result of a heart attack or some other natural cause?'

'Sadly, that does seem to stretch the bounds of credibility. We know for certain that both victims were poisoned. We should know exactly which poison by tomorrow. There's a tiny chance it could have been accidental or even suicide, but really, I don't think any of us believe that.' He shrugged. 'Who knows? And I don't like it either, you being cooped up here with these people. That's why we've kept a couple of constables on hand to watch over things. But it's a case of keeping you all here in one place, rather than have a killer 'at large' in public, according to the chief super. I think he assumes someone knows who it is and is shielding them, and that in time, they will start to give themselves away. Or perhaps the killer will confess and save us all a lot of bother, though that seems unlikely.'

'I know it's not your fault, darling, but I just want to go home. I miss Watson and Hastings.'

'And there I was hoping it was me you wanted to see,' he said with a pretend sulky look.

She laughed. 'Oh darling, I do!' She kissed his cheek and snuggled against him. 'It's really starting to be miserable, staying here. Florentina Coyle just gets drunk and argumentative, and Christiana, well, it's just so awkward. One feels like one is trespassing on her grief. Even though, I'm certain, that once the shock lessens, she'll soon get over the loss of Sebastian.'

There wasn't anything he could say to make things better. He kissed her again. That made him feel better at least, but she just sighed as she turned to lean back against his shoulder.

'I suppose no one's said anything to indicate they

know something useful?' He remembered he wasn't supposed to be discussing the case, but she was already shaking her head.

'No. Except that it's now confirmed that Christiana is...'

'Is what?' His interest was piqued, so she said,

'If I tell you, you've got to promise not to say anything to Inspector Rhodes. I don't want him going off like a bull in a china shop.'

She was waiting for a response so he nodded, adding, 'I can't promise, obviously. But I'll only tell him if it seems crucial to the case.'

That was as good as she would get, she knew. 'All right. Well, it's not much really, only what we suspected: Christiana has actually admitted to me that she has been having an affair with Boxhall.'

'She admitted it?' He was immediately alert.

Dottie's heart sank. This was going to be a disaster, she could already tell. 'Look, don't forget you promised—all right, *not* a promise, but you said...'

'Yes, yes, I know, love. But don't you see, that gives either or indeed both of them a definite motive?'

The sinking feeling worsened. He was actually excited about it.

'No, you can't... I promised!'

'Look, we already guessed that was what was going on, so it's not really anything new. You've just confirmed it, that's all. As it is, we've already been instructed to have another heart-to-heart with Boxhall first thing tomorrow. Just tell me everything she said. How long has it been going on?'

So she told him all about seeing them together earlier, and exactly what Christiana had told her, hoping she would not have to stand by and watch as Christiana and Boxhall were arrested in the middle of dinner.

It was almost eleven o'clock when she went back into the house. She didn't see anyone as she went in at the side door, or when she went through the back hall, the entrance hall, and up the stairs. She reached her room without seeing another soul. It seemed as though everyone had already turned in for the night. She would be glad to do so herself.

When she reached her room, she turned on the little lamp by the window, turned it off, then on, then off again as a signal to William that she had reached her room safely.

Outside in the darkness, she saw his headlamps flash once, twice, in response, as he drove slowly along the gravel lane, then she heard the sound of the car's engine change as he sped up and soon the car was out of sight. She felt his absence, missing him already. If only he'd been able to stay with her. The last thing she'd said to him was, 'Don't forget to feed the kittens when you get back,' then he'd reminded her that his next-door neighbour was doing that as he was staying in Berkshire for the night. What a pity he couldn't have stayed in this house. Just knowing he was there would have been a comfort, even if they didn't see one another.

She hoped the cats wouldn't have forgotten her by the time she next saw them. No doubt they would have grown a lot in that short time, too. She could picture herself and William, there at the kitchen table, whilst the cats tucked into their meal then sat washing on their cosy cushion by the stove. Soon, she reminded herself. Soon she and William would be married and it would be her home too.

She sat on the chair in the bay window, forbidding herself to dwell on the warm domestic scene she missed so much.

'Soon,' she repeated to herself again. She smiled to recall that he'd asked about her dress-fitting and listened patiently and with every appearance of interest as she'd told him all about it. Dear man, she thought. But that then reminded her of the sabotage incidents which had definitely caught his interest too. She frowned to think of those again. How she hoped the situation didn't escalate, that was the last thing she wanted.

There was a tap on the door. Then her mother's voice, saying softly,

'Dorothy, dear, are you still awake?'

Dottie hurried to let her mother in. Lavinia was in her nightdress, dressing-gown and slippers, her hair in long plaits over her shoulders, making her look, in Dottie's opinion, far younger than her daughter.

'I hope I'm not disturbing you, dear. I can't seem to get to sleep.'

'It's all right. I'm not ready for bed yet, in any case. I was just sitting, thinking.'

'How is William?'

'How did you...?' She laughed. 'He's very well. Very apologetic for keeping us all here and understanding that it's difficult. They are staying in Berkshire for tonight and coming back here tomorrow to continue their enquiries. I doubt we'll be able to return to London for a few more days at least.'

'Dear, sweet boy,' Mrs Manderson said fondly about the six-foot-tall policeman who was not a boy of ten but was almost thirty years of age. 'Did he tell you if they've found out anything?'

Dottie shook her head. 'Not really. Only that they are treating both deaths as deliberate poisonings. I wish he could tell me more, but obviously that's too much to expect, and completely against the rules. I told him about Christiana's affair with Boxhall. I hadn't planned to, but then I felt I should. And now I feel terrible for telling William something so private.'

'You shouldn't, dear, they've hardly been discreet. I should think everyone already knows all about it. Besides, the police need to know these things. Unfortunately, there is little place for secrets and confidences in a police investigation.'

'Gosh,' Dottie said. Her mother was getting far too good at this.

*

Chapter Seventeen

'Where the devil have you been, Hardy? We were due at Mrs Milner's five minutes ago.'

It was now Saturday morning, William came hurrying from the office of the local sergeant, where he had arranged to take a couple of private telephone calls. They weren't anything he could tell Rhodes about. Yet. But they had certainly given him plenty of food for thought. So he simply apologised and waited for the irritated inspector to precede him from the room. As he went by, Spence, as so often, couldn't resist a jibe at Hardy's expense.

'One more thing and they'll bust you down to constable at this rate! You just don't know how to do your job, do you?'

Hardy said nothing. He told himself that it wouldn't be long and Spence would be smiling on the other side of his face.

Boxhall met them at the door and led them through to the late Mr Milner's study. 'If you'll wait

in here, inspector, I'll let Mrs Milner know you have
arrived.'

'As a matter of fact, it's you I want to speak to first
of all. Sergeant Spence will speak with Mrs Milner.
Please call her.'

Boxhall was momentarily thrown by this
disclosure, but like all good butlers, he rallied
quickly. 'Perhaps it would be better to interview Mrs
Milner in here, and myself in my sitting-room?'

'Good idea.'

Boxhall left the room, and Rhodes turned to tell
his men: 'Hardy, you're with me. Spence, you and
Kerridge can speak with Mrs Milner, as we discussed
earlier.'

'Yes sir.'

'It will come as quite the shock for Mrs Milner to
hear that her husband was definitely murdered.'
Hardy suggested. It was not a welcome comment.

'Unless she killed him, of course. Which she most
likely did.' Spence smirked. 'Women always choose
poison, don't they? Everyone knows that.'

At the same time, Rhodes said, 'So much the
better. We want her off-guard. Women spill the
beans when they're worried about being caught out.
We want her to know we're onto her, and that it's
useless to deny anything.'

William's heart sank. He had a very bad feeling
about this.

Spence chimed in again: 'Inspector, don't you
think we should excuse Hardy from these interviews.
After all, his fancy woman is a close friend of Mrs
Milner. Manderson could be keeping all kinds of
things back from us, and at the same time be telling
her cronies our every move.

Rhodes frowned as he mulled this over. But
William, goaded by Spence and his self-satisfied

smirk, quickly said, 'Sir, I would *never* divulge confidential police intelligence to any civilian, not even to *Miss* Manderson, my *fiancée*, I can assure you.'

Rhodes was irritated again now. He snapped at William, 'All right, all right. Don't have a tantrum. Just make sure you keep your mouth shut when you are spending time with Miss Manderson. *And* her mother. Remember I'm watching you. You've got to prove yourself to me and the chief super or you'll be out on your ear. Understand?

William, in his meekest voice, said simply, 'Yes, sir'. He had to be content with that. Clearly their tentative friendship of the previous evening had vanished with the morning dew.

Boxhall was on his way back to them, his arm outstretched to indicate for them to follow him.

'This way please, gentlemen.' He held open the baize door for them.

'*My* lead, sergeant,' Rhodes cautioned softly.

'Yes sir,' Hardy responded once more.

They settled themselves in Boxhall's room, Boxhall in his armchair, Rhodes on the hard upright chair, which left Hardy to lean against the mantelpiece, his notebook and pencil ready.

'Thank you for giving us a few moments of your time, Mr Boxhall. We just have a few things we'd like to clear up.'

Boxhall was nodding, intently focussed on the inspector's face, his foot tapping incessantly which Hardy noted as a sign of nerves.

'First of all,' Rhodes continued, 'I'd like you to tell me again what happened the evening before Mr Milner died. Last Saturday evening.'

Boxhall nodded again. 'Of course, inspector. Well, Mr Milner had been feeling unwell for most of the day, and indeed the previous day. He had been drinking heavily. Rum and blackcurrant. Someone had told him it was an excellent remedy for colds and so forth. He took to it rather. I should say he had at least half a dozen of those during the course of the afternoon and early part of the evening.'

'Was he an habitual drinker?' Rhodes asked.

'Oh definitely. Though he'd usually stick to Scotch. That evening there was also wine at the table, white and red, and the gentlemen had port after dinner, once the ladies had left them.'

'So he was pretty well plastered?'

A ghost of a smile crossed Boxhall's face. 'Er—well, yes, you could say that.'

'Was he a jovial drunk?'

'Not really, inspector, he could get quite loud, quite forceful with his opinions—he was fond of his own opinion at the best of times. And he could be argumentative.'

'Violent? Aggressive?' Hardy looked up from his notebook to ask.

Boxhall nodded but said nothing. His knee was still bouncing.

'Is it true he struck his wife in front of everyone that Saturday evening?' Hardy asked further. He didn't glance at the inspector but was aware of Rhodes looking at him. And no doubt glaring rather than simply looking.

'Yes, that's correct.' Boxhall was looking down at his folded hands.

Hardy glanced again at Rhodes, who shrugged as if to say, Go on then, keep going.

Hardy said, 'Were you there when that happened?'

Boxhall shook his head.

'So you heard about it later? Who told you?'

'I know what you're doing,' Boxhall said abruptly.

'You're trying to say that I killed him and this was the reason. Well, I didn't, it wasn't. Though I felt like punching him, but Christiana would never allow that. She'd worry about me losing my job.'

'You won't need that job much longer, at any rate.' Hardy suggested gently.

Boxhall's head jerked up again. 'What? What are you talking about? Why do you say that?'

Hardy was satisfied. Boxhall had no idea about the will.

Rhodes said, 'You've just inherited a decent amount of money. You'll probably be set for life, never have to work again. Mamie Cotton left pretty much all she owned to you.' Rhodes was watching the butler closely.

Boxhall stared. 'What?' It came out rather more abruptly than his usual courteous butler tones.

'You didn't know?' Hardy asked, his tone gentle still. 'Mrs Cotton left everything to you in her will.'

'But... but...' Boxhall was floundering. He looked from one to the other of them, confused, unable to think of another thing to say.

Meanwhile, in the study, Spence and Kerridge were staring at the open doorway through which Christiana Milner had just walked, stiff with offence. After a couple of seconds, Kerridge said,

'D'you want me to fetch her back, sarge?'

'No need,' Spence told him, leaning back in his seat, arms folded across his chest, a smug grin on his face. 'She'll be back, Kerridge. Just give her a moment.'

They gave her half an hour, and she failed to appear. Spence, annoyed with her for proving him wrong, said, 'Well, serves her right if we throw the book at her and her bit on the side. They're obviously in it together. She had her chance to tell us her side of the story. Now she'll have to take what's dished out to her.'

'Yes, sarge.' Kerridge was thinking, not for the first time, that Spence was an idiot. 'Um, what shall we say to the boss?'

'Leave him to me. You don't need to worry about him.'

In the butler's sitting-room, Hardy handed the solicitor's business card to Boxhall, who took it, but looked at it rather as if he expected it to bite him.

'You'll need that. That's the chap who is dealing with Mamie's will and so forth. He wanted us to let him know when her funeral is to be held, as he wants to pay his respects. I imagine her funeral is another thing that will land on your plate, so I'll leave that with you. Telephone to his office, arrange to speak with him. Once we give you permission to leave the house, of course.'

Boxhall nodded, in a daze, still staring at the business card that he held between thumb and forefinger as if he didn't trust it.

Rhodes cleared his throat. 'Now then, setting all that on one side, there are still a number of questions I must ask you. If you're up to it,' he added in a softer tone. He and Hardy exchanged a nod. Hardy was pleased that the aggressive manner had fallen away.

Boxhall put the card in his jacket pocket, shook himself then turned and gave them his full attention once more. 'Of course.'

'I want you to tell me what you can remember about the night Harold Bassington died.'

'Bassington?' Boxhall was utterly astonished.

Rhodes nodded. 'Everyone had skied to some lodge in the French Alps?'

'I didn't, nor the maid. We went up on a cart hauled by a tractor. But Mr Bassington and his cronies—and his wife too, of course, Mrs Milner, Mrs Bassington as she was then, obviously. They got a ski-lift up to the top stage of the ski-run, about halfway up the mountain then they skied down to the lodge.'

'And who were these 'cronies'?'

Boxhall shrugged, 'Well, it was everyone who's here now. Except Mrs Penterman. She remained at the hotel in the valley. I believe she had a sprained ankle or something like that. Otherwise, it's the same people as are here now: Lord Dalbury, Mr Parkes, the major, Miss Sweeney and Miss Coyle. Mrs Milner, as she is now, and the late Mr Milner. Not Mrs and Miss Manderson, and not Mrs Cotton. But the rest of them...'

'I see. And apparently, that evening, Mr Bassington had to make an urgent trip out?'

'That's right, inspector. Well, I don't know if it was really urgent, but it was something he had a bee in his bonnet about, and once he has—had, I should say—adopted a point of view, pride would not allow him to change his mind, no matter how ridiculous it seems with hindsight. Very much the same kind of man as Mr Milner, in fact. An odious fellow, and not even slightly missed.'

'Hmm. I imagine not. What was the reason for this emergency trip?'

'Apparently Chris—Mrs Mil—er—Mrs Bassington had two hundred pounds in her handbag which she'd left in her hotel room. Mr Bassington was furious and insisted he had to go and fetch it, said someone might steal the money. I think Mrs Bassington had mentioned it to someone and they had unfortunately passed it on to him without her knowledge.'

'Any idea who that was?'

Boxhall shook his head.

'If you had to make a guess?'

Boxhall still shook his head. 'No, sorry, I don't have any idea. It could have been any of them. They'd all been chatting in the lounge, sometimes altogether, sometimes in twos and threes, so anyone could have simply overheard. I just don't know. Mrs Milner didn't remember saying anything to one particular person. But then she was upset as she knew to expect retribution when he got back. He meted out punishment just as Mr Milner did. Bastards, both of them. That poor woman.'

'So did you see him leave?' Hardy asked.

'No. I was in the kitchen getting another round of drinks—nothing changes, does it? I saw him getting ready, but I went back to the kitchen. Annoyed, if I'm honest. It seemed like a suicidal mission but he wouldn't listen to reason. So I left him to it. But I did hear the front door bang. When I heard the door bang again a few minutes later, I assumed he'd had a change of heart and returned. I went out into the lobby to see him. But no, he had gone. It was someone else coming in.'

'Who?' Hardy and Rhodes glanced at each other; this could be vital information.

Boxhall gave them both a grin. 'You're excited about this, aren't you? But I'm afraid it won't help you.'

Rhodes snapped at him, 'Well come on man, who was it?'

'It was Mr Milner.'

They sat back in their seats, anticipation gone like the air from a balloon.

'He noticed me standing there in the doorway to the kitchen. I said something like, 'Oh, sir, sorry, I thought Mr Bassington had changed his mind and come back inside.' But he just laughed and said that he had gone out in the hope of catching him, to call him back, but it was too late, Mr Bassington was already out of sight. "I'm afraid we won't see him again tonight," he said.'

'Was Mr Milner wearing full skiing gear?'

Boxhall said, 'Not full gear, no, sir. But he had on his padded jacket, boots and a hat, and I think perhaps his goggles too, though I'm not sure. Not skiing trousers nor gloves. And all the skis apart from Mr Bassington's were still in the locker by the door. Although...' He frowned, a thought had stuck him. 'Hmm. Strange.'

'What's strange?' asked Inspector Rhodes.

'Well, I noticed it at the time, but I suppose I forgot it. It didn't seem important.'

'Forgot what?'

'The shelf with the other implements, sir, ice breakers and picks, shovels, trowels, things used to cut through or get rid of the ice and snow. The shelf had come down at one end, everything was in a jumble on the floor.' Boxhall shook his head over it. 'No doubt Mr Bassington knocked it down when he collected his ski poles, they were stored just beneath the shelf.'

Hardy made a note of this in his daybook, though suspecting it would turn out to be completely irrelevant. 'Probably too late to find out more now. Did anything seem out of place or missing? Or— just—not right in some way?'

Boxhall said, 'Sorry sir, I really couldn't tell you after all this time.'

'And where was everyone just then, do you know?'

'Not really. I remember they were all in the lounge when I went into the kitchen for the second round of drinks. When I came back, Mrs Milner was there with Major Forsythe. But I was only in the room for a moment or two, so anyone could have returned.'

'All right. Well thank you, Mr Boxhall, that's been most helpful. We'll leave you to get on. Thanks again,' Rhodes said, and he and Hardy left, almost immediately followed out by Boxhall who turned towards the kitchen.

When Rhodes and Hardy came out of the butler's room and returned to the main hall, they bumped into Dalbury. He was ready for an argument.

'Look here,' he began, his voice already rising with his temper. 'When are you going to let us leave? I have business to attend to, why are you keeping us here? It's a total disregard for our rights. Oh, and my mother too. She's elderly, she relies on seeing me regularly. In fact, it's about time you got her jewels back too! Why are you wasting time here instead of getting to the bottom of that matter? It's utterly outrageous.'

The gentleman had finally run out of steam and stood there glaring at them.

Rhodes turned to William and said,

'I'll leave Lord Dalbury to you, Hardy.' And he simply turned and walked away.

Dalbury was practically apoplectic with rage. Hardy, sighing deeply, half-turned to go back to Boxhall's sitting-room, then nodded at his lordship and said, 'Do come inside, Lord Henry, and take a seat.'

'Well, I...' But Dalbury couldn't think of anything to say that he hadn't already said. He found himself following Hardy inside.

Hardy took his seat on the upright chair and motioned Dalbury into the armchair opposite.

'Please sit down, sir. I was about to order some tea.

I know that will seem like wasting time to you, sir, but I can assure you that I've had nothing all day, and I'm believe it'll be a useful way to further our conversation.'

Dalbury, still speechless, could only nod. William went and popped his head around the kitchen door. One of the young maids he'd seen before came over to him.

'Sir? What can I get you?'

'I'd like some tea please, er, Janet isn't it? Tea for two, we're using Mr Boxhall's room again.'

'Yes sir.' She bobbed then almost ran to fill the kettle, blushing furiously that the good-looking policeman had remembered her name and even smiled at her. Hardy returned to the sitting-room.

'Now look,' Dalbury began.

Hardy held up both hands. 'I can assure you that we are working very hard to find your mother's missing jewels. The fact that we are here doesn't mean work has stopped on that front. Quite the opposite.'

Dalbury leaned back in his seat. He raised his eyebrows. 'Ah!' he said, as if it had all just fallen into place in his mind. He leaned forward and tapped his nose. 'I believe I understand you, Insp—er—Sergeant, isn't it?'

Hardy smiled but said nothing.

Dalbury, freely interpreting this to mean great deeds were afoot in a secretive, Sherlockian manner, smiled again. He sat back again now, calm and relaxed, his hands folded on his stomach.

Hardy was unwilling to turn to business just yet— he suspected that as soon as they did, the tea would arrive and interrupt things. So he simply said,

'I hope your mother is recovering from the shock of her jewels being taken?'

Dalbury was only halfway through his description of his mother's ills when Janet knocked on the door. Hardy leapt up to meet her, relieving her of the tray and setting it on the table. He smiled, thanked her and off she went, blushing all over again at his charm.

Dalbury finished his comments about his mother, they poured their tea, and finally settled back into their seats, sending watchful glances at one another.

Hardy said, 'I'd like to ask you about Mr Milner. Did he have any enemies, as far as you knew?'

'Enemies?' Yet Dalbury didn't seem surprised to be asked such a thing. 'I don't think he had any enemies as such. He was not especially popular—he could be arrogant, was often crass, and treated women abominably. But he could if he wished turn on the charm and be a very pleasant fellow. Sadly, he didn't often wish to be that way.'

Hardy nodded, drank some tea, then said, 'And is that what he did after Mr Bassington died? Turned on the charm for Mrs Bassington as she was then?'

Dalbury shrugged. 'Well, yes, that's exactly what he did. He said to me she was worth the effort. He only ever wanted the status, the money. He worked very hard to overcome her grief and make her think he loved her, then he coaxed her into marriage. After that...Well...'

'He didn't need to bother anymore?'

'Exactly.'

Hardy nodded. 'And what about Mr Bassington. Did he have any enemies?'

'He had political opponents, people who envied his success in political life. But he wasn't a particularly sociable chap. He was often surrounded by people, hangers-on, and I include myself in that, but he wasn't close to any of them. It was just part of playing the game for him. All he really wanted deep down was to be left alone in his fernery. He studied botany and chemistry at Oxford. He should have been a botanist, he loved plants. But he also craved adulation, and of course, the good life.'

'I see. I've heard he was very similar in temperament to Mr Milner.'

'Definitely. Two men cut from the same cloth.'

'But no one amongst his acquaintance you can think of who had a motive to kill the man?'

'Good Lord, no.' Dalbury was rather taken aback by that. 'Unless it was his wife, desperate to be free of him.' He sat back, holding up his hand. 'No, no, please, don't take that seriously, that was crass, a stupid thing to say. Christiana would never... She's just not the type. She would suffer and continue to do her duty as a wife. She's rather saintly, but a bit of a doormat if we're honest. Not my type at all.'

'I believe you're engaged to Miss Sweeney?'

Dalbury shrugged. 'Yes.'

Hardy shot him a look. 'You don't sound especially enthused.'

Dalbury spread his hands. 'To be honest, I'm thinking of breaking it off. We're just not suited.' He gave a rueful smile. 'If Christiana is too much of a doormat, Penny is too much the other way. Unpredictable, unreliable. Not interested in anything but having a good time. And, well, in all honesty, I don't think I have the funds to support the lifestyle she is expecting. Bad investments lately.'

Hardy nodded. 'Speaking of bad investments, how much did Mr Milner owe you and Mr Parkes, exactly? It's in the terms of his will, you know. We spoke to his solicitor and his bank manager yesterday, but this is your chance to tell me yourself.'

Dalbury was clearly surprised that Hardy knew

about that but didn't waste anyone's time trying to deny it. He said, 'Ah. Well, if you really must know, it is a little over £35,000.'

Hardy had been expecting a large number, but even so, he was shocked. He let out a low whistle. 'And that was from...?'

'Failed investments. Milner went in with his eyes open, we told him the scheme might not work out, that it was a terrific risk, but he was very keen to attempt it. A pride thing, just like Bassington. If it had come off, it could have been worth a million pounds. As it was, sadly...'

Hardy ignored that finessing, and said, 'Was that before or after Mr Bassington died?'

'After. Well, about the same time, really. I'd planned to tell both Bassington and Milner that week whilst we were away. Once Harold was out of the way, that was probably the main incentive for Milner to pursue Christiana. He knew he'd need a good-sized pot of cash to bail himself out. And she was the only way he was going to get it.'

'In that case, Lord Dalbury, do you think Sebastian Milner killed Harold Bassington?'

'Oh, absolutely,' said Lord Dalbury.

*

Chapter Eighteen

Dottie giggled. 'I feel as though we're playing truant, or something. Thank you so much, darling!' She leaned across to kiss his cheek, though he wasn't able to take his eyes off the road.

'Where are we going, William, dear?' Mrs Manderson pushed herself forward to peer between the seats at them.

'I thought we'd go for an afternoon tea at a rather nice hotel in Windsor.' He briefly grinned at Mrs Manderson in the rear-view mirror. 'My treat, of course.'

They both protested but he held firm, adding, 'I know you're keen to get out of the house for a while, and Rhodes and Kerridge have driven back to London.'

'And Sergeant Spence? Where's he?'

'He's gone to another one of his 'meetings' as he calls them. Not that I believe that for a second. I suspect he's met some young woman that he's seeing.

Anyway, it means I'm free for a couple of hours. I thought we could discuss things.'

Dottie turned in her seat to exchange an excited look with her mother.

They arrived at the hotel and were shown to their table. It was beside a window overlooking a terrace with handsome pots of brightly coloured geraniums in every corner. Through the open windows, a gentle breeze blew, bringing the soothing sound of raindrops.

Mrs Manderson sighed. 'I can't tell how wonderful it is to be out of that house, William. Thank you so much, dear. This is just perfect.'

'I'm glad you like it. Things have been difficult for you both, cooped up in the house like that, especially since you were only going to stay for a couple of days. I'm not at all happy that you've been detained, but unfortunately, I don't have any say in the matter. Hopefully we'll get all this cleared up in just another day or two.'

'Does that mean you've found out something new?' Dottie asked him. Under the table she was crossing her fingers. She longed for this all to be over and to go home.

'Well,' he said, leaning closer, and keeping his voice down. 'I can tell you a few things, but you absolutely cannot tell anyone, or I will definitely get the sack.' He gave Dottie a mock-severe look. 'And that will mean your wedding plans will be over, young lady.'

She just laughed. 'You're not getting out of it that easily. But go on, tell us what you've found out.'

Relenting with a grin, he repeated what they'd discovered from the solicitors, and the conversations with Boxhall and Dalbury. By then he'd also finished his finger-sandwiches, his cakes, and the dainty little savouries. He pushed his plate away looking disappointed. 'I hardly noticed I was eating all that.'

'So you now believe that Sebastian Milner murdered Christiana's first husband?' Dottie asked.

'Yes, but I honestly don't think we've any hope of proving it, short of an eye-witness. I might try talking to some of the others, in case any of them have something to add, but I'd have expected them to have come forward at the time if that were the case. Not that it really matters now, because we must concentrate on the two current investigations, and not get side-tracked onto a suspicious but inconclusive third. He's dead, so we can't bring him to justice, there's little point in pursuing it.'

'How is the investigation into those jewellery robberies going?' Dottie asked. 'Have there been any more?'

He shook his head. 'Nothing that's been reported. It's frustrating. We know that the thieves must have got their information from somewhere, but we just don't know where.'

'Presumably a member of staff knows something,' Mrs Manderson commented. 'They would know who was in what room, and whether they appeared to have a lot of valuables with them. Though of course, that's only to be expected if they are well-to-do and staying for more than a day or two.'

'True,' said William. 'In fact, we did bring in Sir Nigel's footman for questioning. He was present on the evening that Lady Cosgrove's things were stolen. And once he realised what had happened, he ran to ring for the police and was heard to say, 'What have I done?''

Dottie leaned forward, excited. 'So he did tell someone Lady Cosgrove was there, and where to find her?'

'Not exactly.' William sighed. 'We couldn't charge him with anything more than accepting a bribe. He told us everything—that he'd spoken with a female guest and she'd offered him ten pounds to leave the side door open on that particular evening. He says he didn't tell anyone which room Lady Cosgrove was in, that he didn't know that himself, but I think we can treat that with the contempt it deserves. It was Lady Cosgrove's maid who told us that her ladyship is known for staying in that same room: the Ormulu bedroom, as it's called, at Sir Nigel's, as no one else likes the room except Lady Cosgrove. Sir Nigel has dismissed the man, but I believe Brownlee when he says he didn't realise what a terrible error of judgement he'd made until it was too late. He's a young fellow, a bit naïve. I felt rather sorry for him really.'

'Very foolish, though, one can't trust a man like that.' Mrs Manderson was shaking her head in disapproval. 'I'm glad Sir Nigel has sacked him. Who was the female guest?'

'We don't know, I'm afraid. We've got someone going back to ask tomorrow.'

'I've managed to find out something that could be useful,' Dottie told him. 'One of the maids at the Milners' is friendly with someone from Sir Nigel's establishment. And Salt told the staff there that the thief who posed as the maid had red hair. She said she didn't think Lady Cosgrove noticed as she was facing the woman whilst Salt was behind her and could see her hair poking out from under the cap at the back of her neck. I know it's only a small detail, but it might help.'

William looked pleased. He reached inside his jacket for his notebook and quickly made a note, then leaned over to kiss Dottie on the cheek. 'Thank you, darling, that might be really useful to know.'

'So if Mr Milner had no enemies as such,' Mrs Manderson said, coming back to the deaths, 'who do you think could have a motive for killing the man, and why?'

William looked at her and laughed. 'Oh, so now there are two of you trying to muscle-in on my case? That's a disgrace! Talk about 'like mother, like daughter'.'

They both just smiled at him. And waited.

'You're both incorrigible!' he said with another laugh. 'Well, tell me what you think, who had the best motive, and also opportunity?'

'When was the poison administered, and how?' Mrs Manderson wanted to know.

He shrugged. 'We're not sure. But it would have been in his food or drink, and later in the evening rather than earlier.'

'If it was later, then presumably that means in his drink? He *did* drink a lot, didn't he?' Dottie glanced at her mother for confirmation.

'Oh yes,' Dottie's mother agreed. 'All his clique did. Far too much. I should think that was the reason for the losses of temper that evening. Mr Milner, and of course, Florentina.'

'Who was once engaged to Mr Milner. Therefore, she had reason to resent him marrying Christiana. Especially as it happened so quickly.' Dottie added.

William just sat back, a little bemused, and wondered how he'd never seen the similarity between them before. He grinned at them both and said, 'You know, for the first time, I'm beginning to see where you get it from... I just can't get over it.'

'Where she gets what from?'

'Where I get what from?' Dottie and her mother asked in unison, Dottie puzzled, her mother more than a little on the defensive.

'Your nosiness! And intelligence, obviously,' he hastily added, sensing this observation wasn't as well received as he'd expected.

'Hmm,' Dottie said doubtfully. 'You just about saved yourself with that last bit,' but Mrs Manderson was shaking her head in disappointment.

'*Tsk tsk*. Oh William, dear.'

'Anyway, coming back to the topic at hand,' Dottie continued, 'Almost anyone could have done it, if they'd had the poison in a little bottle or something about their person. Mamie. She was furious with Milner for his treatment of Christiana.'

'As were Anabella and the gallant major of course,' Lavinia pointed out.

'Yes! And then, what if Dalbury or Parkes were desperate for that money that he owed them? Or they might have been afraid he would tell other people about their confidence tricks or whatever they are up to, and that they'd lose business.'

'Or,' said Lavinia, 'they may have feared he'd simply changed his will. Much as I hate to admit it, it could even have been that delightful young Mr Boxhall. Though I very much hope it wasn't him. It would be lovely if Christiana and he could have their happiness at last.'

'All right,' said William, butting in. 'Enough about Milner. Who would have had a motive or the opportunity to get rid of Mamie Cotton?'

'Ah well,' Mrs Manderson said, with a glance at her daughter. 'That's easy.'

Dottie was nodding. 'Oh definitely,' she said. 'It must have been because she either witnessed something or was blackmailing whoever poisoned Mr Milner. Otherwise, I don't see why...'

'Hmm, I think I would agree with you on that.

Though occasionally it's the first murder that's the self-protective one and the second one is the real target. But that just brings us back once again to the beginning: *Who?*'

Both of his companions shrugged.

'No idea,' Dottie said. 'The possibilities must be the same as for Mr Milner's death, I should think. The same pool of suspects. No one else had left the house or arrived apart from Mr Milner, metaphorically speaking.'

Anabella and the major were waiting for them as soon as they entered the house.

Anabella grabbed Dottie's arm and pulled her towards the morning-room.

'The others are outside,' she said. 'Not sure what they're doing, but so long as it keeps them out of our hair. Now then,' and she closed the door behind the four of them and turned to Dottie, eyes gleaming with excitement. 'So, what did you find out?'

Dottie laughed. 'What makes you think...'

'Oh tish! It's perfectly obvious that your young man is very quick-witted, and I'm guessing he doesn't miss much. So spill! What did he tell you? And don't bother fobbing me off with all that, 'I can't possibly divulge the police's case' nonsense.'

Dottie looked from Anabella to Tom, who shrugged, and with a grin said, 'You may as well tell her. She's like a dog with a bone. She'll just keep worrying away at you until you give in.'

Dottie glanced at her mother who also shrugged. Dottie sighed.

'Oh, very well, but he didn't tell us much. Just that they now know that both Mr Milner and Mamie were definitely poisoned. But that was all he was able or willing to tell me. Nothing we didn't already know,

I'm afraid.'

Anabella and Tom looked rather disappointed. Dottie hoped this was enough to appease them, because she was definitely not prepared to tell them anything more.

'Definitely poisoned?' Anabella asked.

'Definitely.' Dottie nodded.

'Huh.' Anabella exchanged a look with Forsythe. Then Forsythe said,

'What kind of poison, do they know?'

Dottie shook her head. 'William didn't say, and I'm afraid it didn't occur to me to ask him.' She laughed on seeing their expressions again. 'Sorry! Perhaps next time, you should give me a list of questions you'd like me to ask him?' She grinned as she said it, not wanting to cause offence.

'Huh,' Anabella said again. She seemed at something of a loss. 'Well, if they're looking for someone who might have administered that poison, I'm assuming they'll speak to Seb and Mamie's nearest and dearest.'

'Which is why they interviewed Christiana as soon as they got here. It's utterly preposterous to imagine that she...' Forsythe began angrily. He halted, paused for a second or two before continuing in a marginally calmer tone. 'I know that they have to ask these questions, but honestly, anyone with half a brain could see that Chris could never be capable of such a thing.'

'True,' Anabella agreed. 'Chris is far too gentle. Killing someone takes calculation and a certain hardness, or so I should think.'

Forsythe said, 'Perhaps they'll speak to all of us again. Was that all you learned, Dottie, or did your chap let anything else slip?'

'That was it, I'm afraid. Or—well—he did say he'd

been threatened with being taken off the case because I'm caught up in it. He made a promise not to tell me anything, so the inspector agreed to allow him to stay with the investigation.'

'Good thing he didn't hear what you just told us, then!' Forsythe chuckled now, his irritation forgotten.

The gong sounded in the hall, making them all start.

'My gosh, I didn't realise it was so late!' Anabella peeked at her watch.

'We'd better go and get changed for dinner, dear,' Mrs Manderson urged her daughter.

'Whatever happens this evening, it can't possibly be as bad as last Saturday night,' Forsythe commented as they went into the hall and headed upstairs.

'True,' Anabella said, and put her arm through his.

Her mother followed after them, but Dottie held back, catching Boxhall's eye. She approached him.

'Yes, Miss Dottie, can I help you at all?' It was his usual polite, professional voice, but he winked at her as he said it, a broad grin on his face.

Dropping her voice, Dottie said, 'I just wondered if you're all right? I understand the police had a few questions for you this morning?'

He nodded, his expression immediately grave. 'Well yes, they did. It started out a bit hostile. The inspector was asking the questions. Put it to me that I'd killed Mr Milner with poison, to get rid of him so I could marry Mrs Milner. Obviously, it's public knowledge that she and I are... And then they suggested I killed Mamie for her money. Bloody ridiculous. Excuse my language. Sorry.'

'It's all right, I quite understand. It must have been a shock to discover Mamie had left her estate to you.'

He shook his head, but not in denial, it was a mixture of sorrow and disbelief, Dottie could see. 'I had no idea. I mean, why? Why would she...?'

'She was fond of you. And she had no family. I'm very happy for you,' Dottie told him.

'I know it's rather soon, but do you know what your plans are for the future? Will you continue to work as a butler?' Mrs Manderson asked.

He exhaled heavily. 'My Lord, I have no idea. I still just can't take it in. It's simply unbelievable. I even pinched myself but that didn't make things any easier to accept. Christiana said I should ring the solicitor first thing on Monday morning.'

'Good idea. How is Christiana? Is she recovering from losing Mamie so soon after Mr Milner?' Dottie asked him, and her mother added,

'Oh yes, poor Christiana. It's such a difficult situation.'

Boxhall said, 'She seems a little better. I think if she didn't have so many people here—you know the ones I mean, I'm sure—she'd feel able to relax a little more. The police questioned her this morning too. Not the inspector and your young man, miss, but the other fellow. Christiana said she felt like calling her solicitor, they made it clear she was their main suspect for Mr Milner's death, she half-expected them to arrest her on the spot. As if she would do such a thing. Your young man even asked me about Mrs Milner's first husband—the night he died. Makes me wonder if they're suspicious about that too now. I just—I just want it all to be over. For Christiana's sake.'

'Of course you do.' Dottie hesitated for a second or two then said, 'Well, we'd better go up, or dinner will be served before we're ready.'

They smiled at him and then left.

With two police constables on the premises at all times—albeit in the kitchen drinking tea and eating apple turnovers, according to Boxhall, Dottie had no qualms about venturing from her room that night. She needed a glass of water and made her way along the brightly-lit upper hall and down the stairs to the kitchen. She passed a pleasant few minutes in conversation with the policemen, Jack and Eddie, then said goodnight. She had only got as far as the door to the study. But as soon as she saw the door was ajar with a light burning inside, she set down the glass of water on the hall table and went to investigate.

Florentina Coyle was there, still fully dressed and standing in front of the bookcase, scouring the shelves.

'Looking for something to help you drift off?' Dottie asked from her place just inside the door.

Florentina jolted then uttered a very unladylike word, adding, 'You startled me!'

Dottie apologised, coming further into the room. She hesitated, half-expecting that Florentina would pour out more of her usual venom. But instead, she turned back to the shelves.

'Yes, I need a book. As a matter of fact I've been finding it hard to sleep since we've all been hauled back here,' Florentina added in a milder tone.

'I know what you mean. It's very awkward, isn't it? And we're all rather on edge, aren't we?'

'It's no wonder,' Florentina hissed, glancing back towards the door. 'Who knows if one of the other guests is a murderer? I mean, I'm almost certain that's what the police think. And they won't let us leave. It's—it's—barbaric! Milo says we're all sitting ducks. And he's right! Anything could happen to us.

It's as if we don't even matter!' She took a breath, trying to calm herself.

'It is a little odd being in here now, isn't it?' Dottie looked about her.

'You don't think it's haunted, do you? By Sebastian, I mean.' Florentina cast anxious looks over her shoulder.

'Not by ghosts, if that's what you mean. But perhaps by memories, who knows? It must have been a dreadful shock for that poor young maid to come into the room just as she did every morning and—what? Find her employer lying on the floor, and beyond anyone's help?' Dottie watched her closely to gauge her response.

'At his desk, you mean.' Florentina nodded eagerly. 'Oh I know. Too gruesome for words. That's why there's that new rug on the floor by his desk. Seb had fallen sideways in his chair, and there was a horrific mess all over the desk and the floor. The smell was...' She shook her head, her expression sorrowful. Her eyes were trained on the spot for a few seconds before she hastily added, 'Or so the maid told me.'

'How awful. The poor man,' Dottie said piously.

Florentina agreed, saying, 'Oh yes, the poor dear man. He was so...' She shook her head, clearly unable to remember even one of his good qualities. But her voice broke as she said softly, 'I shall miss him a great deal.'

'Had you known him long? Him and Christiana.'

'I had known Seb for about ten years, I suppose. He was at school with my uncle, my father's younger brother, and quite often visited us with my uncle and his family. It was my uncle who introduced him to Harold Bassington, another old school-friend. I adored Sebastian,' she added, again in that gentle voice Dottie had never heard before. Florentina was studying her nails now, and Dottie could sense the emotion in her. 'It's silly, but I was devastated when Seb broke off our engagement to marry Christiana. I blamed her for that, of course, probably unfairly—he wasn't a man to commit himself unless it suited his purposes. And her bank account was a lot bigger than mine. Not that I realised that back then, it's amazing how quickly you can come to your senses. I'd always thought Seb was well off, but now according to Penelope, it seems he was badly overdrawn at the bank. You just can't tell, can you?'

'No, you can't,' Dottie agreed.

'At one time he was everything to me. But seeing how he treated Christiana was a terrible shock. The things he used to say about her when she wasn't around. I realise now that he probably was the same about me—running me down behind my back. Penny said he did. Soon he'd have been losing his temper with me if I didn't do everything just so, and lashing out. He was a lot older than me, but he always seemed so confident, so sophisticated. Just one of those schoolgirl crushes. But one always hopes, I suppose. We women always think we can change a man. Tame him. My mother thought the same about my father. I should have learned from her. But Seb and I—we were so much in with the same crowd. Then almost as soon as Harold died, he dropped me like a hot coal and turned to Christiana instead. And it was obvious they weren't at all happy.'

Dottie acted surprised. 'Really? How sad. I'm afraid I only got to know them recently.'

'Weren't you involved with Christiana's brother Peter?'

'Not really involved,' Dottie said. 'We went out a few times. He's a terribly good dancer. But that's really all...'

Florentina smiled. 'Well one can't spend one's whole life dancing, can one?'

Dottie smiled back, and echoed Florentina's words. 'Well, no, one can't. And you and Parkes? Are you...? Should we expect a happy announcement anytime soon?'

'Milo? Good God, no! He couldn't be serious about anything other than money. And he hasn't even got any of that. Oh, he's a nice chap, good for a fun evening on the town. But it's not serious.'

'And Penelope, are she and Dalbury serious?'

Florentina shrugged. 'I'm not sure, to be honest. They are engaged, but... again I don't think they are truly happy. One minute she says she adores the man, the next she can't stand him, and says that if she never sees him again, that would be perfect.'

'Sounds like love to me,' Dottie said with a laugh. 'What do her parents think?'

'Oh, well there's only her mother, her father left when she was a girl. But no, her mother's not too keen on Dalbury, mainly because she thinks Dalbury is too much above their own class, too wealthy. As if that could be possible. How can anyone be *too* wealthy? In any case, he's not as wealthy as people think. He's on his uppers until his mother dies and leaves him all her property.'

'Oh dear.' Dottie didn't quite know what to say to that, but she wanted to keep the conversation going if she could. Anything to build some kind of acceptance between them. They had no choice but to spend a lot of time together at the moment, so it would be easier if they were friends.

'Yes, Penny's not from wealth, nor am I if it comes to that.' Florentina gave a shrug, as if it didn't bother her, but her expression told another story.

'Oh dear,' Dottie repeated. 'It's difficult. Trying to

find someone who fits in with your family. Who sees things as you do. What about your family? Do they nag you to find the right man and settle down?'

'Just a bit.' She gave a rueful smile, then almost at random she grabbed a book off the shelf. Dottie didn't have a chance to see what it was, although both the books on either side appeared to be guides to European wildflowers. Florentina was looking down at the cover of the book, but as if she didn't really see it.

'What's on your mind?' Dottie asked her gently.

Florentina looked up, and immediately looked away again, biting her lip. She was near to tears, Dottie thought.

'If there's something on your mind, something worrying you, you can tell me. I promise it won't go any further.'

'Meaning you won't tell your boyfriend the policeman?' There was a sarcastic edge to Florentina's voice, but it was nothing like the bite of the Florentina of previous evenings.

'No,' said Dottie. 'I won't. I swear to you.'

Florentina nodded. For a moment she seemed to waver, tempted to give in, but then she took a deep breath, straightened her back and Dottie could see that the moment had passed.

'Well goodnight. See you at breakfast, Dottie!'

Disappointed, Dottie said goodnight too, and followed after Florentina at a leisurely pace, only remembering her glass of water when she was almost at the top of the stairs.

*

Chapter Nineteen

It had been a wearisome day—and with little in the way of achievement to show for the long hours of poking through the dead man's possessions, friendships and business dealings.

When William got his hat down off the stand in the corner of the Windsor police station office and slapped it on his head, Rhodes who was just returned once more from a lightning-quick trip to London, surprised him by saying,

'Hang on, and I'll walk out with you.'

Kerridge and Spence both glanced up from their desks. Kerridge continued to stare at them, chewing his thumbnail, but Spence frowned then turned back to whatever it was he was doing. William didn't exactly know what he was working on. Presumably Rhodes had tasked him with something relating to their investigation, but from where William stood it looked as though Spence was making a show of being busy but not actually doing anything. If I was in charge, he thought... then reminded himself, that in fact, he was not.

'Don't stay too much longer,' Rhodes said to Spence. He grabbed his hat, raincoat and briefcase then accompanied William out.

All the way down the stairs, through the lobby and out into the street, William waited to see if Rhodes would say something to him. It had seemed significant, him telling William to wait for him.

The street was busy with people everywhere making their way home, and cars, lorries, and buses all threading their way along narrow streets, children playing, young boys and old men selling newspapers on the corners, people crossing the roads, and of course the constant obstacles of horses and carts.

Without any discussion the two men crossed the street. The pub they'd visited before was only a little further on, and William was half-expecting Rhodes to suggest a drink before going back to their rooms.

Abruptly Rhodes said, 'I know that, like me, you've got nothing better to do with your time, seeing that your young lady is stuck at Mrs Milner's, and I have to admit, I don't fancy going straight back to my hotel room just to sit there twiddling my thumbs. I could do with a bite to eat. I spotted a place just along here earlier, does decent food at a reasonable price. What d'you say?'

'I say, that's the best idea you've had today. Sir,' William added hastily, wondering if he'd been too informal, especially after annoying Rhodes so much earlier in the day.

But Rhodes actually laughed. He clapped William on the shoulder, saying, 'Good man. Come on, then, this way.'

It was a small but busy café that Rhodes chose. He pointed to a table near the back by the kitchen. The waft of food that came from there made William's stomach growl.

A plump, attractive young woman came over, gave them both a broad wink, then said, 'Right then, gents, what can I get you?'

They gave their order and off she went again, leaving them to make somewhat awkward conversation. William was still wondering if Rhodes had a purpose in inviting him.

Rhodes said, 'So when's the big day, then? Your wedding to Miss Manderson?'

'August the third,' William said with a grin, leaning back in his seat. 'Pretty soon.'

The waitress came over to set down their cutlery and a large pot of tea along with the necessary items. Heavy cheap pottery cups and saucers followed, then she left them.

'Very nice,' Rhodes commented, and it took William a second to realise he was referring to the wedding date rather than the quality of the tea. 'Known her long, have you?'

'About a year and a half.' William was puzzled. How much detail did Rhodes want? Was he just being friendly, passing the time until their food arrived? Or was he trying to find out something? William explained as briefly as he could how Dottie and he had met, some nineteen months earlier.

'She stayed with a dying man? A complete stranger?' Rhodes' tone was one of surprise.

William nodded. 'She didn't feel that it would be right to leave the poor fellow on his own.'

Rhodes said nothing but was clearly thinking about it.

Their food arrived, and they concentrated on eating. It was only when they had almost finished their meal that Rhodes said,

'I suppose she does know what she's letting herself in for, does she, being a policeman's wife?'

William glanced up. Before he had a chance to reply, Rhodes held up a hand in a kind of apology.

'Oh, I know, I know. It's none of my business. Let's just call it fatherly concern.'

Rhodes was probably only ten or twelve years older than himself, nevertheless, William nodded. 'That's quite all right, sir. But yes, as a matter of fact, she knows what to expect.'

'It can hit a woman hard, having her man go off at all hours, or missing his dinner and so forth. Not to mention cutting short all those visits with the in-laws.'

William grinned. 'She's a good one, sir. She understands.'

Rhodes nodded and pushed his empty plate away. 'Good, good. Well then, you're a lucky chap. They're not all so happy with the hours we sometimes have to do, take it from me.'

So that was it, William thought. Rhodes' wife must have left him, not willing to put up with the unsociable hours.

'I'll remind her what to expect, sir. Thanks for the suggestion.'

Rhodes nodded again. 'Good luck to you both. She is a very pretty and intelligent young lady.'

'Yes sir, she is.'

'Her mother's a bit scary, though. Doesn't suffer fools, I'm certain.'

William laughed. 'She seems happy to put up with me!'

The waitress came to clear away their empty plates; they paid their bill then left. As they walked along the road, they reached the pub. From inside came the gentle sound of conversation and laughter.

The smell of hops hung on the warm evening air.

'Shall we, sergeant?'

William nodded. 'Another excellent idea, sir. I'll get them in.'

They found a table, and carried their drinks across, sitting down to face one another.

William regarded Rhodes with some concern. Now his complexion appeared greyer, his eyes deeply circled and bloodshot. The case—or cases, William reminded himself—were taking their toll. He felt sorry for the man.

'Why don't we talk over what we've got so far?' William suggested.

Rhodes seemed to rouse himself, coming back from far away. He reached for his glass and took a drink of stout. Setting the glass back on the table, in a low, colourless voice, he said, 'I expect you think I'm handling this very badly. Not doing things the way you would in my position.'

There seemed to be no resentment behind his words, just a deep sense of failure. It came off him almost in waves, William thought. The man was ready to give up.

'Not at all,' William said. 'None of us works the same way, but I'm sure I would have done everything just as you have. You have nothing to reproach yourself for.'

'Nothing?' Rhodes tone was bitterly ironic. 'Two deaths within a day of one another? Four jewellery snatches in London, all conducted in the same manner? You would call that a good job well done, would you?' He drank his glass down to the halfway mark, then wiped his mouth on the back of his hand.

'I'd say you're doing the best you can with the information you have so far. Of course, I have an advantage over you.'

'Oh really? Well, I am surprised. Do tell.' Rhodes' tone was even more bitter.

William was not surprised the man was angry and inclined to lash out. This was it. Chief Superintendent Smithers would not be happy, but William was ready to lay his cards on the table.

'It's easy. You see, since I came to work with you, I've discovered that Sergeant Spence is taking payments to conceal evidence and tamper with statements. Exactly what he and someone who owes him money have accused you of doing.'

Rhodes had his glass almost to his mouth. He froze. The glass hovered mid-air for easily fifteen seconds before he set it down with a bang, drawing looks from all around them. He leaned forward, and almost with a snarl, said, *'What did you say?'*

William leaned forward. 'You were right previously when you suggested I was here to spy on you. I am. But although my investigation only started a little more than two weeks ago, and we have necessarily been hampered by the demands of the two cases we are working on, I firmly believe that you are an exemplary officer. However, Sergeant Spence— outwardly respectable, law abiding, and honest—has in reality manipulated some of your cases, accepted bribes, and in secret falsely accused you of crooked practices. That's why I was delayed this morning, I had a couple of calls with Scotland Yard, with officers who are making enquiries on my behalf into yourself and Sergeant Spence. Two credible witnesses have been found who will testify against him, and other useful facts have been uncovered. I am to deliver my report to the chief super the day after tomorrow. I have no doubt that he will authorise me to place Spence under arrest. And I will need your help to do that. I understand that in asking, I'm putting you in a difficult position.'

Rhodes looked as though he had suffered a great shock. But he was breathing easier, William noticed, and his skin was returning to a normal colour.

Rhodes drained his glass and looked as though he could do with another. William went to get them two more half-pints of ale.

As soon as William returned, Rhodes nodded, took another long swig then said,

'I'll admit I've had concerns about Spence, but I honestly had no idea... I once asked him about a couple of things. A witness statement went missing, and there were a couple of minor 'misunderstandings'. But I mentioned them to him, and he just laughed. He wasn't at all concerned. When I said that I had no choice but to report him, he said it would never happen, that he had evidence of a compromising nature against me. I-I'm ashamed to say I overlooked what happened, fearful I would lose my job.'

William nodded. 'I suspected as much. Can you tell me what it is Spence has over you? If it's no longer a secret, then it can no longer harm you.'

Rhodes laugh was still bitter. He shook his head. 'You have no idea what you are asking...'

'Are you a homosexual?'

That surprised the man. 'What? No, of course not... You know I was married.'

William shrugged. 'I know several men who are both, and it's an ever-present worry to them if it should become known. You might be surprised to know they very often are married men.'

'No, it was... I...' He looked down at his hands, struggling to find a way to get started, William thought, but then he just took a deep breath and came out with it. 'I was a member of the Communist

Party for years, ever since university. And four years ago I leaked information to the Party about a secret Government meeting where I was part of the body providing a security detail. The result was that Party members very publicly disrupted the meeting, causing trouble and wrecking the talks, which had to be abandoned, and could possibly have resulted to a small degree in what is going on now on the Continent.

'Spence, well, he may appear to be a good honest working-class lad, but he belongs to all the right clubs, hobnobs with all the right people to get on in life, and quite a few wrong ones too. Three of the Party members told Spence at that it was I who leaked the information. He has held this over me for—four—years.' He looked down at his clasped hands, which trembled. 'He's held it over me... I thought it would kill me, the shame,' he repeated in a near whisper.

William patted his shoulder, and said,

'Drink up, you need it. Then we'll go back to the hotel. It'll be easier to talk there.'

'What do you think they will do to me when they find out? Will I lose my job?' Then, immediately, Rhodes shook his head. 'What am I saying? Of course, I'll lose my job and rightly so. It's just... It's really all I've got. Since Paulette left me.'

William said, 'I can't say for sure, of course. But Smithers is a decent old stick under all that bluster. I imagine you'll be censured, probably have to promise to keep out of the political side of things...'

'Oh I will!' Rhodes assured him. 'I've already stopped. I haven't had anything to do with the Party since that event four years ago. That brought me to my senses.'

William nodded. 'I imagine that's all Smithers will

require you to do. After all, we can't afford to lose good officers. Not in these volatile times. Not a man of your experience.'

Rhodes, looking almost cheerful now, picked up his glass of stout and clinking it against William's, he said, 'You're a good man, Hardy. I'm grateful to you for any help you can give. And of course I will give you all the help and cooperation I can.'

It was just half-past eight on Monday 17th June when Christiana Milner, her guests, along with Boxhall and Mrs Warboys were herded into police cars and driven to Windsor for the inquests into the deaths of Sebastian Milner and Esmerelda Cotton.

The procedures were to be held consecutively; the venue was a small meeting hall a few minutes' walk from the police station. One by one, they filed in, guided to their rows of seats by a clerk.

Dottie looked across to where Hardy sat on a bench to one side of the coroner's throne-like seat. He was behind Inspector Rhodes and Sergeant Spence. Hidden from the view of the inspector, he was able to smile and nod to her, which lifted her spirits.

'All rise.' The clerk of the court instructed them, then announced that the session had begun. The coroner immediately read out a brief statement to the effect that enquiries into the death by iodine poisoning of Sebastian Wilcott Milner were ongoing, and he declared the inquest adjourned for one week.

There was no time to exchange comments with her mother on her left or Christiana on her right as the coroner moved on directly to announce:

'Furthermore, the enquiries by the police into the death by chloral hydrate poisoning on Monday 10th of June 1935 of Esmerelda Cotton, known as Mamie

Cotton, is likewise adjourned for one week. That is all.'

With a sharp tap of his gavel on the wooden tabletop, the coroner gathered up his few papers and rose, stepping down from his seat to a rising babble as the onlookers turned to one another and began their speculations.

Behind Dottie, Dalbury was crossly saying, "I can't bloody well believe it. We were dragged all the way over here for nothing. What an absolute waste of time!"

There were nods and murmurs of agreement.

Dottie's hopes of snatching a moment or two with William were thwarted. The constable who had driven them from the house began directing them out of the building to where the cars waited to take them back once more.

In the car, Christiana stared out at the street, lost in her thoughts, whilst Anabella in the front passenger seat turned several times to cast anxious looks at her. Mrs Manderson leaned towards Dottie to whisper,

'It was just like a production line in a factory. No pause, no comment, just 'adjourned' and 'likewise adjourned'.'

'Yes.' Dottie couldn't think of anything else to add. She was wondering if there were any books in Christiana's study that could tell her about the properties of iodine or chloral hydrate.

They arrived back at Christiana's house at twenty minutes past nine.

They went up to their rooms to take off hats, jackets and outdoor shoes. Dottie remembered that Mamie had called for the iodine from the medicine chest on the Saturday night when Sebastian had slapped Christiana, and her cheek had been caught by his ring.

'And it was Sebastian who was poisoned with the iodine, not Mamie,' she mused as she stood by the window looking out.

Was it possible that Mamie had been so enraged by Sebastian's actions that she removed the iodine from the medicine chest then poisoned Sebastian with it? Iodine would be on hand in most homes, every medicine chest had some. But chloral hydrate? And who had killed Mamie? Was it possible that there were not just two victims but also two killers? It seemed highly unlikely, but perhaps she had been wrong to assume that there was one killer with one motive.

She left her room—somewhat reluctantly—and returned to the morning-room. Only her mother and Anabella were there, almost inevitably they were deep in discussion about poison.

After lunch, Dottie was sitting in the garden a little apart from the more energetic ones who were playing tennis once again, apparently untroubled by the soaring temperatures. She was holding a glass of lemon cordial in both hands, and in fact had been holding it for half an hour, just enjoying the coolness on her palms and occasionally raising the glass to place against her cheek or forehead. It didn't matter that she was in the shade, it was almost as hot here as in the full sun on this airless afternoon.

Beside her, Mrs Manderson was asleep in her deckchair, the book she had been reading having slipped from her hand onto the grass, snapping shut on the page that had failed to hold her interest. It was slightly more than a week since Sebastian had been found dead in his study by a maid, and a week since Mamie had been killed. Their closest friends were right in front of Dottie, playing tennis and laughing as if they hadn't a care in the world. Did they even think of Sebastian or Mamie, here, in what had been Sebastian's home, enjoying the amenities he and his wife had provided for them? It was truly peculiar, she thought.

But Dottie was not really seeing the tennis match. Nor the flowers blooming madly in the borders or the neat beds ablaze with summer colour. She was lost in her thoughts. She should have been thinking of William and their upcoming marriage, making plans for their lives together, or at the very least, planning the décor of their bedroom. That awful Victorian brown and cream paper had got to go. Perhaps something in pastel shades, flowers or a dainty stripe? But she kept becoming distracted.

It was Mamie Cotton's face she saw, whether she closed her eyes or kept them open, staring unseeing at Christiana Milner's guests as they laughed and leapt about, shouting encouragement—or playful insults—to one another.

Dottie almost recoiled as she recalled the moment when Florentina had slapped Mamie. There had been a real fury behind that slap. But had that been the end of Florentina's rage? Or had she taken an even more shocking step to punish Mamie? And for what, Dottie pondered. For not being taken in by Florentina's falsified airs and graces? For laughing at her behind her hand?

Why had that mattered so much to Florentina? In a day or two, they should have all left, gone back to their normal lives. If Florentina had hated Mamie so much, she need never have seen her again after that weekend. What did it matter if one old woman had punctured her pride a little with some throwaway comment or another? It wasn't as if Florentina held back when it came to wounding insults. Nor had her dearest friend Penelope.

Had Florentina's temper been relieved by striking Mamie, or had that just fuelled her desire to hurt Mamie even more? Dottie found she couldn't stop staring at the four of them, at first one then the next, and all the while asking herself if any of them had the necessary hatred for Sebastian or for Mamie that would be required to commit murder.

'Dottie, are you sure you don't want a game?' Milo called. His sudden question made her jump. He wiped his forehead and neck with a towel and flopped into a deckchair nearby, causing her mother to stir briefly in the neighbouring chair before falling asleep once more. The others were right behind him, smiling their knowing sarcastic smiles at her then exchanging looks. Clearly, they had been talking about her, but she didn't care. Let them laugh, let them think whatever they liked, she didn't care.

All she wanted to do now was to go home. She said a smiling, 'No thanks.' And sipped her lemon cordial.

As the afternoon wore on, Dottie grew tired of sitting in her chair. Her mother awoke refreshed, and after a cup of tea and some cucumber sandwiches, was wondering what to do to while away the time until dinner.

'How about a walk around the garden?' Mrs Manderson suggested.

'Good idea, Mother. I'm so bored.'

It was still sunny even though it was almost evening. Soon they'd have to go in for dinner, but for now, arm in arm with her mother, Dottie wandered into the rose walk for the second time in as many days.

Without discussion, they paused by the bench where Mamie had been found, and stood looking at the scene. Not that there was much to see, Dottie reflected. In many ways it seemed unchanged. The roses still bloomed and filled the air with their lovely rich scent.

'It's the same, yet somehow completely different,' Mrs Manderson commented.

Dottie nodded. 'Just what I was thinking. The first time we came along here, I thought how lovely it was, what a charming place to sit for a while. And now it's tainted.' She reached out a hand to touch a rose, fully open, and even though her touch was soft, the rose's petals faltered then one by one drifted to the ground, leaving no sign of its beauty.

'My goodness,' said her mother, 'That's quite a metaphor, isn't it?'

'Indeed.'

Dottie moved to seat herself in the place where Mamie had been found, feeling slightly irreligious, but at the same time, impatient with herself for her silliness. She could see her mother was a little surprised but nevertheless sat beside her. They remained there for several minutes without speaking.

Dottie looked about her. She looked at the roses, looked up and down the walk, seeing the other benches, one to the left, one to the right, both on the other side of the walk, facing into the garden that could be seen here and there through the stems of the roses and their trellis.

'It's odd,' she murmured. 'If I chose to sit here, I'd want to face the garden, rather than the house. It's prettier.'

Getting up, she went along to the bench on the left. Mrs Manderson watched her with interest. Dottie sat on the other bench. Yes, she thought, it was just as she'd expected. You could see part of the lawn and the far shrubbery, but not much else, but it was a more charming view than staring at the back of the house. She got up and walked back, past her mother, and seated herself on the other bench. Here, the view was much the same, just from a slightly different perspective. She returned to Mamie's place.

'Why did she choose this spot?'

'Perhaps she didn't care where she sat. Or didn't care about the view. Perhaps she just wanted to smell the roses and enjoy their beauty? She was, after all, a florist,' her mother suggested.

'True.' Still Dottie mulled it over. Chewing her lip, she stared through the gap in the roses. 'What room is that?'

Her mother leaned towards her to see through the same gap Dottie was looking through. 'Mr Milner's study.'

'Of course,' Dottie said, and her mind began to worry away at this realisation. It felt like a moment of great significance.

After a few moments in her reverie, Dottie began to look about her. There was nothing remarkable about the bench. It was just a bench, wooden, plain, somewhere to sit for a while out of the glare of the sun, and enjoy the roses. The roses!

'Ouch! Blast it!'

'Be careful, dear, some of those roses have huge thorns.'

Dottie rolled her eyes. It was a bit late to remind her of that now. She rubbed the scratch on the back of her hand. Fortunately, the wound was nothing too serious. With great care, she parted some of the lower leaves to peer at the ground beneath the bench. It was a tangle of stems and shoots, a torn handkerchief, long forgotten, and heaps of partially rotted leaved. An earthy waft assaulted her nostrils.

But then—as she was about to straighten up, defeated—she saw it: the slightest glint of light on a hard narrow edge. Reaching in carefully, she grasped it and drew her hand out. She held up her find for them both to see.

It was a small crystal tumbler. It had been lying on its side. Some of the fluid it had contained was collected in the lowest point of the curving glass wall. Just a dreg. Not even half a teaspoonful.

'Of course, it may simply be rainwater, discoloured by age and dirt,' her mother murmured softly. 'But we must be careful with it. Perhaps this might work.'

'This' was Mrs Manderson's shawl that she'd brought with her in case of a cool breeze. If only there *was* a breeze, Dottie thought.

With great delicacy they wrapped the glass in one end of the shawl, then positioned the shawl over Mrs Manderson's forearm, so that it appeared as though she was simply carrying her bunched-up shawl back into the house.

'I suppose there's nothing else?' she asked anxiously.

Dottie was leaning over the bench, checking the area all around. 'No, nothing.' Her tone was regretful, but at least they had a small prize to hand over to the police—one the police themselves surely ought to have discovered. Here in Mamie's favourite spot, it had suddenly dawned on Dottie that there may be something, some small clue, and now sure enough, here it was.

'If only there is enough of the contents to test,' Mrs Manderson hazarded. 'That would be so exciting.'

They hurried back to the house and sought out the constable who was stationed in the back regions of the property. He was supposedly on duty and on high alert, keeping the household safe, his eyes peeled for a murderer. But he was currently 'testing' a cherry tart fresh from the oven, under the beady eyes of Mrs Warboys.

He was reluctant to leave to speak with them privately in Mr Boxhall's sitting-room, glancing back towards the kitchen with great sorrow. Until that is, he'd finally understood what they were telling him. Mrs Manderson set down the glass with great care on the butler's table, still with its tiny dribble of brownish liquid.

To her relief the constable made no attempt to grab the item. Realising it could be useful evidence, he procured a clean duster and a small wicker basket.

'I'll get this to Sergeant Spence immed...'

'Sergeant *Hardy*,' Dottie corrected him. She wouldn't put it past Spence to suggest she'd put the glass under the rose herself.

He nodded gravely. 'I'll get this to Sergeant Hardy within the hour, miss. My relief will be here by then and I can cycle back to the police station with it myself. If the sergeant isn't there, who should I...?'

'Inspector Rhodes. No one other than those two gentlemen must be given the glass until it's been examined by an expert,' Dottie told him, and was pleased, yet a little surprised, that her took her instructions very seriously.

'Yes, ma'am. You can leave that to me.'

'And don't mention it to anyone, either.' Dottie advised.

A little reluctantly the two women left, but Dottie was aware of a growing thrill of excitement. What if this discovery proved to be really important?

That evening, after dinner, Florentina suggested putting on the radio. She wanted dance music, of course, but a news programme was already on, and the men immediately perked up, interested in developments on the Continent. A heated debate started up between them.

As always at any mention of what everyone called the 'inevitable' war, Dottie's arms prickled with goosebumps, and a shiver went down her spine. Surely not *war*? Not here? Not now? What if William had to go and fight? What if he was hurt? Killed? How could she bear it? And not just William, but George, and all the other men. All the young men of every nation in Europe and even beyond would inevitably be caught up in it. And not only the men. Women. Children. Young and old. Rich and poor. Town and country. All at risk of damage, of injury, or even death. Please, God, surely not a war?

She was shaking, but she only knew about it when the soft chattering of her cup in its saucer finally broke into her thoughts, and she looked down to see the cup vibrating. She set the cup and saucer down and clasped her hands tightly together in her lap.

Conversational inspiration struck, and she said, 'So Anabella, how long are you planning to stay in England?'

Anabella, too, looked relieved to have something safe, even mundane to talk about. She exchanged a loving smile with Major Forsythe and said,

'Well, do you know, I think I might just stay here a little longer than planned. Not sure what it is, but something here definitely seems to be drawing me.' She grinned at Dottie, who, happier now they were discussing a cheery topic, grinned back.

'Something? Or perhaps someone?'

'That too!'

'I don't think we'll be staying here too much longer though, especially if war is in the air. I've got a strange feeling I might end up working on the other side of the pond in the near future.' Tom Forsythe said. 'And if this crazy dame,' and here he attempted an American drawl, failing horribly, 'will have me, I'll marry her like a shot, and we'll live happily ever after in some smart suburb of New York.'

'Wonderful,' Dottie said. 'Congratulations! I expect you can hardly wait!'

Anabella pulled a face. 'Sadly I shall have to, my divorce still has to come through. That's going to take quite some time. Looks like it'll be a year or two before we can make the official announcement, I guess. But that is the plan. My father is keen to take Tom into his firm, and the money should be pretty good, let me tell you. And much as I love London, and Windsor is so cute, I can't wait to get back to the States, and with this guy on my arm, too!'

At last a dance programme began, and they waited attentively to see what the first song would be. The announcer said,

'And now without further ado, we cross the airwaves to the Continental Ballroom on The Strand where Ray Noble and his Mayfair Dance Orchestra are about to play their popular new piece, *Midnight, the Stars, and You,* accompanied of course by vocalist Al Bowlly.'

Dottie smiled. It was one of her favourite tunes. She settled back in her seat, her eyes closed as she listened to the opening bars. Someone nearby cleared his throat, and she opened her eyes to see Tom Forsythe now standing in front of her.

'Shall we?' He crooked his elbow ready to lead her into the middle of the floor.

'Why not,' she said. And they joined the others in a foxtrot. What was the point of moping about, Dottie asked herself. It wouldn't bring back Mamie, or even Sebastian. Soon, surely, the police would have a break-through and arrest the person responsible, then she and everyone else could go back to their lives. She glanced at Forsythe as she thought this.

'Anything wrong?' he asked, brows creased with concern.

She smiled and shook her head. 'No. I've just realised, there's no point in sitting around sombrely.'

'True,' he said. 'It won't bring back the old girl.'

'Nor Sebastian.'

'Nor him.' But he said it with a broad smile.

The musical introduction came to an end and Mr Bowlly's distinctive voice began the song:

Midnight with the stars and you,
Midnight and a rendezvous
Your eyes held a message tender
Saying 'I surrender all my love to you.'

As Dottie moved to the music, Forsythe's arm at her back, his rough right hand holding her left, all she could think was, where is William. All she wanted was to be dancing with him.

*

Chapter Twenty

'Message for you from Sergeant Spence, inspector,' was how Constable Kerridge greeted Rhodes and Hardy the following morning when they reached their borrowed office at Windsor police station. 'In fact,' Kerridge continued, consulting his daybook, 'there are two messages from him.'

'Go ahead.' Rhodes stared down at Kerridge, obviously praying for good news, as was Hardy.

'The first is that the chief super is blowing a gasket at how long things are taking. Says you'd better get it all wrapped up within the next twenty-four hours or he's taking you off the case.' Kerridge glanced up, worried that this might be one of those 'shoot the messenger' situations. 'Sorry sir, I told the sarge to tell the boss that we're making progress. But then he asked me what the progress was and I didn't quite know what to say.'

Rhodes, thin-lipped but otherwise making no response, simply said, 'And?'

'And,' Kerridge flipped to the next page of his notes. 'Spence says that no one's heard of our man, no sign of him whatsoever. The date and place of birth are verified, but that's about all.'

'Interesting.' Rhodes exchanged a look with Hardy. This was progress, after all.

Hardy said, 'I've got an idea. Ask Spence to get onto Oxford University and find out if our man was enrolled at any of the colleges. Or failing that, get a list of all Harold Bassington's contemporaries. He studied botany and chemistry.'

'Yes sir.' Kerridge made a careful note then pulled the telephone apparatus towards him. They left him to it and went into the inner office.

'So what do you think of that?'

'It's just as we suspected, sir,' Hardy said. He pulled out a seat and sat down. Rhodes stood by the window staring down at the busy street below.

There was a tap on the door. It was Kerridge.

'Sorry sir, forgot to say, I've had a call from the pathologist. He's already tested that glass Miss Manderson handed in last night. It contains traces of gin, laced with what would have been a lethal dose of chloral hydrate. There are some fingerprints, but they're smudged, he's not sure they'll be usable. He said he'd keep trying.'

'Thanks. That's excellent news.' Rhodes smiled for the first time that morning.

Hardy leaned back in his chair, stretching cramped shoulders. 'Things are hotting up nicely,' he remarked. 'I'm not sure it's quite enough. We still need something more.'

'Yes. I suppose we could bring him in, see if he'll crack under pressure, but I'm not hopeful.'

'No.' Hardy got to his feet, paced a bit then came over to the window and leaned against the frame, arms folded. 'So, Mamie Cotton was sitting in her favourite spot that everyone in the house knew about. Our chap pops out to speak with her, taking with him a glass of gin laced with a little something special.'

'Hmm.' Rhodes leaned against the opposite window frame, his arms folded too. He frowned as he mulled the situation over. 'We know it wasn't during the evening before she was found, because the doctor stated her body was still almost the normal temperature. She had to have died that morning.'

'Would she be likely to drink gin at that time of day, though?'

Rhodes laughed. 'From what we've been told, she was quite a character, living by her own rules. I think it's entirely possible she might fancy a G and T for breakfast.'

'No one saw a person talking to her, or at least, no one *remembers* or *admits* to seeing anyone.'

'No. The maid said Boxhall sent her to look for Mrs Cotton when the old lady failed to come in to breakfast. That wasn't until half-past eight. But that seems to be the only time anyone thought about her or talked about her.'

'Apart from our killer, that is.'

'Exactly, sergeant.'

At the same time as this conversation was taking place at the police station, a few miles away in West Halliford, Dottie and her mother came into the dining-room for a late breakfast and found to their delight that Christiana was there with Anabella. And no one else.

'Where is everyone?' Dottie enquired.

'Tom's gone out for a cigarette and a wander around the grounds,' Anabella said, 'I think he's a bit fed up being shut up indoors so much, he's very grumpy at the moment, he's been snapping at me quite a bit lately. The sooner we can get back to normal, the better, I say. But the others seem happy enough. They are already out there having a game of tennis. Too energetic for me, I must say.'

'And too early!' Dottie said. 'Though I might have a game later. Might.'

'What have you done to your hand, Dottie?'

Dottie glanced down ruefully at the scratch. 'I got a bit too close to some roses last evening,' she admitted. She added, trying not to sound as though she was giving herself an alibi, 'I just wanted to smell them all.'

'Oh, I did the same, as did Tom when he tried to untangle my skirt hem from the roses' clutches.' Anabella smiled and held out her arm to show the scratch on the back of her wrist.

'But the roses are heavenly, aren't they?' Christiana smiled. 'Worth the occasional wounding.'

Her mother said, 'Perhaps we could borrow a little of your iodine from the medicine chest? We should have used it at the time, but it completely slipped my mind to do that. But I wouldn't like it to become infected.'

Christiana was already on her feet. 'Certainly, I'll just go and fetch it.' And she was out of the room even as Dottie opened her mouth to say that after breakfast would be soon enough. Two minutes later Christiana returned looking puzzled. She held the bottle up for them to see.

'I can't understand it,' she said, her brow furrowed. 'It's completely empty. But the other evening, when Mamie... It was a full bottle, so it can't have been used up already...' Her voice trailed off as she realised the implication. She sank down heavily in her seat, her expression stricken. 'My word! I've just realised... Why didn't I think of that before?' She glanced from Dottie to her mother then finally to Anabella. Realisation dawned. 'You all knew! My goodness, why am I so slow to put two and two together?'

Anabella patted her arm. 'You've had plenty on your mind without that. Don't worry about it.'

'But... that means it was our—*my*—iodine that was used to kill Mamie and Seb? Oh, that's awful!' She set the bottle down on the side-table with a firm click.

'Just Mr Milner, I fear,' Mrs Manderson said gently. 'The blue-black of his rum and blackcurrant drink would have perfectly disguised the dark colour of the iodine. And he wouldn't have smelled the iodine because of his heavy cold. I'm afraid it was a very clever ploy. But with Mamie, something else was used. The police said Mamie was killed with chloral hydrate, didn't they? A different poison altogether.'

'Where on earth would someone have got something like that?' Christiana wondered, shaking her head, her brows drawn together. 'They must have brought it with them, surely?'

'I have an idea about that,' Mrs Manderson said. 'But I need to ask William...' she fell silent, staring towards the window.

'And you're sure it was a new bottle? The iodine?' Dottie asked.

Christiana nodded immediately. 'Oh yes, we watched Mamie remove the foil seal, didn't we, Bella?' Her eyes filled with tears as she remembered that awful evening. Anabella slipped her hand through Christiana's arm.

'We certainly did.' Anabella agreed.

'What happened to the medicine chest once you'd used the iodine?' Dottie wanted to know. 'Did Mamie take it and put it back in its place? Where was it usually kept?'

Christiana, wiping her eyes, cast about her. 'It's usually kept on a shelf in Paul's sitting-room. But I didn't see what happened to it. I'm sorry, I'm afraid I don't know. I wasn't attending.'

Mrs Manderson nodded and patted her arm. 'No, dear, of course you weren't. You were understandably distracted.'

But Anabella said, 'It was I who picked up the chest to take it back. I was going to give it to Paul, but Mamie took it from me, saying it was better if I stayed with Chris. "Don't leave her alone," Mamie said. So she took it and left the room. But she came back almost right away.'

'Oh?' Dottie queried.

'Yes. I didn't ask her, but she said something like, "Someone saved me the trouble." Then she said, if we didn't mind, she'd leave us to talk. I assumed she meant she needed to use the lavatory, but she didn't come back for almost half an hour.'

Dottie nodded, her mind racing. 'I see.'

And indeed, she did see.

For where else would Mamie have gone at that point to seek solace or some peace and quiet but to her beloved rose walk? From that vantage point at a crucial moment, Dottie now knew, Mamie would have seen exactly what had happened that evening—thanks to that excellent view of Mr Milner's study window.

Then, the following evening, after dark, Mamie had met the killer there at the rose walk to confront them—Dottie had seen someone there smoking a cigarette, heard the sound of voices. It was so frustrating that she couldn't identify the other voice; she had heard Mamie's distinctive tones, but the other voice had been a mere rumble, apart from that one sentence, 'I thought I might find you out here'. But even though she knew it was a man speaking, she hadn't heard quite enough to be able to identify him. That it was someone who knew Mamie's habits well was clear, but that could apply to any of the men on the premises. Dottie fumed to remember denying her curiosity to peek around the door when she heard Mamie and the man coming back upstairs later.

But it was easy to imagine what had happened. Perhaps Mamie had gone so far as to suggest she might go to the police if the perpetrator didn't pay her a certain sum of money in exchange for her silence. By doing that, she had sealed her own fate. The killer would have had to act quickly: she was a garrulous old woman who enjoyed a drink. They must have been concerned she would hint at, or just declare outright, what she had seen.

Dottie was relieved to hear the sound of voices in the hall: Inspector Rhodes and her own William had just arrived. She went out to meet them, and her mother, sensing an interesting conversation was about to take place, followed close on her heels.

They were enjoying coffee in the butler's sitting-room. Two more chairs had been brought in to accommodate the four of them. Mrs Manderson had been pressed to take the only armchair, the others all stating they were perfectly comfortable on the upright chairs. For a few seconds they stared at one another. Dottie was nervous. The Inspector didn't look very happy about the way things had begun. No doubt having a couple of women interfering in police matters was new to him.

She held out the medicine chest to him. 'This is where the killer got the iodine from,' she told them.

Rhodes pulled a handkerchief from his pocket and took the dark-coloured glass vial from the chest. He scrutinised it, turning it this way and that under the light. There was no exterior window in the room, just the interior one that looked out onto the kitchen corridor. The only light came from the single bulb surrounded by a lacy lampshade in faded turquoise.

'It looks very clean,' he grumbled.

'I'm sorry, but it may have Mrs Milner's prints on it. She picked it up when she went to check on the medicine chest. She assured me that she only held it by the metal lid.' Dottie bit her lip, waiting to see if he castigated her. But he just gave a resigned shrug, then wrapping the vial in his handkerchief, he placed it into his jacket pocket.

'We must keep in mind that she could have used that as a convenient opportunity to account for her prints being on the bottle, however,' he pointed out.

Hardy nodded, but added, 'Yes, true, although no legal chap will let that go. He'd be bound to point out that as it's her property and found in her house, it would be quite likely to have her prints on it.'

Reluctantly Rhodes admitted the truth of that. 'Well, that accounts for the iodine, anyway. We now know that whoever the killer is, he or she didn't bring it with them.'

'He,' Dottie and Mrs Manderson said together.

Inspector Rhodes frowned at them. '*He or she* didn't bring it with them,' he repeated. 'Or at least, I assume not. There could be another bottle, I suppose. But nothing has been discovered during our searches.'

'Not that they were very thorough,' Mrs Manderson remarked.

The air was immediately tense. Inspector Rhodes did not appreciate her criticism, she realised. She held up a hand to apologise. 'I'm sorry. It isn't my place to say such things. I was referring to the glass that my daughter found amongst the roses.'

'Sergeant Spence had instructions to search most diligently. I know he and Kerridge and a couple of constables went over the house very thoroughly. I believe we didn't understand at that time just how much Mrs Cotton enjoyed sitting on that bench out there.'

'Of course. Once again, inspector, I apologise.'

Ruffled feathers had been smoothed. Rhodes continued.

'Now we just need to know how the killer got his...' he caught Dottie and Mrs Manderson's eyes again, '*Or her*... hands on the other stuff, the chloral hydrate.'

'Ah,' said Mrs Manderson. 'I may be able to help you there.'

Hardy was certain he heard Rhodes emit a soft groan. There was definitely a roll of the eyes. Hardy hid a smile, able to sympathise to an extent over the annoying sensation of having a laywoman explain his job to him. But, Hardy thought, he himself had become quite used to it. It had been a great help on a number of occasions.

With a heavy tone, but nevertheless preserving his good manners, Rhodes said, 'Do go on, Mrs Manderson.'

'You might not think it to look at me now, but at school I was considered quite the scientist. Not that girls were encouraged to be scientific when I was young, of course, it was very much considered a male discipline. But I was good at chemistry, not quite so good at other scientific disciplines such as physics, but also good at botany—that was what I really loved, and I had something of a flair for it. You do, you know, when you love something. You learn as much about it as you can. It was a revelation to me, on a par with discovering a new world, to look down the lens of a microscope...' Mrs Manderson said.

She paused and glanced around. They weren't exactly hanging on her every word, but they were still more or less attending. She continued:

'We used to make our own slide samples. That was one of the basic skills one had to learn to pass the examination. How to create your own slides to study under the microscope. You know, little samples of leaves or petals, or sepals, or...' She paused, noting they were glazing over slightly at this. She hurried along.

'We girls always wanted pretty things, I suppose, so it was rather fun to do. The process with the plant sections and the chloral hydrate—it could be used to produce some truly lovely samples that we then mounted—and framed like a little picture to put on the wall or use in other decorative ways. Oh, we loved it! Dottie, dear, I'm sure you remember the little botanical pictures on the wall in your father's study? I made those for him.'

Dottie nodded, remembering. There were two framed pictures of a single petal of some unknown origin, and two similar ones of leaves. She always thought them a trifle dull. But now that she knew her mother had actually created them herself, she was definitely going to look at them more closely—and admire them.

The two men, who at first had looked as if they may die of boredom, were now giving her close attention.

Mrs Manderson continued, 'Of course, chloral hydrate is also *notoriously* addictive. Quite a few people of our acquaintance many years ago became terribly addicted, and it haunted them all their lives. There was quite the fashion for it, once it was realised the Victorian use of opium was far too dangerous. Not that chloral hydrate proved to be less so. Quite the reverse! It was thought to be a way to cope with pain or simply to relax, but soon it became impossible for its users to live without it.'

'And Mamie was sitting out there in her favourite spot under the roses, all alone, after she had been given it, with no one close by to call to for help.' Dottie shook her head sorrowfully. 'The poor woman. It was such a wicked thing to do to her.'

'But I'm getting sidetracked.' Mrs Manderson said. 'This is a somewhat rambling explanation. You wondered, inspector, and William dear, how your killer had got hold of the poison. Well, it was like this. Mrs Milner's first husband used chloral hydrate in his fernery, which is in the garden. He was, she told us, a keen botanist and amateur photographer. Much of his equipment is still there on the shelves of the fernery. Dottie and I saw it all on the day that we arrived.'

The two police officers were on the edge of their seats by now, suddenly understanding the lady's slightly long-winded reminiscences. They exchanged a look, and neither Dottie nor Lavinia were surprised that they rose as one and ran from the room without so much as a backward glance.

The two women followed them at a more leisurely pace.

By the time Dottie and Mrs Manderson reached the fernery, expecting to see the men outside, frustrated by the locked door, the two police officers were right inside.

Dottie and her mother exchanged a look.

'That wasn't open before,' Dottie said.

'No, it wasn't.' Mrs Manderson peeked around the door. Her tentative sniffs at the air were greeted by an earthy but not unpleasant aroma. William glanced back at her.

'Is it all right to come in?' she asked him.

He looked at his colleague, who nodded, seemingly now resigned to their involvement. In turn, William nodded to Mrs Manderson, who nodded to her daughter and the two of them stepped inside.

'Up there, was it?' Rhodes asked Mrs Manderson.

She nodded. 'Yes, but...'

'It's not there now.' He stood on a chair and peered at the surface of the top shelf. 'There's ethanol, and distilled water, but...' He pointed. 'There's just a ring in the dust at this end. I imagine that's where the chloral hydrate was.'

Mrs Manderson said, 'I'm not certain, but I definitely had the impression there was at least one other bottle on the shelf. A large one of brown glass with a poison symbol on the label. That was how I knew, you see.'

The inspector stepped down again. 'Well, whoever it is, he or she has gone off with the goods, all right.'

'I'll go back to the house and ask Mrs Milner who borrowed the key,' William said.

'No, it's Paul Boxhall you need to speak to,' Dottie told him. 'When we asked before, Christiana told us the key was most likely kept in his room.'

'Like everything else,' Rhodes said, his tone heavily ironic. 'Funny that. All the useful stuff being kept in our main suspect's private sitting-room!'

'Your main suspect, you mean. I've already told you what I think,' Hardy was heard to say.

Dottie and Mrs Manderson exchanged a worried look.

Returning to the house, and having missed breakfast, the two women joined the others for mid-morning coffee in the drawing-room, whilst Rhodes and Hardy collared Boxhall as he returned from delivering the tray.

'A word, Boxhall,' Rhodes said. His tone brooked no argument although Boxhall did cock an eyebrow at him. But he'd been insulted by worse people than the inspector in his time, and more or less took it in his stride. They returned once again to the butler's sitting-room.

'Where do you keep the medicine chest?' Rhodes demanded immediately.

Hardy thought it would be more helpful if Rhodes employed a little less aggression and a little more tact. Boxhall was now looking irritated. He took up a stance by the door, arms folded in the classically uncooperative style. He nodded curtly towards one of the shelves in the alcove to the left of the chimney breast.

Thinking the man appeared poised for flight, Hardy thanked him and smiled. Then he added, 'And what about the key to the fernery. I believe that's kept in here too?'

He was gratified to see Boxhall relax a little. 'That little cupboard on the other side of the chimney. It's usually on the bottom row, but someone's borrowed it and not brought it back yet.' He turned towards Rhodes, 'Mrs Milner came for the iodine earlier, if that's what you want the medicine chest for.'

'Thank you, but we already have that,' Rhodes nodded. 'We just wanted to see the place where it was kept.'

Hardy said, 'On the night Mr Milner hit his wife, the iodine was used. Who came and got the medicine chest from you?'

'It was Mamie.'

Hardy nodded. 'And who brought it back?'

Boxhall told him the name. Hardy and Rhodes exchanged a look.

'And,' Rhodes asked now, 'is that the same person who took the key for the fernery?'

'Yes.' Boxhall looked from one to the other of them, clearly puzzled.

'Do us a favour, will you?' Rhodes said. 'Get the two constables on duty and have them wait outside the terrace doors. Just in case.'

Rhodes nodded to Boxhall and left the room, Hardy following close behind. Hardy said, 'I just need to make a telephone call. I'd like you to come with me.'

*

Chapter Twenty-one

In the drawing-room, Mrs Manderson poured coffee for herself and Dottie, then taking her cup, she went to sit beside Anabella and the major, opposite Christiana. Dottie set down her cup and crossed the room to Florentina. Florentina had been on the point of going outside with her coffee: her friends were already out there on the terrace.

'Are you sleeping any better?' Dottie asked her, keeping her voice low.

Florentina glanced at her then glanced away. 'Not really. I expect I'll be all right once I get away from here.'

'Yes, I know what you mean. Look, I need to ask you something. It may be important. And if your answer is what I'm expecting, I'll have to tell my fiancé what you said. But,' Dottie continued hastily, seeing Florentina was already on the point of turning away, 'I don't believe anything will come of it. And it will ease your mind to have it out in the open. I really think you'll sleep all the better for it.'

'Oh you do, do you?' Florentina said, a feeble attempt at her former cutting sarcasm. Then she sighed. 'What is it?'

'Why did you allow everyone, including the police, to believe that it was the maid who discovered Mr Milner's body? I know it was you who found him. You were already in the morning-room crying on Penelope's shoulder when the rest of us came downstairs having just heard the news.'

Florentina stared at her for a long minute. Dottie began to think she wasn't going to answer.

But then, with the slightest lift of her shoulder, and a somewhat sardonic quirk of her lips, she said, 'I don't know why you bothered asking. You obviously know why.'

Dottie nodded. 'You'd been having an affair with Mr Milner. But that doesn't explain... Unless you were using the study for your—er—liaisons?'

Florentina shook her head. 'He'd arranged to come to my room. But with all that I drank that evening, I just fell asleep. It was early the next morning when I awoke. He'd hadn't joined me. I went looking for him, but he wasn't in his bedroom. As I passed by the top of the stairs, I saw the light was still on in the hall below even though it was fully daylight outside, so I went down to see if I could find him. And I—I did, in his study. He was... I was too late... He was already...' her voice failed her. She pressed her free hand to trembling lips. 'The maid came in right behind me. It was her who screamed. That brought Paul Boxhall running downstairs. He found me in a terrible state, as you can imagine, and he sent another maid to get Penelope to come and comfort me. He had enough to do with phoning for a doctor and breaking the news to Christiana. I—I hoped she wouldn't need to know about the affair. I do like her, it was just...'

'I understand.' Dottie nodded and patted her arm. 'Thank you.'

'So you see, I have a motive...'

'No, not at all. At the most you have an opportunity. But in spite of his arrogance and his appalling treatment of his wife—and his treatment of you too—you loved him, didn't you?'

Florentina gave the curtest of nods. 'Well, now you know, so you can report me. If your boyfriend wants me, he'll find me on the terrace with my friends, drinking my cold coffee.'

And she pushed wide open the already-ajar door and went down the steps, head held high. Dottie closed the door behind her.

'Frank? It's Bill. Look, sorry, I've got to be quick. Can you just tell me, did the fingerprints from the bedroom door at Sir Nigel's match any of the ones Sergeant Kerridge handed to you a few days ago? They did? Just two? And whose prints were they? Ah, thanks, just as we suspected. Thumb and forefinger of the left hand, and a couple of smudged ones? Right, I've got that. And the other thing? Yes? That's excellent. Well done. Thanks a lot, I'll let you get back to Foul-up.'

Hardy hung up the telephone receiver then turned to face Rhodes. 'Did you hear all that?'

'Yes, and no.' Rhodes stared at him. 'Tell me.'

'Not here,' Hardy said. 'Let's pop back to the butler's sitting-room.'

'It's becoming our new office.'

'Very handy,' Hardy agreed.

Boxhall was nowhere to be seen, so the police officers made themselves comfortable.

'The fingerprints?' Rhodes prompted.

'Ah yes, and the other thing.'

'Other thing?'

'I asked Sergeant Maple to look into the background of Sergeant Spence.'

'*Spence*? Well, I know he had a troubled childhood,' Rhodes said. 'Father abandoned the family. Spence grew up in poverty.'

'Yes. He did. He and his mother. Along with his younger sister.'

Rhodes rocked back in his seat, eyebrows almost disappearing beneath his hairline. 'Surely you don't mean...?'

Hardy nodded. 'I do. Now then, coming to the fingerprints found at Sir Nigel Ponsonby's house. There were none on the handle of the door—or rather, no usable ones, there was just a mess of prints. But on the edge of the door, where the 'maid' peeked around at Lady Cosgrove—there were some prints from where the woman touched the door to push it open with her left hand, her right being on the handle itself, presumably. Those prints will make the pretty bow on the top of our gift to the chief super.'

Rhodes face practically split in two with the breadth of his smile. 'Well, well, well,' he said.

Hardy grinned back. 'Now then, let's get back to other, more pressing matters.'

'Indeed,' said Rhodes leaping tohis feet with renewed energy, and bounded from the room, Hardy following in his wake.

The two policemen came into the drawing-room to find a peaceful scene: four ladies and a gentleman were drinking coffee and chatting amiably.

Hardy heard Mrs Manderson say, 'Major Forsythe,' to which the gentleman smiled and said,

'Oh Mrs Manderson, Tom, please. I'm sure we know each other well enough by now.'

'Of course, dear.' Mrs Manderson inclined her head.

'You wished to ask me something, Mrs Manderson?' If he had expected her to say, do call me Lavinia, that didn't happen, but nevertheless she leaned forward and said,

'I was recalling your story about the egg in vinegar. You were telling it to Mr Milner over dinner one evening, I believe. I'm afraid I only caught part of it, but I was intrigued. Do tell me the story again.'

Rhodes was about to interrupt these gentle proceedings when he felt Hardy's warning hand on his arm.

Hardy came forward, said, 'Oh don't mind us, we're just here for the coffee. Do go on, major.' And he stole his fiancée's cup and drained it, then reached for a shortbread slice before settling himself back in an armchair. Rhodes did the same, although he was fortunate enough to find an unused cup and pour himself a fresh, full cup of hot coffee.

'Well, er,' Forsythe glanced about him, surprised to find he was the focus of everyone's attention, then continued. 'It's a silly thing really. Not at all interesting.'

'Oh, do go on, Tom, sweetheart, we'd love to hear it again,' Anabella urged. She glanced at the others. 'It is a funny story.'

'I don't know about that,' he responded with a self-deprecating grin.

'Don't be silly, of course it is. And so clever,' she told Dottie and Mrs Manderson. 'I had no idea it could do that.'

'All right. Well, it was just that when I was at university, many moons ago now, I played a prank on a chap. You may have heard of him, his name was Harold Bassington. In fact, it was due to this prank that we became such good friends. You see, we were two young chaps sharing a room. He had bought half a dozen eggs for his meals, and we were larking about one evening, having a few drinks. Then I said to him, 'I bet you five pounds that I can eat those eggs without cracking the shells.' And he said, 'You're on!'"

Forsythe glanced about him, pleased to see all eyes on him; one or two were smiling already. He really had a good way with telling a story, Dottie thought, a born raconteur, and he enjoyed the attention.

'Well, go on,' Christiana said with a smile, indulging him. 'Tell everyone how you did it.'

'It was like this,' Forsythe said. 'Quite easy really. When Harold had gone to bed, I put two of the eggs into a jug and filled the jug with vinegar. The next day, we overslept—hungover, obviously, to my shame—and we had to scramble, no pun intended, out of bed and run straight to our lectures. But... When we got back that evening, I reminded poor old Harold of our agreement, then showed him the eggs—now completely free of their shells. He was speechless, until I explained of course. And then he was pretty annoyed—tried to say I'd cheated. But he stumped up the fiver anyway. I treated him to fish and chips as an apology, *sans* vinegar as I'd used it all on the eggs.'

'How did the eggshells come off?' Dottie asked.

'Well, the vinegar dissolved them. Because you see, vinegar contains acetic acid. When you soak something like eggs in it, it eats away at the shells.' Forsythe looked around the little circle with a triumphant grin.

Beyond them, outside on the terrace, Hardy could

see the two constables were standing ready, along with Paul Boxhall, and drawing some worried looks from the other guests who occupied the sun loungers. A glance sideways showed him that the inspector had also noticed this.

Rhodes set down his cup. 'Very nice coffee, better than the liquid stuff you usually get, I must say. And a very good story, major. You were quite the chemist in your younger days, it seems.'

Hardy wondered if he imagined Forsythe's eyes narrow very slightly, or the tension now evident in the set of his shoulders. Hardy looked away, not wanting to spook the fellow.

It was Dottie who said, 'But of course, that's exactly what you have been for your entire professional life, isn't it, Tom? Your chemistry studies at Oxford set you up perfectly for that life.'

His eyes snapped to hers, an involuntary intake of breath answering her as eloquently as any words.

Hardy said, 'You were a teacher of chemistry at a boys' school in Leicestershire until five years ago, when an aunt died and left you a sum of money in her will. That enabled you to reinvent yourself, didn't it?'

Dottie saw the bewildered look on Christiana's face, and more especially on her friend's. Dottie's heart ached for Anabella—she would bear the grief of this.

'Now look,' Forsythe began, attempting a smile, but the room was quieter, cooler. He shrugged. He knew it was already too late. He sat back, finished his drink and his cake, whilst Rhodes took up Hardy's story.

'The money enabled you to present yourself in a new light. You could be more exotic, more exciting. People would look up to you, see you as someone with authority, power, even. You probably persuaded Bassington to back you up. You thought it sounded more interesting, more appealing to the opposite sex perhaps, to tell people you were a soldier—a major, no less—rather than an ordinary person, a teacher. No doubt it was useful to be able to disappear for a while then return and say you'd been away on His Majesty's service, very hush-hush, and all the women would have thought you a brave adventurer, saving the nation from harm.'

'But really, you only had one object,' Dottie pointed out. 'Christiana and her fortune.'

'Her money had nothing to do with it! I loved her.' He snarled at Dottie.

Christiana gasped. But it was Anabella who had her hands to her mouth, her face white, her eyes wide with shock.

Dottie simply rolled her eyes. 'Oh of course it did. You were just like Harold Bassington and Sebastian Milner, desperate to woo her money, and to have the hand of a gentle, trusting woman on your arm.'

Forsythe was now opting for a disbelieving smile and a shake of the head. 'No, you're being ridiculous, this is all utter nonsense.'

'Did you kill Harold Bassington?' Dottie asked abruptly, and the suddenness of it surprised him.

'What? Now look, I've gone along with this...' His attempt to laugh his way out of it failed horribly as he struggled to control his temper.

Hardy said, 'You objected to Bassington's treatment of the woman you loved, and so you killed him. It's really that simple. But then what did she do?'

Rhodes continued, addressing not Forsythe but Hardy. 'I'll tell you what she did. She looked in the wrong direction. There was Forsythe, ready to offer comfort and solace, even adoration, but did she turn to him? No. She turned to Milner—another tyrant in the same vein.'

'Which meant he had to go, too. He lashed out at her, abusing her horribly, and in doing so, signed his own death warrant,' Hardy pointed out. Rhodes nodded.

'Exactly, sergeant. And then, as if things weren't bad enough already, Mamie Cotton just happens to be sitting out on her bench and sees what he did, then threatens to tell unless he pays up. So, she had to go too, didn't she, Forsythe? A necessary evil, her death. Because you really did like her, didn't you? It cut you up to get rid of her, but I doubt she could be trusted to keep quiet. Probably went so far as to ask you for money to buy her silence.' He gave a short laugh, 'Well, well, the things we do for love, eh?'

'You can't bring Bassington's death down on me,' Forsythe sneered.

'No, that's very true. Mr Boxhall told us he saw Mr Milner coming into the lodge after Bassington left. No doubt that's another good reason for getting rid of Milner. He'd have been able to tell us he saw you out there.'

'No, he didn't see me! He'd already...' Too late, Forsythe shut his mouth.

'Already gone back inside? Thank you for telling us that, *Mr* Forsythe.'

Rhodes gestured to the waiting constables. They came into the room and stationed themselves by the doors to the terrace—just in case Mr Forsythe should think of attempting to escape. Dalbury, Parkes and the two women, along with Paul Boxhall, all came in, staring at those present in bewilderment, understanding that they had missed something.

'Please stand, Mr Forsythe,' Rhodes said. Then,

'Hardy, you can do the honours.'

Hardy nodded. 'Certainly, inspector. Thomas Forsythe, I am arresting you for the wilful murders of Sebastian Milner and Esmeralda Cotton. You do not have to say anything...'

Over his words, a babble of questions and comments broke out from the house guests. Forsythe ignored all of this. He held out his hands. William put the handcuffs on him. The chemistry teacher, with no loss of his usual poised self-possession, smiled politely and said,

'Well, well. One can't outrun one's fate, I suppose. So let's be off.'

As they led him past the others, past his ex-love, Anabella, he turned to give her a sad smile.

'I'm very sorry, my dear. You were charming, but just not quite what I was looking for. God bless you.'

He made to pat her arm, but was restrained by William, and couldn't quite reach her. Nonetheless, Anabella shrank back as if she'd been burned. She stumbled another step, covering her face with her hands, her shoulders heaving with the weight of her grief. Christiana's arm came about her in a protective way. Christiana glared, her eyes snapping at him, furious.

'How could you?' she raged.

Forsythe responded with a shout, 'The way he treated you! Always ill-mannered, always sneering at you, taking advantage of your good nature, not even remaining true to you after, what, just a year of marriage? And then, Saturday night! Really, that was the final straw. Mamie handed me the medicine chest that evening, said she'd just treated the scratch on your cheek with iodine but that she feared it may leave a scar, and then it all simply came to me. How I could do it. He didn't deserve you, and I hated him for what he did. I wanted to beat him to a pulp, but then a better idea came to me.'

'It didn't 'just come to you' at all. You planned it,' Dottie stated.

Forsythe stared at her. His lip curled. 'What?'

'You're trying to claim it all just happened on the spur of the moment, that you lost control of your emotions, your actions. But in fact, you planned the murder of Sebastian Milner and carried it out meticulously. Since I came here, several times I've been told, 'someone told him'. *Someone* told Harold Bassington his wife had left a large sum of money in her handbag in the hotel—knowing he'd feel compelled to act on that. All you had to do was wait until he went outside, then go after him. I doubt you even had to go very far. And then, s*omeone* told Sebastian Milner that rum and blackcurrant was good for a cold. That way the iodine could be disguised, and he drank his poison willingly. You were that someone. You manipulated both men in your determination to get Christiana to yourself.'

'And Mamie?' Mrs Manderson asked.

Dottie told her, 'Yes. In just the same way, he planned Mamie's death the night before he killed her. He knew he'd find her in her favourite spot. He went out there for a smoke. I heard him say to her, 'I thought I might find you here'. But she wasn't prepared to forget what she'd seen from her bench, was she, and she was adamant she would use it to her advantage.'

He sighed. 'I really regret that. I adored Mamie, she was such a character. But unreliable. She just wouldn't have held her tongue, I knew it immediately. She wanted money. I knew that even if I could afford to pay her what she asked—which I couldn't—she would come back time and again for more, always threatening to expose me. It would have hung over my head all my life. So I'm afraid I just had to make an end of it.'

'Of her, you mean.' Christina's voice was shaking with rage and grief.

Finally, he had the grace to hang his head in shame. Only to raise his chin in defiance, saying in a strong, clear voice, 'Just once. I wanted you to look at me. Just once, Christiana, my love. To see you look at me with the same adoration you had for that butler.' He pointed a shaking finger at Boxhall's chest. 'I loved you, why couldn't you see that? My only love. I did it all for you. It was all because of you.'

'Because of me? How could it have been? Or do you mean, because I chose them over you?' She was shaking her head slightly. To her, he was making no sense at all.

'Because they weren't worthy. None of them—*none of them*—ever loved you the way I did. None of them deserved to stand beside you. I—I worshipped you. To me you were the whole world, and everything in it. You—my dearest Christiana—you were everything. Still are everything. You are incomparable.'

'But I'm... I'm no one. I'm just ordinary.' She couldn't have sounded more surprised, and Dottie thought she understood, thought she would have felt the same confusion that Christiana felt at being so elevated in one man's eyes. This kind of love was not love at all, it was... What was it? Dottie struggled to name it. It was pure madness, surely?

He shook his head in a pitying response to Christiana. He reached for her but she stepped aside, frustrating him.

'My darling! How can you say that? You are my whole world. I love you. I've worshipped you from the moment I saw you, but... Well, I suppose I was just never quite enough, was I? Even as a major in the British Army. Yet somehow I always thought, I hoped,' he added, his voice low, sorrowful, 'I hoped you might at last look in my direction, when all the others were gone. But you never did...'

'I think that's quite enough,' William said, attempting to move him on.

Forsythe struggled, turning back in a panic now he knew this would be the last time he saw her. 'Christiana! Darling! Please... think of me kindly!'

But it was too late to plead for her good wishes. In a frigid voice, she said, 'I shall never think of you at all. All those deaths! You are a *monster*!'

And she turned away to put her arm around Anabella's heaving shoulders once more.

His eyes were downcast, his expression masked, rigid as the police, with no further impediment, marched him out of the house into the waiting car.

The car sped away almost immediately, its bell clanging loudly all the way. For several seconds they stood there in a confounded silence, dwelling on what had happened.

Then Dottie said, 'Shall we sit down?' To Boxhall she said, 'Perhaps we could have some more coffee?' Taking Anabella's other arm, she and Christiana led her to a sofa. The others, still stunned by what had just happened, followed on behind them.

The following morning the awkward process of taking their leave began. It's doubtful whether any house guests had ever been so keen to get away, longing to put the whole of the recent events behind them, as those who left Mrs Milner's residence after not one weekend but almost two full weeks of enforced incarceration.

Everyone had a hug for Christiana, and a slightly

uncomfortable handshake for a relaxed-looking and gravely smiling Boxhall, standing at her side now as if he was the master of the house. Which he now was, Dottie realised. Christiana herself looked radiantly happy, despite the recent death of her husband, the loss of one of her dearest friends, and the fact that these atrocities had been committed by a man she had always viewed as a reliable gentleman, friend, and ally, and the future husband of her closest friend, Anabella.

Anabella was the first to leave, almost running to the taxicab Boxhall had ordered for her. It came right up to the front door in a hail of gravel that had them all leaping back out of the way. Tearfully she waved and promised to write to Christiana and Dottie too.

Dottie and her mother came next to say goodbye, William standing to one side, ready to ride back with them in Dottie's car. Rhodes had gone on ahead with Spence and Kerridge in the police car.

'What are your plans for the coming weekend?' Christiana asked, prepped by Dottie earlier as part of a new plan.

Dottie tried to look as though she was thinking about it.

Her mother chipped in with, 'Well, we were invited to a weekend house-party at Sir Stanley Sissons' home in Gladstone Avenue, in Kensington.' She pulled a face of dismay, and Dottie, taking her cue, nodded vigorously and said,

'My word, yes. Good grief, I don't think I want to do that, do you? Shall I telephone to Sir Stanley and explain? I'm sure he'll understand.'

Only her mother, William and Christiana knew that Sir Stanley was in fact her father, though not the man who had raised her as his own child.

Mrs Manderson said, 'Good idea. Yes, he's such a

sweet man, he certainly would see the problem. Another time, perhaps. Although I had been looking forward to meeting Mrs Gascoigne.' She gave Dottie a direct look.

Dottie responded, 'Oh definitely.' She turned to Christiana. 'Mrs Flora Gascoigne, the great London socialite. Her husband is George Gascoigne de la Gascoigne, head of the family estate in Hertfordshire, and extremely wealthy.'

Christiana nodded, pretending she had no idea that Flora was actually Dottie's sister. 'Oh yes, dear Flora, she's such a sweetheart. I met her last year at Sir Nigel's. They say her diamond necklace is two hundred years old, and worth more than ten thousand pounds!'

'I had been looking forward to seeing it. One hears so many interesting stories about its history. Still, as I say, perhaps another time,' Mrs Manderson added, then glanced at her watch. 'Dottie, dear, it's getting late.'

'And Mrs Gascoigne is such a dear woman, so gentle, so kind and will do anything for anyone.' Dottie made a show of glancing about her. 'Dear me, yes, Mother, we must get going, or we'll be late for lunch!'

They said goodbye once again to Christiana and all the others, then went to the car.

The final group said farewell, and followed close behind the Mandersons, getting into two cars parked close to Dottie's. There was a nod and a wave from Florentina, nothing at all from Penelope, a curt nod from Parkes, then a broad grin and a wave from Dalbury.

As Dottie turned the car and headed for the road, her mother let out a long held breath.

'My goodness, dear, I'm so relieved to finally get

away from that place! It'll be wonderful to get home.'

'Absolutely! I feel better already.'

'All the same, Dottie dear,' Lavinia said, and Dottie shot her a surprised look. Her mother almost never called her Dottie. 'It's been the most exciting adventure.' Her smile faded a little as she recalled the actual events. She added, 'Of course, it was dreadfully sad about poor Mamie. She was a highly unusual and entertaining woman, I would have loved to get to know her better.'

'Yes,' Dottie said. 'She was quite something.'

'But all the same, it's been terribly exciting.'

'That's it!' William said from the rear seat. 'As soon as we are married, I shall put my foot down and forbid the two of you from going anywhere alone together, you just can't be trusted to keep out of trouble.'

He'd been joking, but even so, felt slightly miffed when Dottie and her mother just looked at one another then burst out laughing. He huffed to himself.

Dottie slammed the car in reverse then headed back to the road and to London.

'As for the jewel robberies,' Dottie said later. 'Mother and I have made a start on bringing that to a conclusion. It's a good thing we shall have your help.'

'Yes, you set the scene perfectly, but that's as far as your involvement goes, don't forget.' William said.

'Like I said, Mother and I have made a start on that...'

Dottie had just halted the car outside Mrs Manderson's home in London. They got out. Already the door of the house was opening, Mr Manderson and a maid were coming out to greet them.

On seeing she wasn't joking, William groaned.

How on earth was he to explain to them...?

'No, you really must leave it all to the police now. No more mischief involving you and your mother! No offense intended, Mrs Manderson,' he hastily added.

Mrs Manderson gave him a smile. 'That's quite all right, William dear.'

Mrs Manderson leaned a little to one side and directed a fluttery wave to her husband who had halted on the top step, uncertain what was going on. Why didn't they simply come inside?

Turning to Dottie, William said, 'All right, let's hear this latest scheme of yours. I'm not agreeing to anything yet, please note. What is it you have in mind? What are you going to do?'

He was holding a couple of hat boxes which were taken from him by the maid.

'Oh, not me, dear,' Dottie told him with a grin. 'I have someone else entirely in mind for it. Two someones actually. In fact, the trap has already been set, in a way. And it will take place at Sir Stanley's London home.'

'Your father?' Belatedly he glanced apologetically at Herbert Manderson, but Herbert just smiled.

'My first father,' Dottie corrected gently, leaning to give her second—most beloved—father a kiss on the cheek. Taking his arm, she smiled at her mother and together they went up the steps into the house.

William groaned again, shaking his head, and wondering what he could do to stop this, short of locking the two women up.

*

Chapter Twenty-two

Flora Gascoigne was humming to herself as she sat at the dressing-table in Sir Stanley's Blue Room.

If truth be told she was feeling rather tense, and the gentle blue décor: soft shades of blue merged with white and touches of gold, was having a delightful calming effect.

She dipped her fingertip into the little pot of make-up and began to sparingly dot it here and there on her face and neck, then oh-so-gently smoothed it into her fine complexion. The routine of preparing to go downstairs to dinner helped to ease her nerves, as did focussing on the dinner itself rather than what was about to happen.

Because her nerves were stretched, she heard the slight sound outside her door; her every sense was on the alert for it. Sure enough there came a timid little knock, not a very loud one, certainly not forceful, yet all the same it made her jump.

This was it. She took a deep breath.

'Come in' she called.

The door opened and a face appeared in the gap, and in the mirror she saw it, a maid's cap on the person's head.

'Excuse me, madam. I'm very sorry to intrude.'

'Not at all, dear.' Flora looked at her enquiringly, without appearing to stare too closely, she gave her a friendly smile then immediately looked away again at her make-up, as if she wasn't especially interested in the new arrival. The maid came into the room and stood there, hands folded neatly in front of her, the suggestion of red hair scraped back under her cap, her pale skin scrubbed free of make-up, freckles undisguised by powder, her ginger eyelashes and eyebrows giving her a sandy-faced look that was pale by comparison with the severe black maid's uniform. She said in a softened, polite voice,

'Excuse me, madam. I'm very sorry to disturb you. Sir Stanley offers his best wishes and asks if you have everything you need?'

Flora smiled back, and in a perfectly natural tone, said, 'Oh, how very kind of him. Please tell him I'm most comfortable, thank you.'

The maid came a little closer now, feeling more secure, no doubt. 'And may I turn down your bed, madam?'

Flora smiled at her kindly and nodded, unconcerned, turning back to the dressing-table mirror. She dusted a little rouge into her forehead with a soft brush then added a sweep of it onto her nose and chin. 'Oh yes, please do.'

The maid bobbed, and turned aside immediately to head towards the bed, turning back the counterpane and sheet, straightening them neatly, then she plumped up the pillows.

'Someone said there was pheasant for dinner,'

Flora remarked. She gently swiped a pink lipstick across her bottom lip, pressed her lips together then applied some to the top lip. She repeated the pressing of the lips then wiped a little excess from the corners of her mouth and checked she had none on her teeth.

'Thank you, madam, I'll tell cook you're looking forward to it. Shall I help you on with your gown, madam?'

'Please.'

The maid came around the bed to grab the dress Flora had draped over the back of a chair. She helped Flora to pass the gown over her head without disrupting her hair.

'Very elegant, madam,' said the maid.

Flora wondered if there was a hint of a smirk behind that bland smile. She decided it was best to ignore it. She began to put on her jewellery, beginning with some diamond drop-earrings. She noticed—without appearing to notice—that the maid was paying close attention, taking in the bracelets and rings that were in the little case on the dressing-table.

She helped Flora to do up her necklace then handed her some rings.

As Flora sat back for a final check of her appearance before going down to dinner, the maid said, 'Before I forget, madam. Sir Stanley has instructed the staff to ask if there was any jewellery or other valuables that need to be placed in the safe overnight. You've probably heard all about them robberies?'

Flora shook her head, willing herself to stay calm. 'My goodness, no, I haven't heard anything about that. We've been out of town for a while.' She had just the right amount of alarm in her voice.

'Just half a mile up the road, the last one was. The thieves got away with a great hoard of diamonds, pearls, all sorts of things. But police haven't got a clue what to do about it. Well, you know what the police are like. Wooden tops, the lot of them. They are probably all in on it, if you ask me. So if you just place your valuables into this little bag Sir Stanley gave me, I'll nip it downstairs, and you'll know everything is safe. If anyone breaks in here, they won't get away with a thing!'

'Excellent,' Flora said. 'Though actually these few things aren't worth all that much. Not compared to my real jewellery. But...' She hunted about her, then with a roll of her eyes, said, 'Oh of course. I left it all in the bigger case in the bathroom. If you take a look, you will see it just on the dresser inside the door.' Flora pointed, and the maid immediately went to look.

Again, Flora found she was holding her breath, on edge to see if the maid took the bait. Incredibly, she did, and Flora softly released her breath.

Sounding completely at ease, the maid said over her shoulder, 'Rightio, madam. I'll just fetch them then I can take them downstairs right away to Sir Stanley. He's waiting down there special.'

She put on the bathroom light, going inside as she did so, and glanced about for the supposed case of jewellery. 'Madam, I can't seem to find the jewellery case, do you know where...' she began.

But Flora came right up behind her, gave her a good hard shove into the room, and slammed the door behind her, turning the key in the lock then putting the back of the chair under for good measure.

'You're going to be sorry you did that, you stupid cow!' bellowed the 'maid'.

'No, I won't, Penelope. It will be you who has all

the time in the world to reflect on what you've just done. The police will be here in about—oh ten seconds—I should think. You know, those 'wooden tops' you so despise. And your brother will get picked up too. You won't be seeing him for a while.' Flora rang the bell. When the real maid that she'd seen earlier came to answer it, Flora said, 'Could you fetch Sir Stanley and Constable Kerridge right away, please? And my sister too, of course.'

'Certainly, madam,' the maid said, eyes round with excitement as she took in the chair Flora had so carefully wedged in place. 'You got her, then?'

'I certainly did,' Flora said with a grin.

There was only one thing left to do.

As soon as she arrived, Dottie quickly donned a maid's uniform Sir Stanley had brought her, whilst Constable Kerridge led the now-silent and sullen Penelope Sweeney into a small sitting-room along the hall to wait until a couple more police officers arrived to take her away.

Dottie added a gingery wig, carefully pinning the little cap on top. She emerged from the bathroom and presented herself to Sir Stanley, who nodded at her and grinned.

'You'll do,' he said. He handed her the jewellery case—empty now—and together they hurried down the back stairs. At the side door they halted. His hand poised on the door latch, he said,

'Ready, Dottie, dear?'

'Yes, I'm ready.' She smiled at him.

He kissed her cheek, 'Do be careful, dear.'

'I will, I promise. Right, here goes.'

She took a deep breath, he opened the door, and she bolted outside, along the winding drive, and got into the waiting car, taking care to keep her head down.

The man in the driver's seat half-turned, saying, 'Hand it over then. For heaven's sake, you took your time. I was starting to panic—thought you'd got caught. I knew it was a bit of risk, doing this one. We need to take a break from it for a while, I reckon.'

He grabbed the case from her, prised it open, and before he could say anything, Dottie said,

'I didn't take nearly as big a risk as the ones you've been taking, Sergeant Spence. But you're right about taking a break. About ten years, I should think.'

His head jerked up as he realised her voice was wrong. She wasn't the woman he'd been expecting. Too late he understood what was happening. He let out a sound that was practically a roar and threw himself at her but she flung herself back against the door, just beyond his reach. He turned back to grab at the steering wheel but before he could stamp down hard on the accelerator, the doors on either side were yanked open, Spence was seized and dragged from the car by uniformed police officers and marched away to a nearby police vehicle where he was bundled in with scant regard for his expensive suit. One of their own had betrayed them, they didn't care if he got a bit rumpled.

Inspector Rhodes leaned in on one side of the car, and William leaned in on the other, helping Dottie to step down from the car, both men anxious to make sure she was safe.

Back in the house, Sir Stanley and Flora regaled guests over dinner with the exciting news of the capture of the jewellery thieves.

A week later, the chief superintendent finally finished his long speech and stood to his feet, and with the warmest smile William had ever witnessed from the man, he reached across his desk to hold out his hand to shake first William's hand and then that of Inspector Rhodes, saying,

'In conclusion then, the Commander of the Metropolitan Police and myself are most grateful for your service. Inspector Rhodes, in case you were doubtful of my confidence in your ability, doubt no longer. Thank you for the excellent work and the most satisfactory outcome of both of your investigations. The Commander is extremely pleased with the results.'

He nodded to Rhodes and beamed a genuinely warm smile at him. Rhodes looked almost overcome, William thought. The inspector even blushed a little.

Then the chief super turned to William too and said, 'And once again, many thanks to you for your, shall we say *unofficial*, investigation. I am pleased to inform you that you are now fully reinstated at the rank of Detective Inspector. Thank you, *Inspector* Hardy.' Almost as an after-thought, the man turned and said, 'By the way, gentlemen, both your next pay packets will include an extra discretionary sum. Might come in handy seeing that you're soon to be a married man, Hardy. Good afternoon to both of you, gentlemen.'

'Thank you, sir,' Rhodes said and turned to head for the door.

'Er—indeed, er good afternoon...' William floundered, but the chief super had already sat down and was attending to other matters. He flapped a hand at Hardy.

'Well, well, off you go, inspector.'

'Yes sir, thank you sir.'

And then they were back in the corridor. William and Rhodes grinned at each other, shook hands, and there was a lot of rather embarrassed back-slapping.

'Thanks so much, Bill,' Rhodes said, and he walked

away before his emotions could get the better of him.

William smiled, shaking his head. Thank God it had all turned out all right. Smithers was not such a bad old stick, all things considered, he thought.

*

Epilogue

Dottie hesitated at the door of the church, her white gown shifting softly in the breeze.

'What is it, my love?' Herbert Manderson saw her glance back toward the beribboned car. 'Have you forgotten something?'

'No, I...' She looked at him. Shaking her head, she stumbled over the words. 'I don't think... I can't...'

He smiled then. He knew now what it was that troubled her. He clasped her hand in both of his. 'It's all right, dear. It's just nerves. You'll be all right once you get inside.' He nodded towards the church door. 'William is waiting for you.'

'What if he doesn't turn up? Or—or if he's changed his mind... or...'

'He's here, dear, and waiting. He loves you.'

She turned a wide-eyed stare at the vast oak doors ahead of her. They stood open, and beyond the gloom of the entry, she could see a small patch of light that was the window at the far end of the church.

Again, she shook her head. 'It's too... It all feels too big, somehow. Such an important... I don't think I can...'

He hugged her. Then straightened her veil. 'It will be all right, Dottie dear. Trust me.'

She saw the bridesmaids waiting for her: William's youngest sister Ellie, dressed in some of the warehouse's finest gowns for young women, as were a couple of Dottie's youngest cousins whom she hadn't seen for more than ten years. Their eyes were bright, their cheeks flushed pink with excitement. She heard the organ begin the opening bars of the Wedding March.

'Come along, my dear, let's not keep them waiting.' And Herbert took his daughter's right arm, whilst Sir Stanley came forward to kiss her cheek, and take her left arm, and with a deep breath, they took one step, then another and at last they entered the church.

They slowly progressed down the aisle. Dottie was unable to glance to either side, afraid she'd lose her nerve completely and give in to the urge to turn, gather up her skirts and run.

At last, they came to the front of the church and halted at the altar-rail. Dottie took her station beside the tall, blond, morning-suited man. The organ ceased its playing, and the vicar came forward to beam at them in a fatherly way, and asked,

'Who giveth this woman unto this man?'

With broad grins, Herbert Manderson and Sir Stanley Sissons stated in unison, 'We do!'

'Then let us begin.' The vicar raised his prayer book and his voice. 'Dearly beloved, we are gathered here today...'

Everything faded as William turned to face her. He could hardly believe this moment had arrived, that it was real and that he was not dreaming but awake.

She was so beautiful. Her face was pale, not, as he'd expected flushed with the joy of the moment or from being the centre of so much close attention. She drew closer to him in a gown he knew she had designed herself. Her eyes, the loveliest eyes he had ever seen, were large pools, she looked almost tearful. He smiled at her. Her answering, tremulous smile engulfed his heart, he would never be free again. He would spend the rest of his life trying with all his might to deserve her.

'I do,' he said at the appropriate moment, and knew immediately he had said it a little too loud, too forcefully, but it made her smile, and her shoulders relaxed. And in response to the same question, she too said, 'I do' though so tremulously softly he doubted anyone beyond the first row of seats—her immediate family and his—would have heard her.

As their first official dance together as man and wife came to an end, Dottie was aware of a touch then a firm pat on the centre of her back. She turned to see her brother-in-law George smirking at her much like an eight-year-old plotting some mischief.

'What are you...?' she began, but William, glancing at his wife's back, reached out to take hold of something. He held it up to show her. It was a cardboard sign which said in large black letters: 'This design £42 12s 6d. Other colours including emerald-green, sapphire-blue, and silver lamé are available.'

George and William both laughed uproariously. Dottie shaking her head and trying not to laugh, attempted a severe look.

'You're such a child!' She told George, sending the two men into more gales of laughter to the great amusement of onlookers.

George kissed her cheek then shook William's

hand. 'Once again, many congratulations to the pair of you!'

Then he strode away to claim his own wife for the next dance, leaving William holding the cardboard sign, trying to push the pin into a corner of it without pricking himself. As Flora and George went past them amongst the other dancers, Flora exchanged an eye roll with her sister, and said, 'Men!'

'Boys, more like!' Dottie returned. She took the sign off William and handed it to a nearby waiter, along with the pin. 'Could you please throw that away?'

He took it from her with a bow and a grin. Dottie turned back to her husband, and placing her hand on his shoulder, they too joined in the dance. They paused slightly for him to bow her back a little and kiss her very thoroughly indeed, to cheers and clapping from their guests. Then the dance resumed.

'Really, Herbert, they are so close together, you could barely call it waltzing,' Lavinia Manderson commented to Herbert.

He said, 'They are so very much in love. What a perfect match they are,' Then he swept Lavinia onto the dancefloor with a flourish, saying, 'Dance with me, my love.'

She swirled into his arms, and as they moved in time to the music, she made a sound that was suspiciously like a giggle.

THE END

About the author

Caron Allan writes cosy murder mysteries, both contemporary and also set in the 1930s. Caron lives in Derby, England with her husband and an endlessly varying quantity of cats and sparrows.

Caron Allan can be found on these social media channels and would love to hear from you:

Instagram: caronsbooks

Twitter: caron_allan

Mastodon social: caron_allan

Facebook: CaronAllanFiction

Pinterest: caronallan

Bluesky: caronallanfiction.bsky.social

Also, if you're interested in news, snippets, Caron's 'quirky' take on life or just want some sneak previews, please sign up to Caron's blog shown below:

caronallanfiction.com/

Also by Caron Allan:

The Friendship Can Be Murder books:

Criss Cross: book 1
Cross Check: book 2
Check Mate: book 3

The Dottie Manderson mysteries:

Night and Day: book 1
The Mantle of God: book 2
Scotch Mist: book 3 a novella
The Last Perfect Summer of Richard Dawlish: book 4
The Thief of St Martins: book 5
The Spy Within: book 6
Rose Petals and White Lace: book 7
Midnight, the Stars, and You: book 8

The Miss Gascoigne mysteries:

A Meeting With Murder: book 1
A Wreath of Lilies: book 2

Others:

Easy Living: a story about life after death, after death, after death

Printed in Dunstable, United Kingdom